Praise for the reigning queen of romance

DIANA PALMER!

"Palmer's talent for character development and ability
to fuse heartwarming romance with nail-biting
suspense shine in *Outsider*."
—*Booklist*

"A gentle escape mixed with real-life menace
for fans of Palmer's more than 100 novels."
—*Publishers Weekly* on *Night Fever*

"The ever-popular and prolific Palmer has penned
another sure hit."
—*Booklist* on *Before Sunrise*

"Nobody does it better."
—*New York Times* bestselling author Linda Howard

"Palmer knows how to make sparks fly…heartwarming."
—*Publishers Weekly* on *Renegade*

"Sensual and suspenseful."
—*Booklist* on *Lawless*

"Diana Palmer is a mesmerizing storyteller
who captures the essence of what a romance should be."
—*Affaire de Coeur*

"Nobody tops Diana Palmer when it comes to delivering pure,
undiluted romance. I love her stories."
—*New York Times* bestselling author Jayne Ann Krentz

Look for Diana Palmer's new hardcover

Heartless

Coming in summer 2009

Also by Diana Palmer

DIANA PALMER

HER KIND OF HERO

HQN™

HQN™

Recycling programs
for this product may
not exist in your area.

ISBN-13: 978-0-373-77381-7
ISBN-10:   0-373-77381-1

HER KIND OF HERO

Copyright © 2009 by Harlequin Books S.A.

The publisher acknowledges the copyright holder
of the individual works as follows:

THE LAST MERCENARY
Copyright © 2001 by Diana Palmer

MATT CALDWELL: TEXAS TYCOON
Copyright © 2000 by Diana Palmer

This edition published by arrangement with Harlequin Books S.A.

® and TM are trademarks of the publisher. Trademarks indicated with
® are registered in the United States Patent and Trademark Office, the
Canadian Trade Marks Office and in other countries.

www.HQNBooks.com

Printed in U.S.A.

CONTENTS

THE LAST MERCENARY

1

It had been a jarring encounter.

Callie Kirby felt chilled, and it wasn't just because it was November in south Texas. She watched the stepbrother she worshiped walk away from her as casually as if he'd moved around an obstacle in his path. In many ways, that was what Callie was to Micah Steele. He hated her. Of course, he hated her mother more. The two Kirby women had alienated him from the father he adored. Jack Steele had found his only son wrapped up in the arms of his young wife—Callie's mother— and an ugly scene had followed. Callie's mother, Anna, was sent packing. So was Micah, living mostly at his father's home while he finished his last year of residency.

That had been six years ago, and the breach still hadn't healed. Jack Steele rarely spoke of his son. That suited Callie. The very sound of his name was painful to her. Speaking to him took nerve, too. He'd once called her a gold digger like her mother, among other insults. Words could hurt. His always had. But she was twenty-two now, and she could hold her own with him. That didn't mean that her knees didn't shake and her heartbeat didn't do a tango while she was holding her own.

She stood beside her little second-hand yellow VW and watched Micah bend his formidable height to open the door of the black convertible Porsche he drove. His thick, short blond hair caught the sunlight and gleamed like gold. He had eyes so dark they looked black, and he rarely smiled. She didn't understand why he'd come home to Jacobsville, Texas, in the first place. He lived somewhere in the Bahamas. Jack had said that Micah inherited a trust fund from his late mother, but he'd sounded curious about his son's luxurious lifestyle. The trust, he told Callie privately, wasn't nearly enough to keep Micah in the Armani suits he wore and the exotic sports cars he bought new every year.

Perhaps Micah had finished his residency somewhere else and was in private practice somewhere. He'd gone to medical school, but she remembered that there had been some trouble in his last year of his residency over a lawsuit, stemming from a surgical procedure he refused to do. Neither she nor his father knew the details. Even when he'd been living with his father, Micah was a clam. After he left, the silence about his life was complete.

He glanced back at Callie. Even at a distance he looked worried. Her heart jumped in spite of her best efforts to control it. He'd had that effect on her from the beginning, from the first time she'd ever seen him. She'd only been in his arms once, from too much alcohol. He'd been furious, throwing her away from him before she could drag his beautiful, hard mouth down onto hers. The aftermath of her uncharacteristic boldness had been humiliating and painful. It wasn't a pleasant memory.

She wondered why he was so concerned about her. It was probably that he was concerned for his father, and she was his primary caretaker. That had to be it. She turned her attention back to her own car.

With a jerk of his hand, he opened the door of the Porsche, climbed in and shot off like a teenager with his first car. The police would get him for that, she thought, if they saw it. For a few seconds, she smiled at the image of big, tall, sexy Micah being put in a jail cell with a man twice his size who liked blondes. Micah was so immaculate, so sophisticated, that she couldn't imagine him ruffled nor intimidated. For all his size, he didn't seem to be a physical man. But he was highly intelligent. He spoke five languages fluently and was a gourmet cook.

She sighed sadly and got into her own little car and started the engine. She didn't know why Micah was worried that she and his father might be in danger from that drug lord everyone locally was talking about. She knew that Cy Parks and Eb Scott had been instrumental in closing down a big drug distribution center, and that the drug lord, Manuel Lopez, had reputedly targeted them for revenge. But that didn't explain Micah's connection. He'd told her that he tipped law enforcement officials to a big drug cargo of Lopez's that had subsequently been captured, and Lopez was out for blood. She couldn't picture her so-straitlaced stepbrother doing something so dangerous. Micah wasn't the sort of man who got involved in violence of any sort. Certainly, he was a far cry from the two mercenaries who'd shut down Lopez's operation. Maybe he'd given the information to the feds for Cy and Eb. Yes, that could have happened, somehow. She remembered what he'd said about the danger to his family and she felt chilled all over again. She'd load that shotgun when she and Jack got home, she told herself firmly, and she'd shoot it if she had to. She would protect her stepfather with her last breath.

As she turned down the street and drove out of town, toward the adult day care center where Jack Steele stayed following his stroke, she wondered where Micah was going in such a hurry. He didn't spend a lot of time in the States. He hadn't for years. He must have been visiting Eb Scott or Cy Parks. She knew they were friends. Odd friends for a tame man like Micah, she pondered. Even if they ran cattle now, they'd been professional mercenaries in the past. She wondered what Micah could possibly have in common with such men.

She was so lost in thought that she didn't notice that she was being followed by a dark, late model car. It didn't really occur to her that anyone would think of harming her, despite her brief argument with Micah just now. She was a nonentity. She had short, dark hair and pale blue eyes, and a nice but unremarkable figure. She was simply ordinary. She never attracted attention from men, and Micah had found her totally resistible from the day they met. Why not? He could have any woman he wanted. She'd seen him with really beautiful women when she and her mother had first come to live with Jack Steele. Besides, there was the age thing. Callie was barely twenty-two. Micah was thirty-six. He didn't like adolescents. He'd said that to Callie, just after that disastrous encounter—among other things. Some of the things he'd said still made her blush. He'd compared her to her mother, and he hadn't been kind. Afterward, she'd been convinced that he was having an affair with her mother, who didn't deny it when Callie asked. It had tarnished him in her eyes and made her hostile. She still was. It was something she couldn't help. She'd idolized Micah until she saw him kissing her mother. It had killed something inside her, made her cold. She wondered if he'd been telling the truth when he said he hadn't seen her mother recently. It hurt to think of him with Anna.

She stopped at a crossroads, her eyes darting from one stop sign to another, looking for oncoming traffic. While she was engrossed in that activity, the car following her on the deserted road suddenly shot ahead and cut across in front of her, narrowly missing her front bumper.

She gasped and hit the brake, forgetting to depress the clutch at the same time. The engine died. She reached over frantically to lock the passenger door, and at the same time, three slim, dark, formidable-looking men surrounded her car. The taller of the three jerked open the driver's door and pulled her roughly out of the car.

She fought, but a hand with a handkerchief was clapped over her nose and mouth and she moaned as the chloroform hit her nostrils and knocked her out flat. As she was placed quickly into the backseat of the other car, another man climbed into her little car and moved it onto the side of the road. He joined his colleagues. The dark car turned around and accelerated back the way it had come, with Callie unconscious in the backseat.

Micah Steele roared away from the scene of his latest disagreement with Callie, his chiseled mouth a thin line above his square jaw. His big hands gripped the steering wheel with cold precision as he cursed his own lack of communication skills. He'd put her back up almost at once by being disparaging about the neat beige suit she was wearing with a plain white blouse. She never dressed to be noticed, only to be efficient. She was that, he had to admit. She was so unlike him. He seemed conservative in his dress and manner. It was a deception. He was unconventional to the core, while Callie could have written the book on proper behavior.

She hadn't believed him, about the danger she and her stepfather—his father—could find themselves in. Manuel Lopez wasn't the man to cross, and he wanted blood. He was going to go to the easiest target for that. He grimaced, thinking how vulnerable Callie would be in a desperate situation. She hated snakes, but he'd seen her go out of her way not to injure one. She was like that about everything. She was a sucker for a hard-luck story, an easy mark for a con artist. Her heart was as soft as wool, and she was sensitive; overly sensitive. He didn't like remembering how he'd hurt her in the past.

He did remember that he hadn't eaten anything since breakfast. He stopped to have a sandwich at a local fast-food joint. Then he drove himself back to the motel he was staying at. He'd been helping Eb Scott and Cy Parks get rid of Lopez's fledgling drug distribution center. Just nights ago, they'd shut down the whole operation and sent most of Lopez's people to jail. Lopez's high-tech equipment, all his vehicles, even the expensive tract of land they sat on, had been confiscated under the Rico statutes. And that didn't even include the massive shipment of marijuana that had also been taken away. Micah himself had tipped off the authorities to the largest shipment of cocaine in the history of south Texas, which the Coast Guard, with DEA support, had appropriated before it even got to the Mexican coast. Lopez wouldn't have to dig too deeply to know that Micah had cost him not only the multimillion-dollar shipment, but the respect of the cartel in Colombia, as well. Lopez was in big trouble with his bosses. Micah Steele was the reason for that. Lopez couldn't get to Micah, but he could get to Micah's family because they were vulnerable. The knowledge of that scared him to death.

He took a shower and stretched out on the bed in a towel, his hands under his damp blond hair while he stared at the ceiling and wondered how he could keep an eye on Callie Kirby and Jack Steele without their knowing. A private bodyguard would stick out like a sore thumb in a small Texas community like Jacobsville. On the other hand, Micah couldn't do it himself without drawing Lopez's immediate retaliation. It was a difficult determination. He couldn't make himself go back to the Bahamas while he knew his father and Callie were in danger. On the other hand, he couldn't stay here. Living in a small town would drive him nuts, even if he had done it in the past, before he went off to medical school.

While he was worrying about what to do next, the telephone rang.

"Steele," he said on a yawn. He was tired.

"It's Eb," came the reply. "I just had a phone call from Rodrigo," he added, mentioning a Mexican national who'd gone undercover for them in Lopez's organization. He'd since been discovered and was now hiding out in Aruba.

"What's happened?" Micah asked with a feeling of dread knotting his stomach.

"He had some news from a friend of his cousin, a woman who knows Lopez. Have you seen Callie Kirby today?" Eb asked hesitantly.

"Yes," Micah said. "About two hours ago, just as she was leaving her office. Why?"

"Rodrigo said Lopez was going to snatch her. He sounded as if they meant to do it pretty soon. You might want to check on her."

"I went to see her. I warned her…!"

"You know Lopez," Eb reminded him somberly. "It won't do her any good even if she's armed. Lopez's men are professionals."

"I'll do some telephoning and get back to you," Micah said quickly, cursing his own lack of haste about safeguarding Callie. He hung up and phoned the adult day care center. Callie would surely be there by now. He could warn her…

But the woman who answered the phone said that Callie hadn't arrived yet. She was two hours late, and her stepfather was becoming anxious. Did Micah know where she was?

He avoided a direct answer and promised to phone her back. Then, with a feeling of utter dread, he climbed into the Porsche and drove past Kemp's law office, taking the route Callie would have taken to the adult day care center.

His heart skipped a beat when he reached the first intersection outside the city. At this time of day, there was very little traffic. But there, on the side of the road, was Callie's yellow VW, parked on the grass with the driver's door wide-open.

He pulled in behind it and got out, cursing as he noted that the keys were still in the ignition, and her purse was lying on the passenger seat. There was no note, no anything.

He stood there, shell-shocked and cold. Lopez had Callie. Lopez had Callie!

After a minute, he phoned Eb on his car phone.

"What do you want me to do?" Eb asked at once, after Micah had finished speaking.

Micah's head was spinning. He couldn't think. He ran a hand through his thick hair. "Nothing. You're newly married, like Cy. I can't put any more women in the firing line. Let me handle this."

"What will you do?" Eb asked.

"Bojo's in Atlanta visiting his brother, but I'll have him meet me in Belize tomorrow. If you have a number for Rodrigo, call it, and tell him to meet me in Belize, too, at the Seasurfer's Bar. Meanwhile, I'll call in the rest of my team." He was remembering phone numbers and jotting them down even as he spoke. "They're taking a holiday, but I can round them up. I'll go in after her."

Eb suggested calling the chief of police, Chet Blake, because he had contacts everywhere, including relatives in positions of power—one was even a Texas Ranger. Micah couldn't argue. If Eb wanted to tell the man, let him. He was going to get to Callie while she was still alive.

"Just remember that somebody in law enforcement is feeding information to Lopez, and act accordingly. I've got to make arrangements about Dad before I leave."

"I'm sorry, Micah."

"It's my fault," Micah ground out furiously. "I shouldn't have left her alone for a minute! I warned her, but what good did that do?"

"Stop that," Eb said at once. "You're no good to Callie unless you can think straight. If you need any sort of help, logistical or otherwise, I have contacts of my own in Mexico."

"I'll need ordinance," Micah said at once. "Can you set it up with your man in Belize and arrange to have him meet us at that border café we used to use for a staging ground?"

"I can. Tell me what you want."

Micah outlined the equipment he wanted, including an old DC-3 to get them into the Yucatán, from which his men would drop with parachutes at night.

"You can fly in under the radar in that," Eb cautioned, "but the DEA will assume you're trying to bring in drugs if they spot you. It'll be tricky."

"Damn!" Micah was remembering that someone in federal authority was on Lopez's payroll. "I had a contact near Lopez, but he left the country. Rodrigo's cousin might help, but he'd be risking his life after this latest tip he fed Rodrigo. So, basically, we've got nobody in Lopez's organization. And if I use my regular contacts, I risk alerting the DEA. Who can I trust?"

"I know someone," Eb said after a minute. "I'll take care of that. Phone me when you're on the ground in Cancún and make sure you've got global positioning equipment with you."

"Will do. Thanks, Eb."

"What are friends for? I'll be in touch. Good luck."

"Thanks."

"Want me to call Cy?"

"No. I'll go by his place on my way out of town and catch him up." He hung up.

He didn't want to leave Callie's car with the door open and her purse in it, but he didn't want to be accused of tampering with evidence later. He compromised by locking it and closing the door. The police would find it eventually, because they patrolled this way. They'd take it from there, but he didn't want anyone in authority to know he was going after Callie. Someone had warned Lopez about the recent devastating DEA raid on his property. That person was still around, and Micah didn't want anyone to guess that he knew about Callie's kidnapping.

* * *

It was hard to think clearly, but he had to. He knew that Callie had a cell phone. He didn't know if she had it with her. Kemp, her boss, had let that slip to Eb Scott during a casual conversation. If Callie had the phone, and Lopez's people didn't know, she might be able to get a call out. He didn't flatter himself that she'd call him. But she might try to call the adult day care center, if she could. It wasn't much, but it gave him hope.

He drove to the center. For one mad instant he thought about speaking to his father in person. But that would only complicate matters and upset the old man; they hadn't spoken in years. He couldn't risk causing his father to have another stroke or a second heart attack by telling him that Callie had been kidnapped.

He went to the office of the nursing director of the center instead and took her into his confidence. She agreed with him that it might be best if they kept the news from his father, and they formulated a cover story that was convincing. It was easy enough for him to arrange for a nurse to go home with his father to Callie's apartment every night and to drive him to the center each day. They decided to tell Jack Steele that one of Callie's elderly aunts had been hurt in a car wreck and she had to go to Houston to see about her. Callie had no elderly aunts, but Jack wouldn't know that. It would placate him and keep him from worrying. Then Micah would have to arrange for someone to protect him from any attempts by Lopez on his life.

He went back to his motel and spent the rest of the night and part of the next day making international phone calls. He knew that Chet Blake, the police chief, would call in the FBI once Callie's disappearance was noted, and that wasn't a bad idea. They would, of course, try to notify Micah, but they wouldn't be able to find him. That meant that Lopez's man in law enforcement would think Micah didn't know that his stepsister had been kidnapped. And that would work to his benefit.

But if Lopez's men carried Callie down to the Yucatán, near Cancún, which was where the drug lord lived these days, it was going to become a nightmare of diplomacy for any U.S. agency that tried to get her out of his clutches, despite international law enforcement cooperation. Micah didn't have that problem. He had Bojo, one of his best mercenaries, with him in the States. It took time to track down the rest of his team, but by dawn he'd managed it and arranged to meet them in Belize that night. He hated waiting that long, and he worried about what Callie was going to endure in the meantime. But any sort of assault took planning, especially on a fortress like Lopez's home. To approach it by sea was impossible. Lopez had several fast boats and guards patrolling the sea wall night and day. It would have to be a land-based attack, which was where the DC-3 came in. The trusty old planes were practically indestructible.

He couldn't get Callie's ordeal out of his mind. He'd kept tabs on her for years without her knowledge. She'd dated one out-of-town auditor and a young deputy sheriff, but nothing came of either relationship. She seemed to balk at close contact with men. That was disturbing to him, because he'd made some nasty allegations about her morals being as loose as her mother's after she'd come on to him under the mistletoe four years ago.

He didn't think words would be damaging, but perhaps they were. Callie had a reputation locally for being as pure as fresh snow. In a small town, where everybody knew everything about their neighbors, you couldn't hide a scandal. That made him feel even more guilty, because Callie had been sweet and uninhibited until he'd gone to work on her. It was a shame that he'd taken out his rage on her, when it was her mother who'd caused all the problems in his family. Callie's innocence was going to cost her dearly, in Lopez's grasp. Micah groaned aloud as he began to imagine what might happen to her now. And it would be his fault.

He packed his suitcase and checked out of the motel. On the way to the airport, he went by Cy Parks's place, to tell him what was going on. Eb was doing enough already; Micah hated the thought of putting more on him. Besides, Cy would have been miffed if he was left out of this. He had his own reasons for wanting Lopez brought down. The vengeful drug lord had endangered the life of Cy's bride, Lisa, and the taciturn rancher wouldn't rest easy until Lopez got what was coming to him. He sympathized with Micah about Callie's kidnapping and Jack Steele's danger. To Micah's relief, he also volunteered to have one of his men, a former law enforcement officer, keep a covert eye on his father, just in case. That relieved Micah's troubled mind. He drove to the airport, left the rented Porsche in the parking lot with the attendant, and boarded the plane to Belize. Then he went to work.

Callie came to in a limousine. She was trussed up like a calf in a bulldogging competition, wrists and ankles bound, and a gag in her mouth. The three men who'd kidnapped her were conversing.

They weren't speaking Spanish. She heard at least one Arabic word that she understood. At once, she knew that they were Manuel Lopez's men, and that Micah had told the truth about the danger she and Jack were in. It was too late now, though. She'd been careless and she'd been snatched.

She lowered her eyelids when one of the men glanced toward her, pretending to still be groggy, hoping for a chance to escape. Bound as she was, that seemed impossible. She shifted a little, noticing with comfort the feel of the tiny cell phone she'd slipped into her slacks' pocket before leaving the office. If they didn't frisk her, she might get a call out. She remembered what she'd heard about Lopez, and her blood ran cold.

She couldn't drag her wrists out of the bonds. They felt like ropes, not handcuffs. Her arm was sore—she wondered if perhaps they'd given her a shot, a sedative of some sort. She must have been out a very long time. It had been late afternoon when she'd been kidnapped. Now it was almost dawn. She wished she had a drink of water....

The big limousine ate up the miles. She had some vague sensation that she'd been on an airplane. Perhaps they'd flown to an airport and the car had picked them up. If only she could see out the window. There were undefined shadows out there. They looked like trees, a lot of trees. Her vision was slightly blurred and she felt as if her limbs were made of iron. It was difficult to concentrate, and more difficult to try to move. What had they given her?

One man spoke urgently to the other and indicated Callie. He smiled and replied with a low, deep chuckle.

Callie noticed then that her blouse had come apart in the struggle. Her bra was visible, and those men were staring at her as if they had every right. She felt sick to her soul. It didn't take knowing the language to figure out what they were saying. She was completely innocent, but before this ordeal was over, she knew she never would be again. She felt a wave of grief wash over her. If only Micah hadn't pushed her away that Christmas. Now it was too late. Her first and last experience of men was going to be a nightmarish one, if she even lived through it. That seemed doubtful. Once the drug lord discovered that Micah had no affection for his stepsister, that he actually hated her and wouldn't soil his hands paying her ransom, she was going to be killed. She knew what happened in kidnappings. Most people knew. It had never occurred to her that she would ever figure in one. How ironic, that she was poor and unattractive, and that hadn't spared her this experience.

She wondered dimly what Micah would say when he knew she was missing. He'd probably feel well rid of her, but he might pay the ransom for her father's sake. Someone had to look after Jack Steele, something his only child couldn't apparently be bothered to do. Callie loved the old man and would have gladly sacrificed her life for him. That made her valuable in at least one way.

The one bright spot in all this was that once word of Callie's kidnapping got out, Micah would hire a bodyguard for Jack whether he wanted one or not. Jack would be safe.

She wished she knew some sort of self-defense, some way of protecting herself, of getting loose from the ropes and the gag that was slowly strangling her. She hadn't had time for lunch the day before and she'd been drugged for the whole night and into the next morning. She was sick and weak from hunger and thirst, and she really had to go to the bathroom. It was a bad day all around.

She closed her eyes and wished she'd locked her car doors and sped out of reach of her assailants. If there was a next time, if she lived to repeat her mistakes, she'd never repeat that one.

She shifted because her legs were cramping and she felt even sicker.

Listening to the men converse in Arabic, she realized her abductors weren't from Mexico. But as she looked out the window now, she could see the long narrow paved ribbon of road running through what looked like rain forest. She'd never been to the Yucatán, but she knew what it looked like from volumes of books she'd collected on Maya relics. Her heart sank. She knew that Manuel Lopez lived near Cancún, and she knew she was in the Yucatán. Her worst fears were realized.

Only minutes later, the car pulled into a long paved driveway through tall steel gates. The gates closed behind them. They sped up to an impressive whitewashed beach house overlooking a rocky bay. It had red ceramic tiles and the grounds were immaculate and full of blooming flowers. Hibiscus in November. She could have laughed hysterically. Back home the trees were bare, and here everything was blooming. She wondered what sort of fertilizer they used to grow those hibiscus flowers so big, and then she remembered Lopez's recent body count. She wondered if she might end up planted in his garden…

The car stopped. The door was opened by a suited dark man holding an automatic rifle of some sort, one of those little snub-nosed machine guns that crooks on television always seemed to carry.

She winced as the men dragged her out of the car and frog-marched her, bonds and all, into the ceramic tile floored lobby. The tile was black and white, like a chessboard. There was a long, graceful staircase and, overhead, a crystal chandelier that looked like Waterford crystal. It probably cost two or three times the price of her car.

As she searched her surroundings, a small middle-aged man strolled out of the living room with his hands in his pockets. He didn't smile. He walked around Callie as if she were some sort of curiosity, his full lips pursed, his small dark eyes narrow and smugly gleaming. He jerked her gag down.

"Miss Kirby," he murmured in accented English. "Welcome to my home. I am Manuel Lopez. You will be my guest until your interfering stepbrother tries to rescue you," he added, hesitating in front of her. "And when he arrives, I will give him what my men have left of you, before I kill him, too!"

Callie thought that she'd never seen such cruelty in a human being's eyes in her life. The man made her knees shake. He was looking at her with contempt and possession. He reached out a stubby hand and ripped her blouse down in front, baring her small breasts in their cotton bra.

"I had expected a more attractive woman," he said. "Sadly you have no attractions with which to bargain, have you? Small breasts and a body that would afford little satisfaction. But Kalid likes women," he mused, glancing at the small, dark man who'd been sitting across from Callie. "When I need information, he is the man who obtains it for me. And although I need no information from you, Miss Kirby," he murmured, "it will please Kalid to practice his skills."

A rapid-fire burst of a guttural language met the statement.

"Español!" Lopez snapped. "You know I do not understand Arabic!"

"The woman," one of the other men replied in Spanish. "Before you give her to Kalid, let us have her."

Lopez glanced at the two thin, unshaven men who'd delivered Callie to him and smiled. "Why not? I make you a present of her. It should arouse even more guilt in her stepbrother to find her...used. But not until I tell you," he added coldly. "For now, take her to the empty servant's room upstairs. And put the gag back in place," he added. "I have important guests arriving. I would not want them to be disturbed by any unexpected noise."

"My stepbrother won't come to rescue me," she said hoarsely, shocked. "He isn't a physical sort of man. Aren't you going to ask him to pay ransom?"

Lopez looked at her as if she were nuts. "Why do you think Steele will not come after you?"

"He's a doctor. Or he was studying to be one. He wouldn't know the first thing about rescuing somebody!"

Lopez seemed to find that amusing.

"Besides that," she added harshly, "he hates me. He'll probably laugh his head off when he knows you've got me. He can't stand the sight of me."

That seemed to disturb Lopez, but after a minute he shrugged. *"No importa,"* he said lightly. "If he comes, that will be good. If not, it will make him even more concerned for his father. Who will be," he added with a cold smile, "next to feel my wrath."

Callie had her mouth open to ask another question, but at a signal from Lopez she was half dragged out of the room, her pale blue eyes as wide as saucers as she shivered with fear.

2

C allie had never been in such danger in her life, although she certainly knew what it was to be manhandled. She'd been in and out of foster care since the age of six. On a rare visit home, one of her mother's lovers had broken her arm when she was thirteen, after trying to fondle her. She'd run from him in horror, and he'd caught up with her at the staircase. A rough scuffle with the man had sent her tumbling down the steps to lie sprawled at the foot of the staircase.

Her mother had been furious, but not at her boyfriend, who said that Callie had called him names and threatened to tell her mother lies about him. After her broken arm had been set in a cast, Anna had taken Callie right back to her foster home, making her out to be incorrigible and washing her hands of responsibility for her.

Oddly, it had been Jack Steele's insistence that he wanted the child that had pushed a reluctant Anna into taking her back, at the age of fifteen. Jack had won her over, a day at a time. When Micah was home for holidays, he'd taunted her, made his disapproval of her so noticeable that her first lesson in the Steele home was learning how to avoid Jack's grown son. She'd had a lot of practice at avoiding men by then, and a lot of emotional scars. Anna had found that amusing. Never much of a mother, she'd ignored Callie to such an extent that the only affection Callie ever got was from Jack.

She closed her eyes. Her own father had ripped her out of his arms when she was six and pushed her away when she begged to stay with him. She was some other man's bastard, he'd raged, and he wanted no part of her. She could get out with her tramp of a mother—whom he'd just caught in bed with a rich friend—and he never wanted to see either of them again. She'd loved her father. She never understood why he couldn't love her back. Well, he thought she wasn't his. She couldn't really blame him for feeling that way.

She was still sitting in a small bedroom that night, having been given nothing to eat or drink. She was weak with hunger and pain, because the bonds that held her wrists and ankles had chafed and all but cut off the circulation. She heard noise downstairs from time to time. Obviously Lopez's visitors had stayed a long time, and been quite entertained, from the sound of things. She could hear the soft whisper of the ocean teasing the shore outside the window. She wondered what they would do with her body, after they killed her. Perhaps they'd throw her out there, to be eaten by sharks.

While she was agonizing over her fate, the sky had darkened. Hours more passed, during which she dozed a little. Then suddenly, she was alone no longer. The door opened and closed. She opened her tired eyes and saw the three men who'd kidnapped her, gathered around her like a pack of dogs with a helpless cat. One of them started stripping her while the others watched. Her cell phone fell out of the pocket of her slacks as they were pulled off her long legs. One of the men tossed it up and laughed, speaking to another man in yet a different foreign language.

Callie closed her eyes, shivering with fear, and prayed for strength to bear what was coming. She wished with all her heart that Micah hadn't pushed her away that last Christmas they'd spent together. Better him than any one of these cold, cruel, mocking strangers.

She heard one of them speaking in rough Spanish, discussing her body, making fun of her small breasts. It was like a playback from one foster home when she was fifteen, where an older son of the family had almost raped her before he was interrupted by the return of his parents. She'd run away afterward, and been sent to another foster home. She'd been saved that time, but she could expect no help now. Micah wouldn't begin to know how to rescue her, even if he was inclined to save her. He probably wouldn't consider ransom, either. She was alone in the world, with no one who would care about her fate. Her mother probably wouldn't even be bothered if she died. Like Micah, she'd blamed Callie for what had happened.

Desperate for some way to endure the ordeal, to block it out, Callie pictured the last time she'd seen her grandmother before she passed away, standing in an arbor of little pink fairy roses, waving. Callie had often stayed with her father's widowed mother when he and Anna were traveling. It was a haven of love. It hadn't lasted. Her grandmother had died suddenly when she was five. Everyone she'd ever loved had left her, in one way or the other. Nobody would even miss her. Maybe Jack would. She spared one last thought for the poor old man who was as alone as she was. But with her out of the way, perhaps Micah would go home again...

There was a loud, harsh shout. She heard the door open, and the men leave. With a shivery sigh, she moved backward until she could ease down into a worn wing chair by the fireplace. It wasn't going to be a long reprieve, she knew. If only she could free herself! But the bonds were cutting into her wrists and ankles. She was left in only a pair of aged white briefs and a tattered white bra, worn for comfort and not for appearance. No one had seen her in her underwear since she was a small child. She felt tears sting her eyes as she sat there, vulnerable and sick and ashamed. Any minute now, those men would be back. They would untie her before they used her. She knew that. She had to try to catch them off guard the instant she was free and run. If she could get into the jungle, she might have a chance. She was a fast sprinter, and she knew woodcraft. It was the last desperate hope she had.

One of the men, the one who'd asked Lopez for her, came back inside for a minute, staring at her. He pulled out a wicked looking little knife and flicked it at one shoulder strap of her bra, cutting right through it.

She called him a foul name in Spanish, making herself understood despite the gag. Her mind raced along. If she could make him angry enough to free her, which he'd have to do if he had rape in mind... She repeated the foul name, with more fervor.

He cursed. But instead of pulling her up to untie her, he caught her by the shoulder and pressed her hard back into the chair, easing the point of the knife against the soft, delicate upper part of her breast.

She moaned hoarsely as the knife lightly grazed her flesh.

"You will learn manners before we finish with you," he drawled icily, in rough Spanish. "You will do what I tell you!"

He made no move to free her. Instead, he jerked down the side of her bra that had been cut, and stared mockingly at her breast.

The prick from the knife stung. She ground her teeth together. What had she been thinking? He wasn't going to free her. He was going to torture her! She felt sick unto death with fear as she looked up into his eyes and realized that he was enjoying both her shame and her fear.

In fact, he laughed. He went back and locked the door. "We don't need to be disturbed, do we?" he purred as he walked back toward her, brandishing the sharp knife. "I have looked forward to this all the way from Texas..."

Her eyes closed. She said a last, silent prayer. She thought of Micah, and of Jack. Her chin lifted as she waited bravely for the impact of the blade.

There was a commotion downstairs and a commotion outside. She'd hoped it might divert the man standing over her with that knife, but he was too intent on her vulnerable state to care what was going on elsewhere. He put one hand on the back of the chair, beside her head, and placed the point of the knife right against her breast.

"Beg me not to do it," he chuckled. "Come on. Beg me."

Her terrified eyes met his and she knew that he was going to violate her. It was in his face. He was almost drooling with pleasure. She was cold all over, sick, resigned. She would die, eventually. But in the meantime, she was going to suffer a fate that would make death welcome.

"Beg me!" he demanded, his eyes flashing angrily, and the blade pushed harder.

There was a sudden burst of gunfire from somewhere toward the front of the house. Simultaneously, there was shattering glass behind the man threatening her, and the sudden audible sound of bullets hitting flesh. The man with the knife groaned once and fell into a silent, red-stained heap at her feet.

Wide-eyed, terrified, shaking, Callie cried out as she looked up into a face completely covered with a black mask, except for slits that bared a little of his eyes and mouth. He was dressed all in black with a wicked looking little machine gun in one hand and a huge knife suddenly in the other. His eyes went to her nicked breast. He made a rough sound and kicked the man on the floor aside as he pulled Callie up out of the chair and cut the bonds at her ankles and wrists.

Her hands and feet were asleep. She almost fell. He didn't even stop to unfasten the gag. Without a word, he bent and lifted her over his shoulder in the classic fireman's carry, and walked straight toward the window. Apparently, he was going out it, with her.

He finished clearing away the broken glass around the window frame and pulled a long black cord toward him. It seemed to be hanging from the roof.

He was huge and very strong. Callie, still in shock from her most recent ordeal, her feet and hands almost numb, didn't try to talk. She didn't even protest. If this was a turf war, and she was being stolen by another drug lord, perhaps he'd just hold her for ransom and not let his men torture her. She had little to say about her own fate. She closed her eyes and noticed that there was a familiar smell about the man who was abducting her. Odd. He must be wearing some cologne that reminded her of Jack, or even Mr. Kemp. At least he'd saved her from the knife.

Her wounded breast hurt, where it was pressed against the ribbed fabric of his long-sleeved shirt, and the small cut was bleeding slightly, but that didn't seem to matter. As long as he got her out of Lopez's clutches, she didn't really care what happened to her anymore. She was exhausted.

With her still over his shoulder, he stepped out onto the ledge, grasped a thick black cord in a gloved hand and, with his rifle leveled and facing forward, he rappelled right out the second-story window and down to the ground with Callie on his shoulder. She gasped as she felt the first seconds of free fall, and her hands clung to his shirt, but he didn't drop her. He seemed quite adept at rappelling.

She'd read about the Australian rappel, where men went down the rope face-front with a weapon in one hand. She'd never seen it done, except on television and in adventure movies. She'd never seen anyone doing it with a hostage over one shoulder. This man was very skillful. She wondered if he really was a rival drug lord, or if perhaps he was one of Eb Scott's mercenaries. Was it possible that Micah would have cared enough to ask Eb to mount her rescue? Her heart leaped at the possibility.

As they reached the ground, she realized that her rescuer wasn't alone. As soon as they were on the ground, he made some sort of signal with one hand, and men dressed in black, barely visible in the security lights dotted along the dark estate, scattered to the winds. Men in suits, still firing after them, began to run toward the jungle.

A four-wheel-drive vehicle was sitting in the driveway with its engine running and the backseat door open, waiting.

Her rescuer threw her inside, climbed in beside her and slammed the door. She pulled the gag off.

"Hit it!" he bit off.

The vehicle spun dirt and gravel as it took off toward the gate. The windows were open. Gunfire hit the side of the door, and was returned by the man sitting beside Callie and the man in the front passenger seat. The other armed man had a slight, neatly trimmed beard and mustache and he looked as formidable as his comrade. The man who was driving handled the vehicle expertly, dodging bullets even as his companions returned fire at the pursuing vehicle. Callie had seen other armed men in black running for the jungle. She revised her opinion that these were rival drug dealers. From the look of these men, they were commandos. She assumed that these three men were part of some sort of covert group sent in to rescue her. Only one person would have the money to mount such an expedition, and she'd have bet money that Eb Scott was behind it somehow. Micah must have paid him to hire these men to come after her.

If he had, she was grateful for his intervention, although she wondered what had prompted it. Perhaps his father had persuaded him. God knew, he'd never have spent that sort of money on her rescue for his own sake. Her sudden disappearance out of his life would have delighted him.

She was chilled and embarrassed, sitting in her underwear with three strange men, but her clothing had been ripped beyond repair. In fact, her rescuer hadn't even stopped to grab it up on his way out of the room where she was being held. She made herself as inconspicuous as possible, grateful that there was no light inside the vehicle, and closed her eyes while the sound of gunfire ricocheted around her. She didn't say a word. Her companions seemed quite capable of handling this new emergency.

She wasn't going to distract them. If she caught a stray bullet, that was all right, too. Anything, even death, would be preferable to what she would endure if Lopez regained custody of her.

Half a mile down the road, there was a deep curve. The big man who'd rescued Callie told the man in front to stop the vehicle. He grabbed a backpack on the floorboard, jumped out, pulled Callie out, and motioned the driver and the man with the beard and mustache to keep going. The big man carried Callie out of sight of the road and dashed her down in the dark jungle undergrowth, his powerful body lying alongside hers in dead leaves and debris while they waited for the Jeep that had been chasing them to appear. Thorns dug into her bare arms and legs, but she was so afraid that she hardly noticed.

Suddenly, the pursuing Jeep came into sight. It braked for the curve, but it barely slowed down as it shot along after the other vehicle. Its taillights vanished around the bend. So far, so good, Callie thought, feeling oddly safe with the warmth and strength of the man lying so close beside her. But she hoped the man who was driving their vehicle and his bearded companion made a clean getaway. She wouldn't want them shot, even to save herself.

"That went well," her companion murmured curtly, rising. He pulled out some sort of electronic gadget and pushed buttons. He turned, sighting along it. "Can you walk?" he asked Callie.

His voice was familiar. Her mind must be playing tricks. She stood up, still in her underwear and barefoot.

"Yes. But I...don't have any shoes," she said hoarsely, still half in shock.

He looked down at her, aiming a tiny flashlight at her body, and a curse escaped his mouth as he saw her mangled bra.

"What the hell did they do to you?" he asked through his teeth.

Amazing, how familiar that deep voice was. "Not as much as they planned to, thanks to you," she said, trying to remain calm. "It's not a bad cut, just a graze. I'll have to have some sort of shoes if we're going to walk. And I...I don't suppose you have an extra shirt?" she added with painful dignity.

He was holding a backpack. He pulled out a big black T-shirt and stuffed her into it. He had a pair of camouflage pants, too. They had to be rolled up, but they fit uncannily well. His face was solemn as he dug into the bag a second time and pulled out a pair of leather loafers and two pairs of socks.

"They'll be too big, but the socks will help them fit. They'll help protect your feet. Hurry. Lopez's men are everywhere and we have a rendezvous to make."

She felt more secure in the T-shirt and camouflage pants. Not wanting to hold him up, she slipped quickly into the two pairs of thick socks and rammed her feet into the shoes. It was dark, but her companion had his small light trained ahead. She noticed that huge knife in his left hand as he started ahead of her. She remembered that Micah was left-handed...

The jungle growth was thick, but passable. Her companion shifted his backpack, so dark that it blended in with his dark gear and the jungle.

"Stay close behind me. Don't speak unless I tell you to. Don't move unless I move."

"Okay," she said in a husky whisper, without argument.

"When we get where we're going, I'll take care of that cut."

She didn't answer him. She was exhausted. She was also dying of thirst and hunger, but she knew there wasn't time for the luxury of food. She concentrated on where she was putting her feet, and prayed that she wouldn't trip over a huge snake. She knew there were snakes and lizards and huge spiders in the jungle. She was afraid, but Lopez was much more terrorizing a threat than a lonesome snake.

She followed her taciturn companion through the jungle growth, her eyes restless, her ears listening for any mechanical sound. The darkness was oddly comforting, because sound traveled so well in it. Once, she heard a quick, sharp rustle of the underbrush and stilled, but her companion quickly trained his light on it. It was only an iguana.

She laughed with delight at the unexpected encounter, bringing a curt jerk of the head from her companion, who seemed to find her amusement odd. He didn't say anything, though. He glanced at his instrument again, stopped to listen and look, and started off again.

Thorns in some of the undergrowth tore at her bare arms and legs, and her face. She didn't complain. Remembering where she'd been just before she was rescued made her grateful for any sort of escape, no matter how physically painful it might be.

She began to make a mental list of things she had to do when they reached safety. First on the list was to phone and see if Jack Steele was all right. He must be worried about her sudden disappearance. She didn't want him to suffer a setback.

Her lack of conversation seemed to puzzle the big man leading her through the jungle. He glanced back at her frequently, presumably to make sure she was behind him, but he didn't speak. He made odd movements, sometimes doubling back on the trail he made, sometimes deliberately snapping twigs and stepping on grass in directions they didn't go. Callie just followed along mindlessly.

At least two hours passed before he stopped, near a small stream. "We should be safe enough here for the time being," he remarked as he put down the backpack and opened it, producing a small bottle of water. He tossed it to Callie. "I imagine you're thirsty."

She opened it with trembling hands and swallowed half of it down at once, tears stinging her eyes at the pleasure of the wetness on her tongue, in her dry mouth.

He set up a small, self-contained light source, revealing his companion. He moved closer, frowning at her enthusiastic swallowing as he drew a first aid kit from his backpack. "When did you last have anything to drink?" he asked softly.

"Day...before yesterday," she choked.

He cursed. In the same instant, he pulled off the mask he'd been wearing, and Callie dropped the water bottle as her eyes encountered the dark ones of her stepbrother, Micah, in the dim light.

He picked up the water bottle and handed it back to her. "I thought it might come as a shock," he said grimly, noting her expression.

"You came after me yourself?" she asked, aghast. "But, how? Why?"

"Lopez has an agent in one of the federal agencies," he told her flatly. "I don't know who it is. I couldn't risk letting them come down here looking for you and having someone sell you out before I got here. Not that it would have been anytime soon. They're probably still arguing over jurisdictions as we speak." He pulled out a foil-sealed package and tossed it to her. "It's the equivalent of an MRE—a meal ready to eat. Nothing fancy, but if you're hungry, you won't mind the taste."

"Thanks," she said huskily, tearing into it with urgent fingers that trembled with hunger.

He watched her eat ravenously, and he scowled. "No food, either?"

She shook her head. "You don't feed people you're going to kill," she mumbled through bites of chicken and rice that tasted freshly cooked, if cold.

He was very still. "Excuse me?"

She glanced at him while she chewed a cube of chicken. "He gave me to three of his men and told them to kill me." She swallowed and averted her eyes. "He said they could do whatever they liked to me first. So they did. At least, they started to, when you showed up. I was briefly alone with a smaller man, Arabic I think, and I tried to make him mad enough to release me so I had one last chance at escape. It made him mad, all right, but instead of untying me, he…put his knife into me." She chewed another cube of chicken, trying not to break down. "He said it was a…a taste of what to expect if I resisted him again. When you came in through the window, he was just about to violate me."

"I'm going to take care of that cut right now. Infection sets in fast in tropical areas like this." He opened the first-aid box and checked through his supplies. He muttered something under his breath.

He took the half-finished meal away from her and stripped her out of the T-shirt. She grimaced and lowered her eyes as her mutilated bra and her bare breast were revealed, but she didn't protest.

"I know this is going to be hard for you, considering what

you've just been through. But try to remember that I'm a doctor," he said curtly. "As near as not, anyway."

She swallowed, her eyes still closed tight. "At least you won't make fun of my body while you're working on it," she said miserably.

He was opening a small bottle. "What's that?"

"Nothing," she said wearily. "Oh God, I'm so tired!"

"I can imagine."

She felt his big, warm hands reach behind her to unfasten the bra and she caught it involuntarily.

He glanced at her face in the small circle of light from the lantern. "If there was another way, I'd take it."

She drew in a slow breath and closed her eyes, letting go of the fabric. She bit her lip and didn't look as he peeled the fabric away from her small, firm breasts.

The sight of the small cut made him furious. She had pretty little breasts, tip-tilted, with dusky nipples. He could feel himself responding to the sight of her, and he had to bite down hard on a wave of desire.

He forced himself to focus on the cut, and nothing else. The bra, he stuffed in his backpack. He didn't dare leave signs behind them. There wasn't much chance that they were closely followed, but he had to be careful.

He had to touch her breast to clean the small cut, and she jerked involuntarily.

"I won't hurt you any more than I have to," he promised quietly, mistaking her reaction for pain. "Grit your teeth."

She did, but it didn't help. She bit almost through her lip as he cleaned the wound. The sight of his big, lean hands on her body was breathtaking, arousing even under the circumstances.

The pain was secondary to the hunger she felt for him, a hunger that had lasted for years. He didn't know, and she couldn't let him know. He hated her.

She closed her eyes while he put a soft bandage over the cleaned wound, taping it in place.

"God in heaven, I thought I'd seen every kind of lowlife on earth, but the guy who did this to you was a class all by himself," he growled.

She remembered the man and shuddered. Micah was pulling the shirt down over her bandaged breast. "It probably doesn't seem like it, but I got off lucky," she replied.

He looked into her eyes. "It's just a superficial wound so you won't need stitches. It probably won't even leave a scar there."

"It wouldn't matter," she said quietly.

"It would." He got up, drawing her up with him. "You're still nervous of me, after all this time."

She didn't meet his eyes. "You don't like me."

"Oh, for God's sake," he burst out, letting go of her shoulders. He turned away to deal with the medical kit. "Haven't you got eyes?"

She wondered what that meant. She was too tired to work it out. She sat down again and picked up her half-eaten meal, finishing it with relish. It was hard to look at him, after he'd seen her like that.

She fingered the rolled-up pair of camouflage pants she was wearing. "These aren't big enough to be yours," she remarked.

"They're Maddie's. She gave me those for you, and the shoes and socks, on the way out of Texas," he commented when he noticed her curious exploration of the pants.

He worked with some sort of electronic device.

"What's that thing?" she asked.

"GPS," he explained. "Global positioning. I can give my men a fix on our position, so they can get a chopper in here to pick us up and pinpoint our exact location. There's a clearing just through there where we'll rendezvous," he added, nodding toward the jungle.

Suddenly she frowned. "Who's Maddie?" she asked.

"Maddie's my scrounger. Anything we need on site that we didn't bring, Maddie can get. She's quite a girl. In fact," he added, "she looks a lot like you. She was mistaken for you at a wedding I went to recently in Washington, D.C."

That was disturbing. It sounded as though he and this Maddie were in partnership or something. She hated the jealousy she felt, when she had no right to be jealous. Old habits died hard.

"Is she here?" she asked, still puzzled by events and Micah's strange skills.

"No. We left her back in the States. She's working on some information I need, about the mole working for the feds, and getting some of your things together to send on to Miami."

She blinked. "You keep saying 'we,'" she pointed out.

His chin lifted. He studied her, unsmiling. "Exactly what do you think I do for a living, Callie?" In the dim light, his blond hair shone like muted moonlight. His handsome face was all angles and shadows. Her vision was still a little blurred from whatever the kidnapper had given her. So was her mind.

"Your mother left you a trust," she pointed out.

"My mother left me ten thousand dollars," he replied. "That wouldn't pay to replace the engine on the Ferrari I drive in Nassau."

Her hands stilled on the fork and tray. Some odd ideas were popping into her head. "You finished your residency?" she fished.

He shook his head. "Medicine wasn't for me."

"Then, what...?"

"Use your mind, Callie," he said finally, irritated. "How many men do you know who could rappel into a drug lord's lair and spirit out a hostage?"

Her breath caught. "You work for some federal agency?"

"Good God!" He got up, moved to his backpack and started repacking it. "You really don't have a clue, do you?"

"I don't know much about you, Micah," she confided quietly as she finished her meal and handed him the empty tray and fork. "That was the way you always wanted it."

"In some cases, it doesn't pay to advertise," he said carelessly. "I used to work with Eb Scott and Cy Parks, but now I have my own group. We hire out to various world governments for covert ops." He glanced at her stunned face. "I worked for the justice department for a couple of years, but now I'm a mercenary, Callie."

She was struck dumb for several long seconds. She swallowed. It explained a lot. "Does your father know?" she asked.

"He does not," he told her. "And I don't want him to know. If he still gives a damn about me, it would only upset him."

"He loves you very much," she said quietly, avoiding his angry black eyes. "He'd like to mend fences, but he doesn't know how. He feels guilty, for making you leave and blaming you for what...what my mother did."

He pulled out a foil sealed meal for himself and opened it before he spoke. "You blamed me, as well."

She wrapped her arms around herself. It was cold in the jungle at night, just like they said in the movies. "Not really. My mother is very beautiful," she said, recalling the older woman's wavy jet-black hair and vivid blue eyes and pale skin. "She was a model just briefly, before she married my...her first husband."

He frowned. "You were going to say, your father."

She shivered. "He said I wasn't his child. He caught her in bed with some rich man when I was six. I didn't understand at the time, but he pushed me away pretty brutally and said not to come near him again. He said he didn't know whose child I was. That was when she put me in foster care."

Micah stared at her, unspeaking, for several long seconds. "Put you in what?"

She swallowed. "She gave me up for adoption on the grounds that she couldn't support me. I went into a juvenile home, and from there to half a dozen foster homes. I only saw her once in all those years, when she took me home for Christmas. It didn't last long." She stared down at the jungle floor. "When she married your father, he wanted me, so she told him I'd been staying with my grandmother. I was in a foster home, but she got me out so she could convince your father that she was a good mother." She laughed hollowly. "I hadn't seen her or heard from her in two years by then. She told me I'd better make a good job of pretending affection, or she'd tell the authorities I'd stolen something valuable—and instead of going back into foster care for two more years, I'd go to jail."

3

Micah didn't say a word. He repacked the first-aid kit into his backpack with quick, angry movements. He didn't look at Callie.

"I guess you know how to use that gun," she said quietly. "If we're found, or if it looks like Lopez is going to catch us, I want you to shoot me. I'd rather die than face what you saved me from."

She said it in such a calm, quiet tone that it made all the more impact.

He looked up, scanning her drawn, white face in the soft light from the lantern. "He won't get you. I promise."

She drew a slow breath. "Thanks." She traced a fingernail over the camouflage pants. "And thanks for coming to get me. Lopez said he didn't have any plans to ransom me. He was going to let his men kill me because he thought it would make you suffer."

"What did you tell him?"

"That you were my worst enemy and you wouldn't care if he killed me," she said carelessly. "But he said you did care about your father, and he was the next victim. I hope you've got someone watching Dad," she added fervently. "If anything happens to him...!"

"You really love him, don't you?" he asked in an odd tone.

"He's the only person in my whole life who ever loved me," she said in a strained whisper.

A harsh sound broke from his lips. He got up and started getting things together. He pulled out what looked like a modified cell phone and spoke into it. A minute later, he put it back into the backpack.

"They're on the way in." He stood over her, his face grim as he picked up the small lantern and extinguished the light. "I know you must be cold. I'm sorry. I planned a quick airlift, so I didn't pack for a prolonged trek."

"It's all right," she said at once. "Cold is better than tortured."

He cursed under his breath as he hefted the backpack. "We have to get to that small clearing on the other side of the stream. It isn't deep, but I can carry you..."

"I'll walk," she said with quiet dignity, standing up. It was still painful to move, because she'd been tied up for so long, but she didn't let on. "You've done enough already."

"I've done nothing," he spat. He turned on his heel and led the way to the bank of the small stream, offering a hand.

She didn't take it. She knew he found her repulsive. He'd even told her mother that. She'd enjoyed taunting Callie with it. Callie had never understood why her mother hated her so much. Perhaps it was because she wasn't pretty.

"Walk where I do," he bit off as he dropped his hand. "The rocks will be slippery. Go around them, not over them."

"Okay."

He glanced over his shoulder as they started over the shallow stream. "You're damned calm for someone who's been through what you have in the past two days."

She only smiled. "You have no idea what I've been through in my life."

He averted his eyes. It was as if he couldn't bear to look at her anymore. He picked his way across to the other bank. Callie followed obediently, her feet cold and wet, her body shivering. Only a little longer, she told herself, and she would be home with Jack. She would be completely safe. Except...Lopez was still out there. She shivered again.

"Cold?" he asked when they were across.

"I'll be fine," she assured him.

He led her through one final tangle of brush, which he cut out of the way with the knife. She could see the silver ripple of the long blade in the dim light of the small flashlight he carried. She put one foot in front of the other and tried to blank out what would happen if Lopez's men caught up with them. It was terrifying.

They made it to the clearing just as a dark, noisy silhouette dropped from the sky and a door opened.

"They spotted us on radar!" came a loud voice from the chopper. "They'll be here in two minutes. Run!"

"Run as if your life depended on it!" Micah told Callie, giving her a push.

She did run, her mind so affected by what she'd already endured that she almost kept up with her long-legged stepbrother. He leaped right up into the chopper and gave her a hand up. She landed in a heap on the dirty floor, and laughed with relief.

The door closed and the chopper lifted. Outside, there were sounds like firecrackers in the wake of the noise the propellers made. Gunfire, Callie knew.

"It always sounds like firecrackers in real life," she murmured. "It doesn't sound that way in the movies."

"They augment the sound in movies, mademoiselle." A gentle hand eased her into a seat on the edge of the firing line Micah and two other men made at the door.

She looked up. There was barely any light in the helicopter, but she could make out a beard and a mustache on a long, lean face. "You made it, too!" she exclaimed with visible relief. "Oh, I'm glad. I felt bad that you and the other man had to be decoys, just to get me out."

"It was no trouble, mademoiselle," the man said gently, smiling at her. "Rest now. They won't catch us. This is an Apache helicopter, one of the finest pieces of equipment your country makes. It has some age, but we find it quite reliable in tight situations."

"Is it yours?" she asked.

He laughed. "You might say that we have access to it, and various other aircraft, when we need them."

"Don't bore her to death, Bojo," a younger voice chuckled.

"Listen to him!" Bojo exclaimed. "And do you not drone on eternally about that small computer you carry, Peter, and its divine functions?"

A dark-haired, dark-eyed young man with white teeth came into view, a rifle slung over his shoulder. "Computers are my specialty," he said with a grin. "You're Callie? I'm Peter Stone. I'm from Brooklyn. That's Bojo, he's from Morocco. I guess you know Micah. And Smith over there—"he indicated a huge dark-eyed man "—runs a seafood restaurant in Charleston, along with our Maddie and a couple of guys we seem to have misplaced..."

"We haven't misplaced them," Micah said curtly. "They've gone ahead to get the DC-3 gassed up."

Bojo grinned. "Lopez will have men waiting at the airport for us."

"While we're taking off where we landed—at Laremos's private airstrip," Micah replied calmly. "And Laremos will have a small army at his airstrip, just in case Lopez does try anything."

"But what about customs?" Callie voiced.

Everybody laughed.

She flushed, realizing now that her captors hadn't gone through customs, and neither had these men. "Okay, I get it, but what about getting back into the States from here? I don't have a passport..."

"You have a birth certificate," Micah reminded her. "It'll be waiting in Miami, along with a small bag containing some of your own clothes and shoes. That's why Maddie didn't come with us," he added smugly.

"Miami?" she exclaimed, recalling belatedly that he'd mentioned that before. "Why not Texas?"

"You're coming back to the Bahamas with me, Callie," Micah replied. "You'll be Lopez's priority now. He'll be out for revenge, and it will take all of us to keep you safe."

She gaped at him. "But, Dad..." she groaned.

"Dad is in good hands. So are you. Now try not to worry. I know what I'm doing."

She bit her lower lip. None of this was making sense, and she was still scared, every time she thought about Lopez. But all these men surrounding her looked tough and battle-hardened, and she knew they wouldn't let her be recaptured.

"Who's Laremos?" Callie asked curiously, a minute later.

"He's retired now," Micah said, coming away from the door. "But he and 'Dutch' van Meer and J. D. Brettman were the guys who taught us the trade. They were the best. Laremos lives outside Cancún on a plantation with his wife and kids, and he's got the equivalent of a small army around him. Even the drug lords avoid his place. We'll get out all right, even if Lopez has his men tracking us."

She averted her eyes and folded her arms tightly around her body.

"You are shivering," Bojo said gently. "Here." He found a blanket and wrapped it around her.

That one simple act of compassion brought all her repressed fear and anguish to the surface. She bawled. Not a sound touched her lips. But tears poured from her eyes, draping themselves hot and wet across her pale cheeks and down to the corner of her pretty bow mouth.

Micah saw them and his face hardened like rock.

She turned her face toward the other side of the helicopter. She was used to hiding her tears. They mostly angered people, made them more hostile. Or they showed a weakness that was readily exploited. It was always better not to let people know they had the power to hurt you.

She wrapped the blanket closer and didn't speak the rest of the way. She closed her eyes, wiping at them with the blanket. Micah spoke in low tones to the other men, and although she couldn't understand what he was saying, she understood that rough, angry tone. She'd heard it enough at home.

For now, all she wanted to do was get to safety, to a place where Lopez and the animals who worked for him couldn't find her, couldn't hurt her. She was more afraid now than she had been on the way out of Texas, because now she knew what re-capture would mean. The darkness was a friend in which she could hide her fear, conceal her terror. The sound of the pro-pellers became suddenly like a mechanical lullaby in her ears, lulling her, like the whispers of the deep voices around her, into a brief, fitful sleep.

She felt an odd lightness in her stomach and opened her eyes to find the helicopter landing at what looked like a small airstrip on private land.

A big airplane, with scars and faded lettering, was waiting with its twin prop engines already running. Half a dozen armed men in camouflage uniforms stood with their guns ready to fire. A tall, imposing man with a mustache came forward. He had a Latin look about him, dark eyes and graceful movement.

He shook hands with Micah and spoke to him quietly, so that his voice didn't carry. Micah listened, and then nodded. They shook hands again. The man glanced at Callie curiously, and smiled in her direction.

She smiled back, her whole young face drawn and fatigued.

Micah motioned to her. "We have to get airborne before Lopez's men get here. Climb aboard. Thanks, Diego!" he called to the man.

"No es nada," came the grinning reply.

"Was that the man you know, with the plantation?" Callie asked when they were inside and the door was closed.

"That was Laremos," he agreed.

"He and his family won't be hurt on our account, will they?" she persisted.

He glanced down at her. "No," he said slowly. His eyes searched hers until she looked away, made uneasy and shivery by the way he was looking at her.

He turned and made his way down the aisle to the cockpit. Two men poked their heads out of it, grinning, and after he spoke to them, they revved up the engines.

The passengers strapped themselves into their seats. Callie started to sit by herself, but Micah took her arm and guided her into the seat beside his. It surprised her, but she didn't protest. He reached across her to fasten her seat belt, bringing his hard, muscular chest pressing gently against her breasts.

She gasped as the pressure made the cut painful.

"God, I'm sorry! I forgot," he said, his hand going naturally, protectively, to her breast, to cup it gently. "Is it bad?"

She went scarlet. Of course, nobody was near enough to see what was going on, but it embarrassed her to have him touch her with such familiarity. And then she remembered that he'd had her nude from the waist up on one side while he cleaned and bandaged that cut.

Her eyes searched his while she tried to speak. Her tongue felt swollen. Her breath came jerkily into her throat and her lips parted under its force. She felt winded, as if she'd fallen from a height.

His thumb soothed the soft flesh around the cut. "When we get to Miami, I'll take you to a friend of mine who's in private practice. We'll get you checked out before we fly out to the Bahamas."

His other arm, muscular and warm, was under her head. She could feel his breath, mint-scented and warm, on her lips as he searched her eyes.

His free hand left her breast and gently cupped her softly rounded chin. "Soft skin," he whispered deeply. "Soft heart. Sweet, soft mouth…"

His lips pressed the words against hers, probing tenderly. He caught her upper lip in both of his and tasted it with his tongue. Then he lifted away to look down into her shocked, curious eyes.

"You should hate me," he whispered. "I hurt you, and you did nothing, nothing at all to deserve it."

She winced, remembering how it had been when he'd lived with his father. "I understood. You resented me. My mother and I were interlopers."

"Your mother, maybe. Never you." He looked formidable, angry and bitter. But his black eyes were unreadable. "I've hesitated to ask. Maybe I don't really want to know. When Lopez had you," he began with uncharacteristic hesitation, "were you raped?"

"No," she said quietly. "But I was about to be. I remember thinking that if it hadn't all gone wrong that Christmas…" Her voice stopped. She was horrified at what she was about to say.

"I know," he interrupted, and he didn't smile. "I thought about it, too. What Lopez's damned henchmen did to you at least wouldn't have been your first experience of intimacy, if I hadn't acted like a prize heel with you!"

He seemed maddened by the knowledge. His hand on her face was hard and the pressure stung.

"Please," she whispered, tugging at his fingers.

He relaxed them at once. "I'm sorry," he bit off. "I'm still on edge. This whole thing has been a nightmare."

"Yes." She searched his black eyes, wishing she knew what he was thinking.

His thumb brushed softly over her swollen mouth. "Lopez will never get the chance to hurt you again," he said quietly. "I give you my word."

She bit her lower lip when his hand lifted away, shy of him. "Do you really think he'll come after me again?"

"I think he'll try," he said honestly.

She shivered, averting her eyes to the aisle beside them. "I hate remembering how helpless I was."

"I've been in similar situations," he said surprisingly. "Once I was captured on a mission and held for execution. I was tied up and tortured. I know how it feels."

She gaped at him, horrified. "How did you escape?"

"Bojo and the others came in after me," he said simply. "Under impossible odds, too." He smiled, and it was the first genuine smile he'd ever given her. "I guess they missed being yelled at."

She smiled back, hesitantly. It was new to relax with Micah, not to be on her guard against antagonistic and sarcastic comments.

He touched her face with a curious intensity in his eyes. "You must have been terrified when you were kidnapped. You've never known violence."

She didn't tell him, but she had, even if not as traumatically as she had at Lopez's. She lowered her gaze to his hard, disciplined mouth. "I never expected to be rescued at all, least of all by you. I wasn't even sure you'd agree to pay a ransom if they'd asked for one."

He scowled. "Why not?"

"You don't like me," she returned simply. "You never did."

He seemed disturbed. "It's a little more complicated than that, Callie."

"All the same, thank you for saving me," she continued. "You risked your own life to get me out."

"I've been risking it for years," he said absently while he studied her upturned face. She was too pale, and the fatigue she felt was visible. "Why don't you try to sleep? It's going to be a long flight."

Obviously he didn't want to talk. But she didn't mind. She was worn-out. "Okay," she agreed with a smile.

He moved back and she leaned her head back, closed her eyes, and the tension of the past two days caught up with her all at once. She fell asleep almost at once and didn't wake up until they were landing.

She opened her eyes to find a hard, warm pillow under her head. To her amazement, she was lying across Micah's lap, with her cheek on his chest.

"Wakey, wakey," he teased gently. "We're on the ground."

"Where?" she asked, rubbing her eyes like a sleepy child.

"Miami."

"Oh. At the airport."

He chuckled. "*An* airport," he corrected. "But this one isn't on any map."

He lifted her gently back into her own seat and got to his feet, stretching hugely. He grinned down at her. "Come on, pilgrim. We've got a lot to do, and not much time."

She let him lead her off the plane. The other men had all preceded them, leaving behind automatic weapons, pistols and other paraphernalia.

"Aren't you forgetting your equipment?" she asked Micah.

He smiled and put a long finger against her mouth. His eyes were full of mischief. He'd never joked with her, not in all the years they'd known each other.

"It isn't ours," he said in a stage whisper. "And see that building, and those guys coming out of it?"

"Yes."

"No," he corrected. "There's no building, and those guys don't exist. All of this is a figment of your imagination, especially the airplane."

"My gosh!" she exclaimed with wide eyes. "We're working for the CIA?"

He burst out laughing. "Don't even ask me who they are. I swore I'd never tell. And I never will. Now let's go, before they get here."

He and the others moved rapidly toward a big sport utility vehicle sitting just off the apron where they'd left the plane.

"Are you sure you cleared this with, uh—" Peter gave a quick glance at Callie "—the man who runs this place?"

"Eb did," Micah told him. "But just in case, let's get the hell out of Dodge, boys!"

He ran for the SUV, pushing Callie along. The others broke into a run, as well, laughing as they went.

There was a shout behind them, but it was still hanging on the air when the driver, one of the guys in the cockpit, burned rubber taking off.

"He'll see the license plate!" Callie squeaked as she saw a suited man with a notepad looking after them.

"That's the idea," the young man named Peter told her with a grin. "It's a really neat plate, too. So is this vehicle. It belongs to the local director of the—" he hesitated "—of an agency we know. We, uh, had a friend borrow it from his house last night."

"We'll go to prison for years!" Callie exclaimed, horrified.

"Not really," the driver said, pulling quickly into a parking spot at a local supermarket. "Everybody out."

Callie's head was spinning. They got out of the SUV and into a beige sedan sitting next to it, with keys in the ignition. She was crowded into the back with Micah and young Peter, while the two pilots, one a Hispanic and the other almost as blond as Micah, crowded Bojo on either side in the front. The driver took off at a sedate pace and pulled out into Miami traffic.

That was when she noticed that all the men were wearing gloves. She wasn't. "Oh, that's lovely," she muttered. "That's just lovely! Everybody's wearing gloves but me. My fingerprints will be the only ones they find, and *I'll* go to prison for years. I guess you'll all come and visit me Sundays, right?" she added accusingly.

Micah chuckled with pure delight. "The guy who owns the SUV is a friend of Eb's, and even though he doesn't show it, he has a sense of humor. He'll double up laughing when he runs your prints and realizes who had his four-wheel drive. I'll explain it to you later. Take us straight to Dr. Candler's office, Don," he told the blond guy at the wheel. "You know where it is."

"You bet, boss," came the reply.

"I'm not going to prison?" Callie asked again, just to be sure.

Micah pursed his lips. "Well, that depends on whether or not the guy at customs recognizes us. I was kidding!" he added immediately when she looked ready to cry.

She moved her shoulder and grimaced. "I'll laugh enthusiastically when I get checked out," she promised.

"He'll take good care of you," Micah assured her. "He and I were at medical school together."

"Is he, I mean, does he do what you do?"

"Not Jerry," he told her. "He specializes in trauma medicine. He's chief of staff at a small hospital here."

"I see," she said, nodding. "He's a normal person."

Micah gave her a speaking glance while the others chuckled.

The hospital where Micah's friend worked was only a few minutes from the airport. Micah took Callie inside while the others waited in the car. Micah had a private word with the receptionist, who nodded and left her desk for a minute. She came back with a tall, dark-headed man about Micah's age. He motioned to Micah.

Callie was led back into an examination room. Micah sank into a chair by the desk.

"Are you going to sit there the whole time?" Callie asked Micah, aghast, when the doctor asked her to remove the shirt she was wearing so he could examine her.

"You haven't got anything that I haven't seen, and I need to explain to Jerry what I did to treat your wound." He proceeded to do that while Callie, uncomfortable and shy, turned her shoulder to him and removed the shirt.

After checking her vital signs, Dr. Candler took the bandage off and examined the small red cut with a scowling face. "How did this happen?" he asked curtly.

"One of Lopez's goons had a knife and liked to play games with helpless women," Micah said coldly.

"I hope he won't be doing it again," the physician murmured as he cleaned and redressed the superficial wound.

"That's classified," Micah said simply.

Callie glanced at him, surprised. His black eyes met hers, but he didn't say anything else.

"I'm going to give you a tetanus shot as a precaution," Dr. Candler said with a professional smile. "But I can almost guarantee that the cut won't leave a scar when it heals. I imagine it stings."

"A little," Callie agreed.

"I need to give her a full examination," Dr. Candler told him after giving Callie the shot. "Why don't you go outside and smoke one of those contraband Cuban cigars I'm not supposed to know you have?"

"They aren't contraband," Micah told him. "It isn't illegal if you get given one that someone has purchased in Cuba. Cobb was down there last month and he brought me back several."

"Leave it to you to find a legal way to do something illegal," Candler chuckled.

"Speaking of which, I'd better give a mutual acquaintance a quick call and thank him for the loan of his equipment." He glanced at Callie and smiled softly. "Then maybe Callie can relax while you finish here."

She didn't reply. He went out and closed the door behind him. She let out an audible sigh of relief.

"Now," Dr. Candler said as he continued to examine her. "Tell me what happened."

She did, still shaken and frightened by what she'd experienced in the last two days. He listened while he worked, his face giving nothing away.

"What happened to the man who did it?" he persisted.

She gave him an innocent smile. "I really don't know," she lied.

He sighed. "You and Micah." He shook his head. "Have you known him long?"

"Since I was fifteen," she told him. "His father and my mother were briefly married."

"You're Callie!" the doctor said at once.

4

The look on Callie's face was priceless. "How did you know?" she asked.

He smiled. "Micah talks about you a lot."

That was a shocker. "I didn't think he wanted anybody to know I even existed," she pointed out.

He pursed his lips. "Well, let's just say that he has ambiguous feelings about you."

Ambiguous. Right. Plainly stated, he couldn't stand her. But if that was true, why had he come himself to rescue her, instead of just sending his men?

She drew in a breath as he tended to her. "Am I going to be okay?"

"You're going to be good as new in a few days." He smiled at her. "Trust me."

"Micah seems to."

"He should. I taught him everything he knows about surgery," he chuckled. "I was a year ahead of him when we were in graduate school, and I took classes for one of the professors occasionally."

She smiled. "You're very good."

"So was he," he replied grimly.

She hesitated, but curiosity prodded her on. "If it wouldn't be breaking any solemn oath, could you tell me why he didn't finish his residency?"

He did, without going into details. "He realized medicine wasn't his true calling."

She nodded in understanding.

"But you didn't hear that from me," he added firmly.

"Oh, I never tell people things I know," she replied easily, smiling. "I work for a lawyer."

He chuckled. "Do tell?"

"He's something of a fire-eater, but he's nice to me. He practices criminal law back in Jacobsville, Texas."

He put the medical equipment to one side and told her she could get dressed.

"I'm going to put you on some antibiotics to fight off infection." He studied her with narrowed eyes. "What you've been through is traumatic," he added as he handed her the prescription bottle. "I'd advise counseling."

"Right now," she said on a long breath, "I'm occupied with just trying to stay alive. The drug dealer is still after me, you see."

His jaw tautened. "Micah will take care of you."

"I know that." She stood up and smiled, extending her hand. "Thanks."

He shook her hand and shrugged. "Think nothing of it. We brilliant medical types feel obliged to minister to the masses…"

"Oh, for God's sake!" Micah groaned as he entered the room, overhearing his friend.

Dr. Candler gave him a look full of frowning mock-hauteur. "And aren't you lucky that I don't have to examine *you* today?" he drawled.

"We're leaving. Right now." He took Callie by the hand and gave the other man a grin. "Thanks."

"Anytime. You take care."

"You do the same."

Callie was herded out the door.

"But, the bill," she protested as he put her out a side door and drew her into the vehicle that was waiting for them with the engine running.

"Already taken care of. Let's get to the airport."

Callie settled into the seat, still worrying. "I don't have anything with me," she said miserably. "No papers, no clothes, no shoes..."

"I told you, Maddie got all that together. It will be waiting for us at the airport, along with tickets and boarding passes."

"What if Lopez has people there waiting for us?" she worried aloud.

"We also have people waiting there for us," Bojo said from the front seat. "Miami is our safest domestic port."

"Okay," she said, and smiled at him.

He smiled back.

Micah and Bojo exchanged a complicated glance. Bojo turned his attention back to the road and didn't say another word all the way to the airport. Callie understood. Micah didn't want her getting too friendly with his people. She didn't take offense. She was used to rejection, after so many years in foster care. She only shrugged and looked out the window, watching palm trees and colorful buildings slide past as they wove through side streets and back onto the expressway.

The airport was crowded. Micah caught her by the arm and guided her past the ticket counter on the way to the concourses.

"But..." she protested.

"Don't argue. Just walk through the metal detector."

He followed close behind her. Neither of them was carrying anything metallic, but Micah was stopped when a security woman passed a wand over the two of them and her detector picked up the residual gunpowder on his hands and clothing. The woman looked at her instrument and then at him, with a wary, suspicious stare.

He smiled lazily at the uniformed woman holding the wand. "I'm on my way to a regional skeet shooting tournament," he lied glibly. "I sent my guns on ahead by express, unassembled. Can't be too careful these days, where firearms are concerned," he added, catching Callie's hand in his. "Right, honey?" he murmured softly, drawing her close.

To Callie's credit, she didn't faint at the unexpected feel of Micah's arm around her, but she tingled from head to toe and her heart went wild.

The airport security woman seemed to relax, and she smiled back. She assumed, as Micah had intended, that he and Callie were involved. "Indeed you can't. Have a good trip."

Micah kept that long, muscular arm around Callie as they walked slowly down the concourse. He looked down, noting the erratic rhythm of her heartbeat at her neck, and he smiled to himself.

"You have lightning-quick reflexes," he remarked after a

minute. "I noticed that in Cancún. You didn't argue, you didn't question anything I told you to do, and you moved almost as fast as I did. You're good company in tight corners."

She shrugged. "When you came in through the window, I didn't know who you were, because of that face mask. Actually," she confessed with a sheepish smile, "at first, I figured you were a rival drug dealer, but I had high hopes that you might be kind enough to just kill me and not torture me first if I didn't resist."

He drew in a sharp breath and the arm holding her contracted with a jerk. "Strange attitude, Callie," he remarked.

"Not at the time. Not to me, anyway." She shivered at the memory and felt his arm tighten almost protectively. They were well out of earshot and sight of the security guard. "Micah, what was that wand she was checking us with?"

"It detects nitrates," he replied. "With it, they can tell if a passenger has had any recent contact with weapons or explosives."

She was keenly aware of his arm still holding her close against his warm, powerful body. "You can, uh, let go now. She's out of sight."

He didn't relent. "Don't look, but there's a security guard with a two-way radio about fifteen feet to your right." He smiled down at her. "And I'll give you three guesses who's on the other end of it."

She smiled back, but it didn't reach her eyes. "The lady with the nitrate wand? We're psyching them out, right?"

He searched her eyes and for a few seconds he stopped walking. "Psyching them out," he murmured. His gaze fell to her soft, full mouth. "Exactly."

She couldn't quite get her breath. His expression was unreadable, but his black eyes were glittering. He watched her blouse shake with the frantic rate of her heartbeats. He was remembering mistletoe and harsh words, and that same look in Callie's soft eyes, that aching need to be kissed that made her look so very vulnerable.

"What the hell," he murmured roughly as his head bent to hers. "It's an airport. People are saying hello and goodbye everywhere..."

His warm, hard mouth covered hers very gently while the sounds of people in transit all around them faded to a dull roar. His heavy brows drew together in something close to anguish as he began to kiss her. Fascinated by his expression, by the warm, ardent pressure of his mouth on hers, she closed her eyes tight, and fantasized that he meant it, that he wasn't pretending for the benefit of security guards, that he was enjoying the soft, tremulous response of her lips to the teasing, expert pressure of his own.

"Boss?"

They didn't hear the gruff whisper.

It was followed by the loud clearing of a throat and a cough.

They didn't hear that, either. Callie was on tiptoe now, her short nails digging into the hard muscles of his upper arms, hanging on Micah's slow, tender kiss with little more than willpower, so afraid that he was going to pull away...!

"Micah!" the voice said shortly.

Micah's head jerked up, and for a few seconds he seemed as disoriented as Callie. He stared blankly at the dark-headed man in front of him.

The man was extending a small case toward him. "Her papers and clothes and shoes and stuff," the man said, nodding toward

Callie and clearing his throat again. "Maddie had me fly them over here."

"Thanks, Pogo."

The big, dark man nodded. He stared with open curiosity at Callie, and then he smiled gently. "It was my pleasure," he said, glancing again at Micah and making an odd little gesture with his head in Callie's direction.

"This is Callie Kirby," Micah said shortly, adding, "my... stepsister."

The big man's eyebrows levered up. "Oh! I mean, I was hoping she wasn't a real sister. I mean, the way you were kissing her and all." He flushed, and laughed self-consciously when Micah glared at him. Callie was scarlet, looking everywhere except at the newcomer.

"You'll miss your flight out of here," Micah said pointedly.

"What? Oh. Yeah." He grinned at Callie. "I'm Pogo. I'm from Saint Augustine. I used to wrestle alligators until Micah here gave me a job. I'm sort of a bodyguard, you know..."

"You're going to be an unemployed bodyguard in twenty seconds if you don't merge with the crowd," Micah said curtly.

"Oh. Well...sure. Bye, now," he told Callie with an ear-to-ear smile.

She smiled back. He was like a big teddy bear. She was sorry they wouldn't get to know each other.

Pogo almost fell over his own feet as he turned, jerking both busy eyebrows at his boss, before he melted into the crowd and vanished.

"Stop doing that," Micah said coldly.

She looked up at him blankly. "Doing what?"

"Smiling at my men like that. These men aren't used to it. Don't encourage them."

Her lips parted on a shaken breath. She looked at him as if she feared for his sanity. "Them?" she echoed, dazed.

"Bojo and Peter and Pogo," he said, moving restlessly. He was jealous, God knew why. It irritated him. "Come on."

He moved away from her, catching her hand tightly and pulling her along with him.

"And don't read anything into what just happened," he added coldly, without looking at her.

"Why would I?" she asked honestly. "You said it was just for appearances. I haven't forgotten how you feel about me, Micah."

He stopped and stared intently down into her eyes. His own were narrow, angry, impatient. She wore her heart where anyone could see it. Her vulnerability made him protective. Odd, that, when she was tough enough to survive captivity by Lopez and still keep her nerve during a bloody breakout.

"You don't have a clue how I feel about you," he said involuntarily. His fingers locked closer into hers. "I'm thirty-six. You're barely twenty-two. The sort of woman I prefer is sophisticated and street-smart and has no qualms about sex. You're still at the kissing-in-parked-cars stage."

She flushed and searched his eyes. "I don't kiss people in parked cars because I don't date anybody," she told him with blunt honesty. "I can't leave Dad alone in the evenings. Besides, too many men around Jacobsville remember my mother, and think I'm like her." Her face stiffened and she looked away. "Including you."

He didn't speak. There was little softness left in him after all the violent years, but she was able to touch some last, sensitive place with her sweet voice. Waves of guilt ran over him. Yes, he'd compared her to her mother that Christmas. He'd said harsh, cruel things. He regretted them, but there was no going back. His feelings about Callie unnerved him. She was the only weak spot in his armor that he'd ever known. And what a good thing that she didn't know that, he told himself.

"You don't know what was really going on that night, Callie," he said after a minute.

She looked up at him. "Don't you think it's time I did?" she asked softly.

He toyed with her fingers, causing ripples of pleasure to run along her spine. "Why not? You're old enough to hear it now." He glanced around them cautiously before he looked at her again. "You were wearing an emerald velvet dress that night, the same one you'd worn to your eighteenth birthday party. They were watching a movie while you finished decorating the Christmas tree," he continued absently. "You'd just bent over to pick up an ornament when I came into the room. The dress had a deep neckline. You weren't wearing a bra under it, and your breasts were visible in that position, right to the nipples. You looked up at me and your nipples were suddenly hard."

She gaped at him. The comment about her nipples was disturbing, but she had no idea what he meant by emphasizing them. "I had no idea I was showing like that!"

"I didn't realize that. Not at first." He held her fingers tighter. "You saw me and came right up against me, drowning me in that floral perfume you wore. You stood on tiptoe, like you did a minute ago, trying to tempt me into kissing you."

She averted her embarrassed eyes. "You said terrible things..."

"The sight of you like that had aroused me passionately," he said frankly, nodding when her shocked eyes jumped to his face. "That's right. And I couldn't let you know it. I had to make you keep your distance, not an easy accomplishment after the alcohol you'd had. For which," he added coldly, "your mother should have been shot! It was illegal for her to let you drink, even at home. Anyway, I read you the riot act, pushed you away and walked down the hall, right into your mother. She recognized immediately what you hadn't even noticed about my body, and she thought it was the sight of her in that slinky silver dress that had caused it. So she buried herself against me and started kissing me." He let out an angry breath. "Your father saw us like that before I could push her away. And I couldn't tell him the truth, because you were just barely eighteen. I was already thirty-two."

The bitterness in his deep voice was blatant. She didn't feel herself breathing. She'd only been eighteen, but he'd wanted her. She'd never realized it. Everything that didn't make sense was suddenly crystal clear—except that comment about his body. She wondered what her mother had seen and recognized about him that she hadn't.

"You never told me."

"You were a child, Callie," he said tautly. "In some ways, you still are. I was never low enough to take advantage of your innocence."

She was almost vibrating with the turmoil of her emotions. She didn't know what to do or say.

He drew in a long, slow breath as he studied her. "Come on," he said, tugging her along. "We have to move or we'll miss our flight." He handed her the case and indicated the ladies' room. "Get changed. I'll wait right here."

She nodded. Her mind was in such turmoil that she changed

into jeans and a long-sleeved knit shirt, socks and sneakers, without paying much attention to what was in the small travel case. She didn't take time to look in any of the compartments, because he'd said to hurry. She glanced at herself in the mirror and was glad she had short hair that could do without a brush. Despite all she'd been through, it didn't look too bad. She'd have to buy a brush when they got where they were going, along with makeup and other toiletries. But that could wait.

Micah was propping up the wall when she came out. He nodded, approving what Maddie had packed for her, and took the case. "Here," he said, passing her a small plastic bag.

Inside were makeup, a brush, a toothbrush, toothpaste and deodorant. She almost cried at the thoughtful gift.

"Thanks," she said huskily.

Micah pulled the tickets and boarding passes out of his shirt pocket. "Get out your driver's license and birth certificate," he said. "We have to have a photo ID to board."

She felt momentary panic. "My birth certificate is in my file at home, and my driver's license is still in my purse, in my car...!"

He laid a lean forefinger across her pretty mouth, slightly swollen from the hard contact with his. "Your car is at your house, and your purse is inside it, and it's locked up tight. I told Maddie to put your birth certificate and your driver's license in the case. Have you looked for them?"

"No. I didn't think..."

She paused, putting the case down on the carpeted concourse floor to open it. Sure enough, her driver's license was in the zipped compartment that she hadn't looked in when she was in the bathroom. Besides that, the unknown Maddie had actually put her makeup and toiletries inside, as well, in a plastic bag. She could have wept at the woman's thoughtfulness, but she wasn't going to tell Micah and make him feel uncomfortable that he'd already bought her those items. She closed it quickly and stuck her license in her jeans pocket.

"Does Maddie really look like me?" she asked on the way to the ticket counter, trying not to sound as if she minded. He'd said they resembled one another earlier.

"At a distance," he affirmed. "Her hair is shorter than yours, and she's more muscular. She was a karate instructor when she signed on with me. She's twenty-six."

"Karate."

"Black belt," he added.

"She seems to be very efficient," she murmured a little stiffly.

He gave her a knowing glance that she didn't see and chuckled softly. "She's in love with Colby Lane, a guy I used to work with at the justice department," he told her. "She signed on with us because she thought he was going to."

"He didn't?"

He shook his head. "He's working for Pierce Hutton's outfit, as a security chief, along with Tate Winthrop, an acquaintance of mine."

"Oh."

They were at the ticket counter now. He held out his hand for her driver's license and birth certificate, and presented them along with his driver's license and passport and the tickets to the agent on duty.

She put the tickets in a neat folder with the boarding passes in a slot on the outside, checked the ID, and handed them back.

"Have a nice trip," she told them. "We'll be boarding in just a minute."

Callie hadn't looked at her boarding pass. She was too busy trying to spot Bojo and Peter and the others.

"They're already en route," Micah told her nonchalantly, having guessed why she was looking around her.

"They aren't going with us?"

He gave her a wry glance. "Somebody had to bring my boat back. I left it here in the marina when I flew out to Jacobsville to help Eb Scott and Cy Parks shut down Lopez's drug operation. It's still there."

"Why couldn't we have gone on the boat, too?"

"You get seasick," he said before he thought.

Her lips fell open. She'd only been on a boat once, with him and her mother and stepfather, when she was sixteen. They'd gone to San Antonio and sailed down the river on a tour boat. She'd gotten very sick and thrown up. It had been Micah who'd looked after her, to his father's amusement.

She hadn't even remembered the episode until he'd said that. She didn't get seasick now, but she kept quiet.

"Besides," he added, avoiding her persistent stare, "if Lopez does try anything, it won't be on an international flight out of the U.S. He's in enough trouble with the higher-ups in his organization without making an assault on a commercial plane just to get even for losing a prisoner."

She relaxed a little, because that had been on her mind.

He took her arm and drew her toward a small door, where a uniformed man was holding a microphone. He announced that they were boarding first-class passengers first, and Micah ushered her right down the ramp and into the plane.

"First class," she said, dazed, as he eased her into a wide, comfortable seat with plenty of leg room. Even for a man of his height, there was enough of it.

"Always," he murmured, amused at her fascination. "I don't like cramped places."

She fastened her seat belt with a wry smile. "Considering the size of you, I can understand that. Micah, what about Dad?" she added, ashamed that she was still belaboring the point.

"Maddie's got him under surveillance. When Pogo goes back, he'll work a split shift with her at your apartment to safeguard him. Eb and Cy are keeping their eyes out, as well. I promise you, Dad's going to be safe." He hesitated, searching her wide, pale blue eyes. "But you're the one in danger."

"Because I got away," she agreed, nodding.

He seemed worried. His dark eyes narrowed on her face. "Lopez doesn't lose prisoners, ever. You're the first. Someone is going to pay for that. He'll make an example of the people who didn't watch you closely enough. Then he'll make an example of you and me, if he can, to make sure his reputation doesn't suffer."

She shivered involuntarily. It was a nightmare that would haunt her forever. She remembered what she'd suffered already and her eyes closed on a helpless wave of real terror.

"You're going to be safe, Callie. Listen," he said, reading her expression, "I live on a small island in the Bahamas chain, not too far from New Providence. I have state-of-the-art surveillance equipment and a small force of mercenaries that even Lopez would hesitate to confront. Lopez isn't the only one who has a reputation in terrorist circles. Before I put together my team and hired out as a professional soldier, I worked for the CIA."

Her eyes widened. She hadn't known that. She hadn't known anything about him.

"They approached me while I was in college, before I changed my course of study to medicine. I was already fluent in French and Dutch, and I picked up German in my sophomore year. I couldn't blend in very well in an Arabic country, but I could pass for German or Dutch, and I did. During holidays and vacations, I did a lot of traveling for the company." He smiled, reminiscing. "It was dangerous work, and exciting. By the time I was in my last year of residency, I knew for a fact that I wouldn't be able to settle down into a medical practice. I couldn't live without the danger. That's when I left school for good."

She was hanging on every word. It was amazing to have him speak to her as an equal, as an adult. They'd never really talked before.

"I wondered," she said, "why you gave it up."

He stretched his long legs out in front of him and crossed his arms over his broad chest. "I had the skills, but as I grew older, the less I wanted roots or anything that hinted at permanence. I don't want marriage or children, so a steady, secure profession seemed superfluous. On the other hand, being a mercenary is right up my alley. I live for those surges of adrenaline."

"None of us ever knew about that," she said absently, trying not to let him see how much it hurt to know that he couldn't see a future as a husband and father. Now that she knew what he really did for a living, she could understand why. He was never going to be a family man. "We thought it was the trust your mother left you that kept you in Armani suits," she added in a subdued tone.

"No, it wasn't. I like my lifestyle," he added with a pointed glance in her direction. He stretched lazily, pulling the silk shirt he was wearing taut across the muscles of his chest. A flight attendant actually hesitated as she started down the aisle, helplessly drinking in the sight of him. He was a dish, all right. Callie didn't blame the other woman for staring, but the flight attendant had blond hair and blue eyes and she was lovely. Her beauty was like a knife in the ribs to Callie, pointing out all the physical attributes she herself lacked. If only she'd been pretty, she told herself miserably, maybe Micah would have wanted more than an occasional kiss from her.

"Would you care for anything to drink, sir?" the flight attendant asked, smiling joyfully as she paused by Micah's side.

"Scotch and soda," he told her. He smiled ruefully. "It's been a long day."

"Coming right up," the woman said, and went at once to get the order.

Callie noticed that she hadn't been asked if she wanted anything. She wondered what Micah would say if she asked for a neat whiskey. Probably nothing, she told herself miserably. He might have kissed her in the airport, but he only seemed irritated by her now.

The flight attendant was back with his drink. She glanced belatedly at Callie and grimaced. "Sorry," she told the other woman. "I didn't think to ask if you'd like something, too?"

Callie shook her head and smiled. "No, I don't want anything, thanks."

"Are you stopping in Nassau or just passing through?" the woman asked Micah boldly.

He gave her a lingering appraisal, from her long, elegant legs to her full breasts and lovely face. He smiled. "I live there."

"Really!" Her eyes lit as if they'd concealed fires. "So do I!"

"Then you must know Lisette Dubonnet," he said.

"Dubonnet," the uniformed woman repeated, frowning. "Isn't her father Jacques Dubonnet, the French ambassador?"

"Yes," he said. "Lisette and I have known each other for several years. We're…very good friends."

The flight attendant looked suddenly uncomfortable, and a little flushed. Micah was telling her, in a nice way, that she'd overstepped her introduction. He smiled to soften the rejection, but it was a rejection, just the same.

"Miss Dubonnet is very lovely," the flight attendant said with a pleasant, if more formal, smile. "If you need anything else, just ring."

"I will."

She went on down the aisle. Beside him, Callie was staring out the window at the ocean below without any real enthusiasm. She hated her own reaction to the news that Micah was involved with some beautiful woman in Nassau. And not only a beautiful woman, but a poised sophisticate, as well.

"You'll like Lisse," he said carelessly. "I'll ask her to go shopping with you. You'll have to have a few clothes. She has excellent taste."

Implying that Callie had none at all. Her heart felt like iron in her chest, heavy and cold. "That would be nice," she said, lying through her teeth. "I won't need much, though," she added, thinking about her small savings account.

"You may be there longer than a day or two," he said in a carefully neutral voice. "You can't wear the same clothes day in and day out. Besides," he added curtly, "it's about time you learned how to dress like a young woman instead of an elderly recluse!"

5

Callie felt the anger boil out of her in waves. "Oh, that's nice, coming from you," she said icily. "When you're the one who started me wearing that sort of thing in the first place!"

"Me?" he replied, his eyebrows arching.

"You said I dressed like a tramp," she began, and her eyes were anguished as she remembered the harsh, hateful words. "Like my mother," she added huskily. "You said that I flaunted my body..." She stopped suddenly and wrapped her arms around herself. She stared out the porthole while she recovered her self-control. "Sorry," she said stiffly. "I've been through a lot. It's catching up with me. I didn't mean to say that."

He felt as if he'd been slapped. Maybe he deserved it, too. Callie had been beautiful in that green velvet dress. The sight of her in it had made him ache. She had the grace and poise of a model, even if she lacked the necessary height. But he'd never realized that his own anger had made her ashamed of her body, and at such an impressionable age. Good God, no wonder she dressed like a dowager! Then he remembered what she'd hinted in the jungle about the foster homes she'd stayed in, and he wondered with real anguish what she'd endured before she came to live in his father's house. There had to be more to her repression than just a few regretted words from him.

"Callie," he said huskily, catching her soft chin and turning her flushed face toward him. "Something happened to you at one of those foster homes, didn't it?"

She bit her lower lip and for a few seconds, there was torment in her eyes.

He drew in a sharp breath.

She turned her face away again, embarrassed.

"Can you talk about it?" he asked.

She shook her head jerkily.

His dark eyes narrowed. And her mother—her own mother—had deserted her, had placed her in danger with pure indifference. "Damn your mother," he said in a gruff whisper.

She didn't look at him again. At least, she thought mistakenly, he was remembering the breakup of his father's marriage, and not her childhood anymore. She didn't like remembering the past.

He leaned back in his seat and stretched, folding his arms over his broad chest. One day, he promised himself, there was going to be a reckoning for Callie's mother. He hoped the woman got just a fraction of what she deserved, for all the grief and pain she'd caused. Although, he had to admit, she had changed in the past year or so.

He wondered if her mother's first husband, Kane Kirby, had contacted Callie recently. Poor kid, he thought. She really had gone through a lot, even before Lopez had her kidnapped. He thought about what she'd suffered at Lopez's hands, and he ached to avenge her. The drug lord was almost certain to make a grab for her again. But this time, he promised himself, Lopez was going to pay up his account in full. He owed Callie that much for the damage he'd done.

It was dark when the plane landed in Nassau at the international airport, and Micah let Callie go ahead of him down the ramp to the pavement. The moist heat was almost smothering, after the air-conditioned plane. Micah took her arm and escorted her to passport control. He glanced with amusement at the passengers waiting around baggage claim for their bags to be unloaded. Even when he traveled routinely, he never took more than a duffel bag that he could carry into the airplane with him. It saved time waiting for luggage to be off-loaded.

After they checked through, he moved her outside again and hailed a cab to take them to the marina, where the boat was waiting.

Another small round of formalities and they boarded the sleek, powerful boat that already contained Micah's men. Callie went below and sat quietly on a comfortable built-in sofa, watching out the porthole as the boat flew out of Prince George Wharf and around the bay. From there, it went out to sea.

"Comfortable?" Micah asked, joining her below.

She nodded. "It's so beautiful out there. I love the way the ships light up at night. I knew cruise ships did, but I didn't realize that smaller ones did, too." She glanced at him in the subdued light of the cabin. "You don't light yours, do you?"

He chuckled. "In my line of work, it wouldn't be too smart, would it?"

"Sorry," she said with a sheepish smile. "I wasn't thinking."

He poured himself a Scotch and water and added ice cubes. "Want something to drink? If you don't want anything alcoholic, I've got soft drinks or fruit juice."

She shook her head. "I'm fine." She laughed. Her eyes caught and held on a vessel near the lighted dock. "Look! There's a white ship with black sails flying a skull and crossbones Jolly Roger flag!"

He chuckled. "That would be Fred Spence. He's something of a local eccentric. Nice boat, though."

She glanced at him. "This one is nice, too."

"It's comfortable on long hauls," he said noncommittally. He dropped down onto the sofa beside her and crossed his long legs. "We need to talk."

"About what?"

"Lopez. I'm putting you under twenty-four-hour surveillance," he said somberly. "If I'm not within yelling distance, one of my men will be. Even when you go shopping with Lisse, Bojo or Peter will go along. You aren't to walk on the beach alone, ever."

"But surely that would be safe...?"

He sat forward abruptly, and his black eyes glittered. "Callie, he has weapons that could pinpoint your body heat and send a missile after it from a distance of half a mile," he said curtly.

She actually gasped. That brought to mind another worry. She frowned. "I'm putting you in jeopardy by being with you," she said suddenly.

"You've got that backward, honey," he said, the endearment coming so naturally that he wasn't even aware he'd used it until he watched Callie's soft complexion flush. "You were in jeopardy in the first place because of me. Why does it make you blush when I call you honey?" he added immediately, the question quick enough to rattle her.

"I'm not used to it."

"From me," he drawled softly. "Or from any man?"

She shifted. "From Dad, maybe."

"Dad doesn't count. I mean single, datable bachelors."

She shook her head. "I don't date."

He'd never connected her solitary existence with himself. Now, he was forced to. He drew his breath in sharply, and got up from the sofa. He took a long sip from his drink, walking slowly over to stare out the porthole at the distant lights of the marina as they left it behind. "I honestly didn't realize how much damage I did to your ego, Callie. I'm really sorry about it."

"I was just as much at fault as you were," she replied evenly. "I shouldn't have thrown myself at you like some drunk prostitute..."

"Callie!" he exclaimed, horrified at her wording.

She averted her eyes and her hands clenched in her lap. "Well, I did."

He put his drink on the bar and knelt just in front of her. He was so tall that his black eyes were even with soft blue ones in the position. His lean hands went to her waist and he shook her very gently.

"I pushed you away because I wanted you, not because I thought you were throwing yourself at me," he said bluntly. "I was afraid that I wouldn't be able to resist you if I didn't do something very fast. I would have explained it to you eventually, if your mother hadn't stepped in and split the family apart, damn her cold heart!"

Her hands rested hesitantly on his broad shoulders, lifted and then rested again while she waited to see if she was allowed to touch him.

He seemed to realize that, because he smiled very slowly and his thumbs edged out against her flat belly in a sensuous stroking motion. "I like being touched," he murmured. "It's all right."

She smiled nervously. "I'm not used to doing it."

"I noticed." He stood up and drew her up with him. The top of her head only came to his nose. He framed her face in his warm, strong hands and lifted it gently. "Want to kiss me?" he asked in a husky whisper, and his eyes fell to her own soft mouth.

She wasn't sure about that. Her hands were on his chest now, touching lightly over the silky fabric. Under it, she could feel thick hair. She was hopelessly curious about what he looked like bare-chested. She'd never seen Micah without a shirt in all the time she'd lived in his house with his father.

"No pressure," he promised, bending. "And I won't make fun of you."

"Make fun of me?" she asked curiously.

"Never mind." He bent and his lips closed tenderly on her upper lip while he tasted the moist inside of it with his tongue. His lips moved to her lower lip and repeated the arousing little caress. His hands were at her waist, but they began to move up and down with a lazy, sensual pressure that made her body go rigid in his arms.

He lifted his mouth from her face and looked down at her with affectionate amusement. "Relax! Why are you afraid of me?" he asked gently. "I wouldn't hurt you, Callie. Not for any reason."

"I know. It's just that..."

"What?" he asked.

Her eyes met his plaintively. "Don't...tease me," she asked with dignity. "I'm not experienced enough to play that sort of game."

The amusement left his face. "Is that what it seems like to you?" he asked. He searched her worried eyes. "Even if I were into game-playing, you'd never be a target. I do have some idea now of what you've been through, in the past and just recently."

She let out the breath she'd been holding. "This Lisette you mentioned. Is she...important to you?"

"We're good friends," he said, and there was a new remoteness in his expression. "You'll like her. She's outgoing and she loves people. She'll help you get outfitted."

Now she was really worried. "I have my credit card, but I can't afford expensive shops," she emphasized. "Could you tell her that, so I won't have to?"

"I can tell her." He smiled quizzically. "But why won't you let me buy you some clothes?"

"I'm not your responsibility, even if you have been landed with me, Micah," she replied. "I pay my own way."

He wondered if she had any idea how few of his female acquaintances would ever have made such a statement to him? It occurred to him that he'd never had a woman refuse a wardrobe.

He scowled. "You could pay me back, if you have to."

She smiled. "Thanks. But I'll buy my own clothes."

His black eyes narrowed on her face. "You were always independent," he recalled.

"I've had to be. I've been basically on my own for a long

time," she said matter-of-factly. "Since I was a kid, really, and my father—I mean, Mother's first husband—threw us out. Mother didn't want the responsibility for me by herself and Kane Kirby didn't want me at all."

"If your father didn't think you were his, why didn't he have a DNA profile run?" he asked with a watchful look.

She drew away from him. "There was no such thing fifteen years ago."

"You could insist that he have it done now, couldn't you?" He gave her an odd look. "Have you spoken to him?"

"He phoned me recently. But I didn't call him back," she said unwillingly. She'd seen her mother's first husband once or twice, during his rare visits to his Jacobsville home. He'd actually phoned her apartment a few weeks ago and left a strange, tentative message asking her to call him back. She never had. His rejection of her still hurt. She didn't see him often. He lived mostly in Miami these days.

"Why not talk to him and suggest the DNA test?" he persisted.

She looked up at him with tired, sad eyes. "Because it would probably prove what my mother said, that I'm not related to him at all." She smiled faintly. "I don't know whose child I am. And it really doesn't matter anymore. Please, just…leave it alone."

He sighed with irritation, as if he knew more than he was telling her. She wondered why he was so interested in her relationship with the man who was supposed to be her own father.

He saw that curiosity in her eyes, and he closed up. He could see years of torment in that sad little face. It infuriated him. "Your mother should be horsewhipped for what she did to you," he said flatly.

She folded her arms across her chest, remembering the loneliness of her young life reluctantly. New homes, new faces, new terrors. She turned back to the porthole. "I used to wish I had someplace to belong," she confessed. "I was always the outsider, in any home where I lived. Until my mother married your father," she added, smiling. "I thought he'd be like all the others, that he'd either ignore me or be too familiar, but he just sort of belonged to me, from the very beginning. He really cared about me. He hugged me, coming and going." She drew in a soft breath. "You can't imagine what it feels like, to have someone hug you, when you've hardly been touched in your whole life except in bad ways. He was forever teasing me, bringing me presents. He became my family. He even made up for my mother. I couldn't help loving him." She turned, surprised to see an odd look of self-contempt on Micah's strong face. "I guess you resented us..."

"I resented your mother, Callie," he interrupted, feeling icy-cold inside. "What I felt for you was a lot more complicated than that."

She gave him a surprised little smile. "But, I'm still my mother's daughter, right? Don't they say, look at the mother and you'll see the daughter in twenty years or so?"

His face hardened. "You'll never be like her. Not in your worst nightmares."

She sighed. "I wish I could be sure of that."

He felt like hitting something. "Do you know where she is?"

"Somewhere in Europe with her new husband, I suppose," she said indifferently. "Dad's lawyer heard from her year before last. She wanted a copy of the final divorce decree, because she was getting married again, to some British nobleman, the lawyer said."

He remembered his own mother, a gentle little brown-eyed woman with a ready smile and open arms. She'd died when he was ten, and from that day on, he and his father had been best friends. Until Anna showed up, with her introverted, nervous teenage daughter. The difference between Anna and his own mother was incredible. Anna was selfish, vain, greedy...he could have laid all seven deadly sins at her feet with ease. But Callie was nothing like her, except, perhaps, her exact opposite.

"You're the sort of woman who would love a big family," he murmured thoughtfully.

She laughed. "What do I know about families?" she responded. "I'd be terrified of bringing an innocent child into this sort of world, knowing what I know about the uncertainties of life."

He shoved his hands into his pockets. Children. He'd never thought about them. But he could picture Callie with a baby in her arms, and it seemed perfectly natural. She'd had some bad breaks, but she'd love her own child. It was sad that she didn't want kids.

"Anyway, marriage is dead last on my list of things to do," she added, uncomfortable because he wasn't saying anything.

"That makes two of us," he murmured. It was the sort of thing he always said, but it didn't feel as comfortable suddenly as it used to. He wondered why.

She turned away from the porthole. "How long will it take us to get to your place?" she asked.

He shrugged. "About twenty more minutes, at this speed," he said, smiling. "I think you'll like it. It's old, and rambling, and it has a history. According to the legend, a local pirate owned it back in the eighteenth century. He kidnapped a highborn

Spanish lady and married her out of hand. They had six children together and lived a long and happy life, or so the legend goes." He studied her curiously. "Isn't there Spanish in your ancestry somewhere?"

Her face closed up. "Don't ask me. My mother always said she descended from what they call 'black Irish,' from when the Spanish armada was shipwrecked off the coast of Ireland. I know her hair was jet-black when she was younger, and she has an olive complexion. But I don't really know her well enough to say whether or not it was the truth."

He bit off a comment on her mother's penchant for lying. "Your complexion isn't olive," he remarked quietly. "It's creamy. Soft."

He embarrassed her. She averted her eyes. "I'm just ordinary."

He shook his head. His eyes narrowed on her pretty bow of a mouth. "You always were unique, Callie." He hesitated. "Callie. What's it short for?" he asked, suddenly curious.

She drew in a slow breath. "Colleen," she replied reluctantly. "But nobody ever calls me that. It's been Callie since I was old enough to talk."

"Colleen what?"

"Colleen Mary," she replied.

He smiled. "Yes. That suits you."

He was acting very strangely. In fact, he had been ever since he rescued her. She wondered if he was still trying to take her mind off Lopez. If he was, it wasn't working. The nightmarish memories were too fresh to forget.

She looked at him worriedly. "Lopez will be looking for me," she said suddenly.

He tautened. "Let him look," he said shortly. "If he comes

close enough to make a target, I'll solve all his problems. He isn't getting his hands on you again, Callie."

She relaxed a little. He sounded very confident. It made her feel better. She moved back into the center of the room, wrapping her arms around herself. "How can people like that exist in a civilized world?" she wanted to know.

"Because governments still can't fight that kind of wealth," he said bluntly. "Money and power make criminals too formidable. But we've got the Rico statutes which help us take away some of that illegal money," he added, "and we've got dedicated people enforcing the law. We win more than we lose these days."

"You sound like a government agent," she teased.

He chuckled. "I do, don't I? I spent several years being one. It sticks." He moved forward, taking his hands out of his pockets to wrap them gently around her upper arms. "I give you my word that I won't let Lopez get you. In case you were worrying about that."

She grimaced. "Does it show?"

"I don't know. Maybe I can read your mind these days," he added, trying to make light of it.

"You're sure? About Dad being safe, I mean?"

"I'm sure about Dad," he returned at once. "Gator may look dumb, but he's got a mind like a steel trap, and he's quick on the draw. Nobody's going to get past him—certainly nobody's going to get past him and Maddie at the same time."

"You like her a lot, I guess?"

He chuckled. "Yes, I do. She's hell on two legs, and one of the best scroungers I've ever had."

"What does Bojo do?"

He gave her a wary appraisal, and it seemed as if he didn't like the question. "Bojo is a small arms expert," he replied. "He also has relatives in most of the Muslim nations, so he's a great source of information, as well. Peter, you met him on the plane, is new with the group. He's a linguist and he's able to pass for an Arab or an Israeli. He's usually undercover in any foreign operation we're hired to undertake. You haven't met Rodrigo yet—he was the pilot of the DC-3 we flew back to Miami. He does undercover work, as well. Don, the blond copilot, is a small arms expert. We have another operative, Cord Romero, who does demolition work for us, but he had an accident and he's out of commission for a while."

"What you and your men do—it's dangerous work."

"Living is dangerous work," he said flatly. "I like the job. I don't have any plans to give it up."

Her eyebrows arched and her pale blue eyes twinkled. "My goodness, did I propose marriage just now and get instant amnesia afterward? Excuse *me!*"

He gaped at her. "Propose marriage...?"

She held up both hands. "Now, don't get ruffled. I understand how men feel about these things. I haven't asked you out, or sent you flowers, or even bought you a nice pair of earrings. Naturally you're miffed because I put the cart before the horse and asked you to give up an exciting job you love for marriage to a boring paralegal."

He blinked. "Callie?" he murmured, obviously fearing for her sanity.

"We'll just forget the proposal," she offered generously.

"You didn't propose!" he gritted.

"See? You've already forgotten. Isn't that just like a man?" she muttered, as she went back to the sofa and sat down. "Now you'll pout for an hour because I rejected you."

He burst out laughing when he realized what she was doing. It took the tension away from their earlier discussion and brought them back to normal. He dropped down into an armchair across from her and folded his arms over his chest.

"Just when I think I've got you figured out, you throw me another curve," he said appreciatively.

"Believe me, if I didn't have a sense of humor, I'd already have smeared Mr. Kemp with honey and locked him in a closet with a grizzly bear."

"Ouch!"

"I thought you lived in Nassau?" She changed the subject.

He shrugged. "I did. This place came on the market three years ago and I bought it. I like the idea of having a defendable property. You'll see what I mean when we get there. It's like a walled city."

"I'll bet there are lots of flowers," she murmured hopefully.

"Millions," he confirmed. "Hibiscus and orchids and bougainvillea. You'll love it." He smiled gently. "You were always planting things when I lived at home."

"I didn't think you noticed anything I did," she replied before she thought.

He watched her quietly. "Your mother spent most of that time ordering you around," he recalled. "If she wanted a soft drink, or a scarf, or a sandwich, she always sent you after it. I don't recall that she ever touched a vacuum cleaner or a frying pan the whole time she was around."

"I learned to cook in the last foster home I stayed in," she said with a smile. "It was the best of the lot. Mrs. Toms liked me. She had five little kids and she had arthritis real bad. She was so sweet that it was a joy to help her. She was always surprised that anyone would want to do things for her."

"Most giving people are," he replied. "Ironically they're usually the last ones people give to."

"That's true."

"What else did she teach you?" he asked.

"How to crochet," she recalled. She sighed. "I can't make sweaters and stuff, but I taught myself how to make hats. I give them to children and old people in our neighborhood. I work on them when I'm waiting for appointments with Dad. I get through a lot."

It was another reminder that she was taking care of his father, something he should have been doing himself—something he would be doing, if Callie's mother hadn't made it impossible for him to be near his parent.

"You're still bitter about Dad," she said, surprising him. "I can tell. You get this terrible haunted look in your eyes when I talk about him."

It surprised him that at her age she could read him so well, when his own men couldn't. He wasn't sure he liked it.

"I miss him," he confessed gruffly. "I'm sorry he won't let me make peace."

She gaped at him. "Whoever told you that?"

He hesitated. "I haven't tried to talk to him in years. So I phoned him a few days ago, before you were kidnapped. He listened for a minute and hung up without saying a word."

"What day was it?"

"It was Saturday. What difference does that make?"

"What time was it?" she repeated.

"Noon."

She smiled gently. "I go to get groceries at noon on Saturdays, because Mrs. Ruiz, who lives next door, comes home for lunch and makes it for herself and Dad and stays with him while I'm away."

"So?"

"So, Mrs. Ruiz doesn't speak English yet, she's still learning. The telephone inhibits her. She'll answer it, but if it's not me, she'll put it right down again." She smiled. "That's why I asked when you called."

"Then, Dad might talk to me, if I tried again," he said after a minute.

"Micah, he loves you," she said softly. "You're the only child he has. Of course he'll talk to you. He doesn't know what really happened with my mother, no more than I did, until you told me the truth. But he realizes now that if it hadn't been you, it would have been some other younger man. He said that, after the divorce was final, she even told him so."

"He didn't try to get in touch with me."

"He was upset for a long time after it happened. So was I. We blamed you both. But that's in the past. He'd love to hear from you now," she assured him. "He didn't think you'd want to talk to him, after so much time had passed and after what he'd said to you. He feels bad about that."

He leaned forward. "If that's so, when he had the heart attack, why wasn't I told?"

"I called the only number I had for you," she said. "I never got an answer. The hospital said they'd try to track you down, but I guess they didn't."

Could it really be that simple? he wondered. "That was at the old house, in Nassau. It was disconnected three years ago. The number I have now is unlisted."

"Oh."

"Why didn't you ask Eb Scott or Cy Parks?"

"I don't know them," she said hesitantly. "And until very recently, when this Lopez thing made the headlines, I didn't know they were mercenaries." She averted her eyes. "I knew you were acquainted with them, but I certainly didn't know that you were one of them."

He took a slow breath. No, he remembered, she didn't know. He'd never shared that bit of information with either her or Jack Steele.

"I wrote to you, too, about the heart attack, at the last address you left us."

"That would have been forwarded. I never got it."

"I sent it," she said.

"I'm not doubting that you did. I'm telling you that it never got to me."

"I'm really sorry," she told him. "I did try, even if it doesn't look like it. I always hoped that you'd eventually phone someone and I'd be able to contact you. When you didn't, well, I guess Dad and I both figured that you weren't interested in what happened back here. And he did say that he'd been very cruel in what he said to you when you left."

"He was. But I understood," he added.

She smiled sadly. "He loves you. When this is over, you should make peace with him. I think you'll find that he'll more than meet you halfway. He's missed you terribly."

"I've missed him, too." He could have added that he'd missed her, as well, but she wasn't likely to believe him.

He started to speak, but he felt the boat slowing. He smiled. "We must be coming up to the pier. Come on. It will be nice to have a comfortable bed to sleep in tonight."

She nodded, and followed him up to the deck.

Her eyes caught sight of the house, on a small rise in the distance, long and low and lighted. She could see arches and flowers, even in the darkness, because of the solar-powered lights that lined the walkway from the pier up to the walled estate. She caught her breath. It was like a house she'd once seen in a magazine and daydreamed about as a child. She had the oddest feeling that she was coming home…

6

"What do you think?" Micah asked as he helped her onto the ramp that led down to the pier.

"It's beautiful," she said honestly. "I expect it's even more impressive in the daylight."

"It is." He hesitated, turning back toward the men who were still on the boat. "Bojo! Make sure we've got at least two guards on the boat before you come up to the house," he called to his associate, who grinned and replied that he would. "Peter can help you," he added involuntarily.

Callie didn't seem to notice that he'd jettisoned both men who'd been friendly with her. Micah did. He didn't like the idea of his men getting close to her. It wasn't jealousy. Of course it wasn't. He was...protecting her from complications.

She looked around as they went up the wide graveled path to the house, frowning as she became aware of odd noises. "What's that sound?" she asked Micah.

He smiled lazily. "My early warning radar."

"Huh?"

He chuckled. "I keep a flock of geese," he explained, nodding toward a fenced area where a group of big white birds walked around and swam in a huge pool of water. "Believe it or not, they're better than guard dogs."

"Wouldn't a guard dog or two be a better idea?"

"Nope. I've got a Mac inside."

Before she could ask any more questions, the solid wood front door opened and a tall, imposing man in khakis with gray-sprinkled black wavy hair stood in their path. He was holding an automatic weapon in one big hand.

"Welcome home, boss," he said in deep, crisply accented British. He grinned briefly and raised two bushy eyebrows at the sight of Callie. "Got her, did you?"

"Got her, and with no casualties," Micah replied, returning the grin. "How's it going, Mac?"

"No worries. But it'll rain soon." He shifted his weight, grimacing a little.

"At least you're wearing the prosthesis, now," Micah muttered as he herded Callie into the house.

Mac rubbed his hip after he closed the door and followed them. "Damned thing feels funny," he said. "And I can't run." He glowered at Micah as if the whole thing was his fault.

"Hey," Micah told him, "didn't I say 'duck'? In fact, didn't I say it twice?"

"You said it, but I had my earphones in!"

"Excuses, excuses. We even took up a collection for your funeral, then you had to go mess everything up by living!" Micah grumbled.

"Oh, sure, after you lot had divided up all my possessions!

Bojo's still got my favorite shirt and he won't give it back! And he doesn't even wear shirts!"

"He's using it to polish his gun," Micah explained. "Says it's the best shine he's ever put on it."

Callie was openly gaping at them.

Micah's black eyes twinkled. "We're joking," he told her gently. "It's the way we let off steam, so that we don't get bogged down in worry. What we do is hard work, and dangerous. We have to have safety valves."

"I'll blow Bojo's safety valve for him if he doesn't give back my shirt!" Mac assured his boss. "And you haven't even introduced us."

Callie smiled and held out her hand. "Hi! I'm Callie Kirby."

"I'm MacPherson," he replied, shaking it. "I took a mortar hit on our last mission, so I've got KP until I get used to this damned prosthesis," he added, lifting his right leg and grimacing.

"You'd better get used to it pretty soon, or you're going to be permanent in that kitchen," Micah assured him. "Now I'd like to get Callie settled. She's been through a lot."

The other man became somber all at once. "She's not what I expected," Mac said reluctantly as he studied her.

"I can imagine," she said with a sad little smile. "You were expecting a woman who was blond and as good-looking as Micah. I know I don't look like him..."

Before she could add that they weren't related, the older man interrupted her. "That isn't what I meant," Mac replied at once.

She shrugged and smiled carelessly. "Of course not. I really am tired," she added.

"Come on," Micah said. "Have you got something for sandwiches?" Micah asked Mac. "We didn't stop for food."

"Sure," Mac replied, visibly uncomfortable. "I'll get right to it."

Micah led Callie down the long hall and turned her into a large, airy room with a picture window overlooking the ocean. Except for the iron bars, it looked very touristy.

"Mac does most of the cooking. We used to take turns, but after he was wounded, and we found out that his father once owned a French restaurant, we gave him permanent KP." He glanced at her with a wry smile. "We thought it might encourage him to put on the prosthesis and try to be rehabilitated. Apparently it's working."

"He's very nice."

He closed the door and turned to her, his face somber. "He meant that the sort of woman I usually bring here is blond and long-legged and buxom, and that they usually ignore the hired help."

She flushed. "You didn't have to explain."

"Didn't I?" His eyes narrowed on her face as a potential complication presented itself when he thought about having Lisette take Callie on that shopping trip. The woman was extremely jealous, and Callie had been through enough turmoil already. "I haven't told Mac or Lisette that we aren't related. It might be as well to let them continue thinking we are, for the time being."

She wondered why, but she wasn't going to lower her pride by asking. "Sure," she said with careful indifference. "No problem." Presumably this Lisette would be jealous of a stepsister, but not of a real one. Micah obviously didn't want to cause waves. She smiled drowsily. "I think I could sleep the clock around."

"If Maddie's her usual efficient self, she should have packed a nightgown for you."

"I don't have a gown," she murmured absently, glancing at the case he'd put down beside the bed.

"Pajamas, then."

"Uh, I don't wear those, either."

He stood up and looked at her pointedly. "What *do* you sleep in?"

She cleared her throat. "Never mind."

His eyebrows arched. "Well, well. No wonder you locked your bedroom door when you lived with us."

"That wasn't the only reason," she said before she thought.

His black eyes narrowed. "You've had a hell of a life, haven't you? And now this, on top of the past."

She bit her lower lip. "This door does have a lock?" she persisted. "I'm sorry. I've spent my life behind locked doors. It's a hard habit to break, and not because of the way I sleep."

"The door has a lock, and you can use it. But I hope you know that you're safe with me," he replied quietly. "Seducing innocents isn't a habit with me, and my men are trustworthy."

"It's not that."

"If you're nervous about being the only woman here, I could get Lisette to come over and spend the night in this room with you," he added.

"No," she said, reluctant to meet his paramour. "I'll be fine."

"You haven't been alone since it happened," he reminded her. "It may be more traumatic than you think, especially in the dark."

"I'll be all right, Micah," she said firmly.

He drew in an irritated breath. "All right. But if you're frightened, I'm next door, through the bathroom."

She gave him a curious look.

"I'll wear pajama bottoms while you're in residence," he said dryly, reading her mind accurately.

She cleared her throat. "Thanks."

"Don't you want to eat something before you go to bed?"

She shook her head. "I'm too tired. Micah, thanks for saving me. I didn't expect it, but I'm very grateful."

He shrugged. "You're family," he said flatly, and she grimaced when he wasn't looking. He turned and went out, hesitating before he closed the door. "Someone will be within shouting distance, night or day."

Her heart ached. He still didn't see her as a woman. Probably, he never would. "Okay," she replied. "Thanks."

He closed the door.

She was so tired that she was sure she'd be asleep almost as soon as her head connected with the pillow. But that wasn't the case. Dressed only in her cotton briefs, she lay awake for a long time, staring at the ceiling, absorbing the shock of the past two days. It seemed unreal now, here where she was safe. As her strung muscles began to relax, she tugged the cool, expensive designer sheet in a yellow rose pattern over her and felt her mind begin to drift slowly into peaceful oblivion.

"Callie? Callie!"

The deep forceful voice combined with steely fingers on her upper arms to shake her out of the nightmare she'd been having. She was hoarse from the scream that had dragged Micah from sleep and sent him running to the connecting door with a skeleton key.

She was sitting up, both her wrists in one of his lean, warm hands, her eyes wide with terror. She was shaking all over, and not from the air-conditioning.

He leaned over and turned on the bedside lamp. His eyes went helplessly to the full, high thrust of her tip-tilted little breasts, their nipples relaxed from sleep. She was so shaken that she didn't even feel embarrassment. Her pale blue eyes were wild with horror.

"You're safe, baby," he said gently. "It's all right."

"Micah!" came a shout from outside the bedroom door. It was Bojo, alert as usual to any odd noise.

"Callie just had a nightmare, Bojo. It's okay. Go back to bed!"

"Sure thing, boss."

Footsteps faded down the corridor.

"I was back in the chair, at Lopez's house. That man had the knife again, and he was cutting me," she choked. Her wild, frightened eyes met Micah's. "You'll shoot me, if they try to take me and you can't stop them, right?" she asked in a hoarse whisper.

"Nobody is going to take you away from here by force," he said gently. "I promise. I can protect you on this island. It's why I brought you here in the first place."

She sighed and relaxed a little. "I'm being silly. It was the dream. It was so real, and I was scared to death, Micah! It all came back the minute I fell asleep!" She shivered. "Can't you hold me?" she asked huskily, her eyes on his muscular, hair-roughened chest. Looking at it made her whole body tingle. "Just for a minute?"

"Are you out of your mind?" he ground out.

She searched his eyes. He looked odd. "Why not?"

"Because…" His gaze fell to her breasts. They were hard-tipped now, visibly taut with desire. His jaw clenched. His hands on her wrists tightened roughly.

"Oh, for heaven's sake. I forgot! Sorry." She tried to cover herself, but his hands were relentless. She cleared her throat and grimaced. "That hurts," she complained on a nervous laugh, tugging at his hands. They loosened, but only a fraction.

"Did you take those pills I gave you to make you sleep?" he asked suddenly.

"Yes. But they didn't keep me asleep." She blinked. She smiled drowsily. She felt very uninhibited. He was looking at her breasts and she liked it. Her head fell back, because he hadn't turned her loose. His hands weren't bruising anymore, but they were holding her wrists firmly. She arched her back sensuously and watched the way his eyes narrowed and glittered on her breasts. She saw his body tense, and she gave a husky, wicked little laugh.

"You like looking at me there, don't you?" she asked, vaguely aware that she was being reckless.

He made a rough sound and met her eyes again. "Yes," he said flatly. "I like it."

"I wanted to take my clothes off for you when I was just sixteen," she confided absently as her tongue ran away with her. "I wanted you to see me. I ached all over when you looked at me that last Christmas. I wanted you to kiss me so hard that it would bruise my mouth. I wanted to unbutton your shirt and pull my dress down and let you hold me like that." She shivered helplessly at the images that rushed into her reeling mind. "You're so sexy, Micah," she whispered huskily. "So handsome. And I was just plain and my breasts were small, nothing like those beautiful, buxom women you always dated. I knew you'd never want me the way I wanted you."

He shook her gently. "Callie, for God's sake, hush!" he grated, his whole body tensing with desire at the imagery she was creating.

She was too relaxed from the sleeping pills to listen to warnings. She smiled lazily. "I never wanted anybody to touch me until then," she said softly. "Men always seemed repulsive to me. Did I ever tell you that my mother's last lover tried to seduce me? I ran from him and he knocked me down the stairs. I broke my arm. My mother said it was my fault. She took me back to the foster home. She said I was a troublemaker, and told lies about what happened."

"Dear God!" he exclaimed.

"So after that, I wore floppy old clothes and no makeup and pulled my hair back so I looked like the plainest old maid on earth, and I acted real tough. They left me alone. Then my mother married your dad," she added. "And I didn't have to be afraid anymore. Except it was worse," she murmured drowsily, "because I wanted you to touch me. But you didn't like me that way. You said I was a tramp, like my mother..."

"I didn't mean it," he ground out. "I was only trying to spare you more heartache. You were just a baby, and I was old enough to know better. It was the only way I knew to keep you at arm's length."

"You wanted my mother," she accused miserably.

"Never!" he said, and sounded utterly disgusted. "She was hard as nails, and her idea of femininity was complete control. She was the most mercenary human being I ever met."

Her pale blue eyes blinked as she searched his black ones curiously. "You said I was, too."

"You're not mercenary, honey," he replied quietly. "You never were."

She sighed, and her breasts rose and fell, drawing his attention again. "I feel so funny, Micah," she murmured.

"Funny, how?" he asked without thinking.

She laughed softly. "I don't know how to describe it. I feel... like I'm throbbing. I feel swollen."

She was describing sexual arousal, and he was fighting it like mad. He drew in a long, slow breath and forced himself to let go of her wrists. Her arms fell to her sides and he stared helplessly at the thrust of her small, firm breasts.

"It's so sad," she sighed. "The only time you've ever looked at me or touched me was because I was hurt and needed medical attention." She laughed involuntarily.

"You have to stop this. Right now," he said firmly.

"Stop what?" she asked with genuine curiosity.

He lifted the sheet and placed it over her breasts, pulling one of her hands up to hold it there.

She glowered at him as he got to his feet. "That's great," she muttered. "That's just great. Are you the guy at a striptease who yells 'put it back on'?"

He chuckled helplessly. "Not usually, no. I'll leave the door between our rooms and the bathroom open. You can sing out if you get scared again."

"Gosh, you're brave," she said. "Aren't you afraid to leave your door unlocked? I might sneak in and ravish you in your sleep."

"I wear a chastity belt," he said with a perfectly straight face.

Her eyes widened and suddenly she burst out laughing.

He grinned. "That's more like it. Now lie back down and stop trying to seduce me. When you wake up and remember the things you've said and done tonight, you'll blush every time you look at me."

She shrugged. "I guess I will." She frowned. "What was in those pills?"

"A sedative. Obviously it has an unpredictable reaction on you," he commented with a long, amused look. "Either that or I've discovered a brand-new aphrodisiac. It makes retiring virgins wanton, apparently."

She glared up at him. "I am not wanton, and it wasn't my fault, anyway. I was very scared and you came running in here to flaunt your bare chest at me," she pointed out.

"You were the one doing the flaunting," he countered. "I'm going to have Lisette buy you some gowns, and while you're here, you'll wear them. I don't keep condoms handy anymore," he added bluntly.

She flushed and gasped audibly. "Micah Steele!" she burst out, horrified at the crude remark.

"Don't pretend you don't know what one is. You're not that naive. But that's the only way I'd ever have sex with you, even if I lost my head long enough to stifle my conscience," he added bluntly. "Because I don't want kids, or a wife, ever."

"I've already told you that I'm not proposing marriage!"

"You tried to seduce me," he accused.

"You tempted me! In fact, you drugged me!"

He was trying valiantly not to laugh. "I never!" he defended himself. "I gave you a mild sedative. A very mild sedative!"

"It was probably Spanish Fly," she taunted. "I've read about what it's supposed to do to women. You gave it to me deliberately so that I'd flash my breasts at you and make suggestive remarks, no doubt!"

He pursed his lips and lifted his chin, muffling laughter. "For the record, you've got gorgeous breasts," he told her. "But I've never seen myself as a tutor for a sensuous virgin. In case you were thinking along those lines."

She felt that compliment down to her toes and tried not to disgrace herself by showing it. Apparently he didn't think her breasts were too small at all. Imagine that! "There are lots of men who'd just love to have sex with me," she told him haughtily.

"What a shame that I'm the only one you'd submit to."

She glared at him. "Weren't you going back to bed?" she asked pointedly.

He sighed. "I might as well, if you're through undressing for me."

"I didn't undress for you! I sleep like this."

"I'll bet you didn't before you moved in with my father and me," he drawled softly.

Her flush was a dead giveaway.

"*And* you never locked your bedroom door at home," he added.

"For all the good it did me," she said grimly.

"I never got my kicks as a voyeur, especially with precocious teenagers," he told her. "You're much more desirable now, with a little age on you. Not," he added, holding up one lean hand, "that I have any plans to succumb. You're a picket-fence sort of woman."

"And you like yours in combat gear, with muscles," she retorted.

His eyes sketched her body under the sheet. "If I ever had the urge to marry," he said slowly, "you'd be at the top of my list of prospects, Callie. You're kindhearted and honest and brave. I was proud of you in the jungle."

She smiled. "Were you, really? I was terribly scared."

"All of us are, when we're being hunted. The trick is to keep going anyway." He pushed her down gently with the sheet up to her neck and her head on the pillow, and he tucked her in very gently. "Go back to sleep," he said, tracing a path down her cheek with a lean forefinger. He smiled. "You can dream about having wild sex with me."

"I don't have a clue about how to have wild sex," she pointed out. She lifted both eyebrows and her eyes twinkled as she gave him a wicked smile. "I'll bet you're great in bed."

"I am," he said without false modesty. "But," he added somberly, "you're a virgin. First times are painful and embarrassing, nothing like the torrid scenes in those romance novels you like to read."

She drew in a drowsy breath. "I figured that."

He had to get out of here. He was aroused already. It wouldn't take much to tempt him, and she'd been through enough already. He tapped her on the tip of her nose. "Sleep well."

"Micah, can I ask you something?" she murmured, blinking as she tried to stay awake.

"Go ahead."

"What did my mother see that made her think she'd enticed you that night we had the blowup?"

"Are you sure you want to know?" he asked. "Because if you do, I'll show you."

Her breath caught in her throat and her heart pounded. She looked at him with uninhibited curiosity and hunger. "I'm sure."

"Okay. Your choice." He unsnapped his pajama bottoms, and let them fall. "She saw this," he said quietly.

Her eyes went to that part of him that the pajamas had

hidden. She wasn't so naive that she hadn't seen statues, and photographs in magazines, of naked men. But he sure didn't look like any of the pictures. There were no white lines on him anywhere. He was solid muscle, tanned and exquisitely male. Her eyes went helplessly to that part of him that was most male, and she almost gasped. He was impressive, even to an innocent.

"Do you understand what you're seeing, Callie?" he asked quietly.

"Yes," she managed in a husky whisper. "You're...you're aroused, aren't you?"

He nodded. "When I got away from you that Christmas night, I was like this, just from being close to you," he explained quietly, his voice strained. "The slacks I was wearing were tailored to fit properly, so it was noticeable. Your mother was experienced, and when she saw it, she thought it was because of her. She was wearing a strappy little silver dress, and she had an inflated view of her own charms. I found her repulsive."

"I didn't know men looked like that." Her lips parted as she continued to stare at him. "Are you...I mean, is that...normal?"

"I do occasionally inspire envy in other men," he murmured with a helpless laugh. He pulled his pajama trousers back up and snapped them in place, almost shivering with the hunger to throw himself down on top of her and ravish her. She had no idea of the effect that wide-eyed curiosity had on him. "Now I'm getting out of here before it gets any worse!" he said in a tight voice. "Good night."

She stretched, feeling oddly swollen and achy. She stretched, feeling unfamiliar little waves of pleasure washing over her at the intimacy they'd just shared. She noticed that his face went even tauter as he watched her stretch. It felt good. But she was really sleepy and her eyelids felt heavy. Her eyes began to close. "Gosh, I'm tired. I think I can sleep…now." Her voice trailed off as she sighed heavily and her whole body relaxed in the first stages of sleep.

He looked at her with pure temptation. She'd been sedated, of course, or she'd never have been so uninhibited with him. He knew that, but it didn't stop the frustrated desire he felt from racking his powerful body.

"I'm so glad that one of us can sleep," he murmured with icy sarcasm, but she was already asleep. He gave her one last, wistful stare, and went out of the room quickly.

The next morning, Callie awoke after a long and relaxing sleep feeling refreshed. Then she remembered what had happened in the middle of the night and she was horrified.

She searched through the bag Micah's friend had packed for her, looking for something concealing and unnoticeable, but there wasn't a change of clothing. She only had the jeans and shirt she'd been wearing the day before. Grimacing, she put them back on and ran a brush through her short dark hair. She didn't bother with makeup at all.

When she went into the kitchen, expecting to find it empty, Micah was going over several sheets of paper with a cup of black coffee in one big hand. He gave her a quick glance and watched the blush cover her high cheekbones. His lean, handsome face broke into a wicked grin.

"Good morning," he drawled. "All rested, are we? Ready for another round of show and tell?"

She ground her teeth together and avoided looking directly at him as she poured herself a cup of coffee from the coffeemaker on the counter and added creamer to it.

"I was drugged!" she said defensively, sitting down at the table. She couldn't make herself look him in the eye.

"Really?"

"You should know," she returned curtly. "You drugged me!"

"I gave you a mild sedative," he reminded her. He gave her a mischievous glance. "But I'll be sure to remember the effects."

She cleared her throat and sipped her coffee. "Can you find me something to do around here?" she asked. "I'm not used to sitting around doing nothing."

"I phoned Lisse about thirty minutes ago," he said. "She'll be over at ten to take you shopping."

"So soon?" she asked curiously.

"You don't have a change of clothes, do you?" he asked.

She shook her head. "No."

"Maddie travels light and expects everyone else to, as well," he explained. "Especially in tight corners. I'll give you my credit card…"

"I have my own with my passport," she said at once, embarrassed. "Thanks, but I pay my own way."

"So you said." He eyed her over his coffee cup. "I won't expect anything in return," he added. "In case that thought crossed your mind."

"I know that. But I don't want to be obligated to you any more than I already am."

"You sound like me, at your age," he mused. "I never liked to accept help, either. But we all come to it, Callie, sooner or later."

She let out a slow breath and sipped more coffee. "I couldn't repay you in a hundred years for what you did for me," she said gently. "You risked your life to get me out of there."

"All in a day's work, honey," he said, and smiled. "Besides," he added, "I had a score to settle with Lopez." His face hardened. "I've got an even bigger one to settle, now. I have to put him out of action, before he organizes his men and goes after Dad!"

7

C allie felt her heart go cold at the words. She'd been through so much herself that she'd forgotten briefly that Jack Steele was in danger, too. Micah had said that Pogo and Maddie would watch over him, but obviously he still had fears.

"You don't think he'll be safe with your people?" she asked worriedly.

"Not if Lopez gets his act together," he said coolly. "Which is why I've had Bojo send him a message in the clear, rubbing it in that I took you away from him."

She felt uneasy. "Isn't that dangerous, with a man like Lopez?"

"Very," he agreed. "But if he's concentrating on me, he's less likely to expend his energy on Dad. Right?"

"Right," she agreed. "What do you want me to do?"

He lowered his eyes to his coffee cup and lifted it to his chiseled mouth. "You do whatever you like. You're here as my guest."

She frowned. "I don't need a holiday, Micah."

"You're getting one, regardless. Today you can go shopping with Lisse. Tomorrow, I'll take you sight-seeing, if you like."

"Is it safe?"

He chuckled. "We won't be alone," he pointed out. "I intend taking Bojo and Peter and Rodrigo along with us."

"Oh."

"Disappointed?" he asked with faint arrogance. "Would you rather be alone with me, on a deserted beach?"

She glared at him. "You stop that."

"Spoilsport. You do rise to the bait so beautifully." He leaned back in his chair and the humor left his eyes. "Bojo's going with you to Nassau. Buy what you like, but make sure you don't bring home low-cut blouses and short-shorts or short skirts. There aren't any other women on this island, except a couple of married middle-aged island women who live with their husbands and families. I don't want anything to divert the men's attention with Lopez on the loose."

"I don't wear suggestive clothing," she pointed out.

"You do around me," he said flatly. "Considering last night's showing, I thought the warning might be appropriate."

"I was drugged!" she repeated, flushing.

"I don't mind if you show your body to me," he continued, as if she hadn't spoken. "I enjoy looking at it. But I'm not sharing the sight. Besides, for the next week or two, you're my sister. I don't want anyone speculating about our exact relationship."

"Why? Because of your friend Lisette?" she asked bitterly.

"Exactly," he said with a poker face. "Lisette and I are lovers," he added bluntly. "The last thing I need is a jealous tug-of-war in a crisis."

She caught her breath audibly. It was cruel of him to say such a thing. Or maybe he was being cruel to be kind, making sure that she didn't get her hopes up.

She lifted her head with postured arrogance. "That's wishful thinking," she said firmly. "I know you're terribly disappointed that I haven't proposed, but you'd better just deal with it."

For an instant he looked shocked, then he laughed. It occurred to him that he'd never laughed as much in his life as he had with her, especially the past couple of days. Considering the life or death situation they'd been in, it was even more incredible. Callie was a real mate under fire. He'd heard stories about wives of retired mercs walking right into fire with their husbands. He'd taken them with a grain of salt until he'd seen Callie in a more desperate situation than any of those wives had ever been in.

"You made me proud, in Cancún," he said after a minute. "Really proud. If we had campfires, you're the sort of woman we'd build into legend around them."

She flushed. "Like Maddie?"

"Maddie's never been in the situation you were in," he said somberly. "I don't even know another woman who has. Despite the nightmares, you held up as well as any man I've ever served with."

She smiled slowly. "A real compliment, wow," she murmured. "If you'll write all that down, I'll have it notarized and hang it behind my desk. Mr. Kemp will be very impressed."

He glowered at her. "Kemp's more likely to hang you on the wall beside it. You're wasted in a law office."

"I love what I do," she protested. "I dig out little details that save lives and careers. Law isn't dry and boring, it's alive. It's history."

"It's a job in a little hick Texas town while you'll eventually dry up and blow away like a sun-scorched creosote bush."

She searched his dark eyes. "That's how it felt to you, I know. You never liked living in Jacobsville. But I'm not like you," she added softly. "I want a neat little house with a flower garden and neighbors to talk to over the fence, and a couple of children." Her face softened as she thought about it. "Not right away, of course. But someday."

"Just the thought of marriage gives me chest pain," he said with veiled contempt. "More often than not, a woman marries for money and a man marries for sex. What difference does a sheet of paper with signatures make?"

"If you have to ask, you wouldn't understand the answer," she said simply. "I guess you don't want kids."

He frowned. He'd never thought about having kids. It was one of those "someday" things he didn't give much time to. He studied Callie and pictured her again with a baby in her arms. It was surprisingly nice.

"It would be hard to carry a baby through jungle under-growth with a rifle under one arm," she answered her own question. "And in your line of work, I don't suppose leaving a legacy to children is much of a priority."

He averted his head. "I expect to spend what I make while I'm still alive," he said.

She looked out over the bay, her eyes narrowing in the glare of the sunlight. The casuarinas lining the beach were towering and their feathery fronds waved gracefully in the breeze that always blew near the water. Flowers bloomed everywhere. The sand was like sugar, white and picturesque.

"It's like a living travel poster," she remarked absently. "I've never seen water that color except in postcards, and I thought it was just a bad color job."

"There are places in the Pacific and the Caribbean like it," he told her. He glanced toward the pier as he heard the sound of a motor. "There's Lisse," he said. "Come and be introduced."

She got up and followed along behind him, feeling like a puppy that couldn't be left alone. As she watched, a gorgeous blonde in a skimpy yellow sundress with long legs and long hair let Micah help her onto the pier. Unexpectedly he jerked her against him and kissed her so passionately that Callie flushed and looked away in embarrassment. He was obviously terrified that she might read something into last night, so he was making his relationship with Lisse very plain.

A few minutes later, Micah put something into Lisse's hand and spoke softly to her. Lisse laughed breathily and said something that Callie couldn't hear. Micah took the blonde by the hand and led her down the pier to where Callie was waiting at a respectful distance.

Up close, the blonde had a blemishless complexion and perfect teeth. She displayed them in a smile that would do credit to a supermodel, which was what the woman really looked like.

"I'm Lisette Dubonnet, but everyone calls me Lisse," she introduced herself and held out a hand to firmly shake Callie's.

"I'm Callie…" she began.

"My sister," Micah interrupted, obviously not trusting her to play along. "She's taking a holiday from her job in Texas. I want you to help her buy some leisure wear. Her suitcase didn't arrive with her."

"Oh," Lisse said, and laughed. "I've had that happen. I know *just* how you feel. Well, shall we go? Micah, are you coming with us?"

Micah shook his head. "I've got things to do here, but Bojo wants to come along, if you don't mind. He has to check on a package his brother is sending over from Georgia."

"He's perfectly welcome," Lisse said carelessly. "Come along, Callie. Callie…what a pretty name. A little rare, I should say."

"It's short for Colleen," Callie told her, having to almost run to keep up with the woman's long strides.

"We'll go downtown in Nassau. There are lots of chic little boutiques there. I'm sure we can find something that will do for you."

"You're very kind…"

Lisse held up an imperative hand as they reached the boat she'd just disembarked from. "It's no bother. Micah never speaks of you. Did he have you hidden in a closet or something?"

"We don't get along very well," Callie formulated. It was the truth, too, mostly.

"And that's very odd. Micah gets along wonderfully with most women."

"But then you're not related to him," Callie pointed out, just managing to clamber aboard the boat before the line was untied by Bojo, who was already there and waiting to leave.

"No, thank God I'm not." Lisse laughed. Even her laugh was charming. "I'd kill myself. Hurry up, Bojo, Dad and I have to go to an embassy ball tonight, so I'm pressed for time!"

"I am coming, mademoiselle!" he said with a grin and leaped down into the boat.

"Let's go, Marchand!" she called to the captain, who replied respectfully and turned the expensive speedboat back into the bay and headed it toward Nassau.

"We could postpone this trip, if you don't have time," Callie offered.

"Not necessary," Lisse said. "I'll have less time later on. I try to do anything Micah asks me to. He's always *so* grateful," she added in a purring tone.

And I can just imagine what form that takes, Callie thought, but she didn't say it. Even so, Bojo heard their conversation, caught Callie's eye, and grinned so wickedly that she cleared her throat and asked Lisse about the history of Nassau to divert her.

Nassau was bustling with tourists. The colorful straw market at the docks was doing a booming business, and fishing boats rocked gently on the waves made by passing boats. Seagulls made passes at the water and flew gracefully past the huge glass windows of the restaurant that sat right on the bay. It was beautiful. Just beautiful. Callie, who'd never been anywhere—well, except for the road trip to Cancún with the drug lord's minions while she was unconscious—thought it was pure delight.

"Don't gawk like a tourist, darling," Lisse scoffed as they made their way past the fishing boats and into an arcade framed in an antique stone arch covered in bougainvillea. "It's only Nassau."

But Callie couldn't help it. She loved the musical accents she caught snatches of as they strolled past shops featuring jewelry with shell motifs and handcrafts from all over Europe, not to mention dress shops and T-shirt shops galore. She loved the stone pathways and the flowers that bloomed everywhere. They went past a food stand and her nose wrinkled.

"I thought I smelled liquor," she said under her breath.

"You did," Lisse said nonchalantly, waving her painted finger-nails in the general direction of the counter. "You can buy any sort of alcoholic drink you want at any of these food stands."

"It's legal?"

"Of course it's legal. Haven't you been anywhere?"

Callie smiled sheepishly. "Not really. Now this is the sort of shop I need," she said suddenly, stopping at a store window displaying sundresses, jeans and T-shirts and sneakers. It also displayed the cards it accepted, and Callie had one of them. "I'll only be a minute…"

"Darling, not there!" Lisse lamented. "It's one of those cheap touristy shops! Micah wants you to use his charge card. I've got it in my pocket. He wants you to wear things that won't embarrass him." She put her fingers over her mouth. "Oh, dear, I forgot, I wasn't to tell you that he said that." She grimaced. "Well, anyway…"

"Well, anyway," Callie interrupted, following Lisse's lead, "this is where I'm shopping, with *my* card. You can wait or come in. Suit yourself."

She turned and left Lisse standing there with her mouth gaping, and she didn't care. The woman was horrible!

After she'd tried on two pairs of jeans, two sundresses, a pair of sandals, one of sneakers and four T-shirts, she felt guilty for the way she'd talked to Micah's woman. But Lisse was hard-going, especially after that kiss she'd witnessed. It had hurt right to the bone, and Lisse's condescending, snappy attitude didn't endear her to Callie, either.

She came back out of the shop with two bags. "Thank you very much. I'd like to go back to the house, now," she told Lisse, and she didn't smile.

Lisse made a moue with her perfect mouth. "I've hurt your feelings. I'm sorry. But Micah told me what to do. He'll be furious with me now."

What a pity. She didn't say it. "He can be furious with me," Callie said, walking ahead of Lisse back the way they'd come. "I buy my own clothes and pay my own way. I'm not a helpless parasite. I don't need a man to buy things for me."

There was a stony silence from behind her. She stopped and turned and said, "Oh, my, did I hurt your feelings? I'm sorry." And with a wicked gleam in her eyes at the other woman's furious flush, she walked back toward the boat.

Bojo knew something was going on, but he was too polite to question Lisse's utter silence all the way back to the pier. He got out first to tie up the boat and reached down to help Callie out, relieving her of her packages on the way. Micah had heard the boat and was strolling down the pier to meet them. There was a scramble as Lisse climbed out of the boat, cursing her captain for not being quick enough to spare her a stumble. She sounded like she was absolutely seething!

"We'd better run for it," Callie confided to Bojo.

"What did you do?" he asked under his breath.

"I called her a parasite. I think she's upset."

He muffled a laugh, nodded respectfully at his boss and herded Callie down the pier at very nearly a run while Micah stood staring after them with a scowl. Seconds later Lisse reached him and her voice carried like a bullhorn.

"She's got the breeding of a howler monkey, and the dress sense of an octopus!" she raged. "I wouldn't take her to the nearest tar pit without a bribe!"

Callie couldn't help it. She broke down and ran even faster, with Bojo right beside her.

Later, of course, she had to face the music. She'd changed into a strappy little blue-and-white-striped sundress. It was ankle-length with a square bodice and wide shoulder straps. Modest even enough for her surroundings. She was barefoot, having disliked the fit of the sandals she'd bought that rubbed against her big toe. Micah came striding toward her where she was lounging under a sea grape tree watching the fishing boats come into the harbor.

Micah was in cutoff denims that left his long, powerful legs bare, and he was wearing an open shirt. His chest was broad and hair-roughened and now Callie couldn't look at it without feeling it under her hands.

"Can't you get along with anyone?" he demanded, his fists on his narrow hips as he glared down at her.

"My boss Mr. Kemp thinks I'm wonderful," she countered.

His eyes narrowed. "You gave Lisse fits, and she only came over to do you a favor, when she was already pressed for time."

Her eyebrows arched over shimmering blue eyes. "You don't think I'm capable of walking into a shop and buying clothes all by myself? Whatever sort of women are you used to?"

"And you called her a parasite," he added angrily.

"Does she work?"

He hesitated. "She's her father's hostess."

"I didn't ask you about her social life, I asked if she worked for her living. She doesn't. And she said that when she did you favors, you repaid her handsomely." She cocked her head up at him. "I suppose, in a pinch, you could call that working for her living. But it isn't a profession I'd want to confess to in public."

He just stood there, scowling.

"I make my own living," she continued, "and pay my own way. I don't rely on men to support me, buy me clothes, or chauffeur me around."

"Lisse is used to a luxurious lifestyle," he began slowly, but without much conviction.

"I'm sure that I've misjudged her," she said placatingly. "Why, if you lost everything tomorrow, I know she'd be the first person to rush to your side and offer to help you make it all back with hard work."

He pursed his lips and thought about that.

"That's what I thought," she said sweetly.

He was glaring again. "I told you to put everything on my card, and get nice things."

"You told Lisse to take me to expensive dress shops so that I wouldn't buy cheap stuff and embarrass you," she countered, getting to her feet. She brushed off her skirt, oblivious to the shocked look on his face, before she lifted her eyes back to his. "I don't care if I embarrass you," she pointed out bluntly. "You can always hide me in a closet when you have guests if you're ashamed of me."

He made a rough sound. "You'd walk right into the living room and tell them why you were hidden."

She shrugged. "Blame it on a rough childhood. I don't like people pushing me around. Especially model-type parasites."

"Lisse is not—" he started.

"I don't care what she is or isn't," she cut him off, "she's not bossing me around and insulting me!"

"What did you tell her about our relationship?" he demanded, and he was angry.

"I told her nothing," she countered hotly. "It's none of her business. But, for the record, if you really were my brother, I'd have you stuffed and mounted and I'd use you for an ashtray!"

She walked right past him and back into the house. She heard muffled curses, but she didn't slow down. Let him fume. She didn't care.

She didn't come out for supper. She sat in a peacock chair out on the patio overlooking the bay and enjoyed the delicious floral smell of the musty night air in the delicious breeze, while sipping a piña colada. She'd never had one and she was curious about the taste, so she'd had Mac fix her one, along with a sandwich. She wasn't really afraid of Micah, but she was hoping to avoid him until they both cooled down.

He came into her room without knocking and walked right out onto the patio. He was wearing a tuxedo with a faintly ruffled fine white cotton shirt, and he looked so handsome that her heart stopped and fluttered at just the sight of him.

"Are you going to a funeral, or did you get a job as a waiter?" she asked politely.

He managed not to laugh. It wasn't funny. She wasn't funny. She'd insulted Lisse and the woman was going to give him fits all night. "I'm taking Lisse to an embassy ball," he said stiffly. "I would have invited you, but you don't have anything to wear," he added with a vicious smile.

"Just as well," she murmured, lifting her glass to him in a mock toast. "It would have blood all over it by the end of the night, if I'm any judge of miffed women."

"Lisse is a lady," he said shortly. "Something you have no concept of, with your ignorance of proper manners."

That hurt, but she smiled. "Blame it on a succession of foster homes," she told him sweetly. "Manners aren't a priority."

He hated being reminded of the life she'd led. It made him feel guilty, and he didn't like it. "Pity," he said scathingly. "You might consider taking lessons."

"I always think that if you're going to fight, you should get down in the mud and roll around, not use words."

"Just what I'd expect from a little savage like you," he said sarcastically.

The word triggered horrible memories. She reacted to it out of all proportion, driven by her past. She leaped to her feet, eyes blazing, the glass trembling in her hand. "One more word, and you'll need a shower and a dry cleaner to get out the door!"

"Don't you like being called a savage?" He lifted his chin as her hand drew back. "You wouldn't daaa....re!"

He got it right in the face. It didn't stay there. It dribbled down onto his spotless white shirt and made little white trickles down over his immaculate black tuxedo.

She frowned. "Damn. I forgot the toast." She lifted the empty glass at him. *"Salud y pesetas!"* she said in Spanish, with a big furious smile. Health and wealth.

His fists clenched at his sides. He didn't say a word. He didn't move a muscle. He just looked at her with those black eyes glittering like a coiling cobra.

She wiggled her eyebrows. "It will be an adventure. Lisse can lick it off! Think of the new experiences you can share...now, Micah," she shifted gears and started backing up.

He was moving. He was moving very slowly, very deliberately, with the steps of a man who didn't care if he had to go to jail for homicide. She noticed that at once.

She backed away from him. He really did look homicidal. Perhaps she'd gone a little too far. Her mouth tended to run away from her on good days, even when she wasn't insulted and hadn't had half a glass of potent piña colada to boot. She wasn't used to alcohol at all.

"Let's be reasonable," she tried. She was still backing up. "I do realize that I might have overreacted. I'll apologize."

He kept coming.

"I'm really sorry," she tried again, holding up both hands, palms toward him, as if to ward him off.

He still kept coming.

"And I promise, faithfully, that I will never do it... *aaaaahh!*"

There was a horrific splash and she swallowed half the swimming pool. She came up soaked, sputtering, freezing, because the water was cold. She clamored over the softly lit water to the concrete edge and grabbed hold of the ladder to pull herself up. It was really hard, because her full skirt was soaked and heavy.

"Like hell you do," he said fiercely, and started to push her back in.

She was only trying to save herself. But she grabbed his arms and overbalanced him, and he went right into the pool with her, headfirst.

This time when she got to the surface, he was right beside her. His black eyes were raging now.

She pushed her hair out of her eyes and mouth. "I'm *really* sorry," she panted.

He was breathing deliberately. "Would you like to explain why you went ballistic for no reason?" he demanded.

She grimaced, treading water and trying not to sink. She

couldn't swim *very well*. She was ashamed of her behavior, but the alcohol had loosened all her inhibitions. She supposed she owed him the truth. She glanced at him and quickly away again. "When that man hit on me and made me break my arm, he told my mother I was a lying little savage and that I needed to be put away. That's when my mother took me back to my foster family and disowned me," she bit off the words, averting her eyes.

There was a long silence. He swam to the ladder, waiting for her to join him. But she was tired and cold and emotionally drained. And when she tried to dog-paddle, her arms were just too tired. She sank.

Powerful arms caught her, easing her to the surface effortlessly so that she could breathe. He sat her on the edge and climbed out, reaching down to lift her out beside him. He took her arm and led her back up the cobblestoned walkway to the patio.

"I can pack and go home tomorrow," she offered tautly.

"You can't leave," he said flatly. "Lopez knows where you are."

She lifted her weary eyes to his hard, cold face. "Poor you," she said. "Stuck with me."

His eyes narrowed. "You haven't dealt with any of it, have you?" he asked quietly. "You're still carrying your childhood around on your back."

"We all do, to some extent," she said with a long sigh. "I'm sorry I ruined your suit. I'm sorry I was rude to Lisse. I'll apologize, if you like," she added humbly.

"You don't like her."

She shrugged. "I don't know her. I just don't have a high opinion of women who think money is what life is all about."

He scowled. "What *is* it all about?" he challenged.

She searched his eyes slowly. "Pain," she said in a husky tone, and she winced involuntarily before she could stop herself. "I'm going to bed. Good night."

She was halfway in the door when he called her back.

She didn't turn. "Yes?"

He hesitated. He wanted to apologize, he really did. But he didn't know how. He couldn't remember many regrets.

She laughed softly to herself. "I know. You wish you'd never been landed with me. You might not believe it, but so do I."

"If you'll give me the name of the shop where you bought that stuff, I'll have them transfer it to my account."

"Fat chance, Steele," she retorted as she walked away.

8

After a restless night, but thankfully with no nightmares, Callie put on a colorful sundress and went out onto the beach barefoot to pick up shells. She met Bojo on the way. He was wearing the long oyster silk hooded djellaba she'd never seen him out of.

He gave her a rueful glance. "The boss had to send to town for a new tuxedo last night," he said with twinkling dark eyes. "I understand you took him swimming."

She couldn't help chuckling. "I didn't mean to. We had a name-calling contest and he lost."

He chuckled, too. "You know, his women rarely accost him. They fawn over him, play up to him, stroke his ego and live for expensive presents."

"I'm his sister," she said neutrally.

"You are not," he replied gently. He smiled at her surprised glance. "He does occasionally share things with me," he added. "I believe the fiction is to protect you from Lisse. She is obsessively jealous of him and not a woman to make an enemy of. She has powerful connections and little conscience."

"Oh, I got to her before I got to him, if you recall," Callie said with a wry glance. She scuffed her toes in the sand, unearthing part of a perfect shell. She bent to pick it up. "I guess I'll be fish food if she has mob connections."

He chuckled. "I wouldn't rule that out, but you are safe enough here," he admitted. "What are you doing?"

"Collecting shells to take back home," she said, her eyes still on the beach. "I've lived inland all my life. I don't think I've ever even seen the ocean. Galveston is on the bay, and it isn't too far from Jacobsville, but I've never been there, either. It just fascinates me!" She glanced at him. "Micah said you were from Morocco. That's where the Sahara Desert is, isn't it?"

"Yes, but I am from Tangier. It is far north of the desert."

"But it's desert, too, isn't it?" she wondered.

He laughed pleasantly. "Tangier is a seaport, mademoiselle. In fact, it looks a lot like Nassau. That's why I don't mind working here with Micah."

"Really?" She just stared at him. "Isn't it funny, how we get mental pictures of faraway places, and they're nothing like what you see when you get there? I've seen postcards of the Bahamas, but I thought that water was painted, because it didn't even look real. But it is. It's the most astonishing group of colors…"

"Bojo!"

He turned to see his boss coming toward them, taciturn and threatening. It was enough for Callie to hear the tone of his voice to know that he was angry. She didn't turn around, assuming he had chores for Bojo.

"See you," she said with a smile.

He lifted both eyebrows. "I wonder," he replied enigmatically, and went down the beach to speak to Micah.

Minutes later, Micah strolled down the beach where Callie was kneeling and sorting shells damp with seawater and coated with sand. He was wearing sand-colored slacks with casual shoes and an expensive silk shirt under a sports coat. He looked elegant and so handsome that Callie couldn't continue looking at him without letting her admiration show.

"Are you here for an apology?" she asked, concentrating on the shells instead of him. Her heart was pounding like mad, but at least her voice sounded calm.

There was a pause. "I'm here to take you sight-seeing."

Her heart jumped. She'd thought that would be the last thing on his mind after their argument the night before. She glanced at his knees and away again. "Thanks for the offer, but I'd rather hunt shells, if it's all the same to you."

He stuck his hands into his pockets and glared at her dark, bent head, his mouth making a thin line in a hard face. He felt guilty about the things he'd said to her the night before, and she'd made him question his whole lifestyle with that remark about Lisse. When he looked back, he had to admit that most of the women in his life had been out for material rewards. Far from looking for love, they'd been looking for expensive jewelry, nights out in the fanciest nightclubs and restaurants, sailing trips on his yacht. Callie wouldn't even let him buy her a decent dress.

He glared at the dress she was wearing with bridled fury. Lisse had spent the evening condemning Callie for everything from her Texas accent to her lack of style. It had been one of the most unpleasant dates of his life, and when he'd refused her offer to stay the night at her apartment, she'd made furious comments about his "unnatural" attraction to his sister. Rather than be accused of perversion, he'd been forced to tell the truth. That had only made matters worse. Lisse had stormed into her apartment house without a word and he knew that she was vindictive. He'd have to watch Callie even more carefully now.

"I guess she gave you hell all night, huh?" Callie asked his shoes. "I'm really sorry."

He let out a harsh breath. His dark eyes went to the waves caressing the white sand near the shore. Bits of seaweed washed up over the occasional shell, along with bits of palm leaves.

"Why don't you want to see Nassau?"

She stood up and lifted one of her bare feet. There was a noticeable blister between her big toe and the next one, on both feet. "Because I'd have to go barefoot. I got the wrong sort of sandals. They've got a thong that goes between your toes, and I'm not used to them. Sneakers don't really go with this dress."

"Not much would," he said with a scathing scrutiny of it. "Half the women on New Providence are probably wearing one just like it."

She glared at him. "Assembly line dresses are part of my lifestyle. I have to live within my means," she said with outraged pride. "I'm sorry if I don't dress up to your exacting standards, but I can't afford haute couture on take-home pay of a little over a hundred and fifty dollars a week!" Her chin tilted with even more hostility. "So spare your blushes and leave me to my shells. I'd hate to embarrass you by wearing my 'rags' out in public."

"Oh, hell!" he burst out, eyes flashing.

He was outraged, but she knew she'd hit the nail on the head. He didn't even try to pretend that he wasn't ashamed to take her out in public. "Isn't it better if I stay here, anyway? Surely I'm safer in a camp of armed men that I would be running around Nassau."

"You seem to be surgically attached to Bojo lately," he said angrily.

She lifted both eyebrows. "I like Bojo," she said. "He doesn't look down on the way I dress, or make fun of my accent, or ignore me when I'm around."

He was almost vibrating with anger. He couldn't remember any woman in his life making him as explosively angry as Callie could.

"Why don't you take Lisse sight-seeing?" she suggested, moving away from him. "You could start with the most expensive jeweler in Nassau and work your way to the most expensive boutique...Micah!"

He had her up in his arms and he was heading for the ocean.

She pushed at his broad chest. "Don't you dare, don't...you... dare, Micah!"

It didn't work. He swung her around and suddenly was about to toss her out right into the waves when the explosion came. There was a ricochet that was unmistakable to Micah, and bark flew off a palm tree nearby. "Bojo!" Micah yelled.

The other man, who was still within shouting distance, came running with a small weapon in his hands. Out beyond the breakers, there was a ship, a yacht, moving slowly. A glint of sunlight reflecting off metal was visible on the deck and the ricocheting sound came again.

"What the...!" she exclaimed, as Micah ran down the beach with her in his arms.

"This way!" Bojo yelled to him, and a sharp, metallic ripple of gunfire sounded somewhere nearby.

The firing brought other men to the beach, one of whom had a funny-looking long tube. It was Peter. Bojo called something to him. He protested, but Bojo insisted. He knelt, resting the tube on his shoulder, sighted and pulled the trigger. A shell flew out of it with a muffled roar. Seconds later, there was a huge splash in the water just off the yacht's bow.

"That'll buy us about a minute. Let's go!" Micah grabbed Callie up in his arms and rushed up the beach to the house at a dead run. His men stopped firing and followed. Micah called something to Bojo in a language Callie had never heard before.

"What was that?" she asked, shocked when he put her down inside the house. "What happened?"

"Lopez happened, unless I miss my guess. I was careless. It won't happen twice," Micah said flatly. He walked away while she was still trying to form questions.

Moments later, Micah went to find Bojo.

"The yacht is gone now, of course," Bojo said angrily. "Peter is upset that I refused to let him blow her up."

"Some things require more authority than I have, even here," Micah said flatly. "But don't think I wasn't tempted to do just that. Lopez knows I have Callie, and he knows where she is now. He'll make a try for her." He looked at Bojo. "She can't be out of our sight again, not for a second."

"I am aware of that," the other man replied. His dark eyes narrowed. "Micah, does she have any idea at all that you're using her as bait?"

"If you so much as mention that to her...!" Micah threatened softly.

"I would not," he assured the older man. "But you must admit, it hardly seems the action of someone who cares for her."

Micah stared him down. "She's part of my family and I'll take care of her. But she's only part of my family because my father married her tramp of a mother. She's managed to endear herself to my father and it would kill him if anything happened to her," he said in a cold tone. "I can't let Lopez get to my father. Using Callie to bait him here, where I can deal with him safely, is the only way I have to get him at all, and I'm not backing down now!"

"As you wish," Bojo said heavily. "At least she has no idea of this."

Micah agreed. Neither of them saw the shadow at the door behind them retreat to a distance.

Callie went back to her room and closed the door very quietly before she let the tears roll down her white face. She'd have given two years of her life not to have heard those cold words from Micah's lips. She knew he was angry with her, but she didn't realize the contempt with which he was willing to risk her life, just to get Lopez. All he'd said about protecting her, keeping her safe, not letting Lopez get to her—it was all lies. He wanted her for bait. That was all she meant to him. He was doing it to save his father from Lopez, not to save her. Apparently she was expendable. Nothing in her life had ever hurt quite so much.

She seemed to go numb from the pain. She didn't feel anything, except emptiness. She sat down in the chair beside the window and looked out over the ocean. The ship that had been there was gone now, but Lopez knew where the house was, and how well it was guarded. Considering his record, she didn't imagine that he'd give up his quest just because Micah had armed men. Lopez had armed men, too, and all sorts of connections. He also had a reputation for never getting bested by anyone. He would do everything in his power to get Callie back, thinking Micah really cared for her. After all, he'd rescued her, hadn't he?

She wrapped her arms around herself, remembering how it had been at Lopez's house, how that henchman had tortured her. She felt sick all over. This was even worse than being in the foster care system. She was all alone. There was no one to offer her protection, to comfort her, to value her. Her whole life had been like that. For just a little while, she'd had some wild idea that she mattered to Micah. What a joke.

At least she knew the truth now, even if she'd had to eaves-drop to learn it. She could only depend on herself. She was going to ask Bojo for a gun and get him to teach her to shoot it. If she had to fend for herself, and apparently she did, she wanted a chance for survival. Micah would probably turn her over to Lopez if he got a guarantee that Lopez would leave his father alone, she reasoned irrationally. The terror she felt was so consuming that she felt her whole body shaking with it.

When Micah opened the door to her room, she had to fight not to rage at him. It wasn't his fault that he didn't care for her, she told herself firmly. And she loved his father as much as he did. She managed to look at him without flinching, but the light in her eyes had gone out. They were quiet, haunted eyes with no life in them at all.

Micah saw that and frowned. She was different. "What's wrong? You're safe," he assured her. "Lopez was only letting us know he's nearby. Believe me, if he'd wanted you dead, you'd be dead."

She swallowed. "I figured that out," she said in a subdued tone. "What now?"

The frown deepened. "We wait, of course. He'll make another move. We'll draw back and let him think we didn't take the threat seriously. That will pull him in."

She lifted her eyes to his face. "Why don't you let me go sight-seeing alone?" she offered. "That would probably do the trick."

"And risk letting him take you again?" he asked solemnly.

She laughed without humor and turned her eyes back to the ocean. "Isn't that what you have in mind already?"

The silence behind her was arctic. "Would you like to explain that question?"

"In ancient times, when they wanted to catch a lion, they tethered a live kid goat to a post and baited him with it. If the goat lived, they turned him loose, but if the lion got him, it didn't really matter. I mean, what's a goat more or less?"

Micah had never felt so many conflicting emotions at the same time. Foremost of them was shame. "You heard me talking to Bojo?"

She nodded.

His indrawn breath was the only sound in the room. "Callie," he began, without knowing what he could say to repair the damage.

"It's okay," she said to the picture window. "I never had any illusions about where I fit in your family. I still don't."

His teeth ground together. Why should it be so painful to hear her say that? She was the interloper. She and her horrible mother had destroyed his relationship with his own father. He was alone because of her, so why should he feel guilty? But he did. He felt guilty and ashamed. He hadn't really meant everything he'd said to Bojo. Somewhere there was a vague jealousy of the easy friendship she had with his right-hand man, with the tenderness she gave Bojo, when she fought Micah tooth and nail.

"I'll do whatever you want me to," she said after a minute. "But I want a gun, and I want to learn how to use it." She stood up and turned to face him, defiant in the shark-themed white T-shirt and blue jeans she'd changed into. "Because if Lopez gets me this time, he's getting a dead woman. I'll never go through that again."

Micah actually winced. "He's not getting you," he said curtly.

"Better me than Dad," she said with a cold smile. "Right?"

He slammed the door and walked toward her. She didn't even try to back up. She glared at him from a face that was tight with grief and misery, the tracks of tears still visible down her cheeks.

"Do you actually think I'd let him take you, even to save Dad?" he demanded furiously. "What sort of man do you think I am?"

"I have no idea," she said honestly. "You're a stranger. You always have been."

He searched her blue eyes with irritation and impatience. "You're a prime example of the reason I prefer mercenary women," he said without thinking. "You're nothing but a pain in the neck."

"Thank you. I love compliments."

"You probably thrive on insults," he bit off. Then he remembered how she'd had to live all those years, and could have slapped himself for taunting her.

"If they're all you ever hear, you get used to them," she

agreed without rancor. "I'm tough. I've had to be. So do your worst, Micah," she added. "Tie me to a palm tree and wait in ambush for Lopez to shoot at me, I don't care."

But she did care. There was real pain in those blue eyes, which she was trying so valiantly to disguise with sarcasm. It hurt her that Micah would use her to draw Lopez in. That led him to the question of why it hurt her. And when he saw that answer in her eyes, he could have gone through the floor with shame.

She...loved him. He felt his heart stop and then start again as the thought went through him like electricity. She almost certainly loved him, and she was doing everything in her power to keep him from seeing it. He remembered her arms around him, her mouth surrendering to his, her body fluid and soft under his hands as she yielded instantly to his ardor. A woman with her past would have a hard time with lovemaking, yet she'd been willing to let him do anything he liked to her. Why hadn't he questioned that soft yielding? Why hadn't he known? And she'd heard what he said to Bojo, feeling that way...

"I swear to you, I won't let Lopez get you," he said in a firm, sincere tone.

"You mean, you'll try," she replied dully. "I want a gun, Micah."

"Over my dead body," he said harshly. "You're not committing suicide."

Her lower lip trembled. She felt trapped. She looked trapped.

That expression ignited him like fireworks. He jerked her into his tall, powerful body, and bent to her mouth before she realized his intent. His warm, hard mouth bit into her lips with ardent insistence as his arms enveloped her completely against him. He felt his body swell instantly, as it always did when he touched her. He groaned against her mouth and deepened the kiss, lost in the wonder of being loved…

Dizzily he registered that she was making a halfhearted effort to push him away. He felt her cold, nervous hands on his chest. He lifted his head and looked at her wary, uncertain little face.

"I won't hurt you," he said softly.

"You're angry," she choked. "It's a punishment…"

"I'm not and it isn't." He bent again, and kissed her eyelids. His hands worked their way up into the thickness of her hair and then down her back, slowly pressing her to him.

She shivered at the feel of him against her hips.

He chuckled at that telltale sign. "Most men would kill to have such an immediate response to a woman. But I don't suppose you know that."

"You shouldn't…"

He lifted his head again and gave her a look full of amused worldly wisdom. "You think I can will it not to happen, I guess?"

She flushed.

"Sorry, honey, but it doesn't work that way." He moved away just enough to spare her blushes, but his hands slid to her waist and held her in front of him. "I want you to stay in the house," he said, as if he hadn't done anything outrageous at all. "Stay away from windows and porches, too."

She searched his eyes. "If Lopez doesn't see me," she began.

"He knows you're here," he said with faint distaste. "I don't want him to know exactly where you are. I'll have men on every corner of the property and the house for the duration. I won't let you be captured."

She leaned her forehead against him, shivering. "You can't imagine...how it was," she said huskily.

His arms tightened, holding her close. He cursed himself for ever having thought of putting her deliberately in the line of fire. He couldn't imagine he'd been that callous, even briefly. It had been the logical thing to do, and he'd never let emotion get in the way of work. But Callie wasn't like him. She had feelings that were easily bruised, and he'd done a lot of damage already. Those nightmares she had should have convinced him how traumatic her captivity had been, but he hadn't even taken that into consideration when he was setting up Lopez by bringing Callie here.

"I'm sorry," he bit off the words. He wondered if she knew how hard it was to say that.

She blinked away sudden tears. "It's not your fault, you're just trying to save Dad. I love Dad, too, Micah," she said at his chest. "I don't blame you for doing everything you can to keep him safe."

His eyes closed and he groaned silently. "I'm going to do everything I can to keep you safe, too," he told her.

She shrugged. "I know." She pulled away from him with a faint smile to soften the rejection. "Thanks."

He studied her face and realized that he'd never really looked at her so closely before. She had a tiny line of freckles just over her straight little nose. Her light blue eyes had flecks of dark blue in them and she had the faintest little dimple in her cheek when she smiled. He touched her pretty mouth with his fingertips. It was slightly swollen from the hungry, insistent pressure of his lips. She looked rumpled from his ardor, and he liked that, too.

"Take a picture," she said uncomfortably.

"You're pretty," he murmured with an odd smile.

"I'm not, and stop trying to flatter me," she replied, shifting away from him.

"It isn't flattery." He bent and brushed his mouth lightly over her parted lips. She gasped and hung there, her eyes wide and vulnerable on his face when he drew back. Her reaction made him feel taller. He smiled softly. "You don't give an inch, do you? I suppose it's hard for you to trust anyone, after the life you've led."

"I trust Dad," she snapped.

"Yes, but you don't trust me, do you?"

"Not an inch," she agreed, pulling away. "And you don't have to kiss me to make me feel better, either."

"It was to make me feel better," he pointed out, smiling at her surprise. "It did, too."

She shifted her posture a little, confused.

His dark eyes slid over her body, noting the little points that punctuated her breasts and the unsteady breathing she couldn't control. Yes, she wanted him.

She folded her arms over her breasts, curious about why he was staring at them. They felt uncomfortable, but she didn't know why.

"I didn't tell Lisse that you were an embarrassment to me," he said suddenly, and watched her face color.

"It's okay," she replied tersely. "I know I don't have good dress sense. I don't care about clothes most of the time."

"I'm used to women who do, and who enjoy letting men pay for them. The more expensive they are, the better." He sounded jaded and bitter.

She studied his hard face, recognizing disillusionment and

reticence. She moved a step closer involuntarily. "You sound...I don't know...cheated, maybe."

"I feel cheated," he said shortly. His eyes were full of harsh memories. "No man likes to think that he's paying for sex."

"Then why do you choose women who want expensive gifts from you?" she asked him bluntly.

His teeth met. "I don't know."

"Don't you, really?" she asked, her eyes soft and curious. "You've always said you don't want to get married, so you pick women who don't want to, either. But that sort of woman only lasts as long as the money does. Or am I wrong?"

He looked down at her from his great height with narrowed eyes and wounded pride. "I suppose you're one of those women who would rush right over to a penniless man and offer to get a second job to help him out of debt!"

She smiled sheepishly, ignoring the sarcasm. "I guess I am." She shrugged. "I scare men off. They don't want me because I'm not interested in what sort of car they drive or the expensive places they can afford to take me to. I like to go walking in the country and pick wildflowers." She peered up at him with a mischievous smile. "The last man I said that to left town two days before he was supposed to. He was doing some accounts for Mr. Kemp and he left skid marks. Mr. Kemp thought it was hilarious. He was a notorious ladies' man, it seems, and he'd actually seduced Mr. Kemp's last secretary."

Micah didn't smile, as she'd expected him to. He looked angry.

She held up a hand. "I don't have designs on you, honest. I know you don't like wildflowers and Lisse is your sort of woman. I'm not interested in you that way, anyhow."

"Considering the way you just kissed me, you might have trouble proving that," he commented dryly.

She cleared her throat. "You kiss very nicely, and I have to get experience where I can."

"Is that it?" he asked dubiously.

She nodded enthusiastically. She swallowed again as the terror of the last hour came back and the eyes she lifted to his were suddenly haunted. "Micah, he's never going to stop, is he?"

"Probably not, unless he has help." He lifted an eyebrow. "I have every intention of helping him, once I've spoken with the authorities."

"What authorities?"

"Never mind. You know nothing. Got it?"

She saluted him. "Yes, sir."

He made a face. "Come on out. We'll have Mac make some sandwiches and coffee. I don't know about you, but I'm hungry."

"I could eat something."

He hesitated before he opened her door. "I really meant what I told you," he said. "Lopez won't get within fifty yards of you as long as there's a breath in my body."

"Thanks," she said unsteadily.

He felt cold inside. He couldn't imagine what had made him tell such lies to Bojo, where she might overhear him. He hadn't meant it, that was honest, but he knew she thought he had. She didn't trust him anymore.

He opened the door to let her go through first. A whiff of the soft rose fragrance she wore drifted up into his nostrils and made his heart jump. She always smelled sweet, and she had a loving nature that was miraculous considering her past. She gave with both hands. He thought of her with Bojo and something snapped inside him.

"Bojo's off limits," he said as she slid past him. "So don't get too attached to him!"

She looked up at him. "What a bunch of sour grapes," she accused, "just because I withdrew my proposal of marriage to you!" She stalked off down the hall.

He opened his mouth to speak, and just laughed instead.

9

They ate lunch, but conversation among the mercenaries was subdued and Callie got curious glances from all of them. One man, the Mexican called Rodrigo, gave her more scrutiny than the rest. He was a handsome man, tall, slender, dark-haired and dark-eyed, with a grace of movement that reminded her of Micah. But he had a brooding look about him, and he seemed to be always watching her. Once, he smiled, but Micah's appearance sent him away before he could speak to her.

After lunch, Callie asked Bojo about him.

"Rodrigo lost his sister to Lopez's vicious temper," he told her. "She was a nightclub singer who Lopez took a fancy to. He forced himself on her after she rejected Lopez's advances and… She died trying to get away from him. Rodrigo knows what was done to you, and he's angry. You remind him of his sister. She, too, had blue eyes."

"But he's Latin," she began.

"His father was from Denmark," he said with a grin. "And blond."

"Imagine that!"

He gave her a wry glance. "He likes you," he said. "But he isn't willing to risk Micah's temper to approach you."

"You do," she said without thinking.

"Ah, but I am indispensable," he told her. "Rodrigo is not. He has enemies in many countries overseas and also, Lopez has a contract out on him. This is the only place he has left to go where he has any hope of survival. He wouldn't dare risk alienating Micah."

She frowned. "I can't think why approaching me would do that. Micah tolerates me, but he still doesn't really like me," she pointed out. "I overheard what he said to you, about using me as bait."

He smiled. "Yes. Curious, is it not, that when one of the other men suggested the same thing, he paid a trip to the dentist?"

"Why?"

"Micah knocked out one of his teeth," he confided. "The men agreed that no one would make the suggestion twice."

She caught her breath. "But I heard him tell you that very thing…!"

"You heard what he wanted me to think," he continued. "Micah is jealous of me," he added outrageously, and grinned. "You and I are friendly and we have no hostility between us. You don't want anything from me, you see, or from him. He has no idea how to deal with such a woman. He has become used to buying expensive things at a woman's whim, yet you refuse even the gift of a few items of necessary clothing." He shrugged. "It is new for him that neither his good looks nor his wealth make an impression on you. I think he finds that a challenge and it irritates him. He is also very private about his affairs. He doesn't want the men to see how vulnerable he is where you are concerned," he mused. "He had to assign me, along with Peter and Rodrigo, to keep a constant eye on you. He didn't like that. Peter and Rodrigo are no threat, of course, but he is afraid that you are attracted to me." He grinned at her surprise. "I can understand why he thinks this. I hardly need elaborate on my attributes. I am urbane, handsome, sophisticated, generous..." He paused to glance at her wide-eyed, bemused face. "Shall I continue? I should hate to miss acquainting you with any of my virtues."

She realized he was teasing then, and she chuckled. "Okay, go ahead, but I'm not making you any marriage proposals."

His eyebrows arched. "Why not?"

"Micah's put me off men," she said, tongue-in-cheek. "He's already upset because I won't propose to him." She gave him a wicked grin. "Gosh, first Micah, then you! Having this much sex appeal is a curse. Even Lopez is mad to have me!"

He grinned back. She was a unique woman, he thought, and bristling with courage and character. He wondered why Micah didn't see her as he did. The other man was alternately scathing about and protective of Callie, as if his feelings were too ambiguous to unravel. He didn't like Bojo spending time with her, but he kept her carefully at arm's length, even dragging Lisse over for the shopping trip and using her as camouflage. Callie didn't know, but Lisse had been a footnote in Micah's life even in the days when he was attracted to her. She hadn't been around much for almost a year now.

"After we deal with Lopez, you must play down your attractions," he teased. "Providing twenty-four-hour protection is wearing on the nerves."

"You're not kidding," she agreed, wandering farther down

the beach. "I'm getting paranoid about dark corners. I always expect someone to be lurking in them." She glanced up at him. "Not rejected suitors," she added wryly.

He clasped his hands behind him and followed along with her, his keen eyes on the horizon, down the beach, up the beach— everywhere. Bojo was certain, as Micah was, that Lopez wasn't likely to give them time to attack him. He was going to storm the island, and soon. They had to be constantly vigilant, if they wanted to live.

"Do you know any self-defense?" Bojo asked her curiously.

"I know a little," she replied. "I took a course in it, but I was overpowered too fast."

"Show me what you know," he said abruptly. "And I will teach you a little more. It never hurts to be prepared."

She did, and he did. She learned enough to protect herself if she had time to use it. She didn't tell him, but she was really scared that Lopez might snatch her out of sight and sound of the mercs. She prayed that she'd have a fighting chance if she was in danger again.

Callie had convinced herself that an attack would come like a wave, with a lot of men and guns. The last thing she expected was that, when she was lying in her own bed, a man would suddenly appear by the bed and slap a chloroformed handkerchief over her mouth and nose. That was what happened. Outside her patio a waiting small boat on the beach was visible only where she was situated. The dark shadow against the wall managed to bypass every single safeguard of Micah's security system. He slipped into Callie's bedroom with a cloth and a bottle of chloroform and approached the bed where she was asleep.

The first Callie knew of the attack was when she felt a man's hand holding her head steady while a foul-smelling cloth was shoved up under her nose. She came awake at once, but she kept her head, even when she felt herself being carried roughly out of her bedroom onto the stone patio. She knew what to expect this time if she were taken, and she remembered vividly what Bojo had taught her that afternoon. She twisted her head abruptly so that the chloroform missed her face and landed in her hair. Then she got her hands up and slammed them against her captor's ears with all her might.

He cried out in pain and dropped her. She hit the stone-floored patio so hard that she groaned as her hip and leg crashed down onto the flagstones, but she dragged herself to her feet and grabbed at a shovel that the yardman had left leaning against a stone bench close beside her. As her assailant ignored the pain in his fury to pay her back, she swung the shovel and hit him right in the head with it. He made a strange sound and crumpled to the patio. Callie stared out toward the boat, where a dark figure was waiting.

Infuriated by the close call, and feeling very proud of the fact that she'd saved herself this time, she raised the shovel over her head. "Better luck next time, you son of a bitch!" she yelled harshly. "If I had a gun, I'd shoot you!"

Her voice brought Micah and two other men running out onto the patio. They were all armed. The two mercs ran toward the beach, firing as they made a beeline toward the little boat, which had powered up and was sprinting away with incredible speed and very little noise.

Micah stood in front of Callie wearing nothing but a pair of black silk boxer shorts. He had an automatic pistol in one hand.

His hair was tousled, as if he'd been asleep. But he was wide-awake now. His face was hard, his dark eyes frightening.

He moved close to her, aware of her body in the thin nylon gown that left her breasts on open display in the light from inside the house. She didn't seem to notice, but he did. He looked at them hungrily before he dragged his gaze back up to her face, fighting a burst of desire as he tried to come to grips with the terror he'd felt when he heard Callie yelling. Thank God she'd had the presence of mind to grab that shovel and knock the man out.

"Are you okay?" he asked curtly.

"I'm better off than he is," she said huskily, swallowing hard. Reaction was beginning to set in now, and her courage was leaking away as the terror of what had almost happened began to tear at her nerves. "He had chloroform. I...I fought free, but...oh, Micah, I was scared to...death!"

She threw herself against him, shuddering in the aftermath of terror. Now that the danger was past, reaction set in with a vengeance. Her arms went under his and around him. Her soft, firm breasts were flattened against his bare stomach because she was so much shorter than he was. Her hands ran over the long, hard muscles of his back, feeling scars there as she pressed closer. He felt the corner of her mouth in the thick hair that covered the hard muscles of his chest. His body reacted predictably to the feel of a near-naked woman and he gasped audibly and stiffened.

Her hips weren't in contact with his, but she felt a tremor run through his powerful body and she pulled back a little, curious, to look up at his strained face. "What's wrong?"

He drew in a steadying breath and moved back. "Nothing!

We'll get this guy inside and question him. You don't need to see it," he added firmly. "You should go back into your room…"

"And do what?" she asked, wide-eyed and hurt by his sudden withdrawal. "You think I can go to sleep now?"

"Stupid assumption," he murmured, moving restively as his body tormented him. "I can call Lisse and let her stay with you."

"No!" She lifted her chin with as much pride as she had left. "I'll get dressed. Bojo will sit up with me if I ask him…"

"The hell he will!" he exploded, his eyes glittering.

She took a step backward. He was frightening when he looked like that. He seemed more like the stranger he'd once been than the man who'd been so kind to her in past days.

"I'll get dressed and you can stay with me tonight," he snapped. "Obviously it's asking too much to expect you to stay by yourself!" That was unfair, he realized at once, and he ground his teeth. He couldn't help it. He was afraid to be in the same room with her in the dark, but not for the reason she thought.

She took another step backward, pride reasserting itself. Her chin came up. "No, thanks!" she said. "If you'll just get me a gun and load it and show me how to shoot it, I won't have any problem with being alone."

She sounded subdued, edgy, still frightened despite that haughty look she was giving him. He was overreacting. It infuriated him that she'd had to rescue herself. It infuriated him that he wanted her. He was jealous of his men, angry that she was vulnerable, and fighting with all his might to keep from giving in to his desire for her. She was a marrying woman. She was a virgin. It was hopeless.

Worst of all, she'd almost been kidnapped again and on his watch. He'd fallen asleep, worn-out by days of wear and tear and frustrated desire. Lopez had almost had her tonight. He blamed himself for not taking more precautions, for putting her in harm's way. He should have protected her. He should have realized that Lopez was desperate enough to try anything, including an assault on the house itself. So much for his security net. Upgrades were very definitely needed. But right now, she needed comfort, and he wasn't giving it to her.

He glanced toward the beach. Out beyond it, the little boat had stilled in the water and seemed to be sinking. A dark figure struck out toward the shore.

"Peter, get him!" Micah yelled.

The young man gave him a thumbs-up signal. The tall young man tossed down his weapon, jerked off his boots and overclothes and dived into the water. The assailant tried to get away, but Peter got him. There was a struggle and seconds later, Peter dragged the man out of the water and stood over him where he lay prone on the beach.

Rodrigo came running back up from the beach just about the time the man who'd tried to carry Callie off woke up and rubbed his aching head.

"I told Peter to take the other man around the side of the house to the boat shed."

"Good work," Micah said.

"Oh, look, he's all right," Callie murmured, her eyes narrowed on the downed man who was beginning to move and groan. "What a shame!"

Micah glanced at her. "Bloodthirsty girl," he chided, and grinned despite his churning emotions.

"Well, he tried to kidnap me," she bit off, finally getting her nerve and her temper back. She remembered the chloroform and her eyes blazed. "All I had to hand was a lousy shovel, that's why he's all right."

He turned to the other man. "Rodrigo, get this guy around to the boat shed to keep Peter's captive company. Strip them both, tie them up and gag them. I've got to make a few preparations and I'll be along to question them. Do *not* tell Bojo anything, except that the police have been notified. You can phone them to pick up Lopez's henchmen an hour from now, no sooner."

"I know what you're thinking. It won't work," Rodrigo said, trying to reason with him. "Lopez will be expecting his men back, if he hasn't already seen what happened."

"Have you got the infrareds on you?"

Rodrigo nodded and pulled out what looked like a fancy pair of binoculars.

"Check the area off the beach for Lopez's yacht."

"It's clear for miles right now. No heat signatures."

"Heat signatures?" Callie murmured.

"We have heat-seeking technology," Micah explained. "We can look right into a house or a room in the dark and see everything alive in it, right through the walls."

"You're kidding!" she exclaimed.

"He's not," Rodrigo said, his dark eyes narrowing as he noted the gown and the pretty form underneath.

Micah knew what the other man was seeing, and it angered him. He stepped in front of Callie, and the action was blatant enough to get Rodrigo moving.

"Where do you think Lopez's yacht is?" Callie asked.

"It'll be somewhere close around. Let's just hope the man Peter caught was too rattled to call Lopez while he was being shot at. I'm sure he had a cell phone. Get out my diving gear and some C-4. And don't say a word to Bojo. Got that? It will work."

"What will work?" Callie asked.

"Never mind," Micah said. "Thanks, Rodrigo. I'm going to get Callie back inside."

"I'll deal with our guest," Rodrigo said, and turned at once to his chore.

Micah drew Callie along with him, from the patio to the sliding glass doors her assailant had forced, and down the hall to her bedroom. On the way, he noticed that two other doors had been opened, as if her captor had looked in them in search of her. His bedroom was closer to the front of the house.

He drew her inside her room and closed the door behind them, pausing to lay the automatic on a table nearby. "Did he hurt you?" he asked at once.

"He dropped me on the patio. I bruised my hip...Micah, no!" she exclaimed, pushing at the big, lean hand that was pulling up her nylon gown.

"I've seen more of you than this," he reminded her.

"But..."

He swept her up in his arms and carried her to the bed, easing her down gently onto the sheet where the covers had been thrown back by her captor. He sat down beside her and pulled up the gown, smiling gently at the pale pink cotton briefs she was wearing.

"Just what I'd expect," he murmured. "Functional, not sexy."

"Nobody sees my underthings except me," she bit off. "Will you stop?"

He pushed the gown up to her waist, ignoring her protests,

and winced when he saw her upper thigh and hip. "You're going to have a whopper of a bruise on your leg," he murmured, drawing down the elastic of the briefs. "Your hip didn't fare much better."

His thumb was against the soft, warm skin of her lower stomach and the other one was poised beside her head on the pillow while he looked at her bruises. She didn't think he was doing it on purpose, but that thumb seemed to be moving back and forth in a very arousing way. Her body liked it. She moved restlessly on the sheet, shivering a little with unexpected pleasure.

"A few bruises are...are better than being kidnapped," she whispered shakily. Her wide eyes met his. "I was so scared, Micah!"

His hand spread on her hip. His narrow black eyes met hers. "So was I, when I heard you shouting," he said huskily. "He almost had you!"

"Almost," she agreed, her breath jerking out. "I'm still shaking."

His fingers contracted. "I'm going to give you a sedative," he said, rising abruptly. "You need to sleep. You never will, in this condition."

He left her there and went to get his medical kit. He was back almost at once. He opened the bag and drew out a small vial of liquid and a prepackaged hypodermic syringe. This would alleviate her fear of being alone tonight and give him time to get his rampaging hormones under control.

She watched him fill the syringe effortlessly. It was a reminder that he'd studied medicine.

"Have you ever thought of going back to finish your residency?" she asked him.

He shook his head. "Too tame." He smiled in her general direction as he finished filling the syringe. "I don't think I could live without adrenaline rushes."

"Doctors have those, too," she pointed out, watching him extend her arm and tap a vein in the curve of her elbow. "You're going to put it in there?" she asked worriedly.

"It's quicker. You won't get addicted to this," he added, because she looked apprehensive. "Close your eyes. I'll try not to hurt you."

She did close her eyes, but she felt the tiny prick of the needle and winced. But it was over quickly and he was dabbing her arm with alcohol on a cotton ball.

"It won't knock you out completely," he said when he'd replaced everything in the kit. "But it will relax you."

She blinked. She felt *very* relaxed. She peered up at him with wide, soft eyes. "I wish you liked me," she said.

His eyebrows levered up. "I do."

"Not really. You don't want me around. I'm not pretty like her."

"Her?"

"Lisse." She sighed and stretched lazily, one leg rising so that the gown fell away from her pretty leg, leaving it bare. "She's really beautiful, and she has nice, big breasts. Mine are just tiny, and I'm so ordinary. Gosh, I'd love to have long blond hair and big breasts."

He glanced at the bag and back at her. "This stuff works on you like truth serum, doesn't it?" he murmured huskily.

She sat up with a misty smile and shrugged the gown off, so that it fell to her waist. Her breasts had hard little tips that aroused him the instant he saw them. "See?" she asked. "They look like acorns. Hers look like cantaloupes."

He couldn't help himself. He stared at her breasts helplessly, while his body began to swell with an urgency that made him shiver. He was vulnerable tonight.

"Yours are beautiful," he said softly, his eyes helplessly tracing them.

"No, they're not. You don't even like feeling them against you. You went all stiff and pushed me away, out on the patio. It's been like that since...Micah, what are you...doing?" she gasped as his hungry mouth abruptly settled right on top of a hard nipple and began to suckle it. "Oh...glory!" she cried out, arching toward him with a lack of restraint that was even more arousing. Her nails bit into his scalp through his thick hair, coaxing him even closer. "I like that. I...really like that!" she whispered frantically. "I like it, I like it, I...!"

"I should be shot for this," he uttered as he suckled her. "But I want you. Oh God, I want you so!" His teeth opened and nipped her helplessly.

She drew back suddenly, apprehensively as she felt his teeth, her eyes questioning.

He could barely breathe, and he knew there was no way on earth he was going to be able to stop. It was already too late. Danger was an aphrodisiac. "You don't like my teeth on you," he whispered. "All right. It's all right. We'll try this."

His fingers traced around her pert breast gently and he bent to take her mouth tenderly under his lips. She had no willpower. She opened her lips for him and clung as he eased her down onto the cool sheets.

"Don't let me do this, Callie," he ground out in a last grab at sanity, even as he shed his boxer shorts. "Tell me to stop!"

"I couldn't, not if it meant my life," she murmured, her body on fire for him. Her mind wasn't even working. She held on for dear life and pulled his mouth down harder on hers. She was shivering with pleasure. "I want you to do it," she whispered brazenly. "I want to feel you naked in my arms. I want to make love...!"

"Callie. Sweet baby!" he whispered hoarsely as he felt her hands searching down his flat belly to the source of his anguish. She touched him and he was lost, totally lost. He pressed her hard into the mattress while his mouth devoured hers. It was too late to pull back, too late to reason with her. She was drugged and uninhibited, and her hands were touching him in a way that pushed him right over the edge.

Callie lifted against him, aware of his nudity and the delight of touching him where she'd never have dreamed of touching him if she hadn't been drugged. But she'd always wanted to touch him like that, and it felt wonderful. Her body moved restlessly with little darts of pleasure as he began to discover her, too.

She enjoyed the feel of his body, the touch of his hands. Her skin felt very hot, and when she realized that the gown and her underwear were gone, it didn't matter, because she felt much more comfortable. Then he started touching her in a way she'd never been touched. She gasped. Her body tensed, but she moved toward his hand, burying her face in his neck as the delicious sensations made her pulse with delight. His skin was damp and very hot. She could hear the rasp of his breathing, she could feel it in her hair as he began to caress her very intimately.

Of course, it was wrong to let him do something so outrageous, but it felt too good to stop. She kept coaxing him with sharp little movements of her hips until he was touching her where her body wanted him to. Now the pleasure was stark and urgent. She opened her legs. Her nails bit into his nape and she clung fiercely.

"It's all right," he whispered huskily. "I won't stop. I'll be good to you."

She clung closer. Her body shivered. She was suddenly open to his insistent exploration and with embarrassment she felt herself becoming very damp where his fingers were. She stiffened.

"It's natural," he breathed into her ear. "Your body is supposed to do this."

"It is?" She couldn't look at him. "It isn't repulsive to you?"

"It's the most exciting thing I've ever felt," he whispered. His powerful body shifted so that he was lying directly over her, his hair-roughened legs lazily brushing against hers while he teased her mouth with his lips and her body with his fingers.

Her arms were curled around his neck and the sensations were so sweet that she began to gasp rhythmically. Her hips were lifting and falling with that same rhythm as she fed on the delicious little jabs of pleasure that accompanied every sensual movement.

He began to shudder, too. It was almost as if he weren't in control of himself. But that was ridiculous. Micah was always in control.

His teeth tugged at her upper lip and then at her lower one, his tongue sliding sinuously inside her mouth in slow, teasing thrusts. She felt her breasts going very tight. He was lying against her in an unexpectedly intimate way. She felt body hair against her breasts and her belly. Then she felt him there, *there,* in a contact that she'd never dreamed of sharing with him.

Despite her languor, her eyes opened and looked straight into his. She could actually see the desire that was riding him, there in his taut face and glittering eyes and flattened lips. He was shivering. She liked seeing him that way. She smiled lazily and deliberately brushed her body up against him. He groaned.

Slowly he lifted himself just a little. "Look down," he whispered huskily. "Look at me. I want you to see how aroused I am for you."

Her eyes traced the path of thick, curling blond-tipped hair from the wedge on his muscular chest, down his flat belly, and to another wedge…heavens! He had nothing on. And more than that, he was…he was…

Her misty gaze shot back up to meet his. She should be protesting. He was so aroused that a maiden lady with silver hair couldn't have mistaken it. She felt suddenly very small and vulnerable, almost fragile. But he wanted her, and she wanted him so badly that she couldn't find a single word of protest. Even if he never touched her again, she'd have this one time to live on for the rest of her miserable, lonely life. She'd be his lover, if only this once. Nothing else mattered. Nothing!

Her body lifted to brush helplessly against his while she looked at him. She was afraid. She was excited. She was on fire. She was wanton…

His hand went between their hips and began to invade her body, where it was most sensitive. Despite the pleasure that ensued, she felt a tiny stab of discomfort.

"I can feel it," he whispered, his eyes darkening as his body went taut. "It's wispy, like a spiderweb." He shifted sensuously. His body began to invade hers in a slow, teasing motion, and he watched her the whole time. "Are you going to let me break it, Callie?" he whispered softly.

"Break…it?"

"Your maidenhead. I want it." He moved his hips down and his whole face clenched as he felt the veil of her innocence begin to separate. His hands clenched beside her head on the pillow and the eyes that looked down into hers were tortured. His whole body shuddered with each slow movement of his hips. "I want…you! Callie!" he groaned hoarsely, his eyes closing. "Callie …baby…let me have you," he whispered jerkily. "Let me have…all of you! Let me teach you pleasure…"

He seemed to be in pain. She couldn't bear that. She slid her calves slowly over his and gasped when she felt his body tenderly penetrating hers with the action, bringing a tiny wave of pleasure. She gasped again.

He arched above her, groaning. His eyes held hers as he moved slowly, carefully. He watched her wince and he hesitated. He moved again, and she bit her lip. He moved one more time, and she tensed and then suddenly relaxed, so unexpectedly that his possession of her was complete in one involuntary movement.

It was incredible, he thought, his body as taut as steel as he looked down into her wide, curious eyes with awe as he became her lover. He could feel her, like a warm silk glove. She was a virgin. He was having her. She was giving herself. He moved experimentally, and her lips parted on a helpless breath.

His lean hands slid under her dark hair and cradled her head while he began to move on her. One of his thighs pushed at hers, nudging it further away from the throbbing center of her body. The motion lifted her against him in a blind grasp at pleasure.

"I never thought…it would be you," she whispered feverishly.

"I never thought it would be anyone else," he replied, his eyes hot and narrow and unblinking. "I watched you when I went completely into you," he whispered and smiled when she gasped. "Now, you can watch me," he murmured roughly. "Watch me. I'll let you see...everything I feel!"

She shivered as his hips began to move sinuously, more insistently, increasing the pleasure.

He caught one of her hands and drew it between them, coaxing it back to his body. He groaned at the contact and guided her fingers to the heart of him.

She let him teach her. It was so sweet, to lie naked in his arms, and watch him make love to her. He was incredibly tender. He gave her all the time in the world before he became insistent, before his kisses devoured, before his hand pinned her hips and his whole body became an instrument of the most delicious torture. He looked down at her with blazing dark eyes, his face clenched in passion, his body shivering with urgency as he poised over her.

"Don't close your eyes," he groaned when stars were exploding in his head. "I want to see them...the very second...that you go over the edge under me!"

The words were as arousing as the sharp, violent motion of his hips as he began to drive into her. She thought he became even more potent as the tempo and the urgency increased. He held her eyes until she became blind with the first stirrings of ecstasy and her sharp, helpless cry of surprised pleasure was covered relentlessly by his mouth.

She writhed under him, sobbing with the sensation of fulfillment, her body riveted to his as convulsions made her ripple like a stormy wave. She clutched his upper arms, her nails biting in, as the ripples became almost painful in their delight. Seconds later, she felt him climax above her. His harsh, shuddering groan was as alien a sound as her own had been seconds before. She wrapped her arms around him and held on for dear life, cuddling him, cradling him, as he endured the mindless riptide and finally, finally, went limp and heavy in her arms with a whispery sigh.

"You looked at me…when it happened," she whispered with wonder. "And I saw you, I watched you." She shivered, holding him tight. Her body rippled with the tiny movement, and she laughed secretly and moaned as she felt the pleasure shoot through her. "Do it again," she pleaded. "Make me scream this time…!"

He was still shivering. "Oh, God, …no!" he bit off. "Be still!" He held her down, hard, drawing in a sharp breath as he fought the temptation to do what she asked. He closed his eyes and his teeth clenched as he jerked back from her abruptly.

She gasped as his weight receded. There was a slight discomfort, and then he was on his feet beside the bed, grabbing up his boxer shorts with a furious hand.

She stared at him with diminishing awareness. She was deliciously relaxed. She felt great. Why was he cursing like that. She blinked vacantly. "You're very angry. What's wrong?"

"What's wrong!" He turned to look down at her. She was sprawled nude in glorious abandon, looking so erotic that he almost went to his knees with the arousal that returned with a vengeance.

She smiled lazily and yawned. "Gosh, that was good. So good!" Her eyelids felt very heavy. She sprawled even more comfortably. "Even better than the last time."

"What last time?" he demanded, outraged.

She yawned again. "That other dream," she mumbled, rolling onto her side. "So many dreams. So embarrassing. So erotic! But this was the best dream, though. The very…best…"

Her voice trailed away and he realized all at once that she'd fallen asleep. She didn't understand what had happened. She'd been full of sedative and she'd let him seduce her, thinking she was just dreaming. She thought the whole thing was nothing more than another dream. No wonder she hadn't protested!

"God in heaven, what have I done!" he asked her oblivious form. There was a smear of blood on the white sheet.

Micah ground his teeth together and damned his lack of control. He hadn't had a woman in a very long time, and he'd wanted Callie since the day he'd met her. But that was no excuse for taking advantage of her while she was under the influence of a sedative. Even if she had come on to him with the most incredibly erotic suggestions. He'd seduced her and that was that.

He went to the bathroom, wet a washcloth and bathed her body as gently as he could. She was sleeping so soundly that she never noticed a thing. He put her briefs and gown back on her and put her under the sheet. He'd have to hope she didn't notice the stain, or, if she did, assumed it was an old one.

He dressed, hating himself, and went out of the room after checking the security net. He still had to go after Lopez, and now his mind was going to be full of Callie sobbing with pleasure under the crush of his body. And what if there were consequences?

10

With a face as grim as death, Micah pulled on his black wet suit and fins and checked the air in his tanks and the mouthpiece and face mask. He sheathed the big knife he always carried on covert missions. To the belt around his waist, he attached a waterproof carry pack. He'd interrogated one of the men, who'd been far too intimidated not to tell him what he wanted to know about Lopez's setup on the yacht, the number and placement of his men and his firepower.

"I should go with you," Rodrigo told him firmly.

"You can't dive," Micah said. "Besides, this is a one-man job. If I don't make it, it will be up to you and Bojo to finish it. But whatever happens," he added curtly, and with a threatening stare, "don't let them get Callie."

"I won't. I swear it," Rodrigo said heavily.

"Tell Bojo where I've gone after I've gone, but only after I'm gone," he added. "Don't let him follow me." He picked up a small device packed with plastique and shoved it into the waterproof bag on his belt and sealed it.

"Once you set the trigger, you'll only have a few minutes to get free of the ship. If the engines fire up while you're placing the bomb, you'll be chum," Rodrigo said worriedly. "You already look exhausted. Even if everything goes right, how will you make that swim and turn around and come back in time?"

"If I can't get free in that amount of time, I'm in the wrong business," he told Rodrigo. "I'd disgrace my expensive government training. How many men on the yacht right now?"

Rodrigo nodded toward the yacht, which had just come into view in the past ten minutes. It was out very far, almost undetectable without exotic surveillance devices. But they had a device that used a heat sensor with a telescopic lens, and they could see inside the ship. "The crew, Lopez, and six henchmen. It's suicide to do this alone."

"I'm not letting him try again," he said shortly, and his eyes were blazing. "I've put Callie's life at risk already, because I was arrogant enough to think she was safe here. She could have been killed tonight while I was asleep in my bed. I won't get over that in a hurry. I'm not going to give her to Lopez, no matter what it costs me." He put a hand on Rodrigo's shoulder. "Listen to me. If anything goes wrong, you tell Bojo that I want him to take care of her from now on. There's enough money in my Swiss account to support her and my father for life, in any style they like. You tell Bojo I said to see that she gets it, less the sum we agreed on for all of you. Promise me!"

"Of course I promise." Rodrigo's eyes narrowed. "You look...different."

I've just seduced a virgin who thinks she was having an erotic dream, he thought with black humor. *No wonder I look different.* "It's been a long night," he said. "Call the police an hour from now." He looked at his expensive commando watch, the one with a tiny sharp knife blade that could be released from the edge of the face with a light touch. "Coming up on fourteen hundred and ten hours…almost… almost…hack!"

Rodrigo had set his watch to the same time. He gave Micah a long, worried look as the taller man put on his face mask and adjusted the mouthpiece.

"Dios te protégé," Rodrigo said gently. God protect you.

Micah smiled and put the mouthpiece in. Seconds later, he was in the water, under the water, headed out toward the yacht. It was a distance of almost half a mile, and Rodrigo was uneasy. But Micah had been a champion swimmer in his school days, and he held some sort of record for being able to hold his breath underwater. He looked very tired, though, and that was going to go against him. Odd, Rodrigo thought, that a man who'd just gotten out of bed should look exhausted. And after the culprits had been dealt with so quickly and effectively, which couldn't have tired him. He hoped Micah would succeed. He checked his watch, glanced at the bound and gagged captives in their underwear, and shrugged.

"How sad for you, *compadres,* that your futures will be seen through vertical bars. But, then, your choice of employer leaves so much to be desired!"

He turned away, recalling that Micah had told him to phone the police an hour after he'd gone. But he hesitated to do that, orders or not. Timing was going to be everything here. If there was a holdup planting the charge, and if Lopez had someone on the payroll in Nassau, the show was over. Lopez would get

word of the failed kidnapping attempt in time to blow Micah
out of the water. Micah couldn't have been thinking straight.
Rodrigo would do that for him. He would watch Micah's back.
Now he prayed that his boss could complete this mission
without discovery. If ever a man deserved his fate, it was Manuel
Lopez. He gave Mexicans a bad name, and for that alone
Rodrigo was anxious to see him go down.

It took Micah a long time to reach the boat. He was exhausted
from the mindless pleasure Callie had given him. Making love with
her just before the most dangerous mission of recent years had to
be evidence of insanity. But it had been so beautiful, so tender. He
could still hear her soft, surprised cries of pleasure. The memory
was the sort a man wouldn't mind going down into the darkness
for. Of course, it wasn't helping him focus on the task at hand. He
forcibly put the interlude to the back of his mind and swam on.

He paused as he reached the huge yacht, carefully working
his way toward the huge propellers at the stern, which were
off right now but would start again eventually. If they started
while he was near them, he'd be caught in their turbulent wake
and dragged right into those cruel blades to be dismembered
before he set the charge. *Not* the end he hoped for.

He kept himself in place with slow movements of his fins
while he shone an underwater light hooked to his belt on the
bomb package enclosed in the waterproof bag. He drew it out,
very carefully, and secured it to a metallic connection behind
the propellers. It stuck like glue. He positioned the light so that
he could work with his hands while he wired the charge into
the propeller system. It was meticulous work, and he was really
tired. But he finally secured the connection and double-checked

the explosive package. Yes. The minute the turbine engines fired, the ship would blow up.

The problem was, he was almost too tired to swim back. He was going to have to give himself thirty minutes to get back to the shore, and pray that Lopez didn't have his men fire up those propellers until he was out of harm's way.

He gave the ship's hull a gentle pat, with a momentary twinge of regret at having to destroy such a beautiful yacht. Then he turned and moved slowly, cautiously, around toward the bow of the ship. There was a ladder hanging down from the side. He passed it with idle curiosity and held onto it while he floated, letting his body relax and rest. He just happened to look up while he was hanging from it.

Just above the surface, a man was aiming an automatic weapon down at him through the water.

He couldn't get away. He was too tired. Besides, the man wasn't likely to miss at this range. Salute the flag and move on, he mused philosophically. Nobody lived forever, and his death would serve a noble cause. All he had to do was make them think he'd come aboard to use the knife on Lopez, so they wouldn't start looking for bombs. They had enough time to find and disarm it if he didn't divert them. The waterproof bag on his hip was going to be hard to explain. So was his flashlight. Fortunately the light fit into the bag and weighed it down. He unhooked the bag and closed it out of sight while the man above motioned angrily for him to come up the ladder. He let the bag drop and it sank even as he started the climb to his own death. He might get a chance at Lopez before they killed him, because Lopez would want to gloat.

He padded onto the deck in his breathing equipment and fins, which the man ordered him in Spanish to take off.

Micah tossed his gear aside, carefully, because the man with the gun was nervous. If he had any chance at all to escape, he could make the distance without his equipment if he swam— assuming he wasn't shot to death in the process. He had to hope for a break, but it wasn't likely. This was the situation that every working mercenary had to consider when he chose the lifestyle. Death could come at any moment, unexpectedly.

He stood glaring down at the smaller man. Even with his automatic weapon, the drug lord's man didn't seem too confident. He backed up two more steps. Micah noted the hasty retreat and tensed to make his move. But only seconds later, Lopez and two more men—armed men—came up on deck.

Lopez stared at Micah for a minute and then recognition flashed in his dark eyes. "Micah Steele, I presume," he drawled in accented English. He put his hands behind him and walked around Micah like an emperor inspecting a new slave. "You lack proficiency, don't you? Were you planning to use this on me while I slept?" he added, jerking the big bowie knife out of its sheath. "A nasty weapon. Very nasty." He put the point against Micah's wet suit just below the nipple. "A hard thrust, and you cease to exist. You were careless. Now you will pay the price for it." His face hardened. "Where are my two men that I sent to reclaim your stepsister?"

Micah smiled calmly. "The police have them by now. I expect they'll spill their guts trying to save themselves."

"They would not dare," Lopez said easily. "They fear me."

"They won't fear you if you're in prison," he replied easily. "Or dead."

Lopez laughed. It amused him that this mercenary wasn't begging for his life. He was used to men who did.

"Your attempt at diversion serves no purpose. We both know that my men are on the way back with their captive even now. In fact," he added with a deliberate smile, "I had a phone call just before you were discovered, telling me that she was safely bound and gagged. Your men are too numerous for them to fight, so they are hiding her some distance from your house until the coast is clear and they can get here with the boat." He chuckled maliciously.

Micah surmised that a cell phone had been discovered on one of the men, and Rodrigo had used it to reassure Lopez. A stroke of genius, and it might have worked, if Micah hadn't been careless and let himself get captured like a raw recruit.

"I am fond of knives," Lopez murmured, and ran his fingers over the carved bone handle almost like a caress. He looked at Micah as he traced the pattern in it. "This time, I will not give your stepsister to my men. I will use the knife on her myself." His eyes were cold, hard, unfeeling. "I will skin her alive," he said softly. "And with every strip that comes off, I will remind her that you were careless enough to let her be apprehended a second time." His eyes blazed. "You invaded my home to take her from me. No one humiliates me in such a manner and lives to gloat about it. You will die and your sister will die, and in such a way that it will frighten anyone who sees it."

Micah studied the little man with contempt, seeing the years of death and torture that had benefited Lopez. The drug lord could buy people, yachts, countries. He had enormous power. But it was power built on a foundation of greed, floored with blood and tears. If ever a man deserved to go down, it was Lopez.

"You are very quiet, Micah Steele," Lopez said suddenly, and his eyes narrowed suspiciously.

"I was thinking that I've never encountered anyone as evil as you, Lopez," he said quietly. "You have no conscience at all."

Lopez shrugged. "I am what I am," he said simply. "In order to accumulate great wealth, one has to be willing to take great risks. I have been poor. I never want to be poor again."

"Plenty of people prefer it to murder."

Lopez only laughed. "You are, how is it said, stalling for time," he said abruptly. "Are you hoping to be rescued? Or are you hoping that perhaps one of your men has checked on your stepsister and found her missing from her room? That is not likely. My men are quite expert. Playing for time will avail you nothing."

Micah could have told him that he was using the time to rest from his exhaustive swim, marshaling his strength for an all-out assault. If they took him down, he vowed, he was at least going to take Lopez with him, even if he died with the drug lord's neck in his hands.

"Or you might think it possible to overpower all of us and escape." He laughed again. "I think that I will wait to begin your interrogation until your stepsister is on board with us. Carlos!" he called to a henchman. "Tell the captain to start the engines and move us a little closer to the island."

Micah's heart stopped dead, but not a trace of fear or apprehension showed on his face. Lopez was watching him very closely, as if he suspected something. Micah simply smiled, considering that it was the fortunes of war that sometimes you didn't win.

At least Callie was safe. He hadn't lost completely as long as she survived. He took a relaxing breath and waited for the explosion.

Lopez's henchman was almost up the steps to the pilothouse when Lopez wheeled suddenly.

"Wait!" Lopez called his man back suddenly and Micah fought to keep from showing his relief. "I do not trust you, Steele," Lopez added. "I think perhaps you want me to go closer to your island, to give your men a shot at us, here on the deck. If so, you are going to be disappointed." He turned to the man, Carlos. "Take him below and tie him up. Then I want you and Juan to take one of the boats and follow in the steps of Ramon and Jorge. They must be somewhere near the house waiting for the mercenaries to give up the search or locate it elsewhere. You can help them bring the girl back."

"*Si, señor,*" Carlos said at once, and stuck the automatic weapon in Micah's back. "You will go ahead of me, *señor,*" he told Micah. "And remember, there will be an armed man at the foot of the steps. Escape is not possible. *¡Vaya!*"

Micah gave Lopez one last contemptuous look before he went down the steps into the bowels of the ship. So far, so good. They were convinced that their men on shore were safe and had Callie. They weren't going to start the ship just yet, thank God. He had one last chance to absolve himself. He was going to take it, regardless of the price.

The henchman tied him up in a chair with nylon cord at his wrists and ankles. The cord was tight enough to cut off the circulation. Micah felt his hands and feet going numb, but he wasn't going to protest.

"What a nice fish we caught," Lopez's man chuckled. "And soon, big fish, we will fillet you and your stepsister together."

His eyes narrowed and he smiled coldly. "You have embarrassed my boss. No one is allowed to do that. You must be made an example of. I would not wish to be in your shoes." He looked pointedly at Micah's bare feet. "Hypothetically speaking," he added. "Enjoy your last minutes of life, *señor*."

The small man left Micah in the stateroom, which was obviously some sort of guest room. There was a bed and a dresser and this chair in it, and it was very small. One of the officers of the ship might sleep here, he reasoned.

Now that he was alone—and he wouldn't be for long—he might have just enough time to free himself. Micah touched the button on his watch that extended the small but very sharp little knife blade concealed in the watch face. He cut himself free with very little effort. But the most dangerous part was yet to come. There were men everywhere, all armed. The one thing he had going for him was that it was dark and Lopez had very few lights on deck at the moment, hoping not to be noticed by Micah's men.

He eased out into the corridor and listened. He heard a man's voice humming a Mexican drinking song off-key nearby. Watching up and down the hall with every step, he eased into the galley. A man just a little smaller than he was stirring something in a very big stainless-steel pot. He was wearing black slacks and a black sweater with an apron over them. Micah smiled.

He caught the man from behind and stunned him. Carefully he eased the cook back behind the stove and began to strip him. He pulled off his scuba gear and donned the cook's outerwear, taking time to dress the cook in his own diving suit. The cook had dark hair, but it wouldn't matter. All he had to do was look like Micah at a distance.

He got the cook over his shoulder and made his way carefully to the ladder that led up onto the deck. Lopez was talking to two other men, and not looking in Micah's direction. What supreme self-confidence, Micah thought. Pity to spoil it.

He slapped the cook and brought him around. In the next instant, he threw the man overboard on the side that faced away from Micah's island.

"*¡Steele ha escapado!*" Micah yelled in Spanish. "*¡Se fue alla, a la izquierda, en el Mar!*" Steele has escaped, he went there, to the left, in the sea!

There was a cry of fury from Lopez, followed by harsh orders, and the sound of running feet. Micah followed the other men, managing to blend in, veering suddenly to the other side of the ship.

Just as he got there, he was faced with a henchman who hadn't followed the others. The man had an automatic weapon in his hands and he was hesitating, his eyes trying to see Micah, who was half in shadow so that his blond hair didn't give the game away. If the man pulled that trigger...

"*Es que usted esta esperando una cerveza?*" he shot at the man angrily. "*¡Vaya! ¡Steele esta alla!*" What are you waiting for, a beer? Get going, Steele's over there!

He hesitated with his heart in his throat, waiting, waiting...

All at once, there was a shout from the other side of the ship. The man who was holding Micah at bay still hesitated, but the noise got louder.

"*¡Vaya!*" he repeated. He waved the man on urgently with a mumbled Spanish imprecation about Steele and his useless escape attempt. In that space of seconds before they discovered the man in the water was not Micah, their escaping captive got over the rail and into the ocean and struck out back toward the shore. He kept his strokes even and quick, and he zigzagged. Even if Lopez's men spotted him, they were going to have to work at hitting him from that distance. Every few yards, he submerged and swam underwater. Any minute now, he told himself, and thanked God he'd had just enough rest to allow him a chance of making it to shore before he was discovered and killed.

He heard loud voices and a searchlight began sweeping the water. Micah dived under again and held his breath. With a little bit of luck, they might pass right over him, in his black clothing. He blended in very well with the ocean.

There was gunfire. He ground his teeth together and prayed they'd miss him. Probably they were shooting blind, hoping to hit him with a lucky shot.

Odd, though, the gunfire sounded closer than that...

He came up for air, to snatch a breath, and almost collided with his own swift motorboat, with Bojo driving it and firing an automatic rifle toward Lopez and his men at the same time.

"Climb in, boss!" Bojo called, and kept shooting.

"Remind me to give you a raise," Micah panted as he dragged himself over the side and into the rocking boat. "Good work. Good work! Now get the hell out of here before they blow us out of the water!"

Bojo swung the boat around masterfully and imitated the same zigzag pattern that Micah had used when he swam.

"Lopez is mad now," Micah said with a glittery smile. "If

there's any justice left in the world, he'll try to move in closer to get a better shot at us."

"We hope," Bojo said solemnly, still dodging bullets.

Micah looked back toward the ship, now clearly visible against the horizon. He thought of all Lopez's helpless victims, of whole families in tiny little Mexican towns who had been mowed down with automatic weapons for daring to help the authorities catch the local pushers. He thought of the hard fight to shut down Lopez's distribution network slated for operation in Jacobsville, Texas. He thought of Callie in that murderous assassin's hands, of the knife cut on her pretty little breast where the point had gone in. He thought of Callie dead, tortured, an anguished expression locked forever into those gentle features. He thought of his father, who would have been Lopez's next target. He thought of Lisa Monroe Parks's young husband in the DEA who'd been killed on Lopez's orders. He thought of all the law enforcement people who'd risked their lives and the lives of their families to stop Lopez.

"It's retribution time, Lopez," Micah said absently, watching the big ship with somber eyes. "Life calls in the bets for us all, sooner or later. But you're overdue, you drug-dealing son of a...!"

Before the last word left his lips, there was a huge fireburst where the ship had been sitting in the water. Flames rolled up and up and up, billowing black smoke into the atmosphere. The sound rocked the boat, and pieces of the yacht began falling from the sky in a wide circumference. Micah and Bojo ducked down in the boat and covered their heads as Bojo increased their speed and changed direction, hoping to miss the heavier metal parts that were raining down with wood and fabric.

They made it to the boat dock and jumped out as the last pieces of what had been Lopez's yacht fell into the water.

Mercenaries came rushing down from the house, all armed, to see what had happened.

"Say goodbye to Lopez," Micah told them, eyes narrowed with cold scrutiny.

They all watched the hull of the ship, still partially intact, start to sink. To their credit, none of them cheered or laughed or made a joke. Human lives had been lost. It was no cause for celebration, not even when the ringleader was as bad as Lopez. It had been necessary to eliminate him. He was crazed with vengeance and dangerous to the world at large.

Rodrigo came up beside them. "Glad to see you still alive, boss," he said.

Micah nodded. "It was close. I was too tired to swim back. He caught me at the ladder like a raw recruit."

There was a faint sound from Peter, the newest of the group. "I thought slips were my signature," he told Micah.

"Even veterans can step the wrong way and die for it," Micah told him gently. "That's why you always do it by the book and make sure you've got backup. I broke all the rules, but I didn't want to put anyone else at risk. I got lucky. Sometimes you don't." He watched the last of Lopez's yacht sink. "What about our two guests?"

"They're still in the shed."

"Load them up and take them in to Nassau and say we'll file charges for trespassing," Micah told Rodrigo.

"I'm on my way."

"We'll have federal agents combing the island by dawn, I guess," one of the other mercenaries groaned.

Micah shook his head. "I was sanctioned. And that's all I intend to say about this, ever," he added when the man seemed set to protest. "Let's see if we can get a little more sleep before dawn."

Mumbled agreement met the suggestion. He walked back into the house and down the hall to his bedroom. Callie's door was still closed. He felt a horrible pang of guilt when he remembered what had happened before he went after Lopez. He was never going to get over what he'd done.

He took a shower and changed into a pair of white striped shorts and a white-and-red patterned silk shirt. He padded down the hall to the kitchen and started to get a beer out of the refrigerator. But it hadn't been a beer sort of night. He turned on his heel and went to the liquor cabinet in his study. He poured himself two fingers of Kentucky bourbon with a little ice and took it back down the hall with him.

At the door of Callie's room, he paused. He opened the door gently and moved in to stand by the bed and look down at her. She was sound asleep, her cheek pillowed on a pretty hand devoid of jewelry. She'd kicked off the sheet and bedspread and her long legs were visible where the gown had fallen away from them. She looked innocent, untouched. He remembered the feel of that soft mouth under his lips, the exquisite loving that had driven every sane thought out of his mind. His body went rigid just from the memory.

She stirred, as if she sensed his presence, but she didn't wake up. The sedative had really kicked in now. She wouldn't wake until dawn, if then.

He reached down a gentle hand and brushed the hair away from the corner of her mouth and her cheek. She wasn't conventionally pretty, but she had an inner beauty that made him feel as if he'd just found spring after a hard winter. He liked to hear her laugh. He liked the way she dressed, so casually and indifferently. She didn't take hours to put on makeup, hours to dress. She didn't complain about the heat or the cold or the food. She was as honest as any woman he'd ever known. She had wonderful qualities. But he was afraid of her.

He'd been a loner most of his life. His mother's death when he was ten had hit him hard. He'd adored his mother. After that, it had been Jack and himself, and they'd grown very close. But when Callie and her mother moved in, everything had changed. Suddenly he was an outsider in his own family. He despised Callie's mother and made no secret of his resentment for both women. That had caused a huge rift between his father and himself, one that had inevitably grown wide enough to divide them altogether.

He'd blamed Callie for the final blow, because he'd convinced himself that she'd found Jack and sent him to the hall to find Micah and Anna kissing. Callie had always denied it, and finally he believed her. It hadn't been pique because he'd rejected her.

He took a sip of the whiskey and stared down at her broodingly. She was part of his life, part of him. He hated knowing that. He hated the memory of her body moving sensuously under his while he seduced her.

And she thought she was dreaming. What if she woke up still believing that? They'd not only had sex, but thanks to him they'd had unprotected sex. His dark eyes slid down her body to her flat belly. Life might already be growing in her womb.

His breath caught. Callie might have his baby. His lips parted as he thought about a baby. He'd never wanted one before. He could see Callie with an infant in her arms, in her heart, in her life. Callie would want his baby.

He felt an alien passion gripping him for the first time. And just as quickly, he considered the difficulty it would engender. Callie might be pregnant. She wouldn't remember how she got that way, either.

He pursed his lips, feeling oddly whimsical for a man who was facing the loss of freedom and perhaps even the loss of his lifestyle and his job. Wouldn't it be something if Callie was pregnant and he was the only one who knew?

11

C allie felt the sun on her face. She'd been dreaming. She'd been in Micah's warm, powerful arms, held tight against every inch of him, and he'd been making ardent love to her. He'd looked down into her wide eyes at the very instant he'd possessed her. He'd watched her become a woman. It seemed so real...

Her eyes opened. Sure it was real. And any minute now, the tooth fairy was going to fly in through the open patio windows and leave her a shiny quarter!

She sat up. Odd, that uncomfortable feeling low in her belly. She shifted and she felt sore. Talk about dreams that seemed real!

She swung her legs off the bed and stood up, stilling for a moment so that the sudden dizziness passed. She turned to make up the bed and frowned. There was a stain on the bottom sheet. It looked like dried blood. Well, so much for the certainty that her period wasn't due for another two weeks, she thought. Probably all the excitement had brought it on sooner.

She went into the bathroom, wondering what she was going to do for the necessary equipment in a house full of men.

But she wasn't having her period. That would mean some spotting had occurred and that frightened her because it wasn't natural. She'd always been regular. She'd have to see a doctor when she got home, she supposed.

She bathed and frowned when she was standing in front of the mirror. There were some very bad bruises on her hip and thigh, and that was when she remembered the terror of the night before. Half asleep, she hadn't really been thinking until she saw the bruises and it began to come back. A man, Lopez's man, had tried to kidnap her. She'd actually knocked him out with a shovel. She smiled as she remembered it. Sadly she'd been less brave when Micah came running out to see about her. He'd carried her in here and given her a sedative. She hoped she hadn't said anything revealing to him. Sedatives made her very uninhibited. But she had no memory past the shot. That might, she concluded, be a good thing.

Dressed in a pink Bermuda shorts set that she'd bought on her shopping trip in Nassau, she put her feet into a new pair of sneakers. Unlike the sandals she couldn't wear, the sneakers were a perfect fit.

She walked back into the bedroom worriedly, wondering what Micah had done with Lopez's men. It seemed very quiet this morning. She was certain Micah had all sorts of surveillance systems set up to make sure Lopez couldn't sneak anybody else in here to make another attempt at kidnapping her. But she felt uneasy, just the same. Lopez would never stop. She knew that she was still in the same danger she'd been in when she first arrived here with Micah.

She felt as if she had a hangover, probably because of that sedative Micah gave her. That explained the erotic dream, as well. She blushed, remembering what an erotic dream it was, too. She brushed her hair, not bothering with makeup, and went down the hall to the kitchen to see if coffee was available.

Bojo was helping himself to a cup. He grinned as she came into the room. "You slept very late."

"I was very tired. Besides, Micah drugged me. That's the second time he's given me a sedative since I've been here. I'm not used to them." She laughed as she took the fresh cup of coffee Bojo handed her. "It's a good thing I fell asleep right away, too, because sedatives generally have a very odd effect on me. I get totally swept away. Where is everybody?" she added, noting that Bojo was the only person in the house.

"Micah has gone to Nassau on business," he told her with a grin. "Lopez seems to have vanished in the night. Not only Lopez, but his very expensive yacht and several of his men. The authorities are justifiably curious."

"Lopez has gone?" she asked, excited. "You mean, he's gone away?"

"Very far away," he said with a grin.

"But he'll just come back." He gave her a wry look and she frowned. "Don't you still have his two henchmen? Micah was going to give those two men to the police," she reminded him. "Maybe they know where he is."

"They were handed over to the police," he agreed. "But they don't know where Lopez is, either."

"You look smug," she accused.

He smiled. "I am. I do know where Lopez is. And I can promise you that he won't be making any more raids on this island."

"Great!" she exclaimed, relieved. "Can you hand him over to the police, too?"

"Lopez can't be handed over." He paused to think. "Well, not in one piece, at least," he added.

"You're sounding very strange," she pointed out.

He poured his own cup of coffee and sat back down at the table. "Lopez's yacht went up in flames last night," he said matter-of-factly. "I am amazed that you didn't hear the explosion. It must have been a fault in the engine, or a gas leak," he added, without meeting her eyes. He shook his head. "A very nasty explosion. What was left of the yacht sank within sight of here."

"His boat sank? He was on it? You're sure? Did you see it go down?" she asked, relieved and horrified at the same time.

"Yes, yes, and yes." He studied her. "Lopez will never threaten you or Micah's father again. You will be able to return home now, to your job and your stepfather. I shall miss you."

"I'll miss you, too, Bojo," she said, but her mind was racing ahead. Lopez was dead. She was out of danger. She could go home. She had to go home, she amended. She would never see Micah again...

Bojo was watching the expressions chase themselves across her face. She was vulnerable, and besides that, she was in love with Micah. It didn't take much guesswork to figure that out, or to make sense of Micah's strange attitude about her. Obviously the boss knew she was in love with him, and he was trying to be kind while making his position to her clear.

He grimaced. The musical tones of his cell phone interrupted his gloomy thoughts. He answered it quickly.

"Yes," he said, glancing warily at Callie. "She's here, having coffee. I'll ask her." He lifted both eyebrows. "Micah is having lunch with Lisse on the bay in Nassau. If you want to join them, I can take you over in the small boat."

Lisse. Why should she think anything had changed? she wondered. Lisse was beautiful and Micah had told her at the beginning that he and Lisse were lovers. They'd been together for a long time, and she was important in the Bahamas, as well as being beautiful. A few teasing kisses for Callie meant nothing to him. She'd been a complete fool. Micah had been kind to her to get her to stay and bait Lopez. That was all it had been. It was an effort to smile, but she did.

"Tell him thanks, but I've got to start packing. If Lopez is really out of the way, I have to go home. Mr. Kemp won't keep my job open forever."

Bojo looked really worried. "Boss, she says she'd rather not." He hesitated, nodded, glanced again at Callie. "Okay. I'll make sure he knows. We'll expect you soon. Yes. Goodbye."

"You look like a bad party," she commented.

"He's bringing Lisse here for lunch," he said reluctantly.

Her heart jumped but she only smiled. "Why not? It's obvious to anybody that he's crazy about her. She's a dish," she added, and then wondered why she should suddenly think about Lisse's bust size when compared to her own.

"She's a cat," Bojo replied tersely. "Don't let her walk on you."

"I never have," she commented. "If we're having lunch, I guess I need to get started fixing it, huh?"

"We have a cook..."

"I'm good," she told him without conceit. "I cook for Dad and me every night. I'm not *cordon-bleu,* but I get compliments."

"Very well." Bojo gave in, hoping the boss wasn't going to fire him for letting her into the kitchen. "Mac went to Nassau with the boss and the other guys, so it would have been cold cuts anyway."

"I make homemade rolls," she told him with a grin. "And I can bake a pound cake."

She got up, looked through the cupboards and refrigerator, found an apron and got busy. It would give her something to do while her heart was breaking.

Two hours later, Micah and Lisse came into the living room together, laughing. Callie peered out from the kitchen. "Food's on the table if you want to sit down," she called gaily.

Micah gaped at her. He'd told Bojo to get Mac to fix lunch. What was Callie doing in the kitchen?

Bojo came out of it, and Micah's face hardened. "I thought I told you to monitor communications for traffic about Lopez," he said coldly.

Bojo knew what was eating him, so he only smiled. "I am. I was just asking Callie for another pot of coffee. We drank the other, between us," he added deliberately.

Micah's eyes flashed like black lightning, but he didn't say another word as Bojo nodded politely at Lisse and walked back toward the communications room.

"Sit down, Lisse," Micah said quietly, pulling out a chair for her at the dining-room table, already laid with silverware and plates and fresh flowers. "I'll be back in a minute."

"I do hope it's going to be something light," Lisse said airily. "I can't bear a heavy meal in the middle of the day."

Micah didn't answer her. He'd run into Lisse in town and

she'd finagled him into lunch. He'd compromised by bringing her here, so that he could see how Callie was feeling after the night before. He was hoping against hope that she remembered what had happened. But the instant she looked at him, he knew she hadn't.

"Hi," she said brightly and with a forced smile. "I slept like two logs. I hope you've got an appetite. I made homemade bread and cake, and steak and salad."

"Lisse will probably only want the salad," he murmured. "But I love cake."

"I remember. Go sit down. I'll bring it."

"You only set two places," he said quietly.

She shrugged. "I'm just cooking it. I wouldn't want to get in the way...Micah!"

While she was talking, he picked her up and carried her out of the kitchen the back way and into the first sprawling bathroom he came to, closing the door behind them.

"You're not the hired help here," he said flatly, staring into her eyes without putting her down. "You don't wait at table. You don't cook. I have a man for that."

"I'm a good cook," she pointed out. "And it's going to get cold if you don't put me down and let me finish."

His eyes dropped to her mouth and lingered there hungrily. "I don't want food." He brought her close and his mouth suddenly went down against hers and twisted ardently, until he forced her lips apart and made her respond to him. He groaned under his breath as her arms reached up to hold him. She made a husky little sound and gave in all at once. It felt so familiar to be held like this, kissed like this. She opened her mouth and felt his tongue go into it. Her body was on fire. She'd never felt such desire. Odd, that her body seemed to have a whole different knowledge of him than her mind did.

He couldn't get enough of her mouth. He devoured it. His powerful arms had a faint tremor when he was finally able to draw back. He looked straight into her eyes, remembering her headlong response the night before, feeling her body yield to him on crisp, white sheets in the darkness. He'd thought of nothing else all day. It was anguish to know that she was totally oblivious to what they'd done together, when the memories were torturing him.

"How long have you been talking to Bojo?" he demanded gruffly.

"Just…just a little while." Her mouth was swollen, but her body was shivering with secret needs. She looked at the tight line of his lips and impulsively reached up to kiss him. Amazingly he kissed her back with ardent insistence.

"Micah!" Lisse's strident voice came floating down the hall, followed by the staccato sound of high heels on wood.

Micah heard her and lifted his head. His mouth, like Callie's, was swollen. He searched her misty eyes intently.

"It's Lisse," she whispered dazedly.

"Yes." He bent and brushed his lips lazily over her own, smiling as she followed them involuntarily.

"She wants her lunch," she persisted.

"I want you," he murmured against her mouth.

The words shocked. Her fingers, linked behind his nape, loosened and she looked worried. "I can't!" she whispered huskily.

"Why can't you?"

"Because I've never…" she began.

Until last night. He almost said it. He thought it. His face hardened as he forced his tongue to be silent. He couldn't tell her. He wanted to. But it was too soon. He had to show her that it wasn't a one-night thing with him. Even more important, he had to convince himself that he could change enough, settle down enough, to give her some security and stability. He knew that he could have made her pregnant. Oddly it didn't worry him. The thought of a child was magical, somehow. He didn't know much about children, except that he was certain he'd love his own. Callie would make a wonderful mother.

He smiled as he bent and kissed her eyelids shut. "Wouldn't you?" he whispered. "If I insisted?"

"I'd hate you," she bit off, knowing that she wouldn't. She loved him endlessly.

"Yes, you might," he said after a minute. "And that's the last thing I want."

"Micah!" Lisse's voice came again, from even farther down the hall.

"Sit. Stay," Callie whispered impishly.

He bit her lower lip and growled deep in his throat. "She insisted on lunch. I compromised. Kiss me again." His mouth drifted lazily over hers.

She did kiss him, because she had no willpower when it came to this. She loved being in his arms, being held by him. She loved him!

After a minute he lifted his head and put her down, with obvious reluctance. "We'd better go before she starts opening doors," he said in a husky tone.

"Would she?" she asked, curious.

"She has before," he confessed with a wry grin. He brushed

back her hair with exquisite tenderness. His eyes held an expression she'd never seen in them. "You look like I've been making love to you," he whispered with a faint smile. "Better fix your face before you come out."

She reached up and touched his swollen mouth with wonder. She was still trying to make herself believe that he'd dragged her in here and kissed her so hungrily. There was something in the back of her mind, something disturbing. She couldn't grasp it. But the most amazing thing was the tenderness he was showing her. It made her breathless.

His lean hand spread against her cheek. His thumb parted her lips as he bent again, as if he couldn't help himself. He kissed her softly, savoring the trembling response of her lips.

"Micah!" Lisse was outside, almost screeching now.

He lifted his head again with a long sigh. "I need to take you out in the boat and drop anchor five miles out," he said heavily. He tapped her nose. "Okay, let's go see if everything's cold before Lisse loses her voice."

He opened the door, checking to see if the coast was clear. "Fix your face," he whispered with a wicked grin and closed the door behind him.

She heard his footsteps moving toward the dining room. Two minutes later, staccato heels made an angry sound passing the bathroom door.

"Micah…!"

"I'm in the dining room, Lisse! Where were you? I've been looking everywhere!"

He was good at improvising, Callie thought as she repaired the damage to her face. She combed her hair with a comb from a tray on the vanity table and wondered at the change in her relationship with Micah. He was very different. He acted as if she'd become suddenly important to him, and not in a conventional way. She couldn't help smiling. It was as if her whole life had changed.

She went back into the kitchen and put everything on the table, after checking that the steak had kept warm on the back of the stove. It had.

Micah got up and set a third place at the table, giving Callie a deliberate look. "You eat in here with us," he said firmly, ignoring Lisse's glare.

"Okay." She put out the last of the food, and butter for the rolls, and sat down. "Micah, will you say grace?" she added.

"Grace?" Lisse's beautiful face widened into shock.

Micah flashed her a disapproving glance and said a brief prayer. He was digging into the food while Lisse, in her gold-trimmed white pantsuit, was still gaping.

"We're very conventional at home," Callie pointed out.

"And traditional," Micah added. "Tradition is important for families."

"But you don't have a family, really, darling," Lisse protested. She helped herself to a couple of forkfuls of salad and a hint of dressing. "Rolls? Thousands of calories, darling, especially with butter!" she told Micah.

"Callie made them for me, from scratch," he said imperturbably. He bit into one and smiled. "These are good," he said.

Callie shrugged. "It's the only thing I do really well. My mother couldn't boil water." That had slipped out and she looked horrified as she met Micah's eyes.

"I think Micah could do very well without hearing about your tramp of a mother, dear," Lisse said haughtily. "He's suffered enough at her hands already. Who was it she threw you over for, darling, that British earl?"

"She didn't throw me over," Micah said through his teeth.

"But she was staying here with you last year…?"

Callie's eyes exploded. She got up, throwing down her napkin. "Is that true?" she demanded.

"It is, but not the way you're assuming it is," he said flatly. "Callie, there's something you need to know."

She turned and walked out of the room.

"What the hell was that in aid of?" Micah demanded of Lisse, with real anger.

"You keep secrets, don't you?" she asked with cold delight. "It's dangerous. And she isn't really your sister, either. I got that out of Bojo. You've even slept with her, haven't you, darling?" she added venomously.

Micah threw down his own napkin and got to his feet. *"Bojo!"* he yelled.

The tall Berber came rushing into the room. His boss never raised his voice!

Micah was almost vibrating with rage. "See Lisse back to Nassau. She won't be coming here again," he added with ice dropping from every syllable.

Lisse put down her fork and wiped her mouth before she got leisurely to her feet. She gave him a cool look. "You use people," she accused quietly. "It's always what *you* want, what *you* need. You manipulate, you control, you…use. I loved you," she added in a husky undertone. "But you didn't care. I was handy and good in bed, and that was what mattered to you. When you didn't want me so much anymore, you threw me out. I was only invited over here this time so that you could show your houseguest that she wasn't the only egg in your basket." She gave him a cold smile. "So how does it feel to be on the receiving end for once, Micah? It's your turn. I wish, I really wish, I could stick around to see the result. She doesn't look like the forgiving sort to me. And I'd know, wouldn't I?"

She turned, leaving Bojo to follow her after a complicated glance in Micah's direction. The boss didn't say a word. Not a single word.

Callie was packing with shaking hands. Micah came to the doorway and leaned against it with his hands in his pockets, watching her glumly.

"Nothing to say?" she asked curtly.

"Nothing you'd listen to," he replied. He shrugged. "Lisse just put me in my place. I didn't realize it, but she's right. I do use people. Only I never meant to use you, in any way."

"You said you weren't having an affair with my mother," she accused as she folded a pair of slacks and put them in her case.

"I'm not. I never have." His chest rose and fell heavily. "But you're not in any mood to listen, are you, baby?"

Baby. She frowned. Baby. Why did that word make her uneasy? She looked at him with honest curiosity.

"I called you that," he said quietly. "You don't remember when, do you?"

She sighed, shaking her head.

"It may be just as well," he said, almost to himself. "For now, it's safe for you to go home. Lopez is dead. His top lieutenants died with him. There's no longer any threat to you or to Dad."

"Yes. What a lucky explosion it was," she added, busy with her case.

"It wasn't luck, Callie," he said shortly. "I swam out to the yacht and planted a block of C-4 next to his propeller shaft."

She turned, gasping. Her hands shook as she fumbled the case closed and sat down heavily on the bed. So that was what they'd been talking about the night before, when Micah had said that "it might work." He could have been killed!

"It was a close call," he added, watching her. "I let myself get caught like a rank beginner. I was too tired to make it back in a loop, so I stopped to rest. One of Lopez's men caught me. Lopez made a lot of threats about what he planned to do to you and Dad, and then he got stupid and had me tied up down below." He extended his arm, showed her his watch, pressed a button, and watched her expression as a knife blade popped out. "Pity his men weren't astute enough to check the watch. They knew what I do for a living, too."

Her eyes were full of horror. Micah had gone after Lopez alone. He'd been captured. If it hadn't been for that watch, he'd be dead. She stared at him as if she couldn't get enough of just looking at him. What difference did it make if he'd had a full-blown affair with her mother? He could be out there with Lopez, in pieces...

She put her face in her hands to hide the tears that over-flowed.

He went to the bed and knelt beside her, pulling her wet face into his throat. He smoothed her hair while she clung to him and let the tears fall. It had been such a traumatic week for her. It seemed that her whole life had been uprooted and stranded. Micah could have been dead. Or, last night, she could have been dead. Pride seemed such a petty thing all of a sudden.

"You could have died," she whispered brokenly.

"So could you." He moved, lifting her into his arms. He dropped into a wide cushioned rattan chair and held her close while the anguish of the night before lanced through her slender body like a tangible thing. She clung to him, shivering.

"I wish I'd known what you were planning," she said. "I'd have stopped you, somehow! Even if it was only to save you so you could go to my...my mother."

He wrapped her up even closer and laid his cheek against her hair with a long sigh. "You still don't trust me, do you, honey?" he murmured absently. "I suppose it was asking too much, considering the way I've treated you over the years." He kissed her dark hair. "You go back home and settle into your old routine. Soon enough, this will all seem like just a bad dream."

She rubbed her eyes with her fists, like a small child. Curled against him, she felt safe, cherished, treasured. Odd, to feel like that with a man who was a known playboy, a man who'd already told her that freedom was like a religion to him.

"You'll be glad to have your house to yourself again," she said huskily. "I guess it really cramped your style having me here. With Lisse, I mean."

He chuckled. "I lied."

"Wh...what?"

"I lied about Lisse being my lover now. What was between us was over years ago." He shrugged. "I brought her over here when you arrived as a buffer."

She sat up, staring at him like a curious cat. "A buffer?"

He smiled lazily. His fingers brushed away the tears that were wetting her cheeks. "Bachelors are terrified of virgins," he commented.

"You don't even like me," she protested.

His dark eyes slid down to her mouth, and even farther, over her breasts, down to her long legs. "You have a heart like marshmallow," he said quietly. "You never avoid trouble or turn down people in need. You take in all sorts of strays. Children love you." He smiled. "You scared me to death."

"Past tense?" she asked softly.

"I'm getting used to you." He didn't smile. His dark eyes narrowed. "It hurt me that Lopez got two men onto my property while I was lying in bed asleep. You could have been kidnapped or killed, no thanks to me."

"You were tired," she replied. "You aren't superhuman, Micah."

He drew in a slow breath and toyed with the armhole of her tank top. His fingers brushed against soft, warm flesh and she had to fight not to lean toward them. "I didn't feel comfortable resting while we were in so much danger. It all caught up with me last night."

She was remembering something he'd said. "You were almost too tired to swim back from Lopez's yacht, you said," she recalled slowly. She frowned. "But you'd just been asleep," she added. "How could you have been tired?"

"Oh, that's not a question you should ask yet," he said heavily. "You're not going to like the answer."

"I'm not?"

He searched her eyes for a long moment. All at once, he stood up, taking her with him. "You'd better finish getting your stuff together. I'll put you on a commercial flight home."

She didn't want to go, but she didn't have an excuse to stay. She looked at him as if she were lost and alone, and his face clenched.

"Don't do that," he said huskily. "The idea is to get you out of here as smoothly as possible. Don't invite trouble."

She didn't understand that taut command. But then, she didn't understand him, either. She was avoiding the one question she should be asking. She gave in and asked it. "Why was my mother here?"

"Her husband has cancer," he said simply. "She phoned here and begged for help. It seems the earl is penniless and she does actually seem to love him. I arranged for him to have an unorthodox course of treatment from a native doctor here. They both stayed with me until he got through it." He put his hands in his slacks pockets. "As much as I hate to admit it, she's not the woman she was, Callie," he added. "And she did one other thing that I admired. She phoned your father and told him the truth about you."

Her heart skipped. "What father? What truth?" she asked huskily.

"Your father was going to phone you and ask you to meet him. Did he?"

She moved restlessly back to her packing. "He phoned and left a message. I didn't have anything to say to him, so I didn't call him back."

"He knows that you're his child," he told her. "Your mother sent him your birth certificate. That's why he's trying to contact you. I imagine he wants to apologize. Your mother does, too, to you and Dad, but she told me she wasn't that brave."

Her eyes met his, haunted. "I went through hell because of her and my father," she said in a tight tone. "You don't know... you can't imagine...what it was like!"

"Yes, I can," he said, and he sounded angry. "He's apparently counting his regrets. He never remarried. He doesn't have any children, except you."

"Then he still doesn't have a child," she said through her teeth.

He didn't reply for several long seconds. "I can understand why you feel that way, about him and your mother. I don't blame you. I just thought I'd tell you what I know. It's up to you, what you do or don't do about it."

She folded one last shirt and put it into the case. "Thanks for telling me." She glanced at him. "Lisse wanted to make trouble."

"Yes, she did, and she was entitled. She's right. I did use her, in a way. Your mother left me very embittered about women," he confessed. "I loved my own mother, but I lost her when I was still in grammar school. In later years, your mother was the very worst example of what a wife should be. She made a very bad impression on me."

"On me, too." She closed the case and turned back to him, her eyes trying to memorize his lean face. "I wish you'd liked me, when I lived in your house," she said abruptly. "It would have meant more than you know."

His eyes narrowed. "I couldn't afford to like you, Callie," he said quietly. "Every time I looked at you, I burned like fire inside. You were just a teenager, a virgin. I couldn't take advantage of you that way."

"We could have been friends," she persisted.

He shook his head. "You know we couldn't. You know why."

She grimaced, averting her face. "It's always sex with you, isn't it?"

"Not anymore." His voice was quiet, solemn. "Those days are past. I'm looking ahead now. I have a future to build."

A bigger army of mercenaries, she decided, and more money. She smiled to herself. Once a mercenary, always a mercenary. He'd be the last mercenary who would ever be able to give up the lifestyle.

"I wish you well," she said. She picked up her case and looked around to make sure she hadn't left anything. "Thanks for saving my life. Twice," she added with a forced grin.

"You're welcome." He moved forward to take the case from her. He studied her face for a long time with narrowed eyes. It was as if he was seeing her for the first time. "It's amazing," he murmured involuntarily, "that it took me so long."

"What took you so long?"

"Never mind," he murmured, and he smiled. "You'll find out soon enough. Come on. I'll drive you into Nassau to the airport."

"Bojo could…"

He put his fingers against her soft mouth, and he didn't smile. "I'll drive you."

She swallowed. The tip of his finger was tracing her upper lip, and it was making her knees weak. "Okay," she said.

He took her hand and led her out to the car.

12

Two weeks later, Callie was back at work and it was as if she'd never been kidnapped by Lopez's men or gone to Nassau with Micah. Despite the excitement and adventure, she hadn't told anyone except Mr. Kemp the truth about what had happened. And she let him think that Lopez had died in a freak accident, to protect Micah.

Micah had walked her to the concourse and kissed her goodbye in such a strange, breathlessly tender way that it had kept her from sleeping much since she'd been back. The look in his eyes had been fascinating, but she was still trying to decide what she'd seen there. He'd said he'd see her soon. She had no idea what he meant. It was like leaving part of herself behind when she got on the plane. She cried all the way to Miami, where she got on a plane to San Antonio and then a charter flight to Jacobsville from there.

Micah's father was much better, and so glad to see her that he cried, too. She dismissed the nurse who'd been staying with him with gratitude and a check, but the nurse refused the check. She'd already been paid her fee, in advance, she told a mystified Callie. She left, and Callie and Jack Steele settled back into their comfortable routine.

"I feel better than I have in years," Jack Steele told her with a grin at supper one evening. "It makes me proud that my son wanted to protect me as well as you."

"Micah loves you terribly," she assured him. "He just has a hard time showing it, that's all."

"You really think so?"

"I do. I'm sure he'll come and see you, if you'll let him."

He gave her a peculiar look and pursed his lips. "I'll let Micah come here if you'll do something for me."

"What?"

He leaned back in his chair, and his features reminded her of Micah in a stubborn mood. "If you'll make peace with your father," he said.

She let out a surprised gasp.

"I knew you'd take it like that," he said. "But he's phoned here every single day since you left. He told me some cock-and-bull story about a drug dealer named Lopez. He said he'd heard from a friend in law enforcement that Lopez had kidnapped you and taken you to Mexico. I thought he was full of bull and I told him so. But he kept phoning. I guess it was a good excuse to mend fences. A man that persistent should at least have a hearing."

She gaped at him. "You...didn't believe him, about Lopez?"

Her tone surprised him. "No, of course not." Her expression was very disturbing. He scowled. "Callie...it wasn't true? You really did go to take care of that aunt Micah told me about?"

"Jack, I don't have a aunt," she said heavily. "Lopez did kidnap me. Micah came and got me out himself. He went right into Lopez's house and rescued me."

"My son, storming drug dealers' lairs?" he exclaimed. "Are you kidding?"

"Oh, I didn't want you to have to find out like this," she groaned. "I should have bitten my tongue through!"

He was shocked. "Micah got you out," he repeated.

She leaned across the table and took his arthritic hands in hers and held them tight. "There's no easy way to say this, but you'll have to know. I'm not sure Micah wants you to know, but I don't have a choice anymore. Dad, Micah is a professional mercenary," she told him evenly. "And he's very good at it. He rappelled from Lopez's roof right into a bedroom and rescued me from a man who was going to kill me. We're both fine. He got me away and out of the country, and took me home with him to Nassau. He lured Lopez in, and…Lopez's boat was blown up in a freak accident."

Jack let out the breath he'd been holding. "The things you learn about people you thought you knew. My own son, and he never told me."

She grimaced. "I'm not sure he ever would. He's very brave, Jack. He isn't really money-hungry, although it sounds as if he is. I'd never have survived without him. His men are just the same, dedicated professionals who really care about what they do. They're not a gang of thugs."

Jack sat back in his chair again, scowling. "You know, it does make some sort of sense. He came home bandaged, you remember that time? And he said he'd had a bad fall. But I saw him accidentally without the bandage and it looked like a bullet wound to me."

"It probably was," she said. "He has scars on his back, too."

She frowned, trying to understand how she knew that. She'd

seen Micah with his shirt unbuttoned in Nassau, but never with it off completely. How would she know he had scars down his back?

She put that thought out of her mind. "There's something else I found out," she added. "My mother was there last year, staying with him."

Jack's face hardened at once.

"No, it's not what you're thinking," she said quickly. "That was my thought, too, but she asked Micah for help. She's married to a British earl who has cancer. There was a clinic near Micah and he let them stay with him while the earl was treated. He's impoverished, and I suspect that Micah paid for the treatments, too, although he didn't admit it." She smiled. "He says Mother is really in love this time. She wanted to make peace with both of us, as well, but she didn't think it would be possible."

"Not for me," Jack said quietly. "She cost me a lot."

"She cost me more," she agreed. "But you can't hate people forever. It only hurts you in the end. You have to forgive unless you want to live in torment forever."

"How did you get so wise, at your age?" he asked, smiling as he tried to lighten the mood.

"I had a lot of hard knocks. I learned early how terrible a thing hatred is." She touched his hand gently. "Micah loves you so much. You can't imagine how it hurt him when we thought he'd betrayed you with Mother. He's been bitter, too."

"I wouldn't let him talk about it," he said. "I should have listened. He's never lied to me, except maybe by omission." He sighed with a wry smile. "I never would have guessed he'd have been in such a profession."

She laughed. "Neither would I." She sighed. "He can't give it up, of course. He told me he had no ambition whatsoever to settle down and have a family. I never really saw him as a family man."

He studied her curiously. "But you wish he was," he said perceptibly.

Her gaze fell to the table. "I love him," she said heavily. "I always have. But he's got all the women in his life that he needs already. Beautiful women. One of them took me shopping when we first got to Nassau."

"You have ties with him that no other woman will ever have. If he didn't care about you, he certainly wouldn't have risked his own life to rescue you," he remarked.

"He did it for you, because he knows you love me," she said. "That's why."

He pursed his lips and his eyes narrowed as he studied her. "Think so? I wonder."

She got up. "I'll fix dinner. Then I guess I'll try to phone my father."

"Remember what you said, about forgiving people, Callie," he reminded her. "Your mother told him a lot of lies. He believed her, but maybe it was easier to believe her, when he knew she was taking you away. He was going to lose you anyway."

"She didn't take me away," she said coldly. "He threw me out, and she put me in foster care immediately."

He grimaced. "Yes, I know. Your father told me. He'd only just found out."

"Found out, how?" she exclaimed.

"Apparently he hired a private detective," he said gently. "He was appalled at how you'd been treated, Callie. He blames himself."

She moved restlessly, her eyes glancing at him. "You're the only father I've ever known."

He grinned. "You'll always have me. But give the man a chance. He's not as bad as you remember him being." The smile faded. "Maybe, like your mother, he's found time to face himself and his mistakes."

She turned away. "Okay. I guess it wouldn't hurt to talk to him."

She phoned, but her father was out of the country. She left a message for him on his answering machine, a stumbling sort of greeting and her phone number. If he hadn't given up on her, he might try again.

The next week dragged. She missed Micah. She felt tired. She wondered if all the excitement of the past few weeks wasn't catching up with her. She also seemed to have stopped having a period. She'd always been regular and never skipped, and then she remembered that odd spotting in Nassau. She grimaced. It must be some sort of female problem. She'd have to make an appointment to see Dr. Lou Coltrain.

She made the appointment from work, just after she got back from lunch. When she hung up, her boss, Blake Kemp, was speaking to someone in his office, the door just having opened so that he could show his client out.

"...yes, he phoned me a couple of days ago," the client was saying. "He used to hate Jacobsville, which makes it even stranger. We were all shocked."

"Yes," Kemp replied. "He had a whole island, didn't he? He's already sold up there, and he's got big plans for the Colbert Ranch property. He owns several thoroughbreds, which he's having shipped here from New Providence. He plans to have one of the best racing stables in Texas, from what he says."

"He says he's giving up the business, as well and coming back here to live."

"That's another odd thing, he mentioned going back to medical school and finishing his residency," Kemp chuckled.

"He's good at what he used to do. He's patched me up enough over the years." The tall man with the green eyes, favoring a burned forearm and hand glanced at Callie and noted her shocked face. "Yes, Callie, I'm talking about your stepbrother. I don't guess you and Jack Steele knew a thing about this, did you?"

She shook her head, too stunned to speak.

"That's like Micah." The client chuckled. "He always was secretive. Well, Callie, you look none the worse for wear after your ordeal."

She finally realized who the client was. That was Cy Parks! She knew that he and Micah were friends, but until recently she hadn't known that they shared the same profession.

"Micah's moving here?" she asked involuntarily.

"He is," Cy told her. "But don't tell him you heard me say so," he added with a twinkle in his green eyes. "I don't need to lose any more teeth."

"Sure thing, Mr. Parks," she said with a smile.

"He couldn't stop talking about how brave you were, you know," he added unexpectedly. "He was so proud of you."

She flushed. "He never said so."

"He doesn't, usually." He smiled. "Your father will enjoy having him home, too."

She nodded. "He's proud of Micah. I had to tell him the truth. He'll be over the moon to think that Micah's coming home. He's missed him."

"That cuts both ways. I'm glad to see him making an attempt to settle down," he added with a chuckle. "I can recommend it highly. I never expected so much happiness in my own life. Lisa's pregnant, you know," he added. "It's going to be a boy. We're both over the moon."

"Babies are nice," Callie said wistfully. "Thanks for telling me about Micah, Mr. Parks."

"Make it Cy," he told her. "I expect we'll be seeing each other again. Kemp, walk me out, I want to ask you something."

"Sure thing."

The men walked out onto the sidewalk and Callie stared at her computer screen with trembling fingers on the keyboard. Micah had sold his island. He was coming to live in Jacobsville. Was Lisse coming with him? Had they made up in spite of what he'd said about her? Was he going to marry the beautiful blonde and set up housekeeping here? If he was, she couldn't bear to stay in Jacobsville!

She felt like bawling. Her emotions had been all over the place lately. Along with the sudden bouts of fatigue and an odd nausea at night, and a missing period, she was likely to cry at the drop of a hat. She remembered a girlfriend having all those same symptoms, but of course, the girlfriend had been pregnant. That wasn't possible in her case. An erotic dream did not produce conception, after all. She was going to see the doctor the next day, anyway. She'd know what was wrong then, if anything was. She hoped it was nothing too terrible.

When she got home that evening, the doctor, the office, everything went right out of her head. There was a black Porsche convertible sitting in the driveway. With her heart pounding like mad, she got out and rushed up the front steps and into the apartment house.

She opened her own door, which was unlocked, and there was Micah, sitting at the dining-room table with Jack Steele while they shared a pot of coffee.

"Micah!" she exclaimed, everything she felt showing helplessly on her face.

He got to his feet, his face somber and oddly watchful. "Hello, Callie," he said quietly.

"I thought…I mean, I didn't think…" The room was swirling around her. She felt an odd numbness in her face and everything went white.

Micah rushed forward and caught her up in his arms before she hit the floor.

"Her bedroom's through there," Jack told him. "She's been acting very odd, lately. Tired and goes to bed early. I'll make another pot of coffee."

"Thanks, Dad."

Micah carried her to her room and laid her down gently on the white coverlet of her bed. Her fingers were like ice. He brushed back her disheveled hair and his heart clenched at just the sight of her. He'd missed her until it was anguish not to hear her voice, see her face.

She moaned and her eyes opened slowly, looking up into his. She was faintly nauseous and her throat felt tight.

"I feel awful, Micah," she whispered. "But I'm so happy to see you!"

"I'm happy to see you, too," he replied, but he didn't look it. He looked worried. His big hand flattened on her belly, resting there very gently. He leaned close and his lips touched her eyelids, closing them. They moved down her face, over her cheeks, to her soft lips and he kissed her with breathless tenderness. "Callie," he whispered, and his lips became hard and insistent, as if he couldn't help himself.

She opened her mouth to him unconsciously, and her arms went around his neck, pulling him down. She forgot about Lisse, about everything. She kissed him back hungrily. All the weeks apart might never have been. She loved him so!

After a long minute, he forced himself to lift his head. He drew in a long, hard breath. He looked down where his hand was resting on her belly. It wasn't swollen yet, but he was certain, somehow, that she was carrying his child.

"Why…are you doing that?" she asked, watching his hand smooth over her stomach.

"I don't know how to tell you," he replied gently. "Callie…do you remember the night Lopez's men tried to kidnap you again? Do you remember that I gave you a sedative?"

"Yes," she said, smiling nervously.

"And you had an…erotic dream," he continued.

"Yes." She shifted on the cover. "I'd rather not talk about it."

"But we have to. Callie, I…"

"How about some coffee?" Jack Steele asked, poking his head through the doorway. "I just made a fresh pot."

"I'd like some," Callie said with a forced smile. "I'd like something to eat, too. I'm so empty!"

"That's what you think," Micah said under his breath. He stared down at her with twinkling eyes and a smile unlike any smile she'd ever seen on his lips before.

"You look very strange," she commented.

He shrugged. "Don't I always?"

She laughed gently. "Cy Parks was in Mr. Kemp's office today," she said as he helped her to her feet. "He said you were moving here…oops! I promised not to say anything, too. Please don't get mad at him, Micah."

"It's no big secret," he said gently. "In small towns, everybody knows what's going on. It's all right."

"You really are coming back here?"

Her wide eyes and fascinated expression made him tingle all over. "I am. I'm going to breed thoroughbreds. It's something I've always had an interest in. I might finish my residency, as well. Jacobsville can always use another doctor."

"I guess so. I have to go see Dr. Lou Coltrain tomorrow. I think I may have a female problem," she said absently as they started out of the bedroom.

"Tomorrow?"

"After lunch," she said. "Don't tell Dad," she said, holding him back by the sleeve before they left the room. "I don't want him to worry. It probably scared him when I fainted. It scared me, too," she confessed.

He touched her hair gently. He wanted to tell her, but he didn't know how. He needed to talk to Lou Coltrain first. This had to be done very carefully, so that Callie didn't feel he was being forced into a decision he didn't want to make.

She searched his eyes. "You look so tired, Micah," she said softly.

"I don't sleep well since you left the island," he replied. "I've worried about you."

"I'm doing okay," she said at once, wanting to reassure him. "I don't even have nightmares." She looked down at her hand on his sleeve. "Micah, is Lisse…I mean, will she come, too?"

"Lisse is history. I told you that when you left. I meant it."

"She's so beautiful," she said huskily.

He frowned, tipping her face up to his with a hand under her chin. "You're beautiful yourself. Didn't you know?" he asked tenderly. "You have this big, open heart that always thinks of other people first. You have a generosity of spirit that makes me feel selfish by comparison. You glow, Callie." He smiled softly. "That's real beauty, the kind you don't buy in the cosmetic section of the department store. Lisse can't hold a candle to you." The smile faded. "No woman on earth could, right now. You're pure magic to me, Callie. You're the whole world."

That sounded serious. She just stared at him, transfixed, while she tried to decipher what he was saying.

"Coffee?" Jack Steele repeated, a little more loudly.

They both jumped when they saw him there. Then they laughed and moved out of the bedroom. Jack poured coffee into mugs and Micah carried Callie hers.

"Feeling better?" Jack asked.

"Oh, yes," she said, the excitement she was feeling so plain on her face that Micah grinned. "Much better!"

Micah stayed near Callie for the rest of the evening, until he had to go. She'd fixed them a meal and had barely been able to eat a bite of it. She had little appetite, but mostly she was too excited. Micah was watching her as if everything she did fascinated him. All her dreams of love seemed to be coming true. She couldn't believe the way he was looking at her. It made her tingle.

She walked out with him after he'd said his good-nights to his father. "You could stay," she said.

"I can't sleep on that dinky little sofa, and Dad's in a twin bed. So unless you're offering to share your nice big double bed...?" he teased as they paused by the driver's side of his car.

She flushed. "Stop that."

He touched her cheek with his fingertips. "There's something I wanted to ask you. I can't seem to find a way to do it."

"What? You can ask me anything," she said softly.

He bent and brushed his mouth over hers. "Not yet. Come here and kiss me."

"We have neighbors..." she protested weakly.

But he'd already lifted her clear of the ground and he was kissing her as if there was no tomorrow. She held on and kissed him back with all her might. Two young boys on skateboards went whizzing by with long, insinuating wolf whistles.

Micah lifted his head and gave them a hard glare. "Everyone's a critic," he murmured.

"I'm not complaining," she whispered. "Come back here..."

He kissed her again and then, reluctantly, put her back on her feet. "Unless you want to make love on the hood of the car, we'd better put on the brakes." He looked around. More people had appeared. Incredible that there would be hordes of passersby at this hour in a small Texas town. He glared at two couples sauntering by. They grinned.

"That's Mr. and Mrs. Harris, and behind them is Mr. Harris's son and Jill Williams's daughter. They're going steady," she explained. "They know me, but I'm not in the habit of being kissed by handsome men in Porsches. They're curious."

He nodded over her shoulder. "And her?"

She followed where he was looking. "That's old Mrs. Smith. She grows roses."

"Yes. She seems to be pruning them." He checked his watch. "Ten o'clock at night is an odd hour to do that, isn't it?"

"Oh, she just doesn't want to look as if she's staring," she explained. "She thinks it would embarrass us." She added in a whisper, "I expect she thinks we're courting."

He twirled a strand of dark hair around his fingers. "Aren't we?" he asked with a gentle smile.

"Courting?" She sounded breathless. She couldn't help it.

He nodded. "You're very old-fashioned, Callie. In some ways, so am I. But you'd better know up-front that I'm not playing."

"You already said you didn't want to settle down," she said, nodding agreement.

"That isn't what I mean."

"Then what do you mean?"

"Hello, Callie!" came an exuberant call from the window upstairs. It was Maria Ruiz, who was visiting her aunt who lived upstairs. She was sixteen and vivacious. "Isn't it a lovely night?"

"Lovely."

"Who's the dish?" the younger woman asked with an outrageous grin. "He's a real hunk. Does he belong to you, or is he up for grabs?"

"Sorry, I'm taken," Micah told her.

"Just my luck," she sighed. "Well, good night!"

She closed the window and the curtain and went back inside.

Callie laughed softly. "She's such a doll. She looks in on Dad when her aunt's working. I told you about her aunt, she doesn't speak any English."

He bent again and kissed her lazily. "You taste like roses," he whispered against her mouth. He enfolded her against him, shivering a little as his body responded instantly to the feel of hers against it and began to swell. He groaned softly as he kissed her again.

"Micah, you're..." She felt the hard crush of his mouth and she moaned, too. It was as if she'd felt him like this before, but in much greater intimacy. It was as if they'd been lovers. She held on tight and kissed him until she was shivering, too.

His mouth slid across her cheek to her ear, and he was breathing as roughly as she was. "I want you," he bit off, holding her bruisingly close. "I want you so much, Callie!"

"I'm sorry," she choked. "I can't...!"

He took deep breaths, trying to keep himself in check. He had to stop this. It was too soon. It was much too soon.

"It may not seem like it, but I'm not asking you to," he said. "It's just that there are things you don't know, Callie, and I don't know how to tell them to you."

"Bad things?"

He let out a slow breath. "Magical things," he whispered, cradling her in his arms as he thought about the baby he was certain she was carrying. His eyes closed as he held her. "The most magical sort of things. I've never felt like this in my life."

She wanted, so much, to ask him what he was feeling. But she was too shy. Perhaps if she didn't push him, he might like her. He sounded as if he did. She smiled, snuggling close to him, completely unintimidated with the hard desire of his body. She loved making him feel this way.

He smoothed over her hair with a hand that wasn't quite steady. His body ached, and even that was sweet. The weeks without her had been pure hell.

"Soon," he said enigmatically. "Very soon."

"What?"

He kissed her hair. "Nothing. I'd better go. Mrs. Smith is cutting the tops off the roses. Any minute now, there won't even be a bud left."

She glanced past his shoulder. She giggled helplessly. The romantic old woman was so busy watching them that she was massacring her prize roses!

"She wins ribbons for them, you know," she murmured.

"She won't have any left."

"She's having the time of her life," she whispered. "Her boyfriend married her sister. They haven't spoken in thirty years and she's never even looked at another man. She reads romance novels and watches movies and dreams. This is as close as she's likely to get to a hot romance. Even if it isn't."

"It certainly is," he whispered wickedly. "And if I don't get out of here *very* soon, she's going to see more than she bargained for. And so are you."

"Really?" she teased.

His hand slid to the base of her spine and pushed her close to him. His eyes held a very worldly amusement at her gasp. "Really," he whispered. He bent and kissed her one last time. "Go inside."

She forced herself to step back from him. "What about Bojo and Peter and Rodrigo and Pogo and Maddie?" she asked suddenly.

"Bojo was being groomed to take over the group. He's good at giving orders, and he knows how we operate. I'll be a consultant."

"But why?" she asked, entranced. "And why come back to Jacobsville to raise horses?"

"When you're ready for those answers I'll give them to you," he said with a gentle smile. "But not tonight. I'll be in touch. Good night."

He was in the car and gone before she could get another word out. Several doors down, Mrs. Smith was muttering as she looked at the rosebuds lying heaped around her feet. The skateboarders went past again with another round of wolf whistles. The couples walking gave her long, wicked grins. Callie went back inside, wondering if she should give them all a bow before she went inside.

13

Micah was ushered back into Dr. Lou Coltrain's office through the back door, before she started seeing her patients. He shook hands with her and took the seat she indicated in her office. She sat down behind her desk, blond and attractive and amused.

"Thanks for taking time to see me this morning," he said. He noted her wry look and chuckled. "Is my head on backward?" he asked.

"You may wish it was," she replied with twinkling dark eyes. "I think I know why you're here. At least two people have hinted to me that Callie Kirby's having what sounds like morning sickness."

He sighed and smiled. "Yes."

"And you're the culprit, unless I miss my guess. Are you here to discuss alternatives?" she asked, suddenly serious.

"I am not!" he said at once. "I want a baby as much as Callie will, when she knows about it."

"When she knows? She doesn't suspect?" she asked, wide-eyed.

He grimaced. "Well, it's like this. Lopez and his thugs—you

know about them?" When she nodded, he sighed. "I was careless and they almost got her a second time in Nassau. She knocked her assailant out with a shovel, but she was really shaken up afterward. I gave her a sedative." His high cheekbones colored and he averted his eyes. "She got amorous and I was already upset and on the edge, and I'd abstained for so damned long. And... well..."

"Then what?" she asked, reading between the lines with avid curiosity.

He shifted in the chair, still avoiding eye contact. "She doesn't remember anything. She thinks it was an erotic dream."

Her intake of breath was audible. "In all my years of medicine..." she began.

"I haven't had that many, but it's news to me, too. The thing is, I'm sure she's pregnant, but she'll have a heart attack if you tell her she is. I have to break it to her. But first I have to find a way to convince her to marry me," he added. "So that she won't spend the rest of our lives together believing that the baby forced me into marriage. It's not like that," he said. He rubbed at a spot on his slacks so that he wouldn't have to meet Lou's intent stare. "She's everything. Everything in the world."

Lou smiled. He wasn't saying the words, but she was hearing them. He loved Callie. So it was like that. The mercenary was caught in his own trap. And, amazingly, he didn't want to get out of it. He wanted the baby!

"What do you want me to do?" she asked.

"I want you to do a blood test and see if she really is pregnant. But if she is, I want you to make some excuse about the results being inconclusive, and you can give her a prescription for some vitamins and ask her to come back in two weeks."

"She'll worry that it's something fatal," Lou advised. "People do."

"Tell her you think it's stress, from her recent ordeal," he persisted. "Please," he added, finding the word hard to say even now. "I just need a little time."

"Just call me Dr. Cupid Coltrain," she murmured. "I guess I'll get drummed out of the AMA, but how can I say no?"

"You're in the business of saving lives," he reminded her. "This will save three of them."

"I hear you're moving back here," she said.

"I am. I'm going to raise thoroughbreds," he added, smiling. "And act as a consultant for Eb Scott when he needs some expertise. That way, I'll not only settle down, I'll have enough of a taste of the old life to satisfy me if things get dull. I might even finish my residency and hit you and Coltrain up for a job."

"Anytime," she said, grinning. "I haven't had a day off in two years. I'd like to take my son to the zoo and not have to leave in the middle of the lions on an emergency call."

He chuckled. "Okay. That's a dare."

She stood up when he did and shook hands again. "You're not what I expected, Mr. Steele," she said after a minute. "I had some half-baked idea that you'd never give up your line of work, that you'd want Callie to do something about the baby."

"I do. I want her to have it," he said with a smile. "And a few more besides, if we're lucky. Callie and I were only children. I'd like several, assorted."

"So would we, but one's all we can handle at the moment. Of course, if you finish your residency and stand for your medical license, that could change," she added, tongue-in-cheek.

He grinned. "I guess it's contagious."

She nodded. "Very. Now get out of here. I won't tell Callie I've ever seen you in my life."

"Thanks. I really mean it."

"Anything for a future colleague," she returned with a grin of her own.

Callie worried all morning about the doctor's appointment, but she relaxed when she was in Lou's office and they'd drawn blood and Lou had checked her over.

"It sounds to me like the aftereffects of a very traumatic experience," Lou said with a straight face. "I'm prescribing a multiple vitamin and I want you to come back and see me in two weeks."

"Will the tests take that long?" Callie asked.

"They might." Lou sighed. "You're mostly tired, Callie. You should go to bed early and eat healthy. Get some sun, too. And try not to worry. It's nothing serious, I'm positive of that."

Callie smiled her relief. "Thanks, Dr. Coltrain!" she said. "Thanks, so much!"

"I hear your stepbrother's moving back to town," Lou said as she walked Callie to the door of the cubicle. "I guess you'll be seeing a lot of him now."

Callie flushed. "It looks that way." Her eyes lit up. "He's so different. I never could have imagined Micah settling for small-town life."

"Men are surprising people," Lou said. "You never know what they're capable of."

"I suppose so. Well, I'll see you in two weeks."

"Count on it," Lou said, patting her on the shoulder. "Lots of rest. And take those vitamins," she added, handing over the prescription.

Callie felt as if she were walking on air. No health problems, just the aftereffects of the kidnapping. That was good news indeed. And when Micah phoned and asked her to come out to the ranch with him and see the house, she was over the moon.

He picked her up after work at her apartment house. "I took Dad out there this morning," he told her with a grin. "He's going to move in with me at the weekend."

Callie's heart jumped. "This weekend?"

He nodded, glancing at her. "You could move in, too."

Her heart jumped, but she knew he didn't mean that the way it sounded. "I like living in town," she lied.

He smiled to himself. He knew what she was refusing. She wasn't about to live in sin with him in Jacobsville, Texas.

He reached for her hand and linked her fingers with his. "Did you go see the doctor?"

"Yes. She said it was stress. I guess it could be. At least, it's nothing extreme."

"Thank God," he said.

"Yes."

He turned down onto a long winding graveled road. Minutes later, they pulled up in front of a big white Victorian house with a turret room and a new tin roof. "It's really old-fashioned and some of the furniture will have to be replaced," he said, helping her out of the car. "But it's got potential. There's a nice rose garden that only needs a little work, and a great place out to the side for a playground. You know, a swing set and all those nice plastic toys kids love so much."

She stared at him. "You have kids?" she asked with an impish smile.

"Well, not yet," he agreed. "But they're definitely in the picture. Don't you like kids?" he asked with apparent carelessness.

"I love them," she said, watching him warily. "I didn't think you did."

He smiled. "I'll love my own, Callie," he said, his fingers contracting in hers. "Just as you'll love them."

"I'll love your kids?" she blurted out.

He couldn't quite meet her eyes. He stared down toward the big barn a few hundred yards behind the house and he linked his fingers tighter with hers. "Have you ever thought," he said huskily, "about making a baby with me?"

Her heart went right up into her throat. She flushed scarlet. But it wasn't embarrassment. It was pure, wild, joy.

He looked down at her then. Everything she thought, felt, was laid out there for him to see. He caught his breath at the depth of those emotions she didn't know he could see. It was more than he'd ever dared hope for.

"I want a baby, Callie," he whispered huskily. He framed her red face in his hands and bent to kiss her eyelids closed. His fingers were unsteady as he held her where he wanted her, while his mouth pressed tender, breathless little kisses all over her soft skin. "I want one so much. You'd make...the most wonderful little mother," he bit off, choked with emotion. "I could get up with you in the night, when the baby cried, and take turns walking the floor. We could join the PTA later. We could make memories that would last us forever, Callie—you and me and a little boy or a little girl."

She slid her arms tight under his and around him and held on for dear life, shaking with delighted surprise. He wasn't joking. He really meant it. Her eyes closed. She felt tears pouring down her cheeks.

He felt them against his thin silk shirt and he smiled as he reached in his pocket for a handkerchief. He drew her away from him and dabbed at the tears, bending to kiss away the traces. "We can build a big playground here," he continued, as if he hadn't said anything earthshaking. "Both of us were only kids. I think two or three would be nice. And Dad would love being a grandfather. He can stay with us and the kids will make him young again."

"I'd love that. I never dreamed you'd want to have a family or settle down. You said…"

He kissed the words back against her lips. "Freedom is only a word," he told her solemnly. "It stopped meaning anything to me when I knew that Lopez had you." The memory of that horror was suddenly on his face, undisguised. "I couldn't rest until I knew where you were. I planned an assault in a day that should have taken a week of preparation. And then I went in after you myself, because I couldn't trust anyone to do it but me." His hands clenched on her shoulders. "When I saw you like that, saw what that animal had done to you…" He stopped and swallowed hard. "My God, if he'd killed you, I'd have cut him to pieces! And then," he whispered, folding her close, shivering with the depth of his feelings, "I'd have picked you up in my arms and I'd have jumped off the balcony into the rocks with you. Because I wouldn't want to live in a world…that didn't hold us both. I couldn't live without you. Not anymore."

There was a faint mist in his black eyes. She could barely see it for the mist in her own. She choked on a sob as she looked up at him. "I love you," she whispered brokenly. "You're my whole life. I never dared to hope that you might care for me, too!"

He folded her against him and held her close, rocking her, his cheek on her dark hair as he counted his blessings. They overwhelmed him. She loved him. His eyes closed. It seemed that love could forgive anything, even his years of unkindness. "I wish I could take back every single hurtful thing I've ever done or said to you."

She smiled tearfully against his broad chest. "It's all right, Micah. Honest it is. Do you really want babies?" she asked dreamily, barely aware of anything he'd said.

"More than anything in the world!"

"I won't sleep with you unless you marry me," she said firmly.

He chuckled. "I'll marry you as soon as we can get a license. But," he added on a long sigh, drawing back, "I'm afraid it's too late for the sleeping together part."

Her thin eyebrows arched up. "What?"

He traced around her soft lips. "Callie, that erotic dream you had…" He actually flushed. "Well, it wasn't a dream," he added with a sheepish grin.

Her eyes widened endlessly. All those explicit things he'd done and said, that she'd done and said, that had seemed like something out of a fantasy. The fatigue, the spotting, the lack of a period, the…

"Oh my God, I'm pregnant!" she exclaimed in a high-pitched tone.

"Oh my God, yes, you are, you incredible woman!" he said with breathless delight. "I'm sorry, but I went to Lou Coltrain behind your back and begged her not to tell you until we came to an understanding. I was scared to death that you'd be off like a shot if you knew it too soon." He shook his head at her surprise. "I've never wanted anything as much as I want this child—except you," he added huskily. "I can't make it without you, Callie. I don't want to try." He glanced around them at the house and the stable. "This is where we start. You and me, a new business, a new life—in more ways than one," he added with a tender hand on her soft abdomen. "I know I'm something of a risk. But I'd never have made the offer to come here unless I'd been sure, very sure, that I could make it work. I want you more than I want the adventure and the freedom. I love you with all my heart. Is that enough?"

She smiled with her heart in her eyes. "It's enough," she said huskily.

He seemed to relax then, as if he'd been holding his breath the whole while. His eyes closed and he shivered. "Thank God," he said reverently.

"You didn't think I was going to say no?" she asked, shocked. "Good Lord, the sexiest man in town offers me a wedding ring and you think I'm going to say no?"

He pursed his lips. "Sexy, huh?"

"You seduced me," she pointed out. "Only a very sexy man could have managed that." She frowned. "Of course, you did drug me first," she added gleefully.

"You were hysterical," he began.

"I was in love," she countered, smiling. "And I wasn't all that sedated." She blushed. "But I did think it was a dream. You see, I'd had sort of the same dream since I was...well, since I was about sixteen."

His lips parted on a shocked breath. "That long?"

She nodded. "I couldn't even get interested in anybody else. But you didn't want me..."

"I did want you," he countered. "That's why I was horrible to you. But never again," he promised huskily. "Never again. I'm going to work very hard at being a good husband and father. You won't regret it, Callie. I swear you won't."

"I know that. You won't regret it, either," she promised. She placed her hand over his big one, that still lay gently against her stomach. "And I never guessed," she whispered, smiling secretly. Her eyes brimmed over with excitement. "I'm so happy," she told him brokenly. "And so scared. Babies don't come with instruction manuals."

"We have Lou Coltrain, who's much better than an instruction manual," he pointed out with a grin. "And speaking of Lou, did you get those vitamins she prescribed?"

"Well, not yet," she began.

"They're prenatal vitamins," he added, chuckling. "You're going to be amazed at how good you feel. Not to mention how lucky you are," he added blithely, "to have a husband who knows exactly what to expect all through your pregnancy." He kissed her softly. "After the baby comes, I might finish my residency and go into practice with the Coltrains," he added.

That meant real commitment, she realized. He was giving up every vestige of the old life for her. Well, almost. She knew he'd keep his hand in with Eb Scott's operation. But the last of

Jacobsville's mercenaries was ready to leave the past behind and start again.

So many beautiful memories are about to be created here, she thought as she looked around her from the shelter of Micah's hard arms. She pressed close with a sigh. "After the pain, the pleasure," she whispered.

"What was that?"

"Nothing. Just something I heard when I was younger." She didn't add that it was something her father had said. That was the one bridge she hadn't yet crossed. It would have to be faced. But, she thought, clinging to Micah in the warmth of the sun, not right now...

Micah drove her by the pharmacy on the way back to her apartment. He stood with her while Nancy, the dark-haired, dark-eyed pharmacist filled the prescription, trying not to grin too widely at the picture they made together.

"I suppose you know what these are for?" Nancy asked Callie.

Callie smiled and looked up at Micah, who smiled back with the same tenderness. "Oh, yes," she said softly.

He pulled her close for an instant, before he offered his credit card to pay for them. "We're getting married Sunday at the Methodist church," Micah told her and the others at the counter. "You're all invited...2:00 p.m. sharp."

Nancy's eyes twinkled. "We, uh, heard that from the minister already," she said, clearing her throat as Callie gaped at her.

Micah chuckled at Callie's expression. "You live in a small town, and you didn't think everybody would know already?"

"But you hadn't told me yet!" she accused.

He shrugged. "It didn't seem too smart to announce that I'd arranged a wedding that you hadn't even agreed to yet."

"And they say women keep secrets!" she said on a rough breath.

"Not half as good as men do, sweetheart," Micah told her gently. He glanced around at a sudden commotion behind them. The two remaining bachelor Hart brothers, Rey and Leo, were almost trampling people in their rush to get to the prescription counter.

"Have to have this as soon as possible, sorry!" Rey exclaimed, pressing a prescription into Nancy's hands with what looked like desperation.

"It's an emergency!" Leo seconded.

Nancy's eyes widened. She looked at the brothers with astonishment. "An emergency? This is a prescription for anti-inflammatories…"

"For our cook," Leo said. "Her hands hurt, she said. She can't make biscuits. We rushed her right over to Lou Coltrain and she said it was arthritis." He grimaced. "*Pleaaase* hurry? We didn't get any breakfast at all!"

Callie had her hand over her mouth trying not to have hysterics. Micah just looked puzzled. Apparently he didn't know about the famous biscuit mania.

Leo sounded as if he was starving. Amazing, a big, tall man with a frame like that attempting to look emaciated. Rey was tall and thin, and he did look as if he needed a feeding. There had been some talk about a new woman out at the ranch recently who was rather mysterious. But if they had a cook with arthritis, she surely wasn't a young cook.

Nancy went to fill the prescriptions.

"Sorry," Rey muttered as he glanced behind him and Leo at the people they'd rushed past to get their prescription filled.

He tried to smile. He wasn't really good at it. He cleared his throat self-consciously. "Chocolates," he reminded Leo.

"Right over there," Leo agreed somberly. "We'd better get two boxes. And some of that cream stuff for arthritis, and there's some sort of joint formula…"

"And the We're Sorry card," Rey added, mumbling something about shortsightedness and loose tongues as they stomped off down the aisle with two pairs of spurs jingling musically from the heels of their boots.

Nancy handed Micah the credit card receipt, which he signed and gave Callie a pert grin as she went back to work.

Callie followed Micah out the door, letting loose a barrage of laughter when they reached the Porsche. By the time they got to her apartment, he was laughing, too, at the town's most notorious biscuit eaters.

Jack Steele was overjoyed at the news they had for him. For the next week he perked up as never before, taking a new interest in life and looking forward to having a daughter-in-law and a grandchild. The news that he was going to live with them disturbed him, he thought they needed privacy, but they insisted. He gave in. There was no mistaking their genuine love for him, or their delight in his company. He felt like the richest man on earth.

Callie, meanwhile, had an unexpected phone call from her father, who was back in town and anxious to see her. She met him in Barbara's café on her lunch hour from the law office, curious and nervous after so many years away from him.

Her father had black hair with silver at his temples and dark blue eyes. He was somber, quiet, unassuming and guilt was written all over him.

After they'd both ordered salads and drinks, her father gave her a long, hesitant scrutiny.

"You look so much like my mother," he said unexpectedly. "She had the same shaped eyes you do, and the same color."

Callie looked down at her salad. "Do I?"

He laid down his fork and leaned forward on his elbows. "I've been an idiot. How do I apologize for years of neglect, for letting you be put through hell in foster homes?" he asked quietly. "When I knew what had happened to you, I was too ashamed even to phone. Your mother had only just told me the truth and after the private detective I hired gave me the file on you, I couldn't take it. I went to Europe and stayed for a month. I don't even remember what I did there." He grimaced at Callie's expression. "I'm so ashamed. Even if you hadn't been my biological child, you'd lived in my house, I'd loved you, protected you." He lowered his shamed eyes to his plate. "Pride. It was nothing but pride. I couldn't bear thinking that you were another man's child. You paid for my cruelty, all those years." He drew in a long breath and looked up at her sadly. "You're my daughter. But I don't deserve you." He made an awkward motion. "So if you don't want to have anything to do with me, that's all right. I'll understand. I've been a dead bust as a father."

She could see the torment in his eyes. Her mother had done something unspeakably cruel to both of them with her lies. The bond they'd formed had been broken, tragically. She remembered the loneliness of her childhood, the misery of belonging nowhere. But now she had Micah and a child on the way, and Jack Steele, as well. She'd landed on her feet, grown strong, learned to cope with life. She'd even fought off drug dealing thugs, all by herself, that night in Nassau when her child had been conceived. She felt so mature now, so capable. She smiled slowly. She'd lectured Micah about forgiveness. Here was her best chance to prove that she believed her own words.

"You're going to be a grandfather," she said simply. "Micah and I are getting married Sunday afternoon at two o'clock in the Methodist church. You and Jack Steele could both give me away if you like." She grinned. "It will raise eyebrows everywhere!"

He seemed shocked. His blue eyes misted and he bit his lip. "A grandfather." He laughed self-consciously and looked away long enough to brush away something that looked suspiciously wet. "I like that." He glanced back at her. "Yes. I'd like to give you away. I'd like to get you back even more, Callie. I'm... sorry."

When he choked up like that, she was beyond touched. She got up from her seat and went around to hug him to her. The café was crowded and she didn't care. She held him close and laid her cheek on his hair, feeling his shoulders shake. It was, in so many ways, one of the most poignant experiences of her young life.

"It's okay, Papa," she whispered, having called him that when she was barely school age. "It's okay now."

He held her tighter and he didn't give a damn that he was crying and half of Jacobsville could see him. He had his daughter back, against all the odds.

Callie felt like that, too. She met Barbara's eyes over the counter and smiled through her tears. Barbara nodded, and smiled, and reached for a napkin. It was so much like a new start.

Everything was fresh and sweet and life was blessed. She was never again going to take anything for granted as long as she lived!

The wedding was an event. Callie had an imported gown from Paris, despite the rush to get it in time. Micah wore a morning coat. All the local mercenaries and the gang from the island, including Bojo, Peter, Rodrigo and Mac were there, along with Pogo and Maddie. And, really, Callie thought, Maddie did resemble her, but the older woman was much more athletic and oddly pretty. She smiled broadly at Callie as she stood beside a man Callie didn't recognize, with jet-black hair and eyes and what was obviously a prosthetic arm. There were a lot of men she didn't know. Probably Micah had contacts everywhere, and when word of the marriage had gotten out, they all came running to see if the rumors were true. Some of them looked astonished, but most were grinning widely.

The ceremony was brief, but beautiful. Micah pulled up the veil Callie wore, and kissed her for the first time as his wife.

"When we're finished, you have to read the inscription in your wedding band," he whispered against her soft mouth.

"Don't make me wait," she teased. "What does it say?"

He clasped her hand to his chest, ignoring the glowing faces of the audience. "It says 'forever,' Callie. And it means forever. I'll love you until I close my eyes for the last time. And even afterward, I'll love you."

She cried as he kissed her. It was the most beautiful thing he'd ever said to her. She whispered the words back to him, under her breath, while a soft sound rippled through the church. The couple at the rose-decked altar were so much in love that they fairly glowed with it.

They walked out under a cloud of rose petals and rice and Callie stopped and threw her bouquet as they reached the limousine that would take them to the airport. They were flying to Scotland for their honeymoon, to a little thatched cottage that belonged to Mac and had been loaned to them for the occasion. A romantic gesture from a practical and very unromantic man, that had touched Callie greatly.

Jack Steele, who was staying at the ranch with Micah's new foreman and his wife, waved them off with tears in his eyes, standing next to Kane Kirby, who was doing the same. The two men had become friends already, both avid poker players and old war movie fanatics.

A flustered blond Janie Brewster had caught the bouquet that Callie threw, and she looked down at it as if she didn't quite know what to do next. Nearby, the whole Hart family was watching, married brothers Corrigan and Simon and Cag, and the bachelor boys, Rey and Leo. It was Leo who was giving Janie an odd look, but she didn't see it. She laughed nervously and quickly handed the bouquet to old Mrs. Smith, Callie's neighbor. Then she ducked into the crowd and vanished, to Callie's amusement.

"The last mercenary," she whispered. "And you didn't get away, after all."

"Not the last," he murmured, glancing toward his old comrades and Peter, their newest member, all of whom were silently easing away toward the parking lot. He smiled down at her. "But the happiest," he added, bending to kiss her. "Wave bye at both our papas and let's go. I can't wait to get you alone, Mrs. Steele!"

She chuckled and blushed prettily. "That makes two of us!"

She waved and climbed into the car with her acres of silk and lace and waited for Micah to pile in beside her. The door closed. The car drove away to the excited cries of good luck that followed it. Inside, two newlyweds were wrapped up close in each others' arms, oblivious to everything else. Micah cradled Callie in his arms and thanked God for second chances. He recalled Callie's soft words: After the pain, the pleasure. He closed his eyes and sighed. The pleasure had just begun.

* * * * *

MATT CALDWELL: TEXAS TYCOON

1

The man on the hill sat on his horse with elegance and grace, and the young woman found herself staring at him. He was obviously overseeing the roundup, which the man at her side had brought her to view. This ranch was small by Texas standards, but around Jacobsville, it was big enough to put its owner in the top ten in size.

"Dusty, isn't it?" Ed Caldwell asked with a chuckle, oblivious to the distant mounted rider, who was behind him and out of his line of sight. "I'm glad I work for the corporation and not here. I like my air cool and unpolluted."

Leslie Murry smiled. She wasn't pretty. She had a plain, rather ordinary sort of face with blond hair that had a natural wave, and gray eyes. Her one good feature besides her slender figure was a pretty bow mouth. She had a quiet, almost reclusive demeanor these days. But she hadn't always been like that. In her early teens, Leslie had been flamboyant and outgoing, a live wire of a girl whose friends had laughed at her exploits. Now, at twenty-three, she was as sedate as a matron. The change in her was shocking to people who'd once known her. She knew Ed Caldwell from college in Houston. He'd graduated in her sophomore year, and she'd quit the following semester to go to work as a paralegal for his father's law firm in Houston. Things had gotten too complicated there, and Ed had come to the rescue once again. In fact, Ed was the reason she'd just been hired as an executive assistant by the mammoth Caldwell firm. His cousin owned it.

She'd never met Mather Gilbert Caldwell, or Matt as he was known locally. People said he was a nice, easygoing man who loved an underdog. In fact, Ed said it frequently himself. They were down here for roundup so that Ed could introduce Leslie to the head of the corporation. But so far, all they'd seen was dust and cattle and hardworking cowboys.

"Wait here," Ed said. "I'm going to ride over and find Matt. Be right back." He urged his horse into a trot and held on for dear life. Leslie had to bite her lip to conceal a smile at the way he rode. It was painfully obvious that he was much more at home behind the wheel of a car. But she wouldn't have been so rude as to have mentioned it, because Ed was the only friend she had these days. He was, in fact, the only person around who knew about her past.

While she was watching him, the man on horseback on the hill behind them was watching her. She sat on a horse with style, and she had a figure that would have attracted a connoisseur of women—which the man on horseback was. Impulsively he spurred his horse into a gallop and came down the rise behind her. She didn't hear him until he reined in and the harsh sound of the horse snorting had her whirling in the saddle.

The man was wearing working clothes, like the other

cowboys, but all comparisons ended there. He wasn't ragged or missing a tooth or unshaven. He was oddly intimidating, even in the way he sat the horse, with one hand on the reins and the other on his powerful denim-clad thigh.

Matt Caldwell met her gray eyes with his dark ones and noted that she wasn't the beauty he'd expected, despite her elegance of carriage and that perfect figure. "Ed brought you, I gather," he said curtly.

She'd almost guessed from his appearance that his voice would be deep and gravelly, but not that it would cut like a knife. Her hands tightened on the reins. "I…yes, he…he brought me."

The stammer was unexpected. Ed's usual sort of girl was brash and brassy, much more sophisticated than this shrinking violet here. He liked to show off Matt's ranch and impress the girls. Usually it didn't bother Matt, but he'd had a frustrating day and he was out of humor. He scowled. "Interested in cattle ranching, are you?" he drawled with ice dripping from every syllable. "We could always get you a rope and let you try your hand, if you'd like."

She felt as if every muscle in her body had gone taut. "I… came to meet Ed's cousin," she managed. "He's rich." The man's dark eyes flashed and she flushed. She couldn't believe she'd made such a remark to a stranger. "I mean," she corrected, "he owns the company where Ed works. Where I work," she added. She could have bitten her tongue for her artless mangling of a straightforward subject, but the man rattled her.

Something kindled in the man's dark eyes under the jutting brow; something not very nice at all. He leaned forward and his eyes narrowed. "Why are you really out here with Ed?" he asked.

She swallowed. He had her hypnotized, like a cobra with a rabbit. Those eyes...those very dark, unyielding eyes...!

"It's not your business, is it?" she asked finally, furious at her lack of cohesive thought and this man's assumption that he had the right to interrogate her.

He didn't say a word. Instead, he just looked at her.

"Please," she bit off, hunching her shoulders uncomfortably. "You're making me nervous!"

"You came to meet the boss, didn't you?" he asked in a velvety smooth tone. "Didn't anyone tell you that he's no marshmallow?"

She swallowed. "They say he's a very nice, pleasant man," she returned a little belligerently. "Something I'll bet nobody in his right mind would dream of saying about you!" she added with her first burst of spirit in years.

His eyebrows lifted. "How do you know I'm not nice and pleasant?" he asked, chuckling suddenly.

"You're like a cobra," she said uneasily.

He studied her for a few seconds before he nudged his horse in the side with a huge dusty boot and eased so close to her that she actually shivered. He hadn't been impressed with the young woman who stammered and stuttered with nerves, but a spirited woman was a totally new proposition. He liked a woman who wasn't intimidated by his bad mood.

His hand went across her hip to catch the back of her saddle and he looked into her eyes from an unnervingly close distance. "If I'm a cobra, then what does that make you, cupcake?" he drawled with deliberate sensuality, so close that she caught the faint smoky scent of his breath, the hint of spicy cologne that clung to his lean, tanned face. "A soft, furry little bunny?"

She was so shaken by the proximity of him that she tried desperately to get away, pulling so hard on the reins that her mount unexpectedly reared and she went down on the ground, hard, hitting her injured left hip and her shoulder as she fell into the thick grass.

A shocked sound came from the man, who vaulted out of the saddle and was beside her as she tried to sit up. He reached for her a little roughly, shaken by her panic. Women didn't usually try to back away from him; especially ordinary ones like this. She fell far short of his usual companions.

She fought his hands, her eyes huge and overly bright, panic in the very air around her. "No...!" she cried out helplessly.

He froze in place, withdrawing his lean hand from her arm, and stared at her with scowling curiosity.

"Leslie!" came a shout from a few yards away. Ed bounced up as quickly as he could manage it without being unseated. He fumbled his way off the horse and knelt beside her, holding out his arm so that she could catch it and pull herself up.

"I'm sorry," she said, refusing to look at the man who was responsible for her tumble. "I jerked the reins. I didn't mean to."

"Are you all right?" Ed asked, concerned.

She nodded. "Sure." But she was shaking, and both men could see it.

Ed glanced over her head at the taller, darker, leaner man who stood with his horse's reins in his hand, staring at the girl.

"Uh, have you two introduced yourselves?" he asked awkwardly.

Matt was torn by conflicting emotions, the strongest of which was bridled fury at the woman's panicky attitude. She acted as if he had plans to assault her, when he'd only been trying to help her up. He was angry and it cost him his temper. "The next time you bring a certifiable lunatic to my ranch, give me some advance warning," the tall man sniped at Ed. He moved as curtly as he spoke, swinging abruptly into the saddle to glare down at them. "You'd better take her home," he told Ed. "She's a damned walking liability around animals."

"But she rides very well, usually," Ed protested. "Okay, then," he added when the other man glowered at him. He forced a smile. "I'll see you later."

The tall man jerked his hat down over his eyes, wheeled the horse without another word and rode back up on the rise where he'd been sitting earlier.

"Whew!" Ed laughed, sweeping back his light brown hair uneasily. "I haven't seen him in a mood like that for years. I can't imagine what set him off. He's usually the soul of courtesy, especially when someone's hurt."

Leslie brushed off her jeans and looked up at her friend morosely. "He rode right up to me," she said unsteadily, "and leaned across me to talk with a hand on the saddle. I just...panicked. I'm sorry. I guess he's some sort of foreman here. I hope you don't get in trouble with your cousin because of it."

"That *was* my cousin, Leslie," he said heavily.

She stared at him vacantly. "That was Matt Caldwell?"

He nodded.

She let out a long breath. "Oh, boy. What a nice way to start a new job, by alienating the man at the head of the whole food chain."

"He doesn't know about you," he began.

Her eyes flashed. "And you're not to tell him," she returned firmly. "I mean it! I will not have my past paraded out again. I came down here to get away from reporters and movie producers, and that's what I'm going to do. I've had my hair cut, bought new clothes, gotten contact lenses. I've done everything I can think of so I won't be recognized. I'm not going to have it all dragged up again. It's been six years," she added miserably. "Why can't people just leave it alone?"

"The newsman was just following a lead," he said gently. "One of the men who attacked you was arrested for drunk driving and someone connected the name to your mother's case. His father is some high city official in Houston. It was inevitable that the press would dig up his son's involvement in your mother's case in an election year."

"Yes, I know, and that's what prompted the producer to think it would make a great TV movie of the week." She ground her teeth together. "That's just what we all need. And I thought it was all over. How silly of me," she said in a defeated tone. "I wish I were rich and famous," she added. "Then maybe I could buy myself some peace and privacy." She glanced up where the tall man sat silently watching the herding below. "I made some stupid remarks to your cousin, too, not knowing who he really was. I guess he'll be down in personnel first thing Monday to have me fired."

"Over my dead body," he said. "I may be only a lowly cousin, but I do own stock in the corporation. If he fires you, I'll fight for you."

"Would you really, for me?" she asked solemnly.

He ruffled her short blond hair. "You're my pal," he said. "I've had a pretty bad blow of my own. I don't want to get serious about anybody ever again. But I like having you around."

She smiled sadly. "I'm glad you can act that way about me. I can't really bear to be…" She swallowed. "I don't like men close to me, in any physical way. The therapist said I might be able to change that someday, with the right man. I don't know. It's been so long…"

"Don't sit and worry," he said. "Come on. I'll take you back to town and buy you a nice vanilla ice-cream cone. How's that?"

She smiled at him. "Thanks, Ed."

He shrugged. "Just another example of my sterling character." He glanced up toward the rise and away again. "He's just not himself today," he said. "Let's go."

Matt Caldwell watched his visitors bounce away on their respective horses with a resentment and fury he hadn't experienced in years. The little blond icicle had made him feel like a lecher. As if she could have appealed to him, a man who had movie stars chasing after him! He let out a rough sigh and pulled a much-used cigar from his pocket and stuck it in his teeth. He didn't light it. He was trying to give up the bad habit, but it was slow going. This cigar had been just recently the target of his secretary's newest weapon in her campaign to save him from nicotine. The end was still damp, in fact, despite the fact that he'd only arrived here from his office in town about an hour ago. He took it out of his mouth with a sigh, eyed it sadly and put it away. He'd threatened to fire her and she'd threatened to quit. She was a nice woman, married with two cute little kids. He couldn't let her leave him. Better the cigar than good help, he decided.

He let his eyes turn again toward the couple growing smaller in the distance. What an odd girlfriend Ed had latched onto this time. Of course, she'd let Ed touch her. She'd flinched away from Matt as if he was contagious. The more he thought about it, the madder he got. He turned his horse toward the bawling cattle in the distance. Working might take the edge off his temper.

Ed took Leslie to her small apartment at a local boarding-house and left her at the front door with an apology.

"You don't think he'll fire me?" she asked in a plaintive tone.

He shook his head. "No," he assured her. "I've already told you that I won't let him. Now stop worrying. Okay?"

She managed a smile. "Thanks again, Ed."

He shrugged. "No problem. See you Monday."

She watched him get into his sports car and roar away before she went inside to her lonely room at the top corner of the house, facing the street. She'd made an enemy today, without meaning to. She hoped it wasn't going to adversely affect her life. There was no going back now.

Monday morning, Leslie was at her desk five minutes early in an attempt to make a good impression. She liked Connie and Jackie, the other two women who shared administrative duties for the vice president of marketing and research. Leslie's job was more routine. She kept up with the various shipments of cattle from one location to another, and maintained the herd records. It was exacting, but she had a head for figures and she enjoyed it.

Her immediate boss was Ed, so it was really a peachy job. They had an entire building in downtown Jacobsville, a beautiful old Victorian mansion, which Matt had painstakingly renovated to use as his corporation's headquarters. There were two floors of offices, and a canteen for coffee breaks where the kitchen and dining room once had been.

Matt wasn't in his office much of the time. He did a lot of traveling, because aside from his business interests, he sat on boards of directors of other businesses and even on the board of trustees of at least one college. He had business meetings in all sorts of places. Once he'd even gone to South America to see about investing in a growing cattle market there, but he'd come home angry and disillusioned when he saw the slash and burn method of pasture creation that had already killed a substantial portion of rain forest. He wanted no part of that, so he turned to Australia instead and bought another huge ranching tract in the Northern Territory there.

Ed told her about these fascinating exploits, and Leslie listened with her eyes wide. It was a world she'd never known. She and her mother, at the best of times, had been poor before the tragedy that separated them. Now, even with Leslie's job and the good salary she made, it still meant budgeting to the bone so that she could afford even a taxi to work and pay rent on the small apartment where she lived. There wasn't much left over for travel. She envied Matt being able to get on a plane— his own private jet, in fact—and go anywhere in the world he liked. It was a glimpse inside a world she'd never know.

"I guess he goes out a lot," she murmured once when Ed had told her that his cousin was away in New York for a cattlemen's banquet.

"With women?" Ed chuckled. "He beats them off with a stick. Matt's one of the most hunted bachelors in south Texas, but he never seems to get serious about any one woman. They're just accessories to him, pretty things to take on the town. You know," he added with a faint smile, "I don't think he really likes women very much. He was kind to a couple of local girls who needed a shoulder to cry on, but that was as far as it went, and they weren't the sort of women to chase him. He's like this because he had a rough time as a child."

"How?" she asked.

"His mother gave him away when he was six."

Her intake of breath was audible. "Why?"

"She had a new boyfriend who didn't like kids," he said bluntly. "He wouldn't take Matt, so she gave him to my dad. He was raised with me. That's why we're so close."

"What about his father?" she asked.

"We...don't talk about his father."

"Ed!"

He grimaced. "This can't go any further," he said.

"Okay."

"We don't think his mother knew who his father was," he confided. "There were so many men in her life around that time."

"But her husband..."

"What husband?" he asked.

She averted her eyes. "Sorry. I assumed that she was married."

"Not Beth," he mused. "She didn't want ties. She didn't want Matt, but her parents had a screaming fit when she mentioned an abortion. They wanted him terribly, planned for him, made room for him in their house, took Beth and him in the minute he was born."

"But you said your father raised him."

"Matt has had a pretty bad break all around. Our grandparents were killed in a car wreck, and then just a few months later, their house burned down," he added. "There was some gossip that it was intentional to collect on insurance, but nothing was ever proven. Matt was outside with Beth, in the yard, early that morning when it happened. She'd taken him out to see the roses, a pretty strange and unusual thing for her. Lucky for Matt, though, because he'd have been in the house, and would have died. The insurance settlement was enough for Beth to treat herself to some new clothes and a car. She left Matt with my dad and took off with the first man who came along." His eyes were full of remembered outrage on Matt's behalf. "Grandfather left a few shares of stock in a ranch to him, along with a small trust that couldn't be touched until Matt was twenty-one. That's the only thing that kept Beth from getting her hands on it. When he inherited it, he seemed to have an instinct for making money. He never looked back."

"What happened to his mother?" she asked.

"We heard that she died a few years ago. Matt never speaks of her."

"Poor little boy," she said aloud.

"Don't make that mistake," he said at once. "Matt doesn't need pity."

"I guess not. But it's a shame that he had to grow up so alone."

"You'd know about that."

She smiled sadly. "I guess so. My dad died years ago. Mama supported us the best way she could. She wasn't very intelligent, but she was pretty. She used what she had." Her eyes were briefly haunted. "I haven't gotten over what she did. Isn't it horrible, that in a few seconds you can destroy your own life and several other peoples' like that? And what was it all for?

Jealousy, when there wasn't even a reason for it. He didn't care about me—he just wanted to have a good time with an innocent girl, him and his drunk friends." She shivered at the memory. "Mama thought she loved him. But that jealous rage didn't get him back. He died."

"I agree that she shouldn't have shot him, but it's hard to defend what he and his friends were doing to you at the time, Leslie."

She nodded. "I know," she said simply. "Sometimes kids get the short end of the stick, and it's up to them to do better with their future."

All the same, she wished that she'd had a normal upbringing, like so many other kids had.

After their conversation, she felt sorry for Matt Caldwell and wished that they'd started off better. She shouldn't have overreacted. But it was curious that he'd been so offensive to her, when Ed said that he was the soul of courtesy around women. Perhaps he'd just had a bad day.

Later in the week, Matt was back, and Leslie began to realize how much trouble she'd landed herself in from their first encounter.

He walked into Ed's office while Ed was out at a meeting, and the ice in his eyes didn't begin to melt as he watched Leslie typing away at the computer. She hadn't seen him, and he studied her with profound, if prejudiced, curiosity. She was thin and not much above average height, with short blond hair that curled toward her face. Nice skin, but she was much too pale. He remembered her eyes most of all, wide and full of distaste as he came close. It amazed him that there was a woman on the planet who could find his money repulsive, even if he didn't appeal to her himself. It was new and unpleasant to discover a woman who didn't want him. He'd never been repulsed by a woman in his life. It left him feeling inadequate. Worse, it brought back memories of the woman who'd rejected him, who'd given him away at the age of six because she didn't want him.

She felt his eyes on her and lifted her head. Gray eyes widened and stared as her hands remained suspended just over the black keyboard.

He was wearing a vested gray suit. It looked very expensive, and his eyes were dark and cutting. He had a cigar in his hand, but it wasn't lit. She hoped he wasn't going to try to smoke it in the confined space, because she was allergic to tobacco smoke.

"So you're Ed's," he murmured in that deep, cutting tone.

"Ed's assistant," she agreed. "Mr. Caldwell..."

"What did you do to land the job?" he continued with a faintly mocking smile. "And how often?"

She wasn't getting what he implied. She blinked, still staring. "I beg your pardon?"

"Why did Ed bring you in here above ten other more qualified applicants?" he persisted.

"Oh, that." She hesitated. She couldn't tell him the real reason, so she told him enough of the truth to distract him. "I have the equivalent of an associate in arts degree in business and I worked as a paralegal for his father for four years in a law office," she said. "I might not have the bachelor's degree that was preferred, but I have experience. Or so Ed assured me," she added, looking worried.

"Why didn't you finish college?" he persisted.

She swallowed. "I had...some personal problems at the time."

"You still have some personal problems, Miss Murry," he replied lazily, but his eyes were cold and alert in a lean, hard face. "You can put me at the top of the list. I had other plans for the position you're holding. So you'd better be as good as Ed says you are."

"I'll give value for money, Mr. Caldwell," she assured him. "I work for my living. I don't expect free rides."

"Don't you?"

"No, I don't."

He lifted the cigar to his mouth, looked at the wet tip, sighed and slipped it back down to dangle, unlit in his fingers.

"Do you smoke?" she asked, having noted the action.

"I try to," he murmured.

Just as he spoke, a handsome woman in her forties with blond hair in a neat bun and wearing a navy-and-white suit, walked down the hall toward him.

He glared at her as she paused in the open door of Ed's office. "I need you to sign these, Mr. Caldwell. And Mr. Bailey is waiting in your office to speak to you about that committee you want him on."

"Thanks, Edna."

Edna Jones smiled. "Good day, Miss Murry. Keeping busy, are you?"

"Yes, ma'am, thank you," Leslie replied with a genuine smile.

"Don't let him light that thing," Edna continued, gesturing toward the cigar dangling in Matt's fingers. "If you need one of these—" she held up a small water pistol "—I'll see that you get one." She smiled at a fuming Matt. "You'll be glad to know that

I've already passed them out to the girls in the other executive offices, Mr. Caldwell. You can count on all of us to help you quit smoking."

Matt glared at her. She chuckled like a woman twenty years younger, waved to Leslie, and stalked off back to the office. Matt actually started to make a comical lunge after her, but caught himself in time. It wouldn't do to show weakness to the enemy.

He gave Leslie a cool glance, ignoring the faint amusement in her gray eyes. With a curt nod, he followed Edna down the hall, the damp, expensive cigar still dangling from his lean fingers.

2

From her first day on the job, Leslie was aware of Matt's dislike and disapproval of her. He piled the work on Ed, so that it would inevitably drift down to Leslie. A lot of it was really unnecessary, like having her type up old herd records from ten years ago, which had never been converted to computer files. He said it was so that he could check progress on the progeny of his earlier herd sires, but even Ed muttered when Leslie showed him what she was expected to do.

"We have secretaries to do this sort of thing," Ed grumbled as he stared at the yellowed pages on her desk. "I need you for other projects."

"Tell him," Leslie suggested.

He shook his head. "Not in the mood he's been in lately," he said with a rueful smile. "He isn't himself."

"Did you know that his secretary is armed?" she asked suddenly. "She carries a water pistol around with her."

Ed chuckled. "Matt asked her to help him stop smoking cigars. Not that he usually did it inside the building," he was quick to add. "But Mrs. Jones feels that if you can't light a cigar, you can't smoke it. She bought a water pistol for herself and armed the other secretaries, too. If Matt even lifts a cigar to his mouth in the executive offices, they shoot him."

"Dangerous ladies," she commented.

"You bet. I've seen..."

"Nothing to do?" purred a soft, deep voice from behind Ed. The piercing dark eyes didn't match the bantering tone.

"Sorry, Matt," Ed said immediately. "I was just passing the time of day with Leslie. Can I do anything for you?"

"I need an update on that lot of cattle we placed with Ballenger," he said. He stared at Leslie with narrowed eyes. "Your job, I believe?"

She swallowed and nodded, jerking her fingers on the keyboard so that she opened the wrong file and had to push the right buttons to close it again. Normally she wasn't a nervous person, but he made her ill at ease, standing over her without speaking. Ed seemed to be a little twitchy, himself, because he moved back to his own office the minute the phone rang, placing himself out of the line of fire with an apologetic look that Leslie didn't see.

"I thought you were experienced with computers," Matt drawled mockingly as he paused beside her to look over her shoulder.

The feel of his powerful body so close behind her made every muscle tense. Her fingers froze on the keyboard, and she was barely breathing.

With a murmured curse, Matt stepped back to the side of the desk, fighting the most intense emotions he'd ever felt. He stuck his hands deep into the pockets of his slacks and glared at her.

She relaxed, but only enough to be able to pull up the file he wanted and print it for him.

He took it out of the printer tray when it was finished and gave it a slow perusal. He muttered something, and tossed the first page down on Leslie's desk.

"Half these words are misspelled," he said curtly.

She looked at it on the computer screen and nodded. "Yes, they are, Mr. Caldwell. I'm sorry, but I didn't type it."

Of course she hadn't typed it, it was ten years old, but something inside him wanted to hold her accountable for it.

He moved away from the desk as he read the rest of the pages. "You can do this file—and the others—over," he murmured as he skimmed. "The whole damned thing's illiterate."

She knew that there were hundreds of records in this particular batch of files, and that it would take days, not minutes or hours, to complete the work. But he owned the place, so he could set the rules. She pursed her lips and glanced at him speculatively. Now that he was physically out of range, she felt safe again. "Your wish is my command, boss," she murmured dryly, surprising a quick glance from him. "Shall I just put aside all of Ed's typing and devote the next few months to this?"

Her change of attitude from nervous kid to sassy woman caught him off guard. "I didn't put a time limit on it," Matt said curtly. "I only said, do it!"

"Oh, yes, sir," she agreed at once, and smiled vacantly.

He drew in a short breath and glared down at her. "You're remarkably eager to please, Miss Murry. Or is it just because I'm the boss?"

"I always try to do what I'm asked to do, Mr. Caldwell," she assured him. "Well, almost always," she amended. "Within reason."

He moved back toward the desk. As he leaned over to put down the papers she'd printed for him, he saw her visibly tense. She was the most confounding woman he'd ever known, a total mystery.

"What would you define as 'within reason'?" he drawled, holding her eyes.

She looked hunted. Amazing, that she'd been jovial and uninhibited just seconds before. Her stiff expression made him feel oddly guilty. He turned away. "Ed! Have you got my Angus file?" he called to his cousin through the open door to Ed's private office.

Ed was off the phone and he had a file folder in his hands. "Yes, sorry. I wanted to check the latest growth figures and projected weight gain ratios. I meant to put it back on your desk and I got busy."

Matt studied the figures quietly and then nodded. "That's acceptable. The Ballenger brothers do a good job."

"They're expanding, did you know?" Ed chuckled. "Nice to see them prospering."

"Yes, it is. They've worked hard enough in their lives to warrant a little prosperity."

While he spoke, Leslie was watching him covertly. She thought about the six-year-old boy whose mother had given him away, and it wrung her heart. Her own childhood had been no picnic, but Matt's upbringing had been so much worse.

He felt those soft gray eyes on his face, and his own gaze jerked down to meet them. She flushed and looked away.

He wondered what she'd been thinking to produce such a reaction. She couldn't have possibly made it plainer that she felt no physical attraction to him, so why the wide-eyed stare? It puzzled him. So many things about her puzzled him. She was neat and attractively dressed, but those clothes would have suited a dowager far better than a young woman. While he didn't encourage short skirts and low-cut blouses, Leslie was covered from head to toe; long dress, long sleeves, high neck buttoned right up to her throat.

"Need anything else?" Ed asked abruptly, hoping to ward off more trouble.

Matt's powerful shoulders shrugged. "Not for the moment." He glanced once more at Leslie. "Don't forget those files I want updated."

After he walked out, Ed stared after him for a minute, frowning. "What files?"

She explained it to him.

"But those are outdated," Ed murmured thoughtfully. "And he never looks at them. I don't understand why he has to have them corrected at all."

She leaned forward. "Because it will irritate me and make me work harder!" she said in a stage whisper. "God forbid that I should have time to twiddle my thumbs."

His eyebrows arched. "He isn't vindictive."

"That's what you think." She picked up the file Matt had left and grimaced as she put it back in the filing cabinet. "I'll start on those when I've finished answering your mail. Do you suppose he wants me to stay over after work to do them? He'd have to pay me overtime." She grinned impishly, a reminder of the woman she'd once been. "Wouldn't that make his day?"

"Let me ask him," Ed volunteered. "Just do your usual job for now."

"Okay. Thanks, Ed."

He shrugged. "What are friends for?" he murmured with a smile.

The office was a great place to work. Leslie had a ball watching the other women in the executive offices lie in wait for Matt. His secretary caught him trying to light a cigar out on the balcony, and she let him have it from behind a potted tree with the water pistol. He laid the cigar down on Bessie David's desk and she "accidentally" dropped it into his half-full coffee cup that he'd set down next to it. He held it up, dripping, with an accusing look at Bessie.

"You told me to do it, sir," Bessie reminded him.

He dropped the sodden cigar back in the coffee and left it behind. Leslie, having seen the whole thing, ducked into the rest room to laugh. It amazed her that Matt was so easygoing and friendly to his other employees. To Leslie, he was all bristle and venom. She wondered what he'd do if she let loose with a water pistol. She chuckled, imagining herself tearing up Main Street in Jacobsville ahead of a cursing Matt Caldwell. It was such a pity that she'd changed so much. Before tragedy had touched her young life, she would have been very attracted to the tall, lean cattleman.

A few days later, he came into Ed's office dangling a cigar from his fingers. Leslie, despite her amusement at the antics of the other secretaries, didn't say a word at the sight of the unlit cigar.

"I want to see the proposal the Cattlemen's Association drafted about brucellosis testing."

She stared at him. "Sir?"

He stared back. She was getting easier on his eyes, and he

didn't like his reactions to her. She was repulsed by him. He couldn't get past that because it destroyed his pride. "Ed told me he had a copy of it," he elaborated. "It came in the mail yesterday."

"Okay." She knew where the mail was kept. Ed tried to ignore it, leaving it in the In box until Leslie dumped it on his desk in front of him and refused to leave until he dealt with it. This usually happened at the end of the week, when it had piled up and overflowed into the out-box.

She rummaged through the box and produced a thick letter from the Cattlemen's Association, unopened. She carried it back through and handed it to Matt.

He'd been watching her walk with curious intensity. She was limping. He couldn't see her legs, because she was wearing loose knit slacks with a tunic that flowed to her thighs as she walked. Very obviously, she wasn't going to do anything to call attention to her figure.

"You're limping," he said. "Did you see a doctor after that fall you took at my ranch?"

"No need to," she said at once. "It was only a bruise. I'm sore, that's all."

He picked up the receiver of the phone on her desk and pressed the intercom button. "Edna," he said abruptly, "set Miss Murry up with Lou Coltrain as soon as possible. She took a spill from a horse at my place a few days ago and she's still limping. I want her x-rayed."

"No!" Leslie protested.

"Let her know when you've made the appointment. Thanks," he told his secretary and hung up. His dark eyes met Leslie's pale ones squarely. "You're going," he said flatly.

She hated doctors. Oh, how she hated them! The doctor at the emergency room in Houston, an older man retired from regular practice, had made her feel cheap and dirty as he examined her and made cold remarks about tramps who got men killed. She'd never gotten over the double trauma of her experience and that harsh lecture, despite the therapists' attempts to soften the memory.

She clenched her teeth and glared at Matt. "I said I'm not hurt!"

"You work here. I'm the boss. You get examined. Period."

She wanted to quit. She wished she could. She had no place else to go. Houston was out of the question. She was too afraid that she'd be up to her ears in reporters, despite her physical camouflage, the minute she set foot in the city.

She drew a sharp, angry breath.

Her attitude puzzled him. "Don't you want to make sure the injury won't make that limp permanent?" he asked suddenly.

She lifted her chin proudly. "Mr. Caldwell, I had an... accident...when I was seventeen and that leg suffered some bone damage." She refused to think about how it had happened. "I'll always have a slight limp, and it's not from the horse throwing me."

He didn't seem to breathe for several seconds. "All the more reason for an examination," he replied. "You like to live dangerously, I gather. You've got no business on a horse."

"Ed said the horse was gentle. It was my fault I got thrown. I jerked the reins."

His eyes narrowed. "Yes, I remember. You were trying to get away from me. Apparently you think I have something contagious."

She could see the pride in his eyes that made him resent her. "It wasn't that," she said. She averted her gaze to the wall. "It's just that I don't like to be touched."

"Ed touches you."

She didn't know how to tell him without telling him everything. She couldn't bear having him know about her sordid past. She raised turbulent gray eyes to his dark ones. "I don't like to be touched by strangers," she amended quickly. "Ed and I have known each other for years," she said finally. "It's...different with him."

His eyes narrowed. He searched over her thin face. "It must be," he said flatly.

His mocking smile touched a nerve. "You're like a steamroller, aren't you?" she asked abruptly. "You assume that because you're wealthy and powerful, there isn't a woman alive who can resist you!"

He didn't like that assumption. His eyes began to glitter. "You shouldn't listen to gossip," he said, his voice deadly quiet. "She was a spoiled little debutante who thought Daddy should be able to buy her any man she wanted. When she discovered that he couldn't, she came to work for a friend of mine and spent a couple of weeks pursuing me around Jacobsville. I went home one night and found her piled up in my bed wearing a sheet and nothing else. I threw her out, but then she told everyone that I'd assaulted her. She had a field day with me in court until my housekeeper, Tolbert, was called to tell the truth about what happened. The fact that she lost the case should tell you what the jury thought of her accusations."

"The jury?" she asked huskily. Besides his problems with his mother, she hadn't known about any incident in his past that might predispose him even further to distrusting women.

His thin lips drew up in a travesty of a smile. "She had me arrested and prosecuted for criminal assault," he returned. "I became famous locally—the one black mark in an otherwise unremarkable past. She had the misfortune to try the same trick later on an oilman up in Houston. He called me to testify in his behalf. When he won the case, he had her prosecuted for fraud and extortion, and won. She went to jail."

She felt sick. He'd had his own dealings with the press. She was sorry for him. It must have been a real ordeal after what he'd already suffered in his young life. It also explained why he wasn't married. Marriage involved trust. She doubted he was capable of it any longer. Certainly it explained the hostility he showed toward Leslie. He might think she was pretending to be repulsed by him because she was playing some deep game for profit, perhaps with some public embarrassment in mind. He might even think she was setting him up for another assault charge.

"Maybe you think that I'm like that," she said after a minute, studying him quietly. "But I'm not."

"Then why act like I'm going to attack you whenever I come within five feet of you?" he asked coldly.

She studied her fingers on the desk before her, their short fingernails neatly trimmed, with a coat of colorless sheen. Nothing flashy, she thought, and that was true of her life lately. She didn't have an answer for him.

"Is Ed your lover?" he persisted coldly.

She didn't flinch. "Ask him."

He rolled the unlit cigar in his long fingers as he watched her. "You are one enormous puzzle," he mused.

"Not really. I'm very ordinary." She looked up. "I don't like doctors, especially male ones..."

"Lou's a woman," he replied. "She and her husband are both physicians. They have a little boy."

"Oh." A woman. That would make things easier. But she didn't want to be examined. They could probably tell from X-rays how breaks occurred, and she didn't know if she could trust a local doctor not to talk about it.

"It isn't up to you," he said suddenly. "You work for me. You had an accident on my ranch." He smiled mirthlessly. "I have to cover my bets. You might decide later on to file suit for medical benefits."

She searched his eyes. She couldn't really blame him for feeling like that. "Okay," she said. "I'll let her examine me."

"No comment?"

She shrugged. "Mr. Caldwell, I work hard for my paycheck. I always have. You don't know me, so I don't blame you for expecting the worst. But I don't want a free ride through life."

One of his eyebrows jerked. "I've heard that one before."

She smiled sadly. "I suppose you have." She touched her keyboard absently. "This Dr. Coltrain, is she the company doctor?"

"Yes."

She gnawed on her lower lip. "What she finds out, it is confidential, isn't it?" she added worriedly, looking up at him.

He didn't reply for a minute. The hand dangling the cigar twirled it around. "Yes," he said. "It's confidential. You're making me curious, Miss Murry. Do you have secrets?"

"We all have secrets," she said solemnly. "Some are darker than others."

He flicked a thumbnail against the cigar. "What's yours? Did you shoot your lover?"

She didn't dare show a reaction to that. Her face felt as if it would crack if she moved.

He stuck the cigar in his pocket. "Edna will let you know when you're to go see Lou," he said abruptly, with a glance at his watch. He held up the letter. "Tell Ed I've got this. I'll talk to him about it later."

"Yes, sir."

He resisted the impulse to look back at her. The more he discovered about his newest employee, the more intrigued he became. She made him restless. He wished he knew why.

There was no way to get out of the doctor's appointment. Leslie spoke briefly with Dr. Coltrain before she was sent to the hospital for a set of X-rays. An hour later, she was back in Lou's office, watching the older woman pore somberly over the films against a lighted board on the wall.

Lou looked worried when she examined the X-ray of the leg. "There's no damage from the fall, except for some bruising," she concluded. Her dark eyes met Leslie's squarely. "These old breaks aren't consistent with a fall, however."

Leslie ground her teeth together. She didn't say anything.

Lou moved back around her desk and sat down, indicating that Leslie should sit in the chair in front of the desk after she got off the examining table.

"You don't want to talk about it," Lou said gently. "I won't press you. You do know that the bones weren't properly set at the time, don't you? The improper alignment is unfortunate, because that limp isn't going to go away. I really should send you to an orthopedic surgeon."

"You can send me," Leslie replied, "but I won't go."

Lou rested her folded hands on her desk over the calendar blotter with its scribbled surface. "You don't know me well enough to confide in me. You'll learn, after you've been in Jacobsville a while, that I can be trusted. I don't talk about my patients to anyone, not even my husband. Matt won't hear anything from me."

Leslie remained silent. It was impossible to go over it again with a stranger. It had been hard enough to elaborate on her past to the therapist, who'd been shocked, to put it mildly.

The older woman sighed. "All right, I won't pressure you. But if you ever need anyone to talk to, I'll be here."

Leslie looked up. "Thank you," she said sincerely.

"You're not Matt's favorite person, are you?" Lou asked abruptly.

Leslie laughed without mirth. "No, I'm not. I think he'll find a way to fire me eventually. He doesn't like women much."

"Matt likes everybody as a rule," Lou said. "And he's always being pursued by women. They love him. He's kind to people he likes. He offered to marry Kitty Carson when she quit working for Dr. Drew Morris. She didn't do it, of course, she was crazy for Drew and vice versa. They're happily married now." She hesitated, but Leslie didn't speak. "He's a dish—rich, handsome, sexy, and usually the easiest man on earth to get along with."

"He's a bulldozer," Leslie said flatly. "He can't seem to talk to people unless he's standing on them." She folded her arms over her chest and looked uncomfortable.

So that's it, Lou thought, wondering if the young woman realized what her body language was giving away. Lou knew instantly that someone had caused those breaks in the younger woman's leg; very probably a man. She had reason to know.

"You don't like people to touch you," Lou said.

Leslie shifted in the chair. "No."

Lou's perceptive eyes went over the concealing garments Leslie wore, but she didn't say another word. She stood up, smiling gently. "There's no damage from the recent fall," she said gently. "But come back if the pain gets any worse."

Leslie frowned. "How did you know I was in pain?"

"Matt said you winced every time you got out of your chair."

Leslie's heart skipped. "I didn't realize he noticed."

"He's perceptive."

Lou prescribed an over-the-counter medication to take for the pain and advised her to come back if she didn't improve. Leslie agreed and went out of the office in an absentminded stupor, wondering what else Matt Caldwell had learned from her just by observation. It was a little unnerving.

When she went back to the office, it wasn't ten minutes before Matt was standing in the doorway.

"Well?" he asked.

"I'm fine," she assured him. "Just a few bruises. And believe me, I have no intention of suing you."

He didn't react visibly. "Plenty have." He was irritated. Lou wouldn't tell him anything, except that his new employee was as closemouthed as a clam. He knew that already.

"Tell Ed I'll be out of the office for a couple of days," he said.

"Yes, sir."

He gave her a last look, turned and walked back out. It wasn't until Matt was out of sight that Leslie began to relax.

3

The nightmares came back that night. Leslie had even expected them, because of the visit to Dr. Lou Coltrain and the hospital's X-ray department. Having to wear high heeled shoes to work hadn't done her damaged leg any good, either. Along with the nightmare that left her sweating and panting, her leg was killing her. She went to the bathroom and downed two aspirin, hoping they were going to do the trick. She decided that she was going to have to give up fashion and wear flats again.

Matt noticed, of course, when he returned to the office three days later. His eyes narrowed as he watched her walk across the floor of her small office.

"Lou could give you something to take for the pain," he said abruptly.

She glanced at him as she pulled a file out of the metal cabinet. "Yes, she could, Mr. Caldwell, but do you really want a comatose secretary in Ed's office? Painkillers put me to sleep."

"Pain makes for inefficiency."

She nodded. "I know that. I have a bottle of aspirin in my

purse," she assured him. "And the pain isn't so bad that I can't remember how to spell. It's just a few bruises. They'll heal. Dr. Coltrain said so."

He stared at her through narrowed, cold eyes. "You shouldn't be limping after a week. I want you to see Lou again..."

"I've limped for six years, Mr. Caldwell," she said serenely. Her eyes kindled. "If you don't like the limp, perhaps you shouldn't stand and watch me walk."

His eyebrows arched. "Can't the doctors do anything to correct it?"

She glared at him. "I hate doctors!"

The vehemence of her statement took him aback. She meant it, too. Her face flushed, her eyes sparkled with temper. It was such a difference from her usual expression that he found himself captivated. When she was animated, she was pretty.

"They're not all bad," he replied finally.

"There's only so much you can do with a shattered bone," she said and then bit her lip. She hadn't meant to tell him that.

The question was in his eyes, on his lips, but it never made it past them. Just as he started to ask, Ed came out of his office and spotted him.

"Matt! Welcome back," he said, extending a hand. "I just had a call from Bill Payton. He wanted to know if you were coming to the banquet Saturday night. They've got a live band scheduled."

"Sure," Matt said absently. "Tell him to reserve two tickets for me. Are you going?"

"I thought I would. I'll bring Leslie along." He smiled at her. "It's the annual Jacobsville Cattlemen's Association banquet. We have speeches, but if you survive them, and the rubber chicken, you get to dance."

"Her leg isn't going to let her do much dancing," Matt said solemnly.

Ed's eyebrows lifted. "You'd be surprised," he said. "She loves Latin dances." He grinned at Leslie. "So does Matt here. You wouldn't believe what he can do with a mambo or a rhumba, to say nothing of the tango. He dated a dance instructor for several months, and he's a natural anyway."

Matt didn't reply. He was watching the play of expressions on Leslie's face and wondering about that leg. Maybe Ed knew the truth of it, and he could worm it out of him.

"You can ride in with us," Matt said absently. "I'll hire Jack Bailey's stretch limo and give your secretary a thrill."

"It'll give me a thrill, too," Ed assured him. "Thanks, Matt. I hate trying to find a parking space at the country club when there's a party."

"That makes two of us."

One of the secretaries motioned to Matt that he had a phone call. He left and Ed departed right behind him for a meeting. Leslie wondered how she was going to endure an evening of dancing without ending up close to Matt Caldwell, who already resented her standoffish attitude. It would be an ordeal, she supposed, and wondered if she could develop a convenient headache on Saturday afternoon.

Leslie only had one really nice dress that was appropriate to wear to the function at the country club. The gown was a long sheath of shimmery silver fabric, suspended from her creamy shoulders by two little spaghetti straps. With it, she wore a silver-and-rhinestone clip in her short blond hair and neat little silver slippers with only a hint of a heel.

Ed sighed at the picture she made when the limousine pulled up in front of the boardinghouse where she was staying. She met him on the porch, a small purse clenched in damp hands, all aflutter at the thought of her first evening out since she was seventeen. She was terribly nervous.

"Is the dress okay?" she asked at once.

Ed smiled, taking in her soft oval face with its faint blush of lipstick and rouge, which was the only makeup she ever wore. Her gray eyes had naturally thick black lashes, which never needed mascara.

"You look fine," he assured her.

"You're not bad in a tux yourself," she murmured with a grin.

"Don't let Matt see how nervous you are," he said as they approached the car. "Somebody phoned and set him off just as we left my house. Carolyn was almost in tears."

"Carolyn?" she asked.

"His latest trophy girlfriend," he murmured. "She's from one of the best families in Houston, staying with her aunt so she'd be on hand for tonight's festivities. She's been relentlessly pursuing Matt for months. Some of us think she's gaining ground."

"She's beautiful, I guess?" she asked.

"Absolutely. In a way, she reminds me of Franny."

Franny had been Ed's fiancée, shot to death in a foiled bank robbery about the time Leslie had been catapulted into sordid fame. It had given them something in common that drew them together as friends.

"That must be rough," Leslie said sympathetically.

He glanced at her curiously as they approached the car. "Haven't you ever been in love?"

She shrugged, tugging the small faux fur cape closer around her shoulders. "I was a late bloomer." She swallowed hard. "What happened to me turned me right off men."

"I'm not surprised."

He waited while the chauffeur, also wearing a tuxedo, opened the door of the black super-stretch limousine for them. Leslie climbed in, followed by Ed, and the door closed them in with Matt and the most beautiful blond woman Leslie had ever seen. The other woman was wearing a simple black sheath dress with a short skirt and enough diamonds to open a jewelry store. No point in asking if they were real, Leslie thought, considering the look of that dress and the very real sable coat wrapped around it.

"You remember my cousin, Ed," Matt drawled, lounging back in the leather seat across from Ed and Leslie. Small yellow lights made it possible for them to see each other in the in-credibly spacious interior. "This is his secretary, Miss Murry. Carolyn Engles," he added, nodding toward the woman at his side.

Murmured acknowledgments followed his introduction. Leslie's fascinated eyes went from the bar to the phones to the individual controls on the air-conditioning and heating systems. It was like a luxury apartment on wheels, she thought, and tried not to let her amusement show.

"Haven't you ever been in a limousine before?" Matt asked with a mocking smile.

"Actually, no," she replied with deliberate courtesy. "It's quite a treat. Thank you."

He seemed disconcerted by her reply. He averted his head and studied Ed. His next words showed he'd forgotten her. "Tomorrow morning, first thing, I want you to pull back every penny of support we're giving Marcus Boles. Nobody, and I mean nobody, involves me in a shady land deal like that!"

"It amazes me that we didn't see through him from the start," Ed agreed. "The whole campaign was just a diversion, to give the real candidate someone to shoot down. He'll look like a hero, and Boles will take the fall manfully. I understand he's being handsomely paid for his disgrace. Presumably the cash is worth his reputation and social standing."

"He's got land in South America. I hear he's going over there to live. Just as well," Matt added coldly. "If he's lucky, he might make it to the airport tomorrow before I catch up with him."

The threat of violence lay over him like an invisible mantle. Leslie shivered. Of the four people in that car, she knew first-hand how vicious and brutal physical violence could be. Her memories were hazy, confused, but in the nightmares she had constantly, they were all too vivid.

"Do calm down, darling," Carolyn told Matt gently. "You're upsetting Ms. Marley."

"Murry," Ed corrected before Leslie could. "Strange, Carolyn, I don't remember your memory being so poor."

Carolyn cleared her throat. "It's a lovely night, at least," she said, changing the subject. "No rain and a beautiful moon."

"So it is," Ed drawled.

Matt gave him a cool look, which Ed met with a vacant smile. Leslie was amused by the way Ed could look so innocent. She knew him far too well to be fooled.

Matt, meanwhile, was drinking in the sight of Leslie in that formfitting dress that just matched her eyes. She had skin like marble, and he wondered if it was as soft to the touch as it seemed. She wasn't conventionally pretty, but there was a quality about her that made him weak in the knees. He was driven to protect her, without knowing why he felt that way about a stranger. It irritated him as much as the phone call he'd fielded earlier.

"Where are you from, Ms. Murbery?" Carolyn asked.

"Miss Murry," Leslie corrected, beating Ed to the punch. "I'm from a little town north of Houston."

"A true Texan," Ed agreed with a grin in her direction.

"What town?" Matt asked.

"I'm sure you won't have heard of it," Leslie said confidently. "Our only claim to fame was a radio station in a building shaped like a ten-gallon hat. Very much off the beaten path."

"Did your parents own a ranch?" he persisted.

She shook her head. "My father was a crop duster."

"A what?" Carolyn asked with a blank face.

"A pilot who sprays pesticides from the air in a small airplane," Leslie replied. "He was killed…on the job."

"Pesticides," Matt muttered darkly. "Just what the ground-water table needs to—"

"Matt, can we forget politics for just one night?" Ed asked. "I'd like to enjoy my evening."

Matt gave him a measured glare with one eye narrowed menacingly. But he relaxed all at once and leaned back in his seat, to put a lazy arm around Carolyn and let her snuggle close to him. His dark eyes seemed to mock Leslie as if comparing her revulsion to Carolyn's frank delight in his physical presence.

She let him win this round with an amused smile. Once, she might have enjoyed his presence just as much as his date was reveling in now. But she had more reason than most to fear men.

* * *

The country club, in its sprawling clubhouse on a man-made lake, was a beautiful building with graceful arches and fountains. It did Jacobsville proud. But, as Ed had intimated, there wasn't a single parking spot available. Matt had the pager number of the driver and could summon the limousine whenever it was needed. He herded his charges out of the car and into the building, where the reception committee made them welcome.

There was a live band, a very good one, playing assorted tunes, most of which resembled bossa nova rhythms. The only time that Leslie really felt alive was when she could close her eyes and listen to music; any sort of music—classical, opera, country-western or gospel. Music had been her escape as a child from a world too bitter sometimes to stomach. She couldn't play an instrument, but she could dance. That was the one thing she and her mother had shared, a love of dancing. In fact, Marie had taught her every dance step she knew, and she knew a lot. Marie had taught dancing for a year or so and had shared her expertise with her daughter. How ironic it was that Leslie's love of dance had been stifled forever by the events of her seventeenth year.

"Fill a plate," Ed coaxed, motioning her to the small china dishes on the buffet table. "You could use a little more meat on those bird bones."

She grinned at him. "I'm not skinny."

"Yes, you are," he replied, and he wasn't kidding. "Come on, forget your troubles and enjoy yourself. Tonight, there is no tomorrow. Eat, drink and be merry."

For tomorrow, you die, came the finish to that admonishing verse, she recalled darkly. But she didn't say it. She put some cheese straws and finger sandwiches on a plate and opted for soda water instead of a drink.

Ed found them two chairs on the rim of the dance floor, where they could hear the band and watch the dancing.

The band had a lovely dark-haired singer with a hauntingly beautiful voice. She was playing a guitar and singing songs from the sixties, with a rhythm that made Leslie's heart jump. The smile on her face, the sparkle in her gray eyes as she listened to the talented performer, made her come alive.

From across the room, Matt noted the abrupt change in Leslie. She loved music. She loved dancing, too, he could tell. His strong fingers contracted around his own plate.

"Shall we sit with the Devores, darling?" Carolyn asked, indicating a well-dressed couple on the opposite side of the ballroom.

"I thought we'd stick with my cousin," he said carelessly. "He's not used to this sort of thing."

"He seems very much at home," Carolyn corrected, reluctantly following in Matt's wake. "It's his date who looks out of place. Good heavens, she's tapping her toe! How gauche!"

"Weren't you ever twenty-three?" he asked with a bite in his voice. "Or were you born so damned sophisticated that nothing touched you?"

She actually gasped. Matt had never spoken to her that way.

"Excuse me," he said gruffly, having realized his mistake. "I'm still upset by Boles."

"So...so I noticed," she stammered, and almost dropped her plate. This was a Matt Caldwell she'd never seen before. His usual smile and easygoing attitude were conspicuous for their absence tonight. Boles must really have upset him!

Matt sat down on the other side of Leslie, his eyes darkening as he saw the life abruptly drain out of her. Her body tensed. Her fingers on her plate went white.

"Here, Carolyn, trade places with me," Matt said suddenly, and with a forced smile. "This chair's too low for me."

"I don't think mine's much higher, darling, but I'll do it," Carolyn said in a docile tone.

Leslie relaxed. She smiled shyly at the other woman and then turned her attention back to the woman on the stage.

"Isn't she marvelous?" Carolyn asked. "She's from the Yucatán."

"Not only talented, but pretty, as well," Ed agreed. "I love that beat."

"Oh, so do I," Leslie said breathlessly, nibbling a finger sandwich but with her whole attention on the band and the singer.

Matt found himself watching her, amused and touched by her uninhibited joy in the music. It had occurred to him that not much affected her in the office. Here, she was unsure of herself and nervous. Perhaps she even felt out of place. But when the band was playing and the vocalist was singing, she was a different person. He got a glimpse of the way she had been, perhaps, before whatever blows of fate had made her so uneasy around him. He was intrigued by her, and not solely because she wounded his ego. She was a complex person.

Ed noticed Matt's steady gaze on Leslie, and he wanted to drag his cousin aside and tell him the whole miserable story. Matt was curious about Leslie, and he was a bulldozer when he wanted something. He'd run roughshod right over her to get his answers, and Leslie would retreat into the shell her experiences had built around her. She was just coming into the sunlight, and here was Matt driving her back into shadow. Why couldn't Matt be content with Carolyn's adoration? Most women flocked around him; Leslie didn't. He was sure that was the main attraction she held for his cousin. But Matt, pursuing her interest, could set her back years. He had no idea what sort of damage he could do to her fragile emotions.

The singer finished her song, and the audience applauded. She introduced the members of the band and the next number, a beautiful, rhythmic feast called "Brazil." It was Leslie's very favorite piece of music, and she could dance to it, despite her leg. She longed, ached, for someone to take her on the dance floor and let her show those stiff, inhibited people how to fly to that poignant rhythm!

Watching her, Matt saw the hunger in her eyes. Ed couldn't do those steps, but he could. Without a word, he handed Carolyn his empty plate and got to his feet.

Before Leslie had a chance to hesitate or refuse outright, he pulled her gently out of her seat and onto the dance floor.

His dark eyes met her shocked pale ones as he caught her waist in one lean, strong hand and took her left hand quite reverently into his right one.

"I won't make any sudden turns," he assured her. He nodded once, curtly, to mark the rhythm.

And then he did something remarkable.

Leslie caught her breath as she recognized his ability. She forgot to be afraid of him. She forgot that she was nervous to be held by a man. She was caught up in the rhythm and the delight of having a partner who knew how to dance to perfection the intricate steps that accompanied the Latin beat.

"You're good," Matt mused, smiling with genuine pleasure as they measured their quick steps to the rhythm.

"So are you." She smiled back.

"If your leg gives you trouble, let me know and I'll get you off the floor. Okay?"

"Okay."

"Then let's go!"

He moved her across the floor with the skill of a professional dancer and she followed him with such perfection that other dancers stopped and got out of the way, moving to the sidelines to watch what had become pure entertainment.

Matt and Leslie, enjoying the music and their own interpretation of it, were blind to the other guests, to the smiling members of the band, to everything except the glittering excitement of the dance. They moved as if they were bound by invisible strings, each to the other, with perfectly matching steps.

As the music finally wound down, Matt drew her in close against his lean frame and tilted her down in an elegant, but painful, finish.

The applause was thunderous. Matt drew Leslie upright again and noticed how pale and drawn her face was.

"Too much too soon," he murmured. "Come on. Off you go."

He didn't move closer. Instead, he held out his arm and let her come to him, let her catch hold of it where the muscle was thickest. She clung with both hands, hating herself for doing something so incredibly stupid. But, oh, it had been fun! It was worth the pain.

She didn't realize she'd spoken aloud until Matt eased her down into her chair again.

"Do you have any aspirin in that tiny thing?" Matt asked, indicating the small string purse on her arm.

She grimaced.

"Of course not." He turned, scanning the audience. "Back in a jiffy."

He moved off in the general direction of the punch bowl while Ed caught Leslie's hand in his. "That was great," he enthused. "Just great! I didn't know you could dance like that."

"Neither did I," she murmured shyly.

"Quite an exhibition," Carolyn agreed coolly. "But silly to do something so obviously painful. Now Matt will spend the rest of the night blaming himself and trying to find aspirin, I suppose." She got up and marched off with her barely touched plate and Matt's empty one.

"Well, she's in a snit," Ed observed. "She can't dance like that."

"I shouldn't have done it," Leslie murmured. "But it was so much fun, Ed! I felt alive, really alive!"

"You looked it. Nice to see your eyes light up again."

She made a face at him. "I've spoiled Carolyn's evening."

"Fair trade," he murmured dryly, "she spoiled mine the minute she got into the limousine and complained that I smelled like a sweets shop."

"You smell very nice," she replied.

He smiled. "Thanks."

Matt was suddenly coming back toward them, with Lou Coltrain by the arm. It looked as if she were being forcibly escorted across the floor and Ed had to hide the grin he couldn't help.

"Well," Lou huffed, staring at Matt before she lowered her gaze to Leslie. "I thought you were dying, considering the way he appropriated me and dragged me over here!"

"I don't have any aspirin," Leslie said uneasily. "I'm sorry…"

"There's nothing to be sorry about," Lou said instantly. She patted Leslie's hand gently. "But you've had some pretty bad bruising and this isn't the sort of exercise I'd recommend. Shattered bones are never as strong, even when they're set properly—and yours were not."

Embarrassed, Leslie bit her lower lip.

"You'll be okay," Lou promised with a gentle smile. "In fact, exercise is good for the muscles that support that bone—it makes it stronger. But don't do this again for a couple of weeks, at least. Here. I always carry aspirin!"

She handed Leslie a small metal container of aspirin and Matt produced another cup of soda water and stood over her, unsmiling, while she took two of the aspirins and swallowed them.

"Thanks," she told Lou. "I really appreciate it."

"You come and see me Monday," Lou instructed, her dark eyes full of authority. "I'll write you a prescription for something that will make your life easier. Not narcotics," she added with a smile. "Anti-inflammatories. They'll make a big difference in the way you get around."

"You're a nice doctor," she told Lou solemnly.

Lou's eyes narrowed. "I gather that you've known some who weren't."

"One, at least," she said in a cold tone. She smiled at Lou. "You've changed my mind about doctors."

"That's one point for me. I'll rush right over and tell Copper," she added, smiling as she caught her redheaded husband's eyes across the room. "He'll be impressed!"

"Not much impresses the other Doctor Coltrain," Matt told her after Lou was out of earshot. "Lou did."

"Not until he knew she had a whole closetful of Lionel electric trains," Ed commented with a chuckle.

"Their son has a lot to look forward to when he grows up," Matt mused. He glanced beside Leslie. "Where's Carolyn?"

"She left in a huff," Ed said.

"I'll go find her. Sure you'll be okay?" he asked Leslie with quiet concern.

She nodded. "Thanks for the aspirin. They really help."

He nodded. His dark eyes slid over her drawn face and then away as he went in search of his date.

"I've spoiled his evening, too, I guess," she said wistfully.

"You can't take credit for that," Ed told her. "I've hardly ever seen Matt having so much fun as he was when he was dancing with you. Most of the women around here can only do a two-step. You're a miracle on the dance floor."

"I love to dance," she sighed. "I always did. Mama was so light on her feet." Her eyes twinkled with fond memories. "I used to love to watch her when I was little and she danced with Daddy. She was so pretty, so full of life." The light went out of her eyes. "She thought I'd encouraged Mike, and the others, too," she said dully. "She...shot him and the bullet went through him, into my leg..."

"So that's how your leg got in that shape."

She glanced at him, hardly aware of what she'd been saying. She nodded. "The doctor in the emergency room was sure it was all my fault. That's why my leg wasn't properly set. He removed the bullet and not much else. It wasn't until afterward that another doctor put a cast on. Later, I began to limp. But there was no money for any other doctor visits by then. Mama was in jail and I was all alone. If it hadn't been for my best friend

Jessica's family, I wouldn't even have had a home. They took me in despite the gossip and I got to finish school."

"I'll never know how you managed that," Ed said. "Going to school every day with the trial making headlines week by week."

"It was tough," she agreed. "But it made me tough, too. Fire tempers steel, don't they say? I'm tempered."

"Yes, you are."

She smiled at him. "Thanks for bringing me. It was wonderful."

"Tell Matt that. It might change him."

"Oh, he's not so bad, I think," she replied. "He dances like an angel."

He stared toward the punch bowl, where Matt was glancing toward him and Leslie. The dark face was harder than stone and Ed felt a tingle of apprehension when Matt left Carolyn and started walking toward them. He didn't like that easygoing stride of Matt's. The only time Matt moved that slowly was when he was homicidally angry.

4

Leslie knew by the look in Matt's eyes that he was furious. She thought his anger must be directed toward her, although she couldn't remember anything she'd done to deserve it. As he approached them, he had his cellular phone out and was pushing a number into it. He said something, then closed it and put it back in his pocket.

"I'm sorry, but we have to leave," he said, every syllable dripping ice. "It seems that Carolyn has developed a vicious headache."

"It's all right," Leslie said, and even smiled as relief swept over her that she hadn't put that expression on his handsome face. "I wouldn't have been able to dance again." Her eyes met Matt's shyly. "I really enjoyed it."

He didn't reply. His eyes were narrow and not very friendly. "Ed, will you go out front and watch for the car? I've just phoned the driver."

"Sure." He hesitated noticeably for a moment before he left.

Matt stood looking down at Leslie with an intensity that made her uncomfortable. "You make yourself out to be a broken stick," he said quietly. "But you're not what you appear to be, are you? I get the feeling that you used to be quite a dancer before that leg slowed you down."

She was puzzled. "I learned how from my mother," she said honestly. "I used to dance with her."

He laughed curtly. "Pull the other one," he said. He was thinking about her pretended revulsion, the way she constantly backed off when he came near her. Then, tonight, the carefully planned capitulation. It was an old trick that had been used on him before—backing away so that he'd give chase. He was surprised that he hadn't realized it sooner. He wondered how far she'd let him go. He was going to find out.

She blinked and frowned. "I beg your pardon?" she asked, genuinely puzzled.

"Never mind," he said with a parody of a smile. "Ed should be outside with the driver by now. Shall we go?"

He reached out a lean hand and pulled her to her feet abruptly. Her face was very pale at the hint of domination not only in his eyes, but the hold he had on her. It was hard not to panic. It reminded her of another man who had used domination; only that time she had no knowledge of how to get away. Now she did. She turned her arm quickly and pushed it down against his thumb, the weakest spot in his hold, freeing herself instantly as the self-defense instructor had taught her.

Matt was surprised. "Where did you learn that? From your mother?" he drawled.

"No. From my Tae Kwon Do instructor in Houston," she returned. "Despite my bad leg, I can take care of myself."

"Oh, I'd bet on that." His dark eyes narrowed and glittered

faintly. "You're not what you seem, Miss Murry. I'm going to make it my business to find out the truth about you."

She blanched. She didn't want him digging into her past. She'd run from it, hidden from it, for years. Would she have to run some more, just when she felt secure?

He saw her frightened expression and felt even more certain that he'd almost been taken for the ride of his life. Hadn't his experience with women taught him how to recognize deceit? He thought of his mother and his heart went cold. Leslie even had a look of her, with that blond hair. He took her by the upper arm and pulled her along with him, noticing that she moved uncomfortably and tugged at his hold.

"Please," she said tightly. "Slow down. It hurts."

He stopped at once, realizing that he was forcing her to a pace that made walking painful. He'd forgotten about her disability, as if it were part of her act. He let out an angry breath.

"The damaged leg is real," he said, almost to himself. "But what else is?"

She met his angry eyes. "Mr. Caldwell, whatever I am, I'm no threat to you," she said quietly. "I really don't like being touched, but I enjoyed dancing with you. I haven't danced...in years."

He studied her wan face, oblivious to the music of the band, and the murmur of movement around them. "Sometimes," he murmured, "you seem very familiar to me, as if I've seen you before." He was thinking about his mother, and how she'd betrayed him and hurt him all those years ago.

Leslie didn't know that, though. Her teeth clenched as she tried not to let her fear show. Probably he had seen her before, just like the whole country had, her face in the tabloid papers as it had appeared the night they took her out of her mother's bloodstained apartment on a stretcher, her leg bleeding profusely, her sobs audible. But then her hair had been dark, and she'd been wearing glasses. Could he really recognize her?

"Maybe I just have that kind of face." She grimaced and shifted her weight. "Could we go, please?" she asked on a moan. "My leg really is killing me."

He didn't move for an instant. Then he bent suddenly and lifted her in his strong arms and carried her through the amused crowd toward the door.

"Mr....Mr. Caldwell," she protested, stiffening. She'd never been picked up and carried by a man in her entire life. She studied his strong profile with fascinated curiosity, too entranced to feel the usual fear. Having danced with him, she was able to accept his physical closeness. He felt very strong and he smelled of some spicy, very exotic cologne. She had the oddest urge to touch his wavy black hair just over his broad forehead, where it looked thickest.

He glanced down into her fascinated eyes and one of his dark eyebrows rose in a silent question.

"You're...very strong, aren't you?" she asked hesitantly.

The tone of her voice touched something deep inside him. He searched her eyes and the tension was suddenly thick as his gaze fell to her soft bow of a mouth and lingered there, even as his pace slowed slightly.

Her hand clutched the lapel of his tuxedo as her own gaze fell to his mouth. She'd never wanted to be kissed like this before. When she'd been kissed during that horrible encounter, it had been repulsive—a wet, invading, lustful kiss that made her want to throw up.

It wouldn't be like that with Matt. She knew instinctively that he was well versed in the art of lovemaking, and that he would be gentle with a woman. His mouth was sensual, wide and chiseled. Her own mouth tingled as she wondered visibly what it would feel like to let him kiss her.

He read that curiosity with pinpoint accuracy and his sharp intake of breath brought her curious eyes up to meet his.

"Careful," he cautioned, his voice deeper than usual. "Curiosity killed the cat."

Her eyes asked a question she couldn't form with her lips.

"You fell off a horse avoiding any contact with me," he reminded her quietly. "Now you look as if you'd do anything to have my mouth on yours. Why?"

"I don't know," she whispered, her hand contracting on the lapel of his jacket. "I like being close to you," she confessed, surprised. "It's funny. I haven't wanted to be close to a man like this before."

He stopped dead in his tracks. There was a faint vibration in the hard arms holding her. His eyes lanced into hers. His breath became audible. The arm under her back contracted, bringing her breasts hard against him as he stood there on the steps of the building, totally oblivious to everything except the ache that was consuming him.

Leslie's body shivered with its first real taste of desire. She laughed shakily at the new and wonderful sensations she was feeling. Her breasts felt suddenly heavy. They ached.

"Is this what it feels like?" she murmured.

"What?" he asked huskily.

She met his gaze. "Desire."

He actually shuddered. His arms contracted. His lips parted

as he looked at her mouth and knew that he couldn't help taking it. She smelled of roses, like the tiny pink fairy roses that grew in masses around the front door of his ranch house. She wanted him. His head began to spin. He bent his dark head and bit at her lower lip with a sensuous whisper.

"Open your mouth, Leslie," he whispered, and his hard mouth suddenly went down insistently on hers.

But before he could even savor the feel of her soft lips, the sound of high heels approaching jerked his head up. Leslie was trembling against him, shocked and a little frightened, and completely entranced by the unexpected contact with his beautiful mouth.

Matt's dark eyes blazed down into hers. "No more games. I'm taking you home with me," he said huskily.

She started to speak, to protest, when Carolyn came striding angrily out the door.

"Does she have to be carried?" the older woman asked Matt with dripping sarcasm. "Funny, she was dancing eagerly enough a few minutes ago!"

"She has a bad leg," Matt said, regaining his control. "Here's the car."

The limousine drew up at the curb and Ed got out, frowning when he saw Leslie in Matt's arms.

"Are you all right?" he asked as he approached them.

"She shouldn't have danced," Matt said stiffly as he moved the rest of the way down the steps to deposit her inside the car on the leather-covered seat. "She made her leg worse."

Carolyn was livid. She slid in and moved to the other side of Leslie with a gaze that could have curdled milk. "One dance and we have to leave," she said furiously.

Matt moved into the car beside Ed and slammed the door. "I thought we were leaving because you had a headache," he snapped at Carolyn, his usual control quite evidently gone. He was in a foul mood. Desire was frustrating him. He glanced at Leslie and thought how good she was at manipulation. She had him almost doubled over with need. She was probably laughing her head off silently. Well, she was going to pay for that.

Carolyn, watching his eyes on Leslie, made an angry sound in her throat and stared out the window.

To Ed's surprise and dismay, they dropped him off at his home first. He tried to argue, but Matt wasn't having that. He told Ed he'd see him at the office Monday and closed the door on his protests.

Carolyn was deposited next. Matt walked her to her door, but he moved back before she could claim a good-night kiss. The way she slammed her door was audible even inside the closed limousine.

Leslie bit her lower lip as Matt climbed back into the car with her. In the lighted interior, she could see the expression on his face as he studied her slender body covetously.

"This isn't the way to my apartment," she ventured nervously a few minutes later, hoping he hadn't meant what he said just before they got into the limousine.

"No, it isn't, is it?" he replied dangerously.

Even as he spoke, the limousine pulled up at the door to his ranch house. He helped Leslie out and spoke briefly to the driver before dismissing him. Then he swung a frightened Leslie up into his arms and carried her toward the front door.

"Mr. Caldwell..." she began.

"Matt," he corrected, not looking at her.

"I want to go home," she tried again.

"You will. Eventually."

"But you sent the car away."

"I have six cars," he informed her as he shifted his light burden to produce his keys from the pocket of his slacks and insert one in the lock. The door swung open. "I'll drive you home when the time comes."

"I'm very tired." Her voice sounded breathless and high-pitched.

"Then I know just the place for you." He closed the door and carried her down a long, dimly lit hallway to a room near the back of the house. He leaned down to open the door and once they were through it, he kicked it shut with his foot.

Seconds later, Leslie was in the middle of a huge king-size bed, sprawled on the beige-brown-and-black comforter that covered it and Matt was removing her wrap.

It went flying onto a chair, along with his jacket and tie. He unbuttoned his shirt and slid down onto the bed beside her, his hands on either side of her face as he poised just above her.

The position brought back terrible, nightmarish memories. She stiffened all over. Her face went pale. Her eyes dilated so much that the gray of them was eclipsed by black.

Matt ignored her expression. He looked down the length of her in the clinging silver dress, his eyes lingering on the thrust of her small breasts. One of his big hands came up to trace around the prominent hard nipple that pointed through the fabric.

The touch shocked Leslie, because she didn't find it revolting or unpleasant. She shivered a little. Her eyes, wide and frightened, and a little curious, met his.

His strong fingers brushed lazily over the nipple and around the contours of her breast as if the feel of her fascinated him.

"Do you mind?" he asked with faint insolence, and slipped one of the spaghetti straps down her arm, moving her just enough that he could pull the bodice away from her perfect little breast.

Leslie couldn't believe what was happening. Men were repulsive to her. She hated the thought of intimacy. But Matt Caldwell was looking at her bare breast and she was letting him, with no thought of resistance. She hadn't even had anything to drink.

He searched her face as his warm fingers traced her breast. He read the pleasure she was feeling in her soft eyes. "You feel like sun-touched marble to my hand," he said quietly. "Your skin is beautiful." His gaze traveled down her body. "Your breasts are perfect."

She was shivering again. Her hands clenched beside her head as she watched him touch her, like an observer, like in a dream.

He smiled with faint mockery when he saw her expression. "Haven't you done this before?"

"No," she said, and she actually sounded serious.

He discounted that at once. She was far too calm and submissive for an inexperienced woman.

One dark eyebrow lifted. "Twenty-three and still a virgin?"

How had he known that? "Well...yes." Technically she certainly was. Emotionally, too. Despite what had been done to her, she'd been spared rape, if only by seconds, when her mother came home unexpectedly.

Matt was absorbed in touching her body. His forefinger traced around the hard nipple, and he watched her body lift to follow it when he lifted his hand.

"Do you like it?" he asked softly.

She was watching him intensely. "Yes." She sounded as if it surprised her that she liked what he was doing.

With easy self-confidence, he pulled her up just a little and pushed the other strap down her arm, baring her completely to his eyes. She was perfect, like a warm statue in beautifully smooth marble. He'd never seen breasts like hers. She aroused him profoundly.

He held her by the upper part of her rib cage, his thumbs edging onto her breasts to caress them tenderly while he watched the expressions chase each other across her face. The silence in the bedroom was broken only by the sound of cars far in the distance and the sound of some mournful night bird outside the window. Closer was the rasp of her own breathing and her heart beating in her ears. She should be fighting for her life, screaming, running, escaping. She'd avoided this sort of situation successfully for six years. Why didn't she want to avoid Matt's hands?

Matt touched her almost reverently, his eyes on her hard nipples. With a faint groan, he bent his dark head and his mouth touched the soft curve of her breast.

She gasped and stiffened. His head lifted immediately. He looked at her and realized that she wasn't trying to get away. Her eyes were full of shocked pleasure and curiosity.

"Another first?" he asked with faint arrogance and a calculating smile that didn't really register in her whirling mind.

She nodded, swallowing. Her body, as if it was ignoring her brain, moved sensuously on the bed. She'd never dreamed that she could let a man touch her like this, that she could enjoy letting him touch her, after her one horrible experience with intimacy.

He put his mouth over her nipple and suckled her so insistently that she cried out, drowning in a veritable flood of shocked pleasure.

The little cry aroused Matt unexpectedly, and he was rougher with her than he meant to be, his mouth suddenly demanding on her soft flesh. He tasted her hungrily for several long seconds until he forced his mind to remember why he shouldn't let himself go in headfirst. He wanted her almost beyond bearing, but he wasn't going to let her make a fool of him.

He lifted his head and studied her flushed face clinically. She was enjoying it, but she needn't think he was going to let her take possession of him with that pretty body. He knew now that he could have her. She was willing to give in. For a price, he added.

She opened her eyes and lay there watching him with wide, soft, curious eyes. She thought she had him in her pocket, he mused. But she was all too acquiescent. That, he thought amusedly, was a gross miscalculation on her part. It was her nervous retreat that challenged him, not the sort of easy conquest with which he was already too familiar.

Abruptly he sat up, pulling her with him, and slid the straps of her evening dress back up onto her shoulders.

She watched him silently, still shocked by his ardor and puzzled at her unexpected response to it.

He got to his feet and rebuttoned his shirt, reaching for his snap-on tie and then his jacket. He studied her there, sitting dazed on the edge of his bed, and his dark eyes narrowed. He smiled, but it wasn't a pleasant smile.

"You're not bad," he murmured lazily. "But the fascinated virgin bit turns me right off. I like experience."

She blinked. She was still trying to make her mind work again.

"I assume that your other would-be lovers liked that wide-eyed, first-time look?"

Other lovers. Had he guessed about her past? Her eyes registered the fear.

He saw it. He was vaguely sorry that she wasn't what she pretended to be. He was all but jaded when it came to pursuing women. He hated the coy behavior, the teasing, the manipulation that eventually ended in his bedroom. He was considered a great catch by single women, rich and handsome and experienced in sensual techniques. But he always made his position clear at the outset. He didn't want marriage. That didn't really matter to most of the women in his life. A diamond here, an exotic vacation there, and they seemed satisfied for as long as it lasted. Not that there were many affairs. He was tired of the game. In fact, he'd never been more tired of it than he was right now. His whole expression was one of disgust.

Leslie saw it in his eyes and wished she could curl up into a ball and hide under the bed. His cold scrutiny made her feel cheap, just as that doctor had, just as the media had, just as her mother had...

He couldn't have explained why that expression on her face made him feel guilty. But it did.

He turned away from her. "Come on," he said, picking up her wrap and purse and tossing them to her. "I'll run you home."

She didn't look at him as she followed him down the length of the hall. It was longer than she realized, and even before they got to the front door, her leg was throbbing. Dancing had been damaging enough, without the jerk of his hand as they left the ballroom. But she ground her teeth together and didn't let her growing discomfort show in her face. He wasn't going to make her feel any worse than she already did by accusing her of putting on an act for sympathy. She went past him out the door he was holding open, avoiding his eyes. She wondered how things could have gone so terribly wrong.

The spacious garage was full of cars. He got out the silver Mercedes and opened the door to let her climb inside, onto the leather-covered passenger seat. He closed her door with something of a snap. Her fingers fumbled the seat belt into its catch and she hoped he wouldn't want to elaborate on what he'd already said.

She stared out the window at the dark silhouettes of buildings and trees as he drove along the back roads that eventually led into Jacobsville. She was sick about the way she'd acted. He probably thought she was the easiest woman alive. The only thing she didn't understand was why he didn't take advantage of it. The obvious reason made her even more uncomfortable. Didn't they say that some men didn't want what came easily? It was probably true. He'd been in pursuit as long as she was backing away from him. What irony, to spend years being afraid of men, running crazily from even the most platonic involvement, to find herself capable of torrid desire with the one man in the world who didn't want her!

He felt her tension. It was all too apparent that she was disappointed that he hadn't played the game to its finish.

"Is that what Ed gets when he takes you home?" he drawled.

Her nails bit into her small evening bag. Her teeth clenched. She wasn't going to dignify that remark with a reply.

He shrugged and paused to turn onto the main highway. "Don't take it so hard," he said lazily. "I'm a little too sophisticated to fall for it, but there are a few rich single ranchers around Jacobsville. Cy Parks comes to mind. He's hell on the nerves, but he is a widower." He glanced at her averted face. "On second thought, he's had enough tragedy in his life. I wouldn't wish you on him."

She couldn't even manage to speak, she was so choked up with hurt. Why, she wondered, did everything she wanted in life turn on her and tear her to pieces? It was like tracking cougars with a toy gun. Just when she seemed to find peace and purpose, her life became nothing but torment. As if her tattered pride wasn't enough, she was in terrible pain. She shifted in the seat, hoping that a change of position would help. It didn't.

"How did that bone get shattered?" he asked conversationally.

"Don't you know?" she asked on a harsh laugh. If he'd seen the story about her, as she suspected, he was only playing a cruel game—the sort of game he'd already accused her of playing!

He glanced at her with a scowl. "And how would I know?" he wondered aloud.

She frowned. Maybe he hadn't read anything at all! He might be fishing for answers.

She swallowed, gripping her purse tightly.

He swung the Mercedes into the driveway of her boardinghouse and pulled up at the steps, with the engine still running. He turned to her. "How *would* I know?" he asked again, his voice determined.

"You seem to think you're an expert on everything else about me," she replied evasively.

His chin lifted as he studied her through narrowed eyes. "There are several ways a bone can be shattered," he said quietly. "One way is from a bullet."

She didn't feel as if she were still breathing. She sat like a statue, watching him deliberate.

"What do you know about bullets?" she asked shortly.

"My unit was called up during Operation Desert Storm," he told her. "I served with an infantry unit. I know quite a lot about bullets. And what they do to bone," he added. "Which brings me to the obvious question. Who shot you?"

"I didn't say... I was shot," she managed.

His intense gaze held her like invisible ropes. "But you were, weren't you?" he asked with shrewd scrutiny. His lips tugged into a cold smile. "As to who did it, I'd bet on one of your former lovers. Did he catch you with somebody else, or did you tease him the way you teased me tonight and then refuse him?" He gave her another contemptuous look. "Not that you refused. You didn't exactly play hard to get."

Her ego went right down to her shoes. He was painting her over with evil colors. She bit her lower lip. It was unpleasant enough to have her memories, but to have this man making her out to be some sort of nymphomaniac was painful beyond words. Her first real taste of tender intimacy had been with him, tonight, and he made it sound dirty and cheap.

She unfastened her seat belt and got out of the car with as much dignity as she could muster. Her leg was incredibly painful. All she wanted was her bed, her heating pad and some more aspirins. And to get away from her tormenter.

Matt switched off the engine and moved around the car, irritated by the way she limped.

"I'll take you to the door...!"

She flinched when he came close. She backed away from him, actually shivering when she remembered shamefully what she'd let him do to her. Her eyes clouded with unshed angry tears, with outraged virtue.

"More games?" he asked tersely. He hadn't liked having her back away again after the way she'd been in his bedroom.

"I don't...play games," she replied, hating the hiccup of a sob that revealed how upset she really was. She clutched her wrap and her purse to her chest, accusing eyes glaring at him. "And you can go to hell!"

He scowled at the way she looked, barely hearing the words. She was white in the face and her whole body seemed rigid, as if she really was upset.

She turned and walked away, wincing inwardly with every excruciating step, to the front porch. But her face didn't show one trace of her discomfort. She held her head high. She still had her pride, she thought through a wave of pain.

Matt watched her go into the boardinghouse with more mixed, confused emotions than he'd ever felt. He remembered vividly that curious "Don't you know?" when he'd asked who shot her.

He got back into the Mercedes and sat staring through the windshield for a long moment before he started it. Miss Murry was one puzzle he intended to solve, and if it cost him a fortune in detective fees, he was going to do it.

5

Leslie cried for what seemed hours. The aspirin didn't help the leg pain at all. There was no medicine known to man that she could take for her wounded ego. Matt had swept the floor with her, played with her, laughed at her naiveté and made her out to be little better than a prostitute. He was like that emergency room doctor so long ago who'd made her ashamed of her body. It was a pity that her first real desire for a man's touch had made her an object of contempt to the man himself.

Well, she told herself as she wiped angrily at the tears, she'd never make that mistake again. Matt Caldwell could go right where she'd told him to!

The phone rang and she hesitated to answer it. But it might be Ed. She picked up the receiver.

"We had a good laugh about you," Carolyn told her outright. "I guess you'll think twice before you throw yourself at him again! He said you were so easy that you disgusted him…!"

Almost shaking with humiliation, she put the receiver down with a slam and then unplugged the phone. It was so close to what Matt had already said that there was no reason not to believe her. Carolyn's harsh arrogance was just what she needed to make the miserable evening complete.

The pain, combined with the humiliation, kept her awake until almost daylight. She missed breakfast, not to mention church, and when she did finally open her eyes, it was to a kind of pain she hadn't experienced since the night she was shot.

She shifted, wincing, and then moaned as the movement caused another searing wave of discomfort up her leg. The knock on her door barely got through to her. "Come in," she said in a husky, exhausted tone.

The door opened and there was Matt Caldwell, unshaven and with dark circles under his eyes.

Carolyn's words came back to haunt her. She grabbed the first thing that came to hand, a plastic bottle of spring water she kept by the bed, and flung it furiously across the room at him. It missed his head, and Ed's, by a quarter of an inch.

"No, thanks," Ed said, moving in front of Matt. "I don't want any water."

Her face was lined with pain, white with it. She glared at Matt's hard, angry face with eyes that would have looked perfectly natural over a cocked pistol.

"I couldn't get you on the phone, and I was worried," Ed said gently, approaching her side of the double bed she occupied. He noticed the unplugged telephone on her bedside table. "Now I know why I couldn't get you on the phone." He studied her drawn face. "How bad is it?"

She could barely breathe. "Bad," she said huskily, thinking what an understatement that word was.

He took her thick white chenille bathrobe from the chair beside the bed. "Come on. We're going to drive you to the emergency room. Matt can phone Lou Coltrain and have her meet us there."

It was an indication of the pain that she didn't argue. She got out of bed, aware of the picture she must make in the thick flannel pajamas that covered every inch of her up to her chin. Matt was probably shocked, she thought as she let Ed stuff her into the robe. He probably expected her to be naked under the covers, conforming to the image he had of her nymphomania!

He hadn't said a word. He just stood there, by the door, grimly watching Ed get her ready—until she tried to walk, and folded up.

Ed swung her up in his arms, stopping Matt's instinctive quick movement toward her. Ed knew for a fact that she'd scream the house down if his cousin so much as touched her. He didn't know what had gone on the night before, but judging by the way Matt and Leslie looked, it had been both humiliating and embarrassing.

"I can carry her," he told Matt. "Let's go."

Matt glimpsed her contorted features and didn't hesitate. He led the way down the hall and right out the front door.

"My purse," she said huskily. "My insurance card..."

"That can be taken care of later," Matt said stiffly. He opened the back door of the Mercedes and waited while Ed slid her onto the seat.

She leaned back with her eyes closed, almost sick from the pain.

"She should never have gotten on the dance floor," Matt said through his teeth as they started toward town. "And then I jerked her up out of her chair. It's my fault."

Ed didn't reply. He glanced over the seat at Leslie with concern in his whole expression. He hoped she hadn't done any major damage to herself with that exhibition the night before.

Lou Coltrain was waiting in the emergency room as Ed carried Leslie inside the building. She motioned him down the hall to a room and closed the door behind Matt as soon as he entered.

She examined the leg carefully, asking questions that Leslie was barely able to answer. "I want X-rays," she said. "But I'll give you something for pain first."

"Thank you," Leslie choked, fighting tears.

Lou smoothed her wild hair. "You poor little thing," she said softly. "Cry if you want to. It must hurt like hell."

She went out to get the injection, and tears poured down Leslie's face because of that tender concern. She hardly ever cried. She was tough. She could take anything—near-rape, bullet wounds, notoriety, her mother's trial, the refusal of her parent to even speak to her...

"There, there," Ed said. He produced a handkerchief and blotted the tears, smiling down at her. "Dr. Lou is going to make it all better."

"For God's sake...!" Matt bit off angry words and walked out of the room. It was unbearable that he'd hurt her like that. Unbearable! And then to have to watch Ed comforting her...!

"I hate him," Leslie choked when he was gone. She actually shivered. "He laughed about it," she whispered, blind to Ed's curious scowl. "She said they both laughed about it, that he was disgusted."

"She?"

"Carolyn." The tears were hot in her eyes, cold on her cheeks. "I hate him!"

Lou came back with the injection and gave it, waiting for it to take effect. She glanced at Ed. "You might want to wait outside. I'm taking her down to X-ray myself. I'll come and get you when we've done some tests."

"Okay."

He went out and joined Matt in the waiting room. The older man's face was drawn, tormented. He barely glanced at Ed before he turned his attention to the trees outside the window. It was a dismal gray day, with rain threatening. It matched his mood.

Ed leaned against the wall beside him with a frown. "She said Carolyn phoned her last night," he began. "I suppose that's why the phone was unplugged."

It was Matt's turn to look puzzled. "What?"

"Leslie said Carolyn told her the two of you were laughing at her," he murmured. "She didn't say what about."

Matt's face hardened visibly. He rammed his hands into his pockets and his eyes were terrible to look into.

"Don't hurt Leslie," Ed said suddenly, his voice quiet but full of venom. "She hasn't had an easy life. Don't make things hard on her. She has no place else to go."

Matt glanced at him, disliking the implied threat as much as the fact that Ed knew far more about Leslie than he did. Were they lovers? Old lovers, perhaps?

"She keeps secrets," he said. "She was shot. Who did it?"

Ed lifted both eyebrows. "Who said she was shot?" he asked innocently, doing it so well that he actually fooled his cousin.

Matt hesitated. "Nobody. I assumed...well, how else does a bone get shattered?"

"By a blow, by a bad fall, in a car wreck..." Ed trailed off, leaving Matt with something to think about.

"Yes. Of course." The older man sighed. "Dancing put her in this shape. I didn't realize just how fragile she was. She doesn't exactly shout her problems to the world."

"She was always like that," Ed replied.

Matt turned to face him. "How did you meet her?"

"She and I were in college together," Ed told him. "We used to date occasionally. She trusts me," he added.

Matt was turning what he knew about Leslie over in his mind. If the pieces had been part of a puzzle, none of them would fit. When they first met, she avoided his touch like the plague. Last night, she'd enjoyed his advances. She'd been nervous and shy at their first meeting. Later, at the office, she'd been gregarious, almost playful. Last night, she'd been a completely different woman on the dance floor. Then, when he'd taken her home with him, she'd been hungry, sensuous, tender. Nothing about her made any sense.

"Don't trust her too far," Matt advised the other man. "She's too secretive to suit me. I thinks she's hiding something... maybe something pretty bad."

Ed didn't dare react. He pursed his lips and smiled. "Leslie's never hurt anyone in her life," he remarked. "And before you get the wrong idea about her, you'd better know that she has a real fear of men."

Matt laughed. "Oh, that's a good one," he said mockingly. "You should have seen her last night when we were alone."

Ed's eyes narrowed. "What do you mean?"

"I mean she's easy," Matt said with a contemptuous smile.

Ed's eyes began to glitter. He called his cousin a name that made Matt's eyebrows arch.

"Easy. My God!" Ed ground out.

Matt was puzzled by the other man's inexplicable behavior. Probably he was jealous. His cell phone began to trill, diverting him. He answered it. He recognized Carolyn's voice immediately and moved away, so that Ed couldn't hear what he said. Ed was certainly acting strange lately.

"I thought you were coming over to ride with me this afternoon," Carolyn said cheerfully. "Where are you?"

"At the hospital," he said absently, his eyes on Ed's retreating back going through the emergency room doors. "What did you say to Leslie last night?"

"What do you mean?"

"When you phoned her!" Matt prompted.

Carolyn sounded vague. "Well, I wanted to see if she was better," she replied. "She seemed to be in a lot of pain after the dance."

"What else did you say?"

Carolyn laughed. "Oh, I see. I'm being accused of something underhanded, is that it? Really, Matt, I thought you could see through that phony vulnerability of hers. What did she tell you I said?"

He shrugged. "Never mind. I must have misunderstood."

"You certainly did," she assured him firmly. "I wouldn't call someone in pain to upset them. I thought you knew me better than that."

"I do." He was seething. So now it seemed that Miss Murry was making up lies about Carolyn. Had it been to get even with him, for not giving in to her wiles? Or was she trying to turn his cousin against him?

"What about that horseback ride? And what are you doing at the hospital?" she added suddenly.

"I'm with Ed, visiting one of his friends," he said. "Better put the horseback ride off until next weekend. I'll phone you."

He hung up. His eyes darkened with anger. He wanted the Murry woman out of his company, out of his life. She was going to be nothing but trouble.

He repocketed the phone and went outside to wait for Ed and Leslie.

A good half hour later, Ed came out of the emergency room with his hands in his pockets, looking worried.

"They're keeping her overnight," he said curtly.

"For a sore leg?" Matt asked with mild sarcasm.

Ed scowled. "One of the bones shifted and it's pressing on a nerve," he replied. "Lou says it won't get any better until it's fixed. They're sending for an orthopedic man from Houston. He'll be in this afternoon."

"Who's going to pay for that?" Matt asked coldly.

"Since you ask, I am," Ed returned, not intimidated even by those glittery eyes.

"It's your money," the older man replied. He let out a breath. "What caused the bone to separate?"

"Why ask a question when you already know the answer?" Ed wanted to know. "I'm going to stay with her. She's frightened."

He was fairly certain that even if Leslie could fake pain, she couldn't fake an X-ray. Somewhere in the back of his mind he found guilt lurking. If he hadn't pulled her onto the dance floor, and if he hadn't jerked her to her feet...

He turned away and walked out of the building without another word. Leslie was Ed's business. He kept telling himself that. But all the way home, his conscience stabbed at him. She couldn't help being what she was. Even so, he hadn't meant to hurt her. He remembered the tears, genuine tears, boiling out of her eyes when Lou had touched her hair so gently. She acted as if she'd never had tenderness in her life.

He drove himself home and tried to concentrate on briefing himself for a director's meeting the next day. But long before bedtime, he gave it up and drank himself into uneasy sleep.

The orthopedic man examined the X-rays and seconded Lou's opinion that immediate surgery was required. But Leslie didn't want the surgery. She refused to talk about it. The minute the doctors and Ed left the room, she struggled out of bed and hobbled to the closet to pull her pajamas and robe and shoes out of it.

In the hall, Matt came upon Ed and Lou and a tall, distinguished stranger in an expensive suit.

"You two look like stormy weather," he mused. "What's wrong?"

"Leslie won't have the operation," Ed muttered worriedly. "Dr. Santos flew all the way from Houston to do the surgery, and she won't hear of it."

"Maybe she doesn't think she needs it," Matt said.

Lou glanced at him. "You have no idea what sort of pain she's in," she said, impatient with him. "One of the bone fragments, the one that shifted, is pressing right on a nerve."

"The bones should have been properly aligned at the time the accident occurred," the visiting orthopedic surgeon agreed. "It was criminally irresponsible of the attending physician to do nothing more than bandage the leg. A cast wasn't even used until afterward!"

That sounded negligent to Matt, too. He frowned. "Did she say why not?"

Lou sighed angrily. "She won't talk about it. She won't listen to any of us. Eventually she'll have to. But in the meantime, the pain is going to drive her insane."

Matt glanced from one set face to the other and walked past them to Leslie's room.

She was wearing her flannel pajamas and reaching for the robe when Matt walked in. She gave him a glare hot enough to boil water.

"Well, at least you won't be trying to talk me into an operation I don't want," she muttered as she struggled to get from the closet to the bed.

"Why won't I?"

She arched both eyebrows expressively. "I'm the enemy."

He stood at the foot of the bed, watching her get into the robe. Her leg was at an awkward angle, and her face was pinched. He could imagine the sort of pain she was already experiencing.

"Suit yourself about the operation," he replied with forced indifference, folding his arms across his chest. "But don't expect me to have someone carry you back and forth around the office. If you want to make a martyr of yourself, be my guest."

She stopped fiddling with the belt of the robe and stared at him quietly, puzzled.

"Some people enjoy making themselves objects of pity to people around them," he continued deliberately.

"I don't want pity!" she snapped.

"Really?"

She wrapped the belt around her fingers and stared at it. "I'll have to be in a cast."

"No doubt."

"My insurance hasn't taken effect yet, either," she said with averted eyes. "Once it's in force, I can have the operation." She looked back at him coldly. "I'm not going to let Ed pay for it, in case you wondered, and I don't care if he can afford it!"

He had to fight back a stirring of admiration for her independent stance. It could be part of the pose, he realized, but it sounded pretty genuine. His blue eyes narrowed. "I'll pay for it," he said, surprising both of them. "It can come out of your weekly check."

Her teeth clenched. "I know how much this sort of thing costs. That's why I've never had it done before. I'd never be able to pay it back in my lifetime."

His eyes fell to her body. "We could work something out," he murmured.

She flushed. "No, we couldn't!"

She stood up, barely able to stand the pain, despite the painkillers they'd given her. She hobbled over to the chair, where her shoes were placed, and eased her feet into them.

"Where are you going?" he asked conversationally.

"Home," she said, and started past him.

He caught her up in his arms like a fallen package and carried her right back to the bed, dumping her on it gently. His arms made a cage as he looked down at her flushed face. "Don't be stupid," he said in a voice that went right through her. "You're no good to yourself or anyone else in this condition. You have no choice."

Her lips trembled as she fought to control the tears. She would be helpless, vulnerable. Besides, that surgeon reminded her of the man at the emergency room in Houston. He brought back unbearable shame.

The unshed tears fascinated Matt. She fascinated him. He didn't want to care about what happened to her, but he did.

He reached down and smoothed a long forefinger over her wet lashes. "Do you have family?" he asked unexpectedly.

She thought of her mother, in prison, and felt sick to her very soul. "No," she whispered starkly.

"Are both your parents dead?"

"Yes," she said at once.

"No brothers, sisters?"

She shook her head.

He frowned, as if her situation disturbed him. In fact, it did. She looked vulnerable and fragile and completely lost. He didn't understand why he cared so much for her well-being. Perhaps it was guilt because he'd lured her into a kind of dancing she wasn't really able to do anymore.

"I want to go home," she said harshly.

"Afterward," he replied.

She remembered him saying that before, in almost the same way, and she averted her face in shame.

He could have bitten his tongue for that. He shouldn't bait her when she was in such a condition. It was hitting below the belt.

He drew in a long breath. "Leave it to Ed to pick up strays, and make me responsible for them!" he muttered, angry because of her vulnerability and his unwanted response to it.

She didn't say a word, but her lower lip trembled and she turned her face away from him. Beside her hip, her hand was clenched so tightly that the knuckles were white.

He shot away from the bed, his eyes furious. "You're having the damned operation," he informed her flatly. "Once you're healthy and whole again, you won't need Ed to prop you up. You can work for your living like every other woman."

She didn't answer him. She didn't look at him. She wanted to get better so that she could kick the hell out of him.

"Did you hear me?" he asked in a dangerously soft tone.

She jerked her head to acknowledge the question but she didn't speak.

He let out an angry breath. "I'll tell the others."

He left her lying there and announced her decision to the three people in the hall.

"How did you manage that?" Ed asked when Lou and Dr. Santos went back in to talk to Leslie.

"I made her mad," Matt replied. "Sympathy doesn't work."

"No, it doesn't," Ed replied quietly. "I don't think she's had much of it in her whole life."

"What happened to her parents?" he wanted to know.

Ed was careful about the reply. "Her father misjudged the position of some electrical wires and flew right into them. He was electrocuted."

He frowned darkly. "And her mother?"

"They were both in love with the same man," Ed said evasively. "He died, and Leslie and her mother still aren't on speaking terms."

Matt turned away, jingling the change in his pocket restlessly. "How did he die?"

"Violently," Ed told him. "It was a long time ago. But I don't think Leslie will ever get over it."

Which was true, but it sounded as if Leslie was still in love with the dead man—which was exactly what Ed wanted. He was going to save her from Matt, whatever it took. She was a good friend. He didn't want her life destroyed because Matt was on the prowl for a new conquest. Leslie deserved something better than to be one of Matt's ex-girlfriends.

Matt glanced at his cousin with a puzzling expression. "When will they operate?"

"Tomorrow morning," Ed said. "I'll be late getting to work. I'm going to be here while it's going on."

Matt nodded. He glanced down the hall toward the door of Leslie's room. He hesitated for a moment before he turned and went out of the building without another comment.

Later, Ed questioned her about what Matt had said to her.

"He said that I was finding excuses because I wanted people to feel sorry for me," she said angrily. "And I do not have a martyr complex!"

Ed chuckled. "I know that."

"I can't believe you're related to someone like that," she said furiously. "He's horrible!"

"He's had a rough life. Something you can identify with," he added gently.

"I think he and his latest girlfriend deserve each other," she murmured.

"Carolyn phoned while he was here. I don't know what was said, but I'd bet my bottom dollar she denied saying anything to upset you."

"Would you expect her to admit it?" she asked. She laid back against the pillow, glad that the injection they'd given her was taking effect. "I guess I'll be clumping around your office in a cast for weeks, if he doesn't find some excuse to fire me in the meantime."

"There is company policy in such matters," he said easily. "He'd have to have my permission to fire you, and he won't get it."

"I'm impressed," she said, and managed a wan smile.

"So you should be," he chuckled. He searched her eyes. "Leslie, why didn't the doctor set those bones when it happened?"

She studied the ceiling. "He said the whole thing was my fault and that I deserved all my wounds. He called me a vicious little tramp who caused decent men to be murdered." Her eyes closed. "Nothing ever hurt so much."

"I can imagine!"

"I never went to a doctor again," she continued. "It wasn't just the things he said to me, you know. There was the expense, too. I had no insurance and no money. Mama had to have a public defender and I worked while I finished high school to help pay my way at my friend's house. The pain was bad, but eventually I got used to it, and the limp." She turned quiet eyes to Ed's face. "It would be sort of nice to be able to walk normally again. And I will pay back whatever it costs, if you and your cousin will be patient."

He winced. "Nobody's worried about the cost."

"He is," she informed him evenly. "And he's right. I don't want to be a financial burden on anyone, not even him."

"We'll talk about all this later," he said gently. "Right now, I just want you to get better."

She sighed. "Will I? I wonder."

"Miracles happen all the time," he told her. "You're overdue for one."

"I'd settle gladly for the ability to walk normally," she said at once, and she smiled.

6

The operation was over by lunchtime the following day. Ed stayed until Leslie was out of the recovery room and out of danger, lying still and pale in the bed in the private room with the private nurse he'd hired to stay with her for the first couple of days. He'd spoken to both Lou Coltrain and the visiting orthopedic surgeon, who assured him that Miss Murry would find life much less painful from now on. Modern surgery had progressed to the point that procedures once considered impossible were now routine.

He went back to work feeling light and cheerful. Matt stopped him in the hall.

"Well?" he asked abruptly.

Ed grinned from ear to ear. "She's going to be fine. Dr. Santos said that in six weeks, when she comes out of that cast, she'll be able to dance in a contest."

Matt nodded. "Good."

Ed answered a question Matt had about one of their accounts and then, assuming that Matt didn't want anything else at the moment, he went back to his office. He had a temporary secretary, a pretty little redhead who had a bright personality and good dictation skills.

Surprisingly, Matt followed him into his office and closed the door. "Tell me how that bone was shattered," he said abruptly.

Ed sat down and leaned forward with his forearms on his cluttered desk. "That's Leslie's business, Matt," he replied. "I wouldn't tell you, even if I knew," he added, lying through his teeth with deliberate calm.

He sighed irritably. "She's a puzzle. A real puzzle."

"She's a sweet girl who's had a lot of hard knocks," Ed told him. "But regardless of what you think you know about her, she isn't 'easy.' Don't make the mistake of classing her with your usual sort of woman. You'll regret it."

Matt studied the younger man curiously and his eyes narrowed. "What do you mean, I think she's 'easy'?" he asked, bristling.

"Forgotten already? That's what you said about her."

Matt felt uncomfortable at the words that he'd spoken with such assurance to Leslie. He glanced at Ed irritably. "Miss Murry obviously means something to you. If you're so fond of her, why haven't you married her?"

Ed smoothed back his hair. "She kept me from blowing my brains out when my fiancée was gunned down in a bank robbery in Houston," he said. "I actually had the pistol loaded. She took it away from me."

Matt's eyes narrowed. "You never told me you were that despondent."

"You wouldn't have understood," came the reply. "Women were always a dime a dozen to you, Matt. You've never really been in love."

Matt's face, for once, didn't conceal his bitterness. "I wouldn't give any woman that sort of power over me," he said in clipped tones. "Women are devious, Ed. They'll smile at you until they get what they want, then they'll walk right over you to the next sucker. I've seen too many good men brought down by women they loved."

"There are bad men, too," Ed pointed out.

Matt shrugged. "I'm not arguing with that." He smiled. "I would have done what I could for you, though," he added. "We have our disagreements, but we're closer than most cousins are."

Ed nodded. "Yes, we are."

"You really are fond of Miss Murry, aren't you?"

"In a big brotherly sort of way," Ed affirmed. "She trusts me. If you knew her, you'd understand how difficult it is for her to trust a man."

"I think she's pulling the wool over your eyes," Matt told him. "You be careful. She's down on her luck, and you're rich."

Ed's face contorted briefly. "Good God, Matt, you haven't got a clue what she's really like."

"Neither have you," Matt commented with a cold smile. "But I know things about her that you don't. Let's leave it at that."

Ed hated his own impotence. "I want to keep her in my office."

"How do you expect her to come to work in a cast?" he asked frankly.

Ed leaned back in his chair and grinned. "The same way I did five years ago, when I had that skiing accident and broke my ankle. People work with broken bones all the time. And she doesn't type with her feet."

Matt shrugged. Miss Murry had him completely confused. "Suit yourself," he said finally. "Just keep her out of my way."

That shouldn't be difficult, Ed thought ruefully. Matt certainly wasn't on Leslie's list of favorite people. He wondered what the days ahead would bring. It would be like storing dynamite with lighted candles.

Leslie was out of the hospital in three days and back at work in a week. The company had paid for her surgery, to her surprise and Ed's. She knew that Matt had only done that out of guilt. Well, he needn't flay himself over what happened. She didn't really blame him. She had loved dancing with him. She refused to think of how that evening had ended. Some memories were best forgotten.

She hobbled into Ed's office with the use of crutches and plopped herself down behind her desk on her first day back on the job.

"How did you get here?" Ed asked with a surprised smile. "You can't drive, can you?"

"No, but one of the girls in my rooming house works in downtown Jacobsville and we're going to become a carpool three days a week. I'm paying my share of the gas and on her days off, I'll get a taxi to work," she added.

"I'm glad you're back," he said with genuine fondness.

"Oh, sure you are," she said with a teasing glance. "I heard all about Karla Smith when the girls from Mr. Caldwell's office came to see me. I understand she has a flaming crush on you."

Ed chuckled. "So they say. Poor girl."

She made a face. "You can't live in the past."

"Tell yourself that."

She put her crutches on the floor beside the desk, and swiveled back in her desk chair. "It's going to be a little difficult for me to get back and forth to your office," she said. "Can you dictate letters in here?"

"Of course."

She looked around the office with pleasure. "I'm glad I got to come back," she murmured. "I thought Mr. Caldwell might find an excuse to let me go."

"I'm Mr. Caldwell, too," he pointed out. "Matt's bark is worse than his bite. He won't fire you."

She grimaced. "Don't let me cause trouble between you," she said with genuine concern. "I'd rather quit…"

"No, you won't," he interrupted. He ruffled her short hair with a playful grin. "I like having you around. Besides, you spell better than the other women."

Her eyes lit up as she looked at him. She smiled back. "Thanks, boss."

Matt opened the door in time to encounter the affectionate looks they exchanged and his face hardened as he slammed it behind him.

They both jumped.

"Jehosophat, Matt!" Ed burst out, catching his breath. "Don't do that!"

"Don't play games with your secretary on my time," Matt returned. His cold dark eyes went to Leslie, whose own eyes went cold at sight of him. "Back at work, I see, Miss Murry."

"All the better to pay you back for my hospital stay, sir," she returned with a smile that bordered on insolence.

He bit back a sharp reply and turned to Ed, ignoring her. "I want you to take Nell Hobbs out to lunch and find out how she's going to vote on the zoning proposal. If they zone that land adjoining my ranch as recreational, I'm going to spend my life in court."

"If she votes for it, she'll be the only one," Ed assured him. "I spoke to the other commissioners myself."

He seemed to relax a little. "Okay. In that case, you can run over to Houlihan's dealership and drive my new Jaguar over here. It came in this morning."

Ed's eyes widened. "You're going to let me drive it?"

"Why not?" Matt asked with a warm smile, the sort Leslie knew she'd never see on that handsome face.

Ed chuckled. "Then, thanks. I'll be back shortly!" He started down the hall at a dead run. "Leslie, we'll do those letters after lunch!"

"Sure," she said. "I can spend the day updating those old herd records." She glanced at Matt to let him know she hadn't forgotten his instructions from before her operation.

He put his hands in the pockets of his slacks and his blue eyes searched her gray ones intently. Deliberately he let his gaze fall to her soft mouth. He remembered the feel of it clinging to his parted lips, hungry and moaning...

His teeth clenched. He couldn't think about that. "The herd records can wait," he said tersely. "My secretary is home with a sick child, so you can work for me for the rest of the day. Ed can let Miss Smith handle his urgent stuff today."

She hesitated visibly. "Yes, sir," she said in a wooden voice.

"I have to talk to Henderson about one of the new accounts. I'll meet you in my office in thirty minutes."

"Yes, sir."

They were watching each other like opponents in a match when Matt made an angry sound under his breath and walked out.

Leslie spent a few minutes sorting the mail and looking over it. A little over a half hour went by before she realized it. A sound caught her attention and she looked up to find an impatient Matt Caldwell standing in the doorway.

"Sorry. I lost track of the time," she said quickly, putting the opened mail aside. She reached for her crutches and got up out of her chair, reaching for her pad and pen when she was ready to go. She looked up at Matt, who seemed taller than ever. "I'm ready when you are, boss," she said courteously.

"Don't call me boss," he said flatly.

"Okay, Mr. Caldwell," she returned.

He glared at her, but she gave him a bland look and even managed a smile. He wanted to throw things.

He turned, leaving her to follow him down the long hall to his executive office, which had a bay window overlooking downtown Jacobsville. His desk was solid oak, huge, covered with equipment and papers of all sorts. There was a kid leather-covered chair behind the desk and two equally impressive wing chairs, and a sofa, all done in burgundy. The carpet was a deep, rich beige. The curtains were plaid, picking up the burgundy in the furniture and adding it to autumn hues. There was a framed portrait of someone who looked vaguely like Matt over the mantel of the fireplace, in which gas logs rested. There were two chairs and a table near the fireplace, probably where Matt and some visitor would share a pot of coffee or a drink. There was a bar against one wall with a mirror behind it, giving an added air of spacious comfort to the high-ceilinged room. The windows were tall ones, unused because the Victorian house that contained the offices had central heating.

Matt watched her studying her surroundings covertly. He closed the door behind them and motioned her into a chair facing the desk. She eased down into it and put her crutches beside her. She was still a little uncomfortable, but aspirin was enough to contain the pain these days. She looked forward to having the cast off, to walking normally again.

She put the pad on her lap and maneuvered the leg in the cast so that it was as comfortable as she could get it.

Matt was leaning back in his chair with his booted feet on the desk and his eyes narrow and watchful as he sketched her slender body in the flowing beige pantsuit she was wearing with a patterned scarf tucked in the neck of the jacket. The outside seam in the left leg of her slacks had been snipped to allow for the cast. Otherwise, she was covered from head to toe, just as she had been from the first time he saw her. Odd, that he hadn't really noticed that before. It wasn't a new habit dating from the night he'd touched her so intimately, either.

"How's the leg?" he asked curtly.

"Healing, thank you," she replied. "I've already spoken to the bookkeeper about pulling out a quarter of my check weekly…"

He leaned forward so abruptly that it sounded like a gunshot when his booted feet hit the floor.

"I'll take that up with bookkeeping," he said sharply. "You've overstepped your authority, Miss Murry. Don't do it again."

She shifted in the chair, moving the ungainly cast, and assumed a calm expression. "I'm sorry, Mr. Caldwell."

Her voice was serene but her hands were shaking on the pad and pen. He averted his eyes and got to his feet, glaring out the window.

She waited patiently with her eyes on the blank pad, wondering when he was going to start dictation.

"You told Ed that Carolyn phoned you the night before we

took you to the emergency room and made some cruel remarks." He remembered what Ed had related about that conversation and it made him unusually thoughtful. He turned and caught her surprised expression. "Carolyn denies saying anything to upset you."

Her expression didn't change. She didn't care what he thought of her anymore. She didn't say a word in her defense.

His dark eyebrows met over the bridge of his nose. "Well?"

"What would you like me to say?"

"You might try apologizing," he told her coldly, trying to smoke her out. "Carolyn was very upset to have such a charge made against her. I don't like having her upset," he added deliberately and stood looking down his nose at her, waiting for her to react to the challenge.

Her fingers tightened around the pencil. It was going to be worse than she ever dreamed, trying to work with him. He couldn't fire her, Ed had said, but that didn't mean he couldn't make her quit. If he made things difficult enough for her, she wouldn't be able to stay.

All at once, it didn't seem worth the effort. She was tired, worn-out, and Carolyn had hurt her, not the reverse. She was sick to death of trying to live from one day to the next with the weight of the past bearing down on her more each day. Being tormented by Matt Caldwell on top of all that was the last straw.

She reached for her crutches and stood up, pad and all.

"Where do you think you're going?" Matt demanded, surprised that she was giving up without an argument.

She went toward the door. He got in front of her, an easy enough task when every step she took required extreme effort.

She looked up at him with the eyes of a trapped animal, resigned and resentful and without life. "Ed said you couldn't fire me without his consent," she said quietly. "But you can hound me until I quit, can't you?"

He didn't speak. His face was rigid. "Would you give up so easily?" he asked, baiting her. "Where will you go?"

Her gaze dropped to the floor. Idly she noticed that one of her flat-heeled shoes had a smudge of mud on it. She should clean it off.

"I said, where will you go?" Matt persisted.

She met his cold eyes. "Surely in all of Texas, there's more than one secretarial position available," she said. "Please move. You're blocking the door."

He did move, but not in the way she'd expected. He took the crutches away from her and propped them against the bookshelf by the door. His hands went on either side of her head, trapping her in front of him. His dark eyes held a faint glitter as he studied her wan face, her soft mouth.

"Don't," she managed tightly.

He moved closer. He smelled of spice and aftershave and coffee. His breath was warm where it brushed her forehead. She could feel the warmth of his tall, fit body, and she remembered reluctantly how it had felt to let him hold her and touch her in his bedroom.

He was remembering those same things, but not with pleasure. He hated the attraction he felt for this woman, whom he didn't, couldn't trust.

"You don't like being touched, you said," he reminded her with deliberate sarcasm as his lean hand suddenly smoothed over her breast and settled there provocatively.

Her indrawn breath was audible. She looked up at him with all her hidden vulnerabilities exposed. "Please don't do this," she whispered. "I'm no threat to Ed, or to you, either. Just...let me go. I'll vanish."

She probably would, and that wounded him. He was making her life miserable. Why did this woman arouse such bitter feelings in him, when he was the soul of kindness to most people with problems—especially physical problems, like hers.

"Ed won't like it," he said tersely.

"Ed doesn't have to know anything," she said dully. "You can tell him whatever you like."

"Is he your lover?"

"No."

"Why not? You don't mind if he touches you."

"He doesn't. Not...the way you do."

Her strained voice made him question his own cruelty. He lifted his hand away from her body and tilted her chin up so that he could see her eyes. They were turbulent, misty.

"How many poor fools have you played the innocent with, Miss Murry?" he asked coldly.

She saw the lines in his face, many more than his age should have caused. She saw the coldness in his eyes, the bitterness of too many betrayals, too many loveless years.

Unexpectedly she reached up and touched his hair, smoothing it back as Lou had smoothed hers back in an act of silent compassion.

It made him furious. His body pressed down completely against hers, holding her prisoner. His hips twisted in a crude, rough motion that was instantly arousing.

She tried to twist away and he groaned huskily, giving her a worldly smile when she realized that her attempt at escape had failed and made the situation even worse.

Her face colored. It was like that night. It was the way Mike had behaved, twisting his body against her innocent one and laughing at her embarrassment. He'd said things, done things to her in front of his friends that still made her want to gag.

Matt's hand fell to her hip and contracted as he used one of his long legs to nudge hers apart. She was stiff against him, frozen with painful memories of another man, another en-counter, that had begun just this way. She'd thought she loved Mike until he made her an object of lustful ridicule, making fun of her innocence as he anticipated its delights for the enjoyment of his laughing friends, grouped around them as he forcibly stripped the clothes away from her body. He laughed at her small breasts, at her slender figure, and all the while he touched her insolently and made jokes about her most intimate places.

She was years in the past, reliving the torment, the shame, that had seen her spread-eagled on the wood floor with Mike's drug-crazed friends each holding one of her shaking limbs still while Mike lowered his nude body onto hers and roughly parted her legs...

Matt realized belatedly that Leslie was frozen in place like a statue with a white face and eyes that didn't even see him. He could hear her heartbeat, quick and frantic. Her whole body shook, but not with pleasure or anticipation.

Frowning, he let her go and stepped back. She shivered again, convulsively. Mike had backed away, too, to the sound of a firecracker popping loudly. But it hadn't been a firecracker. It had been a bullet. It went right through him, into Leslie's leg. He looked surprised. Leslie remembered his blue eyes as the life visibly went out of them, leaving them fixed and blank just before he fell heavily on her. There had been such a tiny hole in his back, compared to the one in his chest. Her mother was screaming, trying to fire again, trying to kill her. Leslie had seduced her own lover, she wanted to kill them both, and she was glad Mike was dead. Leslie would be dead, too!

Leslie remembered lying there naked on the floor, with a shattered leg and blood pouring from it so rapidly that she knew she was going to bleed to death before help arrived…

"Leslie?" Matt asked sharply.

He became a white blur as she slid down the wall into oblivion.

When she came to, Ed was bending over her with a look of anguished concern. He had a damp towel pressed to her forehead. She looked at him dizzily.

"Ed?" she murmured.

"Yes. How are you?"

She blinked and looked around. She was lying on the big burgundy leather couch in Matt's office. "What happened?" she asked numbly. "Did I faint?"

"Apparently," Ed said heavily. "You came back to work too soon. I shouldn't have agreed."

"But I'm all right," she insisted, pulling herself up. She felt nauseous. She had to swallow repeatedly before she was able to move again.

She took a slow breath and smiled at him. "I'm still a little weak, I guess, and I didn't have any breakfast."

"Idiot," he said, smiling.

She smiled back. "I'm okay. Hand me my crutches, will you?"

He got them from where they were propped against the wall, and she had a glimpse of Matt standing there as if he'd been carved from stone. She took the crutches from Ed and got them under her arms.

"Would you drive me home?" she asked Ed. "I think maybe I will take one more day off, if that's all right?"

"That's all right," Ed assured her. He looked across the room. "Right, Matt?"

Matt nodded, a curt jerk of his head. He gave her one last look and went out the door.

The relief Leslie felt almost knocked her legs from under her. She remembered what had happened, but she wasn't about to tell Ed. She wasn't going to cause a breach between him and the older cousin he adored. She, who had no family left in the world except the mother who hated her, had more respect for family than most people.

She let Ed take her home, and she didn't think about what had happened in Matt's office. She knew that every time she saw him from now on, she'd relive those last few horrible minutes in her mother's apartment when she was seventeen. If she'd had anyplace else to go, she'd leave. But she was trapped, for the moment, at the mercy of a man who had none, a victim of a past she couldn't even talk about.

Ed went back to the office determined to have it out with Matt. He knew instinctively that Leslie's collapse was caused by something the other man did or said, and he was going to stop the treatment Matt was giving her before it was too late.

It was anticlimactic when he got into Matt's office, with his speech rehearsed and ready, only to find it empty.

"He said he was going up to Victoria to see a man about some property, Mr. Caldwell," one of the secretaries commented. "Left in a hurry, too, in that brand-new red Jaguar. We hear you got to drive it over from Houlihan's."

"Yes, I did," he replied, forcing a cheerful smile. "It goes like the wind."

"We noticed," she murmured dryly. "He was flying when he turned the corner. I hope he slows down. It would be a pity if he wrecked it when he'd only just gotten it."

"So it would," Ed replied. He went back to his own office, curious about Matt's odd behavior but rather relieved that the showdown wouldn't have to be faced right away.

7

Matt was doing almost a hundred miles an hour on the long highway that led to Victoria. He couldn't get Leslie's face out of his mind. That hadn't been anger or even fear in her gray eyes. It went beyond those emotions. She had been terrified; not of him, but of something she could see that he couldn't. Her tortured gaze had hurt him in a vulnerable spot he didn't know he had. When she fainted, he hated himself. He'd never thought of himself as a particularly cruel man, but he was with Leslie. He couldn't understand the hostility she roused in him. She was fragile, for all her independence and strength of will. Fragile. Vulnerable. Tender.

He remembered the touch of her soft fingers smoothing back his hair and he groaned out loud with self-hatred. He'd been tormenting her, and she'd seen right through the harsh words to the pain that lay underneath them. In return for his insensitivity, she'd reached up and touched him with genuine compassion. He'd rewarded that exquisite tenderness with treatment he wouldn't have offered to a hardened prostitute.

He realized that the speed he was going exceeded the limit by a factor of two and took his foot off the pedal. He didn't even know where the hell he was going. He was running for cover, he supposed, and laughed coldly at his own reaction to Leslie's fainting spell. All his life he'd been kind to stray animals and people down on their luck. He'd followed up that record by torturing a crippled young woman who felt sorry for him. Next, he supposed, he'd be kicking lame dogs down steps.

He pulled off on the side of the highway, into a lay-by, and stopped the car, resting his head on the steering wheel. He didn't recognize himself since Leslie Murry had walked into his life. She brought out monstrous qualities in him. He was ashamed of the way he'd treated her. She was a sweet woman who always seemed surprised when people did kind things for her. On the other hand, Matt's antagonism and hostility didn't seem to surprise her. Was that what she'd had the most of in her life? Had people been so cruel to her that now she expected and accepted cruelty as her lot in life?

He leaned back in the seat and stared at the flat horizon. His mother's desertion and his recent notoriety had soured him on the whole female sex. His mother was an old wound. The assault suit had made him bitter, yet again, despite the fact that he'd avenged himself on the perpetrator. But he remembered her coy, sweet personality very well. She'd pretended innocence and helplessness and when the disguise had come off, he'd found himself the object of vicious public humiliation. His name had been cleared, but the anger and resentment had remained.

But none of that excused his recent behavior. He'd overreacted with Leslie. He was sorry and ashamed for making her suffer for something that wasn't her fault. He took a long breath and put the car in gear. Well, he couldn't run away. He might as well go back to work. Ed would probably be waiting with blood in his eye, and he wouldn't blame him. He deserved a little discomfort.

Ed did read him the riot act, and he took it. He couldn't deny that he'd been unfair to Leslie. He wished he could understand what it was about her that raised the devil in him.

"If you genuinely don't like her," Ed concluded, "can't you just ignore her?"

"Probably," Matt said without meeting his cousin's accusing eyes.

"Then would you? Matt, she needs this job," he continued solemnly.

Matt studied him sharply. "Why does she need it?" he asked. "And why doesn't she have anyplace to go?"

"I can't tell you. I gave my word."

"Is she in some sort of trouble with the law?"

Ed laughed softly. "Leslie?"

"Never mind." He moved back toward the door. He stopped and turned as he reached it. "When she fainted, she said something."

"What?" Ed asked curiously.

"She said, 'Mike, don't.'" He didn't blink. "Who's Mike?"

"A dead man," Ed replied. "Years dead."

"The man she and her mother competed for."

"That's right," Ed said. "If you mention his name in front of her, I'll walk out the door with her, and I won't come back. Ever."

That was serious business to Ed, he realized. He frowned thoughtfully. "Did she love him?"

"She thought she did," Ed replied. His eyes went cold. "He destroyed her life."

"How?"

Ed didn't reply. He folded his hands on the desk and just stared at Matt.

The older man let out an irritated breath. "Has it occurred to you that all this secrecy is only complicating matters?"

"It's occurred. But if you want answers, you'll have to ask Leslie. I don't break promises."

Matt muttered to himself as he opened the door and went out. Ed stared after him worriedly. He hoped he'd done the right thing. He was trying to protect Leslie, but for all he knew, he might just have made matters worse. Matt didn't like mysteries. God forbid that he should try to force Leslie to talk about something she only wanted to forget. He was also worried about Matt's potential reaction to the old scandal. How would he feel if he knew how notorious Leslie really was, if he knew that her mother was serving a sentence for murder?

Ed was worried enough to talk to Leslie about it that evening when he stopped by to see how she was.

"I don't want him to know," she said when Ed questioned her. "Ever."

"What if he starts digging and finds out by himself?" Ed asked bluntly. "He'll read everyone's point of view except yours, and even if he reads every tabloid that ran the story, he still won't know the truth of what happened."

"I don't care what he thinks," she lied. "Anyway, it doesn't matter now."

"Why not?"

"Because I'm not coming back to work," she said evenly, avoiding his shocked gaze. "They need a typist at the Jacobsville sewing plant. I applied this afternoon and they accepted me."

"How did you get there?" he asked.

"Cabs run even in Jacobsville, Ed, and I'm not totally penniless." She lifted her head proudly. "I'll pay your cousin back the price of my operation, however long it takes. But I won't take one more day of the sort of treatment I've been getting from him. I'm sorry if he hates women, but I'm not going to become a scapegoat. I've had enough misery."

"I'll agree there," he said. "But I wish you'd reconsider. I had a long talk with him…"

"You didn't tell him?" she exclaimed, horrified.

"No, I didn't tell him," he replied. "But I think you should."

"It's none of his business," she said through her teeth. "I don't owe him an explanation."

"I know it doesn't seem like it, Leslie," he began, "but he's not a bad man." He frowned, searching for a way to explain it to her. "I don't pretend to understand why you set him off, but I'm sure he realizes that he's being unfair."

"He can be unfair as long as he likes, but I'm not giving him any more free shots at me. I mean it, Ed. I'm not coming back."

He leaned forward, feeling defeated. "Well, I'll be around if you need me. You're still my best friend."

She reached out and touched his hand where it rested on his knee. "You're mine, too. I don't know how I'd have managed if it hadn't been for you and your father."

He smiled. "You'd have found a way. Whatever you're lacking, it isn't courage."

She sighed, looking down at her hand resting on his. "I don't know if that's true anymore," she confessed. "I'm so tired of fighting. I thought I could come to Jacobsville and get my life in order, get some peace. And the first man I run headlong into is a male chauvinist with a grudge against the whole female sex. I feel like I've been through the wringer backward."

"What did he say to you today?" he asked.

She blotted out the physical insult. "The usual things, most vividly the way I'd upset Carolyn by lying about her phone call."

"Some lie!" he muttered.

"He believes her."

"I can't imagine why. I used to think he was intelligent."

"He is, or he wouldn't be a millionaire." She got up. "Now go home, Ed. I've got to get some rest so I can be bright and cheerful my first day at my new job."

He winced. "I wanted things to be better than this for you."

She laughed gently. "And just think what a terrible world we'd have if we always got what we think we want."

He had to admit that she had a point. "That sewing plant isn't a very good place to work," he added worriedly.

"It's only temporary," she assured him.

He grimaced. "Well, if you need me, you know where I am."

She smiled. "Thanks."

He went home and ate supper and was watching the news when Matt knocked at the door just before opening it and walking in. And why not, Ed thought, when Matt had been raised here, just as he had. He grinned at his cousin as he came into the living room and sprawled over an easy chair.

"How does the Jag drive?" he asked.

"Like an airplane on the ground," he chuckled. He stared at the television screen for a minute. "How's Leslie?"

He grimaced. "She's got a new job."

Matt went very still. "What?"

"She said she doesn't want to work for me anymore. She got a job at the sewing plant, typing. I tried to talk her out of it. She won't budge." He glanced at Matt apologetically. "She knew I wouldn't let you fire her. She said you'd made sure she wanted to quit." He shrugged. "I guess you did. I've known Leslie for six years. I've never known her to faint."

Matt's dark eyes slid to the television screen and seemed to be glued there for a time. The garment company paid minimum wage. He doubted she'd have enough left over after her rent and grocery bill to pay for the medicine she had to take for pain. He couldn't remember a time in his life when he'd been so ashamed of himself. She wasn't going to like working in that plant. He knew the manager, a penny-pinching social climber who didn't believe in holidays, sick days, or paid vacation. He'd work her to death for her pittance and complain because she couldn't do more.

Matt's mouth thinned. He'd landed Leslie in hell with his bad temper and unreasonable prejudice.

Matt got up from the chair and walked out the door without a goodbye. Ed went back to the news without much real enthusiasm. Matt had what he wanted. He didn't look very pleased with it, though.

After a long night fraught with even more nightmares, Leslie got up early and took a cab to the manufacturing company, hobbling in on her crutches to the personnel office where Judy

Blakely, the personnel manager, was waiting with her usual kind smile.

"Nice to see you, Miss Murry!"

"Nice to see you, too," she replied. "I'm looking forward to my new job."

Mrs. Blakely looked worried and reticent. She folded her hands in a tight clasp on her desk. "Oh, I don't know how to tell you this," she wailed. She grimaced. "Miss Murry, the girl you were hired to replace just came back a few minutes ago and begged me to let her keep her job. It seems she has serious family problems and can't do without her salary. I'm so sorry. If we had anything else open, even on the floor, I'd offer it to you temporarily. But we just don't."

The poor woman looked as if the situation tormented her. Leslie smiled gently. "Don't worry, Mrs. Blakely, I'll find something else," she assured the older woman. "It's not the end of the world."

"I'd be furious," she said, her eyes wrinkled up with worry. "And you're being so nice...I feel like a dog!"

"You can't help it that things worked out like this." Leslie got to her feet a little heavily, still smiling. "Could you call me a cab?"

"Certainly! And we'll pay for it, too," she said firmly. "Honestly, I feel so awful!"

"It's all right. Sometimes we have setbacks that really turn into opportunities, you know."

Mrs. Blakely studied her intently. "You're such a positive person. I wish I was. I always seem to dwell on the negative."

"You might as well be optimistic, I always think," Leslie told her. "It doesn't cost extra."

Mrs. Blakely chuckled. "No, it doesn't, does it?" She phoned the cab and apologized again as Leslie went outside to wait for it.

She felt desolate, but she wasn't going to make that poor woman feel worse than she already did.

She was tired and sleepy. She wished the cab would come. She eased down onto the bench the company had placed out front for its employees, so they'd have a place to sit during their breaks. It was hard and uncomfortable, but much better than standing.

She wondered what she would do now. She had no prospects, no place to go. The only alternative was to look for something else or go back to Ed, and the latter choice wasn't a choice at all. She could never look Matt Caldwell in the face again without remembering how he'd treated her.

The sun glinted off the windshield of an approaching car, and she recognized Matt's new red Jaguar at once. She stood up, clutching her purse, stiff and defensive as he parked the car and got out to approach her.

He stopped an arm's length away. He looked as tired and worn-out as she did. His eyes were heavily lined. His black, wavy hair was disheveled. He put his hands on his hips and looked at her with pure malice.

She stared back with something approaching hatred.

"Oh, what the hell," he muttered, adding something about being hanged for sheep, as well as lambs.

He bent and swooped her up in his arms and started walking toward the Jaguar. She hit him with her purse.

"Stop that," he muttered. "You'll make me drop you. Considering the weight of that damned cast, you'd probably sink halfway through the planet."

"You put me down!" she raged, and hit him again. "I won't go as far as the street with you!"

He paused beside the passenger door of the Jag and searched her hostile eyes. "I hate secrets," he said.

"I can't imagine you have any, with Carolyn shouting them to all and sundry!"

His eyes fell to her mouth. "I didn't tell Carolyn that you were easy," he said in a voice so tender that it made her want to cry.

Her lips trembled as she tried valiantly not to.

He made a husky sound and his mouth settled right on her misty eyes, closing them with soft, tender kisses.

She bawled.

He took a long breath and opened the passenger door, shifting her as he slid her into the low-slung vehicle. "I've noticed that about you," he murmured as he fastened her seat belt.

"Noticed...what?" she sobbed, sniffling.

He pulled a handkerchief out of his dress slacks and put it in her hands. "You react very oddly to tenderness."

He closed the door on her surprised expression and fetched her crutches before he went around to get in behind the wheel. He paused to fasten his own seat belt and give her a quick scrutiny before he started the powerful engine and pulled out into the road.

"How did you know I was here?" she asked when the tears stopped.

"Ed told me."

"Why?"

He shrugged. "Beats me. I guess he thought I might be interested."

"Fat chance!"

He chuckled. It was the first time she'd heard him laugh naturally, without mockery or sarcasm. He shifted gears. "You don't know the guy who owns that little enterprise," he said conversationally, "but the plant is a sweatshop."

"That isn't funny."

"Do you think I'm joking?" he replied. "He likes to lure illegal immigrants in here with promises of big salaries and health benefits, and then when he's got them where he wants them, he threatens them with the immigration service if they don't work hard and accept the pittance he pays. We've all tried to get his operation closed down, but he's slippery as an eel." He glanced at her with narrowed dark eyes. "I'm not going to let you sell yourself into that just to get away from me."

"Let me?" She rose immediately to the challenge, eyes flashing. "You don't tell me what to do!"

He grinned. "That's better."

She hit her hand against the cast, furious. "Where are you taking me?"

"Home."

"You're going the wrong way."

"My home."

"No," she said icily. "Not again. Not ever again!"

He shifted gears, accelerated, and shifted again. He loved the smoothness of the engine, the ride. He loved the speed. He wondered if Leslie had loved fast cars before her disillusionment.

He glanced at her set features. "When your leg heals, I'll let you drive it."

"No, thanks," she almost choked.

"Don't you like cars?"

She pushed back her hair. "I can't drive," she said absently.

"What?"

"Look out, you're going to run us off the road!" she squealed.

He righted the car with a muffled curse and downshifted. "Everybody drives, for God's sake!"

"Not me," she said flatly.

"Why?"

She folded her arms over her breasts. "I just never wanted to."

More secrets. He was becoming accustomed to the idea that she never shared anything about her private life except, possibly, with Ed. He wanted her to open up, to trust him, to tell him what had happened to her. Then he laughed to himself at his own presumption. He'd been her mortal enemy since the first time he'd laid eyes on her, and he expected her to trust him?

"What are you laughing at?" she demanded.

He glanced at her as he slowed to turn into the ranch driveway. "I'll tell you one day. Are you hungry?"

"I'm sleepy."

He grimaced. "Let me see if I can guess why."

She glared at him. His own eyes had dark circles. "You haven't slept, either."

"Misery loves company."

"You started it!"

"Yes, I did!" he flashed back at her, eyes blazing. "Every time I look at you, I want to throw you down on the most convenient flat surface and ravish you! How's that for blunt honesty?"

She stiffened, wide-eyed, and gaped at him. He pulled up at his front door and cut off the engine. He turned in his seat and looked at her as if he resented her intensely. At the moment, he did.

His dark eyes narrowed. They were steady, intimidating. She glared into them.

But after a minute, the anger went out of him. He looked at her, really looked, and he saw things he hadn't noticed before. Her hair was dark just at her scalp. She was far too thin. Her eyes had dark circles so prominent that it looked as if she had two black eyes. There were harsh lines beside her mouth. She might pretend to be cheerful around Ed, but she wasn't. It was an act.

"Take a picture," she choked.

He sighed. "You really are fragile," he remarked quietly. "You give as good as you get, but all your vulnerabilities come out when you've got your back to the wall."

"I don't need psychoanalysis, but thanks for the thought," she said shortly.

He reached out, noticing how she shrank from his touch. It didn't bother him now. He knew that it was tenderness that frightened her with him, not ardor. He touched her hair at her temple and brushed it back gently, staring curiously at the darkness that was more prevalent then.

"You're a brunette," he remarked. "Why do you color your hair?"

"I wanted to be a blonde," she replied instantly, trying to withdraw further against the door.

"You keep secrets, Leslie," he said, and for once he was serious, not sarcastic. "At your age, it's unusual. You're young and until that leg started to act up, you were even relatively healthy. You should be carefree. Your life is an adventure that's only just beginning."

She laughed hollowly. "I wouldn't wish my life even on you," she said.

He raised an eyebrow. "Your worst enemy," he concluded for her.

"That's right."

"Why?"

She averted her eyes to the windshield. She was tired, so tired. The day that had begun with such promise had ended in disappointment and more misery.

"I want to go home," she said heavily.

"Not until I get some answers out of you...!"

"You have no right!" she exploded, her voice breaking on the words. "You have no right, no right...!"

"Leslie!"

He caught her by the nape of the neck and pulled her face into his throat, holding her there even as she struggled. He smoothed her hair, her back, whispering to her, his voice tender, coaxing.

"What did I ever do to deserve you?" she sobbed. "I've never willingly hurt another human being in my life, and look where it got me! Years of running and hiding and never feeling safe...!"

He heard the words without understanding them, soothing her while she cried brokenly. It hurt him to hear her cry. Nothing had ever hurt so much.

He dried the tears and kissed her swollen, red eyes tenderly, moving to her temples, her nose, her cheeks, her chin and, finally, her soft mouth. But it wasn't passion that drove him now. It was concern.

"Hush, sweetheart," he whispered. "It's all right. It's all right!"

She must be dotty, she thought, if she was hearing endearments from Attila the Hun here. She sniffed and wiped her eyes again, finally getting control of herself. She sat up and he let her, his arm over the back of her seat, his eyes watchful and quiet.

She took a steadying breath and slumped in the seat, exhausted.

"Please take me home," she asked wearily.

He hesitated, but only for a minute. "If that's what you really want."

She nodded. He started the car and turned it around.

He helped her to the front door of the boardinghouse, visibly reluctant to leave her.

"You shouldn't be alone in this condition," he said flatly. "I'll phone Ed and have him come over to see you."

"I don't need..." she protested.

His eyes flared. "The hell you don't! You need someone you can talk to. Obviously it isn't going to be your worst enemy, but then Ed knows all about you, doesn't he? You don't have secrets from him!"

He seemed to mind. She searched his angry face and wondered what he'd say if he knew those secrets. She gave him a lackluster smile.

"Some secrets are better kept," she said heavily. "Thanks for the ride."

"Leslie."

She hesitated, looking back at him.

His face looked harder than ever. "Were you raped?"

8

The words cut like a knife. She actually felt them. Her sad eyes met his dark, searching ones.

"Not quite," she replied tersely.

As understatements went, it was a master stroke. She watched the blood drain out of his face, and knew he was remembering, as she was, their last encounter, in his office, when she'd fainted.

He couldn't speak. He tried to, but the words choked him. He winced and turned away, striding back to the sports car. Leslie watched him go with a curious emptiness, as if she had no more feelings to bruise. Perhaps this kind detachment would last for a while, and she could have one day without the mental anguish that usually accompanied her, waking and sleeping.

She turned mechanically and went slowly into the house on her crutches, and down the hall to her small apartment. She had a feeling that she wouldn't see much of Matt Caldwell from now on. At last she knew how to deflect his pursuit. All it took was the truth—or as much of it as she felt comfortable letting him know.

* * *

Ed phoned to check on her later in the day and promised to come and see her the next evening. He did, arriving with a bag full of the Chinese take-out dishes she loved. While they were eating it, he mentioned that her job was still open.

"Miss Smith wouldn't enjoy hearing that," she teased lightly.

"Oh, Karla's working for Matt now."

She stared down at the wooden chopsticks in her hand. "Is she?"

"For some reason, he doesn't feel comfortable asking you to come back, so he sent me to do it," he replied. "He realizes that he's made your working environment miserable, and he's sorry. He wants you to come back and work for me."

She stared at him hard. "What did you tell him?"

"What I always tell him, that if he wants to know anything about you, he can ask you." He ate a forkful of soft noodles and took a sip of the strong coffee she'd brewed before he continued. "I gather he's realized that something pretty drastic happened to you."

"Did he say anything about it to you?"

"No." He lifted his gaze to meet hers. "He did go to the road-house out on the Victoria highway last night and wreck the bar."

"Why would he do something like that?" she asked, stunned by the thought of the straitlaced Mather Caldwell throwing things around.

"He was pretty drunk at the time," Ed confessed. "I had to bail him out of jail this morning. That was one for the books, let me tell you. The whole damned police department was standing around staring at him openmouthed when we left. He was only ever in trouble once, a woman accused him of assault—and he was cleared. His housekeeper testified that she'd been there the whole time and she and Matt had sent the baggage packing. But he's never treed a bar before."

She remembered the stark question he'd asked her and how she'd responded. She didn't understand why her past should matter to Matt. In fact, she didn't want to understand. He still didn't know the whole of it, and she was frightened of how he'd react if he knew. That wonderful tenderness he'd given her in the Jaguar had been actually painful, a bitter taste of what a man's love would be like. It was something she'd never experienced, and she'd better remember that Matt was the enemy. He'd felt sorry for her. He certainly wasn't in love with her. He wanted her, that was all. But despite her surprising response to his light caresses, complete physical intimacy was something she wasn't sure she was capable of responding to. The memories of Mike's vicious fondling made her sick. She couldn't live with them.

"Stop doing that to yourself," Ed muttered, dragging her back to the present. "You can't change the past. You have to walk straight into the future without flinching. It's the only way, to meet things head-on."

"Where did you learn that?" she asked.

"Actually I heard a televised sermon that caught my attention. That's what the minister said, that you have to go boldly forward and meet trouble head-on, not try to run away from it or hide." He pursed his lips. "I'd never heard it put quite that way before. It really made me think."

She sipped coffee with a sad face. "I've always tried to run. I've had to run." She lifted her eyes to his. "You know what they would have done to me if I'd stayed in Houston."

"Yes, I do, and I don't blame you for getting out while you could," Ed assured her. "But there's something I have to tell you now. And you're not going to like it."

"Don't tell me," she said with black humor, "someone from the local newspaper recognized me and wants an interview."

"Worse," he returned. "A reporter from Houston is down here asking questions. I think he's traced you."

She put her head in her hands. "Wonderful. Well, at least I'm no longer an employee of the Caldwell group, so it won't embarrass your cousin when I'm exposed."

"I haven't finished. Nobody will talk to him," he added with a grin. "In fact, he actually got into Matt's office yesterday when his secretary wasn't looking. He was only in there for a few minutes, and nobody knows what was said. But he came back out headfirst and, from what I hear, he ran out the door so fast that he left his briefcase behind with Matt cursing like a wounded sailor all the way down the hall. They said Matt had only just caught up with him at the curb when he ran across traffic and got away."

She hesitated. "When was this?"

"Yesterday." He smiled wryly. "It was a bad time to catch Matt. He'd already been into it with one of the county commissioners over a rezoning proposal we're trying to get passed, and his secretary had hidden in the bathroom to avoid him. That was how the reporter got in."

"You don't think he…told Matt?" she asked worriedly.

"No. I don't know what was said, of course, but he wasn't in there very long."

"But, the briefcase…"

"…was returned to him unopened," Ed said. "I know because

I had to take it down to the front desk." He smiled, amused. "I understand he paid someone to pick it up for him."

"Thank God."

"It was apparently the last straw for Matt, though," he continued, "because it wasn't long after that when he said he was leaving for the day."

"How did you know he was in jail?"

He grimaced. "Carolyn phoned me. He'd come by her place first and apparently made inroads into a bottle of Scotch. She hid the rest, after which he decided to go and get his own bottle." He shook his head. "That isn't like Matt. He may have a drink or two occasionally, but he isn't a drinker. This has shocked everybody in town."

"I guess so." She couldn't help but wonder if it had anything to do with the way he'd treated her. But if he'd gone to Carolyn, perhaps they'd had an argument and it was just one last problem on top of too many. "Was Carolyn mad at him?" she asked.

"Furious," he returned. "Absolutely seething. It seems they'd had a disagreement of major proportions, along with all the other conflicts of the day." He shook his head. "Matt didn't even come in to work today. I'll bet his head is splitting."

She didn't reply. She stared into her coffee with dead eyes. Everywhere she went, she caused trouble. Hiding, running—nothing seemed to help. She was only involving innocent people in her problems.

Ed hesitated when he saw her face. He didn't want to make things even worse for her, but there was more news that he had to give her.

She saw that expression. "Go ahead," she invited. "One more thing is all I need right now, on top of being crippled and jobless."

"Your job is waiting," he assured her. "Whenever you want to come in."

"I won't do that to him," she said absently. "He's had enough."

His eyes became strangely watchful. "Feeling sorry for the enemy?" he asked gently.

"You can't help not liking people," she replied. "He likes most everybody except me. He's basically a kind person. I just rub him the wrong way."

He wasn't going to touch that line. "The same reporter who came here had gone to the prison to talk to your mother," he continued. "I was concerned, so I called the warden. It seems…she's had a heart attack."

Her heart jumped unpleasantly. "Will she live?"

"Yes," he assured her. "She's changed a lot in six years, Leslie," he added solemnly. "She's reconciled to serving her time. The warden says that she wanted to ask for you, but that she was too ashamed to let them contact you. She thinks you can't ever forgive what she said and did to you."

Her eyes misted, but she fought tears. Her mother had been eloquent at the time, with words and the pistol. She stared at her empty coffee cup. "I can forgive her. I just don't want to see her."

"She knows that," Ed replied.

She glanced at him. "Have you been to see her?"

He hesitated. Then he nodded. "She was doing very well until this reporter started digging up the past. He was the one who suggested the movie deal and got that bit started." He sighed angrily. "He's young and ambitious and he wants to make a name for himself. The world's full of people like that, who don't care what damage they do to other peoples' lives as long as they get what they want."

She was only vaguely listening. "My mother...did she ask you about me?"

"Yes."

"What did you tell her?" she wanted to know.

He put down his cup. "The truth. There really wasn't any way to dress it up." His eyes lifted. "She wanted you to know that she's sorry for what happened, especially for the way she treated you before and after the trial. She understands that you don't want to see her. She says she deserves it for destroying your life."

She stared into space with the pain of memory eating at her. "She was never satisfied with my father," she said quietly. "She wanted things he couldn't give her, pretty clothes and jewelry and nights on the town. All he knew how to do was fly a crop-dusting plane, and it didn't pay much..." Her eyes closed. "I saw him fly into the electrical wires, and go down," she whispered gruffly. "I saw him go down!" Her eyes began to glitter with feeling. "I knew he was dead before they ever got to him. I ran home. She was in the living room, playing music, dancing. She didn't care. I broke the record player and threw myself at her, screaming."

Ed grimaced as she choked, paused, and fought for control. "We were never close, especially after the funeral," she continued, "but we were stuck with each other. Things went along fairly well. She got a job waiting tables and made good tips when she was working. She had trouble holding down a job because she slept so much. I got a part-time job typing when I was sixteen, to help out. Then when I'd just turned seventeen, Mike came into the restaurant and started flirting with her. He was so handsome, well-bred and had nice manners. In no time, he'd moved in with us. I was crazy about him, you know the way a young girl has crushes on older men. He teased me, too. But he had a drug habit that we didn't know about. She didn't like him teasing me, anyway, and she had a fight with him about it. The next day, he had some friends over and they all got high." She shivered. "The rest you know."

"Yes." He sighed, studying her wan face.

"All I wanted was for her to love me," she said dully. "But she never did."

"She said that," he replied. "She's had a lot of time to live with her regrets." He leaned forward to search her eyes. "Leslie, did you know that she had a drug habit?"

"She what?" she exclaimed, startled.

"Had a drug habit," he repeated. "That's what she told me. It was an expensive habit, and your father got tired of trying to support it. He loved her, but he couldn't make the sort of money it took to keep her high. It wasn't clothes and jewelry and parties. It was drugs."

She felt as if she'd been slammed to the floor. She moved her hands over her face and pushed back her hair. "Oh, Lord!"

"She was still using when she walked in on Mike and his friends holding you down," he continued.

"How long had she been using drugs?" she asked.

"A good five years," he replied. "Starting with marijuana and working her way up to the hard stuff."

"I had no idea."

"And you didn't know that Mike was her dealer, either, apparently."

She gasped.

He nodded grimly. "She told me that when I went to see her, too. She still can't talk about it easily. Now that she has a good grip on reality, she sees what her lifestyle did to you. She had hoped that you might be married and happy by now. It hurt her deeply to realize that you don't even date."

"She'll know why, of course," she said bitterly.

"You sound so empty, Leslie."

"I am." She leaned back. "I don't care if the reporter finds me. It doesn't matter anymore. I'm so tired of running."

"Then stand and deliver," he replied, getting to his feet. "Come back to work. Let your leg heal. Let your hair grow out and go back to its natural color. Start living."

"Can I, after so long?"

"Yes," he assured her. "We all go through periods of anguish, times when we think we can't face what lies ahead. But the only way to get past it is to go through it, straight through it. No detours, no camouflage, no running. You have to meet problems head-on, despite the pain."

She cocked her head and smiled at him with real affection. "Were you ever a football coach?"

He chuckled. "I hate contact sports."

"Me, too." She brushed her short hair back with her hands. "Okay. I'll give it a shot. But if your cousin gives me any more trouble..."

"I don't think Matt is going to cause you any more problems," he replied.

"Then, I'll see you on Thursday morning."

"Thursday? Tomorrow is just Wednesday..."

"Thursday," she said firmly. "I have plans for tomorrow."

And she did. She had the color taken out of her hair at a local beauty salon. She took her contact lenses to the local optometrist and got big-lensed, wire-framed glasses to wear. She bought clothes that looked professional without being explicit.

Then, Thursday morning, cast and crutches notwithstanding, she went back to work.

She'd been at her desk in Ed's office for half an hour when Matt came in. He barely glanced at her, obviously not recognizing the new secretary, and tapped on Ed's door, which was standing open.

"I'm going to fly to Houston for the sale," he told Ed. He sounded different. His deep voice held its usual authority, but there was an odd note in it. "I don't suppose you were able to convince her to come back...why are you shaking your head?"

Ed stood up with an exasperated sigh and pointed toward Leslie.

Matt scowled, turning on his heel. He looked at her, scowled harder, moved closer, peering into her upturned face.

She saw him matching his memory of her with the new reality. She wondered how she came off, but it was far too soon to get personal.

His eyes went over her short dark hair, over the feminine but professional beige suit she was wearing with a tidy patterned blouse, lingering on the glasses that she'd never worn before in his presence. His own face was heavily lined and he looked as if he'd had his own share of turmoil since she'd seen him last. Presumably he was still having problems with Carolyn.

"Good morning, Miss Murry," he murmured. His eyes didn't smile at her. He looked as if his face was painted on.

That was odd. No sarcasm, no mockery. No insolent sizing up. He was polite and courteous to a fault.

If that was the way he intended to play it...

"Good morning, Mr. Caldwell," she replied with equal courtesy.

He studied her for one long moment before he turned back to Ed. "I should be back by tonight. If I'm not, you'll have to meet with the county commission and the zoning committee."

"Oh, no," Ed groaned.

"Just tell them we're putting up a two-story brick office building on our own damned land, whether they like it or not," Matt told him, "and that we can accommodate them in court for as many years as it takes to get our way. I'm tired of trying to do business in a hundred-year-old house with frozen pipes that burst every winter."

"It won't sound as intimidating if I say it."

"Stand in front of a mirror and practice looking angry."

"Is that how you did it?" Ed murmured dryly.

"Only at first," he assured the other man, deadpan. "Just until I got the hang of it."

"I remember," Ed chuckled. "Even Dad wouldn't argue with you unless he felt he had a good case."

Matt shoved his hands into his pockets. "If you need me, you know the cell phone number."

"Sure."

Still he hesitated. He turned and glanced at Leslie, who was opening mail. The expression on his face fascinated Ed, who'd known him most of his life. It wasn't a look he recognized.

Matt started out the door and then paused to look back at Leslie, staring at her until she lifted her eyes.

He searched them slowly, intently. He didn't smile. He didn't speak. Her cheeks became flushed and she looked away. He made an awkward movement with his shoulders and went out the door.

Ed joined her at her desk when Matt was out of sight. "So far, so good," he remarked.

"I guess he really doesn't mind letting me stay," she murmured. Her hands were shaking because of that long, searching look of Matt's. She clasped them together so that Ed wouldn't notice and lifted her face. "But what if that reporter comes back?"

He pursed his lips. "Odd, that. He left town yesterday. In a real hurry, too. The police escorted him to the city limits and the sheriff drove behind him to the county line."

She gaped at him.

He shrugged. "Jacobsville is a small, close-knit community and you just became part of it. That means," he added, looking almost as imposing as his cousin, "that we don't let outsiders barge in and start harassing our citizens. I understand there's an old city law still on the books that makes it a crime for anyone to stay in a local place of lodging unless he or she is accompanied by at least two pieces of luggage or a trunk." He grinned. "Seems the reporter only had a briefcase. Tough."

"He might come back with a trunk and two suitcases," she pointed out.

He shook his head. "It seems that they found another old law which makes it illegal for a man driving a rental car to park it anywhere inside the city limits. Strange, isn't it, that we'd have such an unusual ordinance."

Leslie felt the first ripple of humor that she'd experienced for weeks. She smiled. "My, my."

"Our police chief is related to the Caldwells," he explained. "So is the sheriff, one of the county commissioners, two volunteer firemen, a sheriff's deputy and a Texas Ranger who was born here and works out of Fort Worth." He chuckled. "The governor is our second cousin."

Her eyes widened. "No Washington connections?" she asked.

"Nothing major. The vice president is married to my aunt."

"Nothing major." She nodded. She let out her breath. "Well, I'm beginning to feel very safe."

"Good. You can stay as long as you like. Permanently, as far as I'm concerned."

She couldn't quite contain the pleasure it gave her to feel as if she belonged somewhere, a place where she was protected and nurtured and had friends. It was a first for her. Her eyes stung with moisture.

"Don't start crying," Ed said abruptly. "I can't stand it."

She swallowed and forced a watery smile to her lips. "I wasn't going to," she assured him. She moved her shoulders. "Thanks," she said gruffly.

"Don't thank me," he told her. "Matt rounded up the law enforcement people and had them going through dusty volumes of ordinances to find a way to get that reporter out of here."

"Matt did?"

He held up a hand as she started to parade her misgivings about what he might have learned of her past. "He doesn't know why the man was here. It was enough that he was asking questions about you. You're an employee. We don't permit harassment."

"I see."

She didn't, but that was just as well. The look Ed had accidentally seen on Matt's face had him turning mental cartwheels. No need to forewarn Leslie. She wasn't ever going to have to worry about being hounded again, not if he knew Matt. And he didn't believe for one minute that his cousin was flying all the way to Houston for a cattle sale that he usually wouldn't be caught dead at. The foreman at his ranch handled that sort of thing, although Leslie didn't know. Ed was betting that Matt had another reason for going to Houston, and it was to find out who hired that reporter and sent him looking for Leslie. He felt sorry for the source of that problem. Matt in a temper was the most menacing human being he'd ever known. He didn't rage or shout and he usually didn't hit, but he had wealth and power and he knew how to use them.

He went back into his office, suddenly worried despite the reassurances he'd given Leslie. Matt didn't know why the reporter was digging around, but what if he found out? He would only be told what the public had been told, that Leslie's mother had shot her daughter and her live-in lover in a fit of jealous rage and that she was in prison. He might think, as others had, that Leslie had brought the whole sordid business on herself by having a wild party with Mike and his friends, and he wouldn't be sympathetic. More than likely, he'd come raging back home and throw Leslie out in the street. Furthermore, he'd have her escorted to the county line like the reporter who'd been following her.

He worried himself sick over the next few hours. He couldn't tell Leslie, when he might only be worrying for nothing. But the thought haunted him that Matt was every bit as dogged as a reporter when it came to ferreting out facts.

In the end, he phoned a hotel that Matt frequented when he was in Houston overnight and asked for his room. But when he was connected, it wasn't Matt who answered the phone.

"Carolyn?" Ed asked, puzzled. "Is Matt there?"

"Not right now," came the soft reply. "He had an appointment to see someone. I suppose he's forgotten that I'm waiting for him with this trolley full of food. I suppose it will be cold as ice by the time he turns up."

"Everything's all right, isn't it?"

"Why wouldn't it be?" she teased.

"Matt's been acting funny."

"Yes, I know. That Murry girl!" Her indrawn breath was audible. "Well, she's caused quite enough trouble. When Matt comes back, she'll be right out of that office, let me tell you! Do you have any idea what that reporter told Matt about her...?"

Ed hung up, sick. So not only did Matt know, but Carolyn knew, too. She'd savage Leslie, given the least opportunity. He had to do something. What?

Ed didn't expect Matt that evening, and he was right. Matt didn't come back in time for the county commission meeting, and Ed was forced to go in his place. He held his own, as Matt had instructed him to, and got what he wanted. Then he went home, sitting on pins and needles as he waited for someone to call him—either Leslie, in tears, or Matt, in a temper.

But the phone didn't ring. And when he went into work the next morning, Leslie was sitting calmly at her desk typing the letters he'd dictated to her just before they closed the day before.

"How did the meeting go?" she asked at once.

"Great," he replied. "Matt will be proud of me." He hesitated. "He, uh, isn't in yet, is he?"

"No. He hasn't phoned, either." She frowned. "You don't suppose anything went wrong with the plane, do you?"

She sounded worried. Come to think of it, she looked worried, too. He frowned. "He's been flying for a long time," he pointed out.

"Yes, but there was a bad storm last night." She hesitated. She didn't want to worry, but she couldn't help it. Despite the hard time he'd given her, Matt had been kind to her once or twice. He wasn't a bad person; he just didn't like her.

"If anything had happened, I'd have heard by now," he assured her. His lips pursed as he searched for the words. "He didn't go alone."

Her heart stopped in her chest. "Carolyn?"

He nodded curtly. He ran a hand through his hair. "He knows, Leslie. They both do."

She felt the life ebb out of her. But what had she expected, that Matt would wait to hear her side of the story? He was the enemy. He wouldn't for one second believe that she was the victim of the whole sick business. How could she blame him?

She turned off the word processor and moved her chair back, reaching for her purse. She felt more defeated than she ever had in her life. One bad break after another, she was thinking, as she got to her feet a little clumsily.

"Hand me my crutches, Ed, there's a dear," she said steadily.

"Oh, Leslie," he groaned.

She held her hand out and, reluctantly, he helped her get them in place.

"Where will you go?" he asked.

She shrugged. "It doesn't matter. Something will turn up."

"I can help."

She looked up at him with sad resignation. "You can't go against your own blood kin, Ed," she replied. "I'm the outsider here. And one way or another, I've already caused too much trouble. See you around, pal. Thanks for everything."

He sighed miserably. "Keep in touch, at least."

She smiled. "Certainly I'll do that. See you."

He watched her walk away with pure anguish. He wished he could make her stay, but even he wouldn't wish that on her. When Matt came home, he'd be out for blood. At least she'd be spared that confrontation.

Leslie didn't have a lot to pack, only a few clothes and personal items, like the photograph of her father that she always carried with her. She'd bought a bus ticket to San Antonio, one of the places nosy reporters from Houston might not think to look for her. She could get a job as a typist and find another place to live. It wouldn't be so bad.

She thought about Matt, and how he must feel, now that he knew the whole truth, or at least, the reporter's version of it. She was sure that he and Carolyn would have plenty to gossip about on the way back home. Carolyn would broadcast the scandal all over town. Even if Leslie stopped working for Matt, she would never live down the gossip. Leaving was her only option.

Running away. Again.

Her hands went to a tiny napkin she'd brought home from the dance that she and Ed had attended with Matt and Carolyn. Matt had been doodling on it with his pen just before he'd pulled Leslie out of her seat and out onto the dance floor. It was a silly sentimental piece of nonsense to keep. On a rare occasion or two, Matt had been tender with her. She wanted to remember those times. It was good to have had a little glimpse of what love might have been like, so that life didn't turn her completely bitter.

She folded her coat over a chair and looked around to make sure she wasn't missing anything. She wouldn't have time to look in the morning. The bus would leave at 6:00 a.m., with or without her. She clumped around the apartment with forced cheer, thinking that at least she'd have no knowing, pitying smiles in San Antonio.

Ed looked up as Matt exploded into the office, stopping in his tracks when he reached Leslie's empty desk. He stood there, staring, as if he couldn't believe what he was seeing.

With a sigh, Ed got up and joined him in the outer office, steeling himself for the ordeal. Matt was obviously upset.

"It's all right," he told Matt. "She's already gone. She said she was sorry for the trouble she'd caused, and that…"

"Gone?" Matt looked horrified. His face was like white stone.

Ed frowned, hesitating. "She said it would spare you the trouble of firing her," he began uneasily.

Matt still hadn't managed a coherent sentence. He ran his hand through his hair, disturbing its neat wave. He stuck his other hand into his pocket and went on staring at her desk as if he expected she might materialize out of thin air if he looked hard enough.

He turned to Ed. He stared at him, almost as if he didn't recognize him. "She's gone. Gone where?"

"She wouldn't tell me," he replied reluctantly.

Matt's eyes were black. He looked back at her desk and

winced. He made a violent motion, pressed his lips together, and suddenly took a deep audible breath and with a furious scowl, he let out a barrage of nonstop curses that had even Ed gaping.

"...and I did *not* say she could leave!" he finished at the end.

Ed managed to meet those flashing eyes, but it wasn't easy. Braver men than he had run for cover when the boss lost his temper. "Now, Matt..."

"Don't you 'Now, Matt' me, dammit!" he raged. His fists were clenched at his sides and he looked as if he really wanted to hit something. Or someone. Ed took two steps backward.

Matt saw two of the secretaries standing frozen in the hall, as if they'd come running to find the source of the uproar and were now hoping against hope that it wouldn't notice them.

No such luck. "Get the hell back to work!" he shouted.

They actually ran.

Ed wanted to. "Matt," he tried again.

He was talking to thin air. Matt was down the hall and out the door before he could catch up. He did the only thing he could. He rushed back to his office to phone Leslie and warn her. He was so nervous that it took several tries and one wrong number to get her.

"He's on his way over there," Ed told her the minute she picked up the phone. "Get out."

"No."

"Leslie, I've never seen him like this," he pleaded. "You don't understand. He isn't himself."

"It's all right, Ed," she said calmly. "There's nothing more he can do to me."

"Leslie...!" he groaned.

The loud roar of an engine out front caught her attention. "Try not to worry," she told Ed, and put the receiver down on an even louder exclamation.

She got up, put her crutches in place and hobbled to open her door just as Matt started to knock on it. He paused there, his fist upraised, his eyes black in a face the color of rice.

She stood aside to let him in, with no sense of self-preservation left. She was as far down as she could get already.

He closed the door behind him with an ultracontrolled softness before he turned to look at her. She went back to her armchair and eased down into it, laying the crutches to one side. Her chin lifted and she just looked at him, resigned to more verbal abuse if not downright violence. She was already packed and almost beyond his reach. Let him do his worst.

Now that he was here, he didn't know what to do. He hadn't thought past finding her. He leaned back against the door and folded his arms over his chest.

She didn't flinch or avert her eyes. She stared right at him. "There was no need to come here," she said calmly. "You don't have to run me out of town. I already have my ticket. I'm leaving on the bus first thing in the morning." She lifted a hand. "Feel free to search if you think I've taken anything from the office."

He didn't respond. His chest rose and fell rhythmically, if a little heavily.

She smoothed her hand over the cast where it topped her kneecap. There was an itch and she couldn't get to it. What a mundane thing to think about, she told herself, when she was confronted with a homicidal man.

He was making her more nervous by the minute. She shifted

in the chair, grimacing as the cast moved awkwardly and gave her a twinge of pain.

"Why are you here?" she asked impatiently, her eyes flashing at him through her lenses. "What else do you want, an apology...?"

"An apology? Dear God!"

It sounded like a plea for salvation. He moved, for the first time, going slowly across the room to the chair a few feet away from hers, next to the window. He eased himself down into it and crossed his long legs. He was still scowling, watching, waiting.

His eyes were appraising her now, not cutting into her or mocking her. They were dark and steady and turbulent.

Her eyes were dull and lackluster as she averted her face. Her grip on the arm of the chair was painful. "You know, don't you?"

"Yes."

She felt as if her whole body contracted. She watched a bird fly past the window and wished that she could fly away from her problems. "In a way, it's sort of a relief," she said wearily. "I'm so tired...of running."

His face tautened. His mouth made a thin line as he stared at her. "You'll never have to run again," he said flatly. "There isn't going to be any more harassment from that particular quarter."

She wasn't sure she was hearing right. Her face turned back to his. It was hard to meet those searching eyes, but she did. He looked pale, worn.

"Why aren't you gloating?" she asked harshly. "You were right about me all along, weren't you? I'm a little tramp who lures men in and teases them...!"

"Don't!" He actually flinched. He searched for words and

couldn't manage to find anything to say to her. His guilt was killing him. His conscience had him on a particularly nasty rack. He looked at her and saw years of torment and self-contempt, and he wanted to hit something.

That expression was easily read in his dark eyes. She leaned her head back against the chair and closed her eyes on the hatred she saw there.

"Everybody had a different idea of why I did it," she said evenly. "One of the bigger tabloids even interviewed a couple of psychiatrists who said I was getting even with my mother for my childhood. Another said it was latent nymphomania…"

"Hell!"

She felt dirty. She couldn't look at him. "I thought I loved him," she said, as if even after all the years, she still couldn't believe it had happened. "I had no idea, none at all, what he was really like. He made fun of my body, he and his friends. They stretched me out like a human sacrifice and discussed…my… assets." Her voice broke. He clenched his hand on the arm of the chair.

Matt's expression, had she seen it, would have silenced her. As it was, she was staring blankly out the window.

"They decided Mike should go first," she said in a husky, strained tone. "And then they drew cards to see which of the other three would go next. I prayed to die. But I couldn't. Mike was laughing at the way I begged him not to do it. I struggled and he had the others hold me down while he…"

A sound came from Matt's tight throat that shocked her into looking at him. She'd never seen such horror in a man's eyes.

"My mother came in before he had time to—" she swallowed "—get started. She was so angry that she lost control entirely.

She grabbed the pistol Mike kept in the table drawer by the front door and she shot him. The bullet went through him and into my leg," she whispered, sickened by the memory. "I saw his face when the bullet hit him in the chest from behind. I actually saw the life drain out of him." She closed her eyes. "She kept shooting until one of the men got the pistol away from her. They ran for their lives, and left us there, like that. A neighbor called an ambulance and the police. I remember that one of them got a blanket from the bedroom and wrapped me up in it. They were all...so kind," she choked, tears filling her eyes. "So kind!"

He put his face in his hands. He couldn't bear what he was hearing. He remembered her face in his office when he'd laughed at her. He groaned harshly.

"The tabloids made it look as if I'd invited what happened," she said huskily. "I don't know how a seventeen-year-old virgin can ask grown men to get high on drugs and treat her with no respect. I thought I loved Mike, but even so, I never did anything consciously to make him treat me that way."

Matt couldn't look at her. Not yet. "People high on drugs don't know what they're doing, as a rule," he said through his teeth.

"That's hard to believe," she said.

"It's the same thing as a man drinking too much alcohol and having a blackout," he said, finally lifting his head. He stared at her with dark, lifeless eyes. "Didn't I tell you once that secrets are dangerous?"

She nodded. She looked back out the window. "Mine was too sordid to share," she said bitterly. "I can't bear to be touched by men. By most men," she qualified. "Ed knew all about me, so he never approached me, that way. But you," she added quietly, "came at me like a bull in a pasture. You scared me to death. Aggression always reminds me of…of Mike."

He leaned forward with his head bowed. Even after what he'd learned in Houston already, he was unprepared for the full impact of what had been done to this vulnerable, fragile creature in front of him. He'd let hurt pride turn him into a predator. He'd approached her in ways that were guaranteed to bring back terrible memories of that incident in her past.

"I wish I'd known," he said heavily.

"I don't blame you," she said simply. "You couldn't have known."

His dark eyes came up glittering. "I could have," he contradicted flatly. "It was right under my nose. The way you downplayed your figure, the way you backed off when I came too close, the way you…fainted—" he had to force the word out "—in my office when I pinned you to the wall." He looked away. "I didn't see it because I didn't want to. I was paying you back," he said on a bitter laugh, "for having the gall not to fall into my arms when I pursued you."

She'd never imagined that she could feel sorry for Matt Caldwell. But she did. He was a decent man. Surely it would be difficult for him to face the treatment he'd given her, now that he knew the truth.

She smoothed her hands over her arms. It wasn't cold in the room, but she was chilled.

"You've never talked about it, have you?" he asked after a minute.

"Only to Ed, right after it happened," she replied. "He's been the best friend in the world to me. When those people started talking about making a television movie of what had happened, I just panicked. They were all over Houston looking for me. Ed offered me a way out and I took it. I was so scared," she whispered. "I thought I'd be safe here."

His fists clenched. "Safe." He made a mockery of the very word.

He got to his feet and moved to the window, avoiding her curious gaze.

"That reporter," she began hesitantly. "He told you about it when he was here, didn't he?"

He didn't reply for a minute. "Yes," he said finally. "He had clippings of the story." She probably knew which ones, he thought miserably, of her being carried out on a stretcher with blood all over her. There was one of the dead man lying on the floor of the apartment, and one of her blond mother shocked and almost catatonic as policemen escorted her to the squad car.

"I didn't connect it when you told Ed you were going to Houston. I thought it was some cattle sale, just like you said," she remarked.

"The reporter ran, but he'd already said that he was working with some people in Hollywood trying to put together a television movie. He'd tried to talk to your mother, apparently, and after his visit, she had a heart attack. That didn't even slow him down. He tracked you here and had plans to interview you." He glanced at her. "He thought you'd be glad to cooperate for a percentage of the take."

She laughed hollowly.

"Yes, I know," he told her. "You're not mercenary. That's one of the few things I've learned about you since you've been here."

"At least you found one thing about me that you like," she told him.

His face closed up completely. "There are a lot of things I like about you, but I've had some pretty hard knocks from women in my life."

"Ed told me."

"It's funny," he said, but he didn't look amused. "I've never been able to come to terms with my mother's actions—until I met you. You've helped me a lot—and I've been acting like a bear with a thorn in its paw. I've mistreated you."

She searched his lean, hard face quietly. He was so handsome. Her heart jumped every time she met his eyes. "Why did you treat me that way?" she asked.

He stuck his hand into his pocket. "I wanted you," he said flatly.

"Oh."

She wasn't looking at him, but he saw her fingers curl into the arm of the chair. "I know. You probably aren't capable of desire after what was done to you. Perhaps it's poetic justice that my money and position won't get me the one thing in the world I really want."

"I don't think I could sleep with someone," she agreed evenly. "Even the thought of it is...disgusting."

He could imagine that it was, and he cursed that man silently until he ran out of words.

"You liked kissing me."

She nodded, surprised. "Yes, I did."

"And being touched," he prompted, smiling gently at the memory of her reaction—astonishing now, considering her past.

She studied her lap. A button on her dress was loose. She'd

have to stitch it. She lifted her eyes. "Yes," she said. "I enjoyed that, too, at first."

His face hardened as he remembered what he'd said to her then. He turned away, his back rigid. He'd made so damned many mistakes with this woman that he didn't know how he was going to make amends. There was probably no way to do it. But he could protect her from any more misery, and he was going to.

He rammed his hands into his pockets and turned. "I went to see that reporter in Houston. I can promise you that he won't be bothering you again, and there won't be any more talk of a motion picture. I went to see your mother, too," he added.

She hadn't expected that. She closed her eyes. She caught her lower lip in her teeth and bit it right through. The taste of blood steeled her as she waited for the explosion.

"Don't!"

She opened her eyes with a jerk. His face was dark and lined, like the downwardly slanted brows above his black eyes. She pulled a tissue from the box on the table beside her and dabbed at the blood on her lip. It was such a beautiful color, she thought irrelevantly.

"I didn't realize how hard this was going to be," he said, sitting down. His head bowed, he clasped his big hands between his splayed knees and stared at the floor. "There are a lot of things I want to tell you. I just can't find the right words."

She didn't speak. Her eyes were still on the blood-dotted tissue. She felt his dark eyes on her, searching, studying, assessing her.

"If I'd…known about your past…" he tried again.

Her head came up. Her eyes were as dead as stone. "You just didn't like me. It's all right. I didn't like you, either. And you couldn't have known. I came here to hide the past, not to talk about it. But I guess you were right about secrets. I'll have to find another place to go, that's all."

He cursed under his breath. "Don't go! You're safe in Jacobsville," he continued, his voice growing stronger and more confident as he spoke. "There won't be any more suspicious reporters, no more movie deals, no more persecution. I can make sure that nobody touches you as long as you're here. I can't...protect you anywhere else," he added impatiently.

Oh, that was just great, she thought furiously. Pity. Guilt. Shame. Now he was going to go to the opposite extreme. He was going to watch over her like a protective father wolf. Well, he could think again. She scooped up one of her crutches and slammed the tip on the floor. "I don't need protection from you or anybody else. I'm leaving on the morning bus. And as for you, Mr. Caldwell, you can get out of here and leave me alone!" she raged at him.

It was the first spark of resistance he'd seen in her since he arrived. The explosion lightened his mood. She wasn't acting like a victim anymore. That was real independence in her tone, in the whole look of her. She was healing already with the retelling of that painful episode in her life.

The hesitation in him was suddenly gone. So was the somber face. Both eyebrows went up and a faint light touched his black eyes. "Or what?"

She hesitated. "What do you mean, or what?"

"If I don't get out, what do you plan to do?" he asked pleasantly.

She thought about that for a minute. "Call Ed."

He glanced at his watch. "Karla's bringing him coffee about now. Wouldn't it be a shame to spoil his break?"

She moved restlessly in the chair, still holding on to the crutch.

He smiled slowly, for the first time since he'd arrived. "Nothing more to say? Have you run out of threats already?"

Her eyes narrowed with bad temper. She didn't know what to say, or what to do. This was completely unexpected.

He studied the look of her in the pretty blue-patterned housedress she was wearing, barefoot. She was pretty, too. "I like that dress. I like your hair that color, too."

She looked at him as if she feared for his sanity. Something suddenly occurred to her. "If you didn't come rushing over here to put me on the bus and see that I left town, why are you here?"

He nodded slowly. "I was wondering when you'd get around to that." He leaned forward, just as another car pulled up outside the house.

"Ed," she guessed.

He grimaced. "I guess he rushed over to save you," he said with resignation.

She glared at him. "He was worried about me."

He went toward the door. "He wasn't the only one," he muttered, almost to himself. He opened the door before Ed could knock. "She's all in one piece," he assured his cousin, standing aside to let him into the room.

Ed was worried, confused, and obviously puzzled when he saw that she wasn't crying. "Are you all right?" he asked her.

She nodded.

Ed looked at her and then at Matt, curious, but too polite to start asking questions.

"I assume that you're staying in town now?" Matt asked her

a little stiffly. "You still have a job, if you want it. No pressure. It's your decision."

She wasn't sure what to do next. She didn't want to leave Jacobsville for another town of strange people.

"Stay," Ed said gently.

She forced a smile. "I guess I could," she began. "For a while."

Matt didn't let his relief show. In a way he was glad Ed had shown up to save him from what he was about to say to her.

"You won't regret it," Ed promised her, and she smiled at him warmly.

The smile set Matt off again. He was jealous, and furious that he *was* jealous. He ran a hand through his hair again and glowered with frustration at both of them. "Oh, hell, I'm going back to work," he said shortly. "When you people get through playing games on my time, you might go to the office and earn your damned paychecks!"

He went out the door still muttering to himself, slammed into the Jaguar, and roared away.

Ed and Leslie stared at each other.

"He went to see my mother," she told him.

"And?"

"He didn't say a lot, except…except that there won't be any more reporters asking questions."

"What about Carolyn?" he asked.

"He didn't say a word about her," she murmured, having just remembered that Ed said Carolyn had gone to Houston with him. She grimaced. "I guess she'll rush home and tell the whole town about me."

"I wouldn't like to see what Matt would do about it, if she did. If he asked you to stay, it's because he plans to protect you."

"I suppose he does, but it's a shock, considering the way he was before he went out of town. Honestly, I don't know what's going on. He's like a stranger!"

"I've never heard him actually apologize," he said. "But he usually finds ways to get his point across, without saying the words."

"Maybe that was what he was doing," she replied, thinking back over his odd behavior. "He doesn't want me to leave town."

"That seems to be the case." He smiled at her. "How about it? You've still got a job if you want it, and Matt's taken you off the endangered list. You're safe here. Want to stay?"

She thought about that for a minute, about Matt's odd statement that she was safe in Jacobsville and she wouldn't be hounded anymore. It was like a dream come true after six years of running and hiding. She nodded slowly. "Oh, yes," she said earnestly. "Yes, I want to stay!"

"Then I suggest you put on your shoes and grab a jacket, and I'll drive you back to work, while we still have jobs."

"I can't go to work like this," she protested.

"Why not?" he wanted to know.

"It isn't a proper dress to wear on the job," she said, rising.

He scowled. "Did Matt say that?"

"I'm not giving him the chance to," she said. "From now on, I'm going to be the soul of conservatism at work. He won't get any excuses to take potshots at me."

"If you say so," he said with a regretful thought for the pretty, feminine dress that he'd never seen her wear in public. So much for hoping that Matt might have coaxed her out of her repressive way of dressing. But it was early days yet.

10

For the first few days after her return to work, Leslie was uneasy every time she saw Matt coming. She shared that apprehension with two of the other secretaries, one of whom actually ripped her skirt climbing over the fence around the flower garden near the front of the building in a desperate attempt to escape him.

The incident sent Leslie into gales of helpless laughter as she told Karla Smith about it. Matt came by her office just as they were discussing it and stood transfixed at a sound he'd never heard coming from Leslie since he'd known her. She looked up and saw him, and made a valiant attempt to stop laughing.

"What's so funny?" he asked pleasantly.

Karla choked and ran for the ladies' room, leaving Leslie to cope with the question.

"Did you say something to the secretaries the other day to upset them?" she asked him right out.

He shifted. "I may have said a word or two that I shouldn't have," was all he'd admit.

"Well, Daisy Joiner just plowed through a fence avoiding you, and half her petticoat's still…out…there!" She collapsed against her desk, tears rolling down her cheeks.

She was more animated than he'd ever seen her. It lifted his heart. Not that he was going to admit it.

He gave her a harsh mock glare and pulled a cigar case out of his shirt pocket. "Lily-livered cowards," he muttered as he took out a cigar, flicked off the end with a tool from his slacks pocket, and snapped open his lighter with a flair. "What we need around here are secretaries with guts!" he said loudly, and flicked the lighter with his thumb.

Two streams of water hit the flame at the same time from different directions.

"Oh, for God's sake!" Matt roared as giggling, scurrying feet retreated down the hall.

"What were you saying about secretaries with guts?" she asked with twinkling gray eyes.

He looked at his drenched lighter and his damp cigar, and threw the whole mess into the trash can by Leslie's desk. "I quit," he muttered.

Leslie couldn't help the twinkle in her eyes. "I believe that was the whole object of the thing," she pointed out, "to make you quit smoking?"

He grimaced. "I guess it was." He studied her intently. "You're settling back in nicely," he remarked. "Do you have everything you need?"

"Yes," she replied.

He hesitated, as if he wanted to say something else and couldn't decide what. His dark eyes swept over her face, as if he were comparing her dark hair and glasses to the blond camouflage she'd worn when she first came to work for him.

"I guess I look different," she said a little self-consciously, because the scrutiny made her nervous. His face gave nothing away.

He smiled gently. "I like it," he told her.

"Did you need to see Ed?" she asked, because he still hadn't said why he was in Ed's office.

He shrugged. "It's nothing urgent," he murmured. "I met with the planning and zoning committee last night. I thought he might like to know how I came out."

"I could buzz him."

He nodded, still smiling. "Why don't you do that?"

She did. Ed came out of his office at once, still uncertain about Matt's reactions.

"Got a minute?" Matt asked him.

"Sure. Come on in." Ed stood aside to let the taller man stride into his office. He glanced back toward Leslie with a puzzled, questioning expression. She only smiled.

He nodded and closed the door, leaving Leslie to go back to work. She couldn't quite figure out Matt's new attitude toward her. There was nothing predatory about him lately. Ever since his return from Houston and the explosive meeting at her apartment, he was friendly and polite, even a little affectionate, but he didn't come near her now. He seemed to have the idea that any physical contact upset her, so he was being Big Brother Matt instead.

She should have been grateful. After all, he'd said often enough that marriage wasn't in his vocabulary. An affair, obviously, was out of the question now that he knew her past. Presumably affection was the only thing he had to offer her. It was a little disappointing, because Leslie had learned in their one early encounter that Matt's touch was delightful. She wished that she could tell him how exciting it was to her. It had been the only tenderness she'd ever had from a man in any physical respect, and she was very curious about that part of relationships. Not with just anyone, of course.

Only with Matt.

Her hands stilled on the keyboard as she heard footsteps approaching. The door opened and Carolyn came in, svelte in a beige dress that made the most of her figure, her hair perfectly coiffed.

"They said he let you come back to work here. I couldn't believe it, after what that reporter told him," the older woman began hotly. She gave Leslie a haughty, contemptuous stare. "That disguise won't do you any good, you know," she added, pausing to dig in her purse. She drew out a worn page from an old tabloid and tossed it onto Leslie's desk. It was the photo they'd used of her on the stretcher, with the caption, Teenager, Lover, Shot By Jealous Mother In Love Triangle.

Leslie just sat and looked at it, thinking how the past never really went away. She sighed wistfully. She was never going to be free of it.

"Don't you have anything to say?" Carolyn taunted.

Leslie looked up at her. "My mother is in prison. My life was destroyed. The man responsible for it all was a drug dealer." She searched Carolyn's cold eyes. "You can't imagine it, can you? You've always been wealthy, protected, safe. How could you understand the trauma of being a very innocent seventeen-year-old and having four grown men strip you naked in a drug-crazed frenzy and try to rape you in your own home?"

Amazingly Carolyn went pale. She hesitated, frowning. Her eyes went to the tabloid and she shifted uneasily. Her hand went out to retrieve the page just as the door to Ed's office opened and Matt came through it.

His face, when he saw Carolyn with the tearsheet in her hand, became dangerous.

Carolyn jerked it back, crumpled it, and threw it in the trash can. "You don't need to say anything," she said in a choked tone. "I'm not very proud of myself right now." She moved away from Leslie without looking at her. "I'm going to Europe for a few months. See you when I get back, Matt."

"You'd better hope you don't," he said in a voice like steel.

She made an awkward movement, but she didn't turn. She squared her shoulders and kept walking.

Matt paused beside the desk, retrieved the page and handed it to Ed. "Burn that," he said tautly.

"With pleasure," Ed replied. He gave Leslie a sympathetic glance before he went back into his office and closed the door.

"I thought she came to make trouble," she told Matt with evident surprise in her expression. Carolyn's abrupt about-face had puzzled her.

"She only knew what I mumbled the night I got drunk," he said curtly. "I never meant to tell her the rest of it. She's not as bad as she seems," he added. "I've known her most of my life, and I like her. She got it into her head that we should get married and saw you as a rival. I straightened all that out. At least, I thought I had."

"Thanks."

"She'll come back a different woman," he continued. "I'm sure she'll apologize."

"It's not necessary," she said. "Nobody knew the true story. I was too afraid to tell it."

He stuck his hands into his pockets and studied her. His face was lined, his eyes had dark circles under them. He looked worn. "I would have spared you this if I could have," he gritted.

He seemed really upset about it. "You can't stop other people from thinking what they like. It's all right. I'll just have to get used to it."

"Like hell you will. The next person who comes in here with a damned tabloid page is going out right through the window!"

She smiled faintly. "Thank you. But it's not necessary. I can take care of myself."

"Judging by Carolyn's face, you did a fair job of it with her," he mused.

"I guess she's not really so bad." She glanced at him and away. "She was only jealous. It was silly. You never had designs on me."

There was a tense silence. "And what makes you think so?"

"I'm not in her league," she said simply. "She's beautiful and rich and comes from a good family."

He moved a step closer, watching her face lift. She didn't look apprehensive, so he moved again. "Not frightened?" he murmured.

"Of you?" She smiled gently. "Of course not."

He seemed surprised, curious, even puzzled.

"In fact, I like bears," she said with a deliberate grin.

That expression went right through him. He smiled. He beamed. Suddenly he caught the back of her chair with his hand and swiveled her around so that her face was within an inch of his.

"Sticks and stones, Miss Murry," he whispered softly, with a lazy grin, and brought his lips down very softly on hers.

She caught her breath.

His head lifted and his dark, quiet eyes met hers and held them while he tried to decide whether or not she was frightened. He saw the pulse throbbing at her neck and heard the faint unsteadiness of her breath. She was unsettled. But that wasn't fear. He knew enough about women to be sure of it.

He chuckled softly, and there was pure calculation in the way he studied her. "Any more smart remarks?" he taunted in a sensual whisper.

She hesitated. He wasn't aggressive or demanding or mocking. She searched his eyes, looking for clues to this new, odd behavior.

He traced her mouth with his forefinger. "Well?"

She smiled hesitantly. All her uncertainties were obvious, but she wasn't afraid of him. Her heart was going wild. But it wasn't with fear. And he knew it.

He bent and kissed her again with subdued tenderness.

"You taste like cigar smoke," she whispered impishly.

"I probably do, but I'm not giving up cigars completely, regardless of the water pistols," he whispered. "So you might as well get used to the taste of them."

She searched his dark eyes with quiet curiosity.

He put his thumb over her soft lips and smiled down at her. "I've been invited to a party at the Ballengers' next month. You'll be out of your cast by then. How about buying a pretty dress and coming with me?" He bent and brushed his lips over her forehead. "They're having a live Latin band. We can dance some more."

She wasn't hearing him. His lips were making her heart beat faster. She was smiling as she lifted her face to those soft kisses, like a flower reaching up to the sun. He realized that and smiled against her cheek.

"This isn't businesslike," she whispered.

He lifted his head and looked around. The office was empty and nobody was walking down the hall. He glanced back down at her with one lifted eyebrow.

She laughed shyly.

The teasing light in his eyes went into eclipse at the response that smile provoked in him. He framed her soft face in his big hands and bent again. This time the kiss wasn't light, or brief.

When she moaned, he drew back at once. His eyes were glittery with strong emotion. He let go of her face and stood up, looking down at her solemnly. He winced, as if he remembered previous encounters when he hadn't been careful with her, when he'd been deliberately cruel.

She read the guilt in his face and frowned. She was totally unversed in the byplay between men and women, well past the years when those things were learned in a normal way.

"I didn't mean to do that," he said quietly. "I'm sorry."

"It's all right," she stammered.

He drew in a long, slow breath. "You have nothing to be afraid of now. I hope you know that."

"I'm not frightened," she replied.

His face hardened as he looked at her. One hand clenched in his pocket. The other clenched at his side. She happened to look down and she drew in her breath at the sight of it.

"You're hurt!" she exclaimed, reaching out to touch the abrasions that had crusted over, along with the swollen bruises that still remained there.

"I'll heal," he said curtly. "Maybe he will, too, eventually."

"He?" she queried.

"Yes. That yellow-backed reporter who came down here looking for you." His face tautened. "I took Houston apart looking for him. When I finally found him, I delivered him to his boss. There won't be any more problems from that direction, ever. In fact, he'll be writing obituaries for the rest of his miserable life."

"He could take you to court..."

"He's welcome, after my attorneys get through with him," he returned flatly. "He'll be answering charges until he's an old man. Considering the difference in our ages, I'll probably be dead by then." He paused to think about that. "I'll make sure the money's left in my estate to keep him in court until every penny runs out!" he added after a minute. "He won't even be safe when I'm six feet under!"

She didn't know whether to laugh or cry. He was livid, almost vibrating with temper.

"But you know what hurts the most?" he added, looking down into her worried eyes. "What he did still wasn't as bad as what I did to you. I won't ever forgive myself for that. Not if I live to be a hundred."

That was surprising. She toyed with her keyboard and didn't look at him. "I thought...you might blame me, when you knew the whole story," she said.

"For what?" he asked huskily.

She moved her shoulders restlessly. "The papers said it was my fault, that I invited it."

"Dear God!" He knelt beside her and made her look at him. "Your mother told me the whole story," he said. "She cried like a baby when she got it all out." He paused, touching her face gently. "Know what she said? That she'd gladly spend the rest of her life where she is, if you could only forgive her for what she did to you."

She felt the tears overflowing. She started to wipe them, but he pulled her face to his and kissed them away so tenderly that they came in a veritable flood.

"No," he whispered. "You mustn't cry. It's all right. I won't let anything hurt you ever again. I promise."

But she couldn't stop. "Oh, Matt...!" she sobbed.

All his protective instincts bristled. "Come here to me," he said gently. He stood up and lifted her into his arms, cast and all, and carried her down the deserted hall to his office.

His secretary saw him coming and opened the door for him, grimacing at Leslie's red, wet face.

"Coffee or brandy?" she asked Matt.

"Coffee. Make it about thirty minutes, will you? And hold my calls."

"Yes, sir."

She closed the door and Matt sat down on the burgundy couch with Leslie in his lap, cradling her while she wept.

He tucked a handkerchief into her hand and rocked her in his arms, whispering to her until the sobs lessened.

"I'm going to replace the furniture in here," he murmured. "Maybe the paneling, too."

"Why?"

"It must hold some painful memories for you," he said. "I know it does for me."

His voice was bitter. She recalled fainting, and coming to on this very couch. She looked up at him without malice or accusation. Her eyes were red and swollen, and full of curiosity.

He traced her cheek with tender fingers and smiled at her. "You've had a rough time of it, haven't you?" he asked quietly. "Will it do any good to tell you that a man wouldn't normally treat a woman, especially an innocent woman, the way those animals treated you?"

"I know that," she replied. "It's just that the publicity made me out to be little more than a call girl. I'm not like that. But it's what people thought I was. So I ran, and ran, and hid...if it hadn't been for Ed and his father, and my friend Jessica, I don't know what I would have done. I don't have any family left."

"You have your mother," he assured her. "She'd like to see you. If you're willing, I'll drive you up there, anytime you like."

She hesitated. "You do know that she's in prison for murder?" she asked.

"I know it."

"You're well-known here," she began.

"Oh, good Lord, are you trying to save me?" he asked with an exasperated sigh. "Woman, I don't give two hoots in hell for gossip. While they're talking about me, they're leaving some other person alone." He took the handkerchief and wiped her cheeks. "But for the record, most reporters keep out of my way." He pursed his lips. "I can guarantee there's one in Houston who'll run the next time he sees me coming."

It amazed her that he'd gone to that much trouble defending her. She lay looking at him with eyes like a cat's, wide and soft and curious.

They had an odd effect on him. He felt his body react to it

and caught his breath. He started to move her before she realized that he was aroused.

The abrupt rejection startled her. All at once she was sitting beside him on the couch, looking stunned.

He got up quickly and moved away, turning his back to her. "How would you like some coffee?" he asked gruffly.

She shifted a little, staring at him with open curiosity. "I...I would, thank you."

He went to the intercom, not to the door, and told his secretary to bring it in. He kept his back to Leslie, and to the door, even when Edna came in with the coffee service and placed it on the low coffee table in front of the sofa.

"Thanks, Edna," he said.

"Sure thing, boss." She winked at Leslie and smiled reassuringly, closing the door quietly behind her.

Leslie poured coffee into the cups, glancing at him warily. "Don't you want your coffee?"

"Not just yet," he murmured, trying to cool down.

"It smells nice."

"Yes, it does, but I've already had a little too much stimulation for the moment, without adding caffeine to the problem."

She didn't understand. He felt her eyes on his stiff back and with a helpless laugh, he turned around. To his amazement, and his amusement, she didn't notice anything wrong with him.

He went back to the couch and sat down, shaking his head as he let her hand him a cupful of fresh coffee.

"Is something wrong?" she asked.

"Not a thing in this world, baby doll," he drawled. "Except that Edna just saved you from absolute ruin and you don't even know it."

Leslie stared into Matt's dancing eyes with obvious confusion.

"Never mind," he chuckled, sipping his coffee. "One day when we know each other better, I'll tell you all about it."

She sipped her coffee and smiled absently. "You're very different since you came back from Houston."

"I've had a bad knock." He put his cup down, but his eyes stayed on it. "I can't remember ever being grossly unfair to anyone before, much less an employee. It's hard for me, remembering some of the things I said and did to you." He grimaced, still not looking straight at her. "It hurt my pride that you'd let Ed get close, but you kept backing away from me. I never stopped to wonder why." He laughed hollowly. "I've had women throw themselves at me most of my adult life, even before I made my first million." He glanced at her. "But I couldn't get near you, except once, on the dance floor." His eyes narrowed. "And that night, when you let me touch you."

She remembered, too, the feel of his eyes and his hands and his mouth on her. Her breath caught audibly.

He winced. "It was the first time, wasn't it?"

She averted her eyes.

"I even managed to soil that one, beautiful memory." He looked down at his hands. "I've done so much damage, Leslie. I don't know how to start over, to begin again."

"Neither do I," she confessed. "What happened to me in Houston was a pretty bad experience, even if I'd been older and more mature when it happened. As it was, I gave up trying to go on dates afterward, because I connected anything physical with that one sordid incident. I couldn't bear it when men wanted to kiss me good-night. I backed away and they thought I was some sort of freak." Her eyes closed and she shuddered.

"Tell me about the doctor."

She hesitated. "He only knew what he'd been told, I guess. But he made me feel like trash." She wrapped both arms around her chest and leaned forward. "He cleaned the wound and bandaged my leg. He said that they could send me back to the hospital from jail for the rest."

Matt muttered something vicious.

"I didn't go to jail, of course, my mother did. The leg was horribly painful. I had no medical insurance and Jessica's parents were simple people, very poor. None of us could have afforded orthopedic surgery. I was able to see a doctor at the local clinic, and he put a cast on it, assuming that it had already been set properly. He didn't do X-rays because I couldn't afford any."

"You're lucky the damage could even be repaired," he said, his eyes downcast as he wondered at the bad luck she'd had not only with the trauma of the incident itself, but with its painful aftermath.

"I had a limp when it healed, but I walked fairly well." She sighed. "Then I fell off a horse." She shook her head.

"I wouldn't have had that happen for the world," he said, meeting her eyes. "I was furious, not just that you'd backed away from me, but that I'd caused you to hurt yourself. Then at the dance, it was even worse, when I realized that all those quick steps had caused you such pain."

"It was a good sort of pain," she told him, "because it led to corrective surgery. I'm really grateful about that."

"I'm sorry it came about in the way it did." He smiled at her new look. "Glasses suit you. They make your eyes look bigger."

"I always wore them until the reporter started trying to sell an idea for a television movie about what happened. I dyed my hair and got contacts, dressed like a dowager, did everything I could to change my appearance. But Jacobsville was my last chance. I thought if I could be found here, I could be tracked anywhere." She smoothed her skirt over the cast.

"You won't be bothered by that anymore," he said. "But I'd like to let my attorneys talk to your mother. I know," he said, when she lifted her head and gave him a worried look, "it would mean resurrecting a lot of unpleasant memories, but we might be able to get her sentence reduced or even get her a new trial. There were extenuating circumstances. Even a good public defender isn't as good as an experienced criminal lawyer."

"Did you ask her that?"

He nodded. "She wouldn't even discuss it. She said you'd had enough grief because of her."

She lowered her eyes back to her skirt. "Maybe we both have. But I hate it that she may spend the rest of her life in prison."

"So do I." He touched her hair. "She really is blond, isn't she?"

"Yes. My father had dark hair, like mine, and gray eyes, too. Hers are blue. I always wished mine were that color."

"I like your eyes just the way they are." He touched the wire rims of her frames. "Glasses and all."

"You don't have any problem seeing, do you?" she wondered.

He chuckled. "I have trouble seeing what's right under my nose, apparently."

"You're farsighted?" she asked, misunderstanding him.

He touched her soft mouth with his forefinger and the smile faded. "No. I mistake gold for tinsel."

His finger made her feel nervous. She drew back. His hand fell at once and he smiled at her surprise.

"No more aggression. I promise."

Her fascinated eyes met his. "Does that mean that you won't ever kiss me again?" she asked boldly.

"Oh, I will," he replied, delighted. He leaned forward. "But you'll have to do all the chasing from now on."

11

Leslie searched his dark eyes slowly and then she began to smile. "Me, chase you?" she asked.

He pursed his lips. "Sure. Men get tired of the chase from time to time. I think I'd like having you pursue me."

Mental pictures of her in a suit and Matt in a dress dissolved her in mirth. But the reversed relationship made her feel warm inside, as if she wasn't completely encased in ice. The prospect of Matt in her arms was exhilarating, even with her past. "Okay, but I draw the line at taking you to football games," she added, trying to keep things casual between them, just for the time being.

He grinned back. "No problem. We can always watch them on TV." The light in her eyes made him light-headed. "Feeling better now?" he asked softly.

She nodded. "I guess you can get used to anything when you have to," she said philosophically.

"I could write you a book on that," he said bitterly, and she remembered his past—his young life marked with such sadness.

"I'm sure you could," she agreed.

He leaned forward with the coffee cup still in his hands. He had nice hands, she thought absently, lean and strong and beautifully shaped. She remembered their touch on her body with delight.

"We'll take this whole thing one step at a time," he said quietly. "There won't be any pressure, and I won't run roughshod over you. We'll go at your pace."

She was a little reluctant. That one step at a time could lead anywhere, and she didn't like the idea of taking chances. He wasn't a marrying man and she wasn't the type for affairs. She did wonder what he ultimately had in mind for them, but she wasn't confident enough of this new relationship to ask. It was nice to have him like this, gentle and concerned and caring. She hadn't had much tenderness in her life, and she was greedy for it.

He glanced suddenly at the thin gold watch on his wrist and grimaced. "I should have been in Fort Worth an hour ago for a meeting with some stock producers." He glanced at her ruefully. "Just look at what you do to me," he murmured. "I can't even think straight anymore."

She smiled gently. "Good for me."

He chuckled, finished his coffee and put down the cup. "Better late than never, I suppose." He leaned down and kissed her, very softly. His eyes held a new, warm light that made her feel funny all over. "Stay out of trouble while I'm gone."

Her eyebrows rose. "Oh, that's cute."

He nodded. "You never put a foot wrong, did you?"

"Only by being stupid and gullible."

His dark eyes went even darker. "What happened wasn't your fault. That's the first idea we have to correct."

"I was madly infatuated for the first time in my life," she said honestly. "I might have inadvertently given him the idea...."

He put his thumb against her soft lips. "Leslie, what sort of decent adult man would accept even blatant signals from a teenager?"

It was a good question. It made her see what had happened from a different perspective.

He gave her mouth a long scrutiny before he abruptly removed his thumb and ruffled her short dark hair playfully. "Think about that. You might also consider that people on drugs very often don't know what they're doing anyway. You were in the wrong place at the wrong time."

She readjusted her glasses as they slipped further on her nose. "I suppose so."

"I'll be in Fort Worth overnight, but maybe we can go out to dinner tomorrow night?" he asked speculatively.

She indicated the cast. "I can see me now, clumping around in a pretty dress."

He chuckled. "I don't mind if you don't."

She'd never been on a real date before, except nights out with Ed, who was more like a brother than a boyfriend. Her eyes brightened. "I'd love to go out with you, if you mean it."

"I mean it, all right."

"Then, yes."

He grinned at her. "Okay."

She couldn't look away from his dark, soft eyes. It felt like electricity flowing between them. It was exciting to share that sort of intimate look. She colored. He arched an eyebrow and gave her a wicked smile.

"Not now," he said in a deep, husky tone that made her blush even more, and turned toward the door.

He opened it. "Edna, I'll be back tomorrow," he told his secretary.

"Yes, sir."

He didn't look back. The outer door opened and closed. Leslie got up with an effort and moved to the office door. "Do you want me to clean up in here?" she asked Edna.

The older woman just smiled. "Heavens, no. You go on back to work, Miss Murry. How's that leg feeling?"

"Awkward," she said, glowering at it. "But it's going to be nice not to limp anymore," she added truthfully. "I'm very grateful to Mr. Caldwell for having it seen to."

"He's a good man," his secretary said with a smile. "And a good boss. He has moods, but most people do."

"Yes."

Leslie clumped her way back down the hall to her office. Ed came out when he heard her rustling paper and lifted both eyebrows. "Feeling better?" he asked.

She nodded. "I'm a watering pot lately. I don't know why."

"Nobody ever had a better reason," he ventured. He smiled gently. "Matt's not so bad, is he?"

She shook her head. "He's not what I thought he was at first."

"He'll grow on you," he said. He reached for a file on his desk, brought it out and perched himself on the edge of her desk. "I need you to answer these. Feel up to some dictation?"

She nodded. "You bet!"

Matt came back late the next morning and went straight to Leslie when he arrived at the office. "Call Karla Smith and ask if she'll substitute for you," he said abruptly. "You and I are going to take the afternoon off."

"We are?" she asked, pleasantly surprised. "What are we going to do?"

"Now there's a leading question," he said, chuckling. He pressed the intercom on her phone and told Ed he was swiping his secretary and then moved back while Leslie got Karla on the phone and asked her to come down to Ed's office.

It didn't take much time to arrange everything. Minutes later, she was seated beside Matt in the Jaguar flying down the highway just at the legal speed limit.

"Where are we going?" she asked excitedly.

He grinned, glancing sideways at the picture she made in that pretty blue-and-green swirl-patterned dress that left her arms bare. He liked her hair short and dark. He even liked her glasses.

"I've got a surprise for you," he said. "I hope you're going to like it," he added a little tautly.

"Don't tell me. You're taking me to see all the big snakes at the zoo," she said jokingly.

"Do you like snakes?" he asked unexpectedly.

"Not really. But that would be a surprise I wouldn't quite like," she added.

"No snakes."

"Good."

He slid into the passing lane and passed several other cars on the four-lane.

"This is the road to Houston," she said, noting a road sign.

"So it is."

She toyed with her seat belt. "Matt, I don't really like Houston."

"I know that." He glanced at her. "We're going to the prison to see your mother."

Her intake of breath was audible. Her hands clenched on her skirt.

He reached a lean hand over and gently pressed both of hers. "Remember what Ed says? Never back away from a problem," he said softly. "Always meet it head-on. You and your mother haven't seen each other in over five years. Don't you think it's time to lay rest to all the ghosts?"

She was uneasy and couldn't hide it. "The last time I saw her was in court, when the verdict was read. She wouldn't even look at me."

"She was ashamed, Leslie."

That was surprising. Her eyes met his under a frown. "Ashamed?"

"She wasn't taking huge amounts of drugs, but she was certainly addicted. She'd had something before she went back to the apartment and found you with her lover. The drugs disoriented her. She told me that she doesn't even remember how the pistol got into her hand, the next thing she knew, her lover was dead and you were bleeding on the floor. She barely remembers the police taking her away." His lips flattened. "What she does remember is coming back to her senses in jail and being told what she did. No, she didn't look at you during the trial or afterward. It wasn't that she blamed you. She blamed herself for being so gullible and letting herself be taken in by a smooth-talking, lying drug dealer who pretended to love her in return for a place to live."

She didn't like the memories. She and her mother had never been really close, but when she looked back, she remembered that she'd been standoffish and difficult, especially after the death of her father.

His hand contracted on both of hers. "I'm going to be right with you every step of the way," he said firmly. "Whatever happens, it won't make any difference to me. I only want to try to make things easier for you."

"She might not want to see me," she ventured.

"She wants to," he said grimly. "Very badly. She realizes that she might not have much time left."

She bit her lower lip. "I never realized she had heart trouble."

"She probably didn't, until she started consuming massive quantities of drugs. The human body can only take so much abuse until it starts rebelling." He glanced at her. "She's all right for now. She just has to take it easy. But I still think we can do something for her."

"A new trial would put a lot of stress on her."

"It would," he agreed. "But perhaps it isn't the sort of stress that would be damaging. At the end of that road, God willing, she might get out on parole."

Leslie only nodded. The difficult part lay yet ahead of her; a reunion that she wasn't even sure she wanted. But Matt seemed determined to bring it about.

It was complicated to get into a prison, Leslie learned at once. There were all sorts of checkpoints and safety measures designed to protect visitors. Leslie shivered a little as they walked down the long hall to the room where visitors were allowed to see inmates. For her, the thought of losing her freedom was akin to fears of a lingering death. She wondered if it was that bad for her mother.

There was a long row of chairs at little cubicles, separated from the prisoners' side by thick glass. There was a small opening in the glass, which was covered with mesh wiring so that people could talk back and forth. Matt spoke to a guard and gestured Leslie toward one of the cubicles, settling her in the straight-backed chair there. Through the glass, she could see a closed door across the long room.

As she watched, aware of Matt's strong, warm hand on her shoulder, the door opened and a thin, drawn blond woman with very short hair was ushered into the room by a guard. She went forward to the cubicle where Leslie was sitting and lifted her eyes to the tense face through the glass. Her pale blue eyes were full of sadness and uncertainty. Her thin hands trembled.

"Hello, Leslie," she said slowly.

Leslie just sat there for a moment with her heart beating half to death. The thin, drawn woman with the heavily lined face and dull blue eyes was only a shadow of the mother she remembered. Those thin hands were so wasted that the blue veins on their backs stood out prominently.

Marie smiled with faint self-contempt. "I knew this would be a mistake," she said huskily. "I'm so sorry..." She started to get up.

"Wait," Leslie croaked. She grimaced. She didn't know what to say. The years had made this woman a stranger.

Matt moved behind her, both hands on her shoulders now, supporting her, giving her strength.

"Take your time," he said gently. "It's all right."

Marie gave a little start as she noticed that Matt was touching Leslie with some familiarity, and Leslie wasn't stiff or protesting. Her eyes connected with his dark ones and he smiled.

Marie smiled back hesitantly. It changed her lined, worn face and made her seem younger. She looked into her daughter's eyes and her own softened. "I like your boss," she said.

Leslie smiled back. "I like him, too," she confessed.

There was a hesitation. "I don't know where to start," she began huskily. "I've rehearsed it and rehearsed it and I simply can't find the words." Her pale eyes searched Leslie's face, as if she was trying to recall it from the past. She winced as she compared it with the terror-stricken face she'd seen that night so long ago. "I've made a lot of mistakes, Leslie. My biggest one was putting my own needs ahead of everybody else's. It was always what *I* wanted, what *I* needed. Even when I started doing drugs, all I thought about was what would make me happy." She shook her head. "Selfishness carries a high price tag. I'm so sorry that you had to pay such a high price for mine. I couldn't even bear to look at you at the trial, after the tabloids came out. I was so ashamed of what I'd subjected you to. I thought of you, all alone, trying to hold your head up with half the state knowing such intimate things about our lives..." She drew in a slow, unsteady breath and she seemed to slump. "I can't even ask you to forgive me. But I did want to see you, even if it's just this once, to tell you how much I regret it all."

The sight of her pinched face hurt Leslie, who hadn't realized her mother even felt remorse. There had been no communication between them. She knew now that Matt had been telling the truth about her mother's silence. Marie was too ashamed to face her, even now. It eased the wound a little. "I didn't know about the drugs," Leslie blurted out abruptly.

Her tone brought Marie's eyes up, and for the first time,

there was hope in them. "I never used them around you," she said gently. "But it started a long time ago, about the time your father…died." The light in her eyes seemed to dim. "You blamed me for his death, and you were right. He couldn't live up to being what I wanted him to be. He couldn't give me the things I thought I deserved." She looked down at the table in front of her. "He was a good, kind man. I should have appreciated him. It wasn't until he died that I realized how much he meant to me. And it was too late." She laughed hollowly. "From then on, everything went downhill. I didn't care anymore, about myself or you, and I went onto harder drugs. That's how I met Mike. I guess you figured out that he was my supplier."

"Matt did," Leslie corrected.

Marie lifted her eyes to look at Matt, who was still standing behind Leslie. "Don't let them hurt her anymore," she pleaded gently. "Don't let that reporter make her run anymore. She's had enough."

"So have you," Leslie said unexpectedly, painfully touched by Marie's concern. "Matt says…that he thinks his attorneys might be able to get you a new trial."

Marie started. Her eyes lit up, and then abruptly shifted. "No!" she said gruffly. "I have to pay for what I did."

"Yes," Leslie said. "But what you did…" She hesitated. "What you did was out of shock and outrage, don't you see? It wasn't premeditated. I don't know much about the law, but I do know that intent is everything. You didn't plan to kill Mike."

The older woman's sad eyes met Leslie's through the glass. "That's generous of you, Leslie," she said quietly. "Very generous, considering the notoriety and grief I caused you."

"We've both paid a price," she agreed.

"You're wearing a cast," her mother said suddenly. "Why?"

"I fell off a horse," Leslie said and felt Matt's hands contract on her shoulders, as if he was remembering why. She reached up and smoothed her hand over one of his. "It was a lucky fall, because Matt got an orthopedic surgeon to operate on my leg and put it right."

"Do you know how her leg was hurt?" the other woman asked Matt with a sad little smile.

"Yes," he replied. His voice sounded strained. The tender, caressing action of Leslie's soft fingers on his hand was arousing him. It was the first time she'd touched him voluntarily, and his head was reeling.

"That's another thing I've had on my conscience for years," the smaller woman told her daughter. "I'm glad you had the operation."

"I'm sorry for the position you're in," Leslie said with genuine sympathy. "I would have come to see you years ago, but I thought...I thought you hated me," she added huskily, "for what happened to Mike."

"Oh, Leslie!" Marie put her face in her hands and her shoulders shook. She wept harshly, while her daughter sat staring at her uncomfortably. After a minute, she wiped the tears from her red, swollen eyes. "No, I didn't hate you! I never blamed you!" Marie said brokenly. "How could I hate you for something that was never your fault? I wasn't a good mother. I put you at risk the minute I started using drugs. I failed you terribly. By letting Mike move in, I set you up for what he and his friends did to you. My poor baby," she choked. "You were so very young, so innocent, and to have men treat you...that way—" She broke off. "That's why I couldn't ask you to come, why I couldn't write or phone. I thought you hated *me!*"

Leslie's fingers clenched around Matt's on her shoulder, drawing strength from his very presence. She knew she could never have faced this without him. "I didn't hate you," she said slowly. "I'm sorry we couldn't talk to each other, at the trial. I...did blame you for Dad," she confessed. "But I was so young when it happened, and you and I had never been particularly close. If we had..."

"You can't change what was," her mother said with a wistful smile. "But it's worth all this if you can forgive me." Her long fingers moved restlessly on the receiver. Her pained eyes met Leslie's. "It means everything if you can forgive me!"

Leslie felt a lump in her throat as she looked at her mother and realized the change in her. "Of course I can." She bit her lip. "Are you all right? Is your health all right?"

"I have a weak heart, probably damaged by all the drugs I took," Marie said without emphasis. "I take medicine for it, and I'm doing fine. I'll be all right, Leslie." She searched the younger woman's eyes intently. "I hope you're going to be all right, too, now that you aren't being stalked by that reporter anymore. Thank you for coming to see me."

"I'm glad I did," Leslie said, and meant it sincerely. "I'll write, and I'll come to see you when I can. Meanwhile, Matt's lawyers may be able to do something for you. Let them try."

There was a hesitation while the other woman exchanged a worried look with Matt.

Both his hands pressed on Leslie's shoulders. "I'll take care of her," he told Marie, and knew that she understood what he was saying. Nobody would bother Leslie again, as long as there was a breath in his body. He had power and he would use it on her daughter's behalf. She relaxed.

"All right, then," she replied. "Thank you for trying to help me, even if nothing comes of it."

Matt smiled at her. "Miracles happen every day," he said, and he was looking at Leslie's small hand caressing his.

"You hold on to him," the older woman told Leslie fervently. "If I'd had a man like that to care about me, I wouldn't be in this mess today."

Leslie flushed. Her mother spoke as if she had a chance of holding on to Matt, and that was absurd. He might feel guilt and sympathy, even regret, but her mother seemed to be mistaking his concern for love. It wasn't.

Matt leaned close to Leslie and spoke. "It's rather the other way around," Matt said surprisingly, and he didn't smile. "Women like Leslie don't grow on trees."

Marie smiled broadly. "No, they don't. She's very special. Take care of yourself, Leslie. I...I do love you, even if it doesn't seem like it."

Leslie's eyes stung with threatening tears. "I love you, too, Mama," she said in a gruff, uneasy tone. She could barely speak for the emotion she felt.

The other woman couldn't speak at all. Her eyes were bright and her smile trembled. She only nodded. After one long look at her daughter, she got up and went to the door.

Leslie sat there for a minute, watching until her mother was completely out of sight. Matt's big hands contracted on her shoulders.

"Let's go, sweetheart," he said gently, and pressed a handkerchief into her hands as he shepherded her out the door.

That tenderness in him was a lethal weapon, she thought. It was almost painful to experience, especially when she knew that it wasn't going to last. He was kind, and right now he was trying to make amends. But she'd better not go reading anything into his actions. She had to take one day at a time and just live for the present.

She was quiet all the way to the parking lot. Matt smoked a cigar on the way, one hand in his pocket, his eyes narrow and introspective as he strode along beside Leslie until they reached the car. He pushed a button on his electronic controller and the locks popped up.

"Thank you for bringing me here," Leslie said at the passenger door, her eyes full of gratitude as they lifted to his. "I'm really glad I came, even if I didn't want to at first."

He stayed her hand as she went to open the door and moved closer, so that she was standing between his long, muscular body and the door. His dark eyes searched hers intently.

His gaze fell to her soft mouth and the intensity of the look parted her lips. Her pulse raced like mad. Her reaction to his closeness had always been intense, but she could almost feel his mouth on her body as she looked up at him. It was frightening to feel such wanton impulses.

His eyes lifted and he saw that expression in her soft, dazed gray eyes. The muscles in his jaw moved and he seemed to be holding his breath.

Around them, the parking lot was deserted. There was nothing audible except the sound of traffic and the frantic throb of Leslie's pulse as she stared into Matt's dark, glittery eyes.

He moved a step closer, deliberately positioning his body so that one long, powerful leg brushed between her good leg and the bulky cast on the other one.

"Matt?" she whispered shakily.

His eyes narrowed. His free hand went to her face and spread against her flushed cheek. His thumb nudged at her chin, lifting it. His leg moved against her thighs and she gasped.

There was arrogance not only in the way he touched her, but in the way he looked at her. She was completely vulnerable when he approached her like this, and he must surely know it, with his experience of women.

"So many women put on an act," he murmured conversationally. "They pretend to be standoffish, they tease, they provoke, they exaggerate their responses. With you, it's all genuine. I can look at you and see everything you're thinking. You don't try to hide it or explain it. It's all right there in the open."

Her lips parted. It was getting very hard to breathe. She didn't know what to say.

His head bent just a little, so that she could feel his breath on her mouth. "You can't imagine the pleasure it gives me to see you like this. I feel ten feet tall."

"Why?" she whispered unsteadily.

His mouth hovered over hers, lightly brushing, teasing. "Because every time I touch you, you offer yourself up like a virgin sacrifice. I remember the taste of your breasts in my mouth, the soft little cries that pulsed out of you when I pressed you down into the mattress under my body." He moved against her, slowly and deliberately, letting her feel his instant response. "I want to take your clothes off and ease inside your body on crisp, white sheets..." he whispered as his hard mouth went down roughly on her soft lips.

She made a husky little cry as she pictured what he was saying to her, pictured it, ached for it. Of all the outrageous, shocking things to say to a woman...!

Her nails bit into his arms as she lifted herself against his arousal and pushed up at his mouth to tempt it into violence. The sudden whip of passion was unexpected, overwhelming. She moaned brokenly and her legs trembled.

He groaned harshly. For a few seconds, his mouth devoured her own. He had to drag himself away from her, and when he did, his whole body seemed to vibrate. There was a flush high on his cheekbones, and his eyes glittered.

She loved the expression on his face. She loved the tremor of the arms propped on either side of her head. Her chin lifted and her eyes grew misty with pleasure.

"Do you like making me this way?" he asked gruffly.

"Yes," she said, something wild and impulsive rising in her like a quick tide. She looked at the pulse in his throat, the quick rhythmic movement of his shirt under the suit he was wearing. Her eyes dropped boldly down his body to the visible effect of passion on him.

His intake of breath was audible as he watched her eyes linger on him, there. His whole body shook convulsively, as if with a fever.

Her eyes went back to his. It was intimate, to look at him this way. She could feel his passion, taste it.

Her hands went to his chest and rested against his warm muscles through the shirt, feeling the soft cushion of hair under it. He wasn't trying to stop her, and she remembered what he'd said to her in his office, that she was going to have to make all the running. Well, why not? She had to find out sooner or later what the limits of her capability were. Now seemed as good a time as any, despite their surroundings. Shyly, involuntarily, her nervous hands slid down to his belt and hesitated.

His jaw clenched. He was helpless. Did she know? Her hands slowly moved over the belt and down barely an inch before they hesitated again. His heavy brows drew together in a ferocious scowl as he fought for control.

He seemed to turn to stone. There was not a trace of emotion on his lean, hard face, but his eyes were glittering wildly.

"Go ahead if you want to. But if you touch me there," he said in a choked, harsh tone, "I will back you into this car, push your skirt up, and take you right here in the parking lot without a second's hesitation. And I won't give a damn if the entire staff of the prison comes out to watch!"

12

The terse threat brought Leslie to her senses. She went scarlet as her hands jerked back from his body.

"Oh, good Lord!" she said, horrified at what she'd been doing.

Matt closed his eyes and leaned his forehead against hers. It was damp with sweat and he shuddered with helpless reaction even as he laughed at her embarrassment.

She could barely get her own breath, and her body felt swollen all over. "I'm sorry, Matt, I don't know what got into me!"

The raging desire she'd kindled was getting the best of him. He'd wanted her for such a long time. He hadn't even thought of other women. "Leslie, I'm fairly vulnerable, and you're starting something both of us know you can't finish," he added huskily.

"I'm...not sure that I can't," she said, surprising both of them. She felt the damp warmth of his body close to hers and marveled at his vulnerability.

His eyes opened. He lifted his head slowly and looked down

at her, his breath on her mouth. "If you have a single instinct for self-preservation left, you'd better get in the car, Leslie."

"Okay," she agreed breathlessly, her heart in her eyes as she looked at him with faint wonder.

She got in on the passenger side and fastened her seat belt. He came around to the driver's side and got into the car.

Her hands were curling in on the soft material of her purse and she looked everywhere except at him. She couldn't believe what she'd done.

"Don't make such heavy weather of it," he said gently. "I did say that you'd have to do the chasing, after all."

She cleared her throat. "I think I took it a little too literally."

He chuckled. The sound was deep and pleasant as the powerful car ate up the miles toward Jacobsville. "You have definite potential, Miss Murry," he mused, glancing at her with indulgent affection. "I think we're making progress."

She stared at her purse. "Slow progress."

"That's the best kind." He changed gears and passed a slow-moving old pickup truck. "I'll drop you by your house to change. We're going out on the town tonight, cast and all."

She smiled shyly. "I can't dance."

"There's plenty of time for dancing when you're back on your feet," he said firmly. "I'm going to take care of you from now on. No more risks."

He made her feel like treasure. She didn't realize she'd spoken aloud until she heard him chuckle.

"That's what you are," he said. "My treasure. I'm going to have a hard time sharing you even with other people." He glanced at her. "You're sure there's nothing between you and Ed?"

"Only friendship," she assured him.

"Good."

He turned on the radio and he looked more relaxed than she'd ever seen him. It was like a beginning. She had no idea where their relationship would go, but she was too weak to stop now.

They went out to eat, and Matt was the soul of courtesy. He opened doors for her, pulled out chairs for her, did all the little things that once denoted a gentleman and proved to her forcefully that he wasn't a completely modern man. She loved it. Old World courtesy was delicious.

They went to restaurants in Jacobsville and Victoria and Houston in the weeks that followed, and Matt even phoned her late at night, just to talk. He sent her flowers at the boarding-house, prompting teasing remarks and secret smiles from other residents. He was Leslie's fellow, in the eyes of Jacobsville, and she began to feel as if her dreams might actually come true—except for the one problem that had never been addressed. How was she going to react when Matt finally made love to her completely? Would she be able to go through with intimacy like that, with her past?

It haunted her, because while Matt had been affectionate and kind and tender with her, it never went beyond soft, brief kisses in his car or at her door. He never attempted to take things to a deeper level, and she was too shy from their encounter at the prison parking lot to be so bold again.

The cast came off just before the Ballengers' party to which all of Jacobsville was invited. Leslie looked at her unnaturally pale leg with fascination as Lou Coltrain coaxed her into putting her weight on it for the first time without the supporting cast.

She did, worried that it wouldn't take her weight, while Matt stood grim-faced next to Lou and worried with her.

But when she felt the strength of the bone, she gasped. "It's all right!" she exclaimed. "Matt, look, I can stand on it!"

"Of course you can," Lou chuckled. "Dr. Santos is the best, the very best, in orthopedics."

"I'll be able to dance again," she said.

Matt moved forward and took her hand in his, lifting it to his mouth. "*We'll* be able to dance again," he corrected, holding her eyes with his.

Lou had to stifle amusement at the way they looked together, the tall dark rancher and the small brunette, like two halves of a whole. That would be some marriage, she thought privately, but she kept her thoughts to herself.

Later, Matt came to pick her up at her apartment. She was wearing the long silver dress with the spaghetti straps, and this time without a bra under it. She felt absolutely vampish with her contacts back in and her hair clean and shining. She'd gained a little weight in the past few weeks, and her figure was all she'd ever hoped it would be. Best of all, she could walk without limping.

"Nice," he murmured, smiling as they settled themselves into the car. "But we're not going to overdo things, are we?"

"Whatever you say, boss," she drawled.

He chuckled as he cranked the car. "That's a good start to the evening."

"I have something even better planned for later," she said demurely.

His heart jumped and his fingers jerked on the steering wheel. "Is that a threat or a promise?"

She glanced at him shyly. "That depends on you."

He didn't speak for a minute. "Leslie, you can only go so far with a man before things get out of hand," he began slowly. "You don't know much about relationships, because you haven't dated. I want you to understand how it is with me. I haven't touched another woman since I met you. That makes me more vulnerable than I would be normally." His eyes touched her profile and averted to the highway. "I can't make light love to you anymore," he said finally, his voice harsh. "The strain is more than I can bear."

Her breath caught. She smoothed at an imaginary spot on her gown. "You want us to…to go on like we are."

"I do not," he said gruffly. "But I'm not going to put any pressure on you. I meant what I said about letting you make the moves."

She turned the small purse over in her hands, watching the silver sequins on it glitter in the light. "You've been very patient."

"Because I was very careless of you in those first weeks we knew each other," he said flatly. "I'm trying to show you that sex isn't the basis of our relationship."

She smiled. "I knew that already," she replied. "You've taken wonderful care of me."

He shrugged. "Penance."

She grinned, because it wasn't. He'd shown her in a hundred nonverbal ways how he felt about her. Even the other women in the office had remarked on it.

He glanced at her. "No comment?"

"Oh, I'm sorry, I was just thinking about something."

"About what?" he asked conversationally.

She traced a sequin on the purse. "Can you teach me how to seduce you?"

The car went off the road and barely missed a ditch before he righted it, pulled onto the shoulder and flipped the key to shut off the engine.

He gaped at her. "What did you say?"

She looked up at him in the dimly lit interior where moonlight reflected into the car. "I want to seduce you."

"Maybe I have a fever," he murmured.

She smiled. She laughed. He made her feel as if she could do anything. Her whole body felt warm and uninhibited. She leaned back in her seat and moved sinuously in the seat, liking the way the silky fabric felt against her bare breasts. She felt reckless.

His gaze fell to the fabric against which her hard nipples were distinctly outlined. He watched her body move and knew that she was already aroused, which aroused him at once.

He leaned over, his mouth catching hers as his lean hand slipped under the fabric and moved lazily against her taut breasts.

She moaned and arched toward his fingers, pulling them back when he would have removed them. Her mouth opened under his as she gave in to the need to experience him in a new way, in a new intimacy.

"This is dangerous." He bit off the words against her mouth.

"It feels wonderful," she whispered back, pressing his hand to her soft skin. "I want to feel you like this. I want to touch you under your shirt..."

He hadn't realized how quickly he could get a tie and a shirt out of the way. He pulled her across the console and against him, watching her pert breasts bury themselves in the thick hair that covered his chest. He moved her deliberately against it and watched her eyes grow languid and misty as she experienced him.

His mouth opened hers in a sensual kiss that was as explicit as lovemaking. She felt his tongue, his lips, his teeth, and all the while, his chest moved lazily against her bare breasts. His hand went to the base of her spine and moved her upon the raging arousal she'd kindled. He groaned harshly, and she knew that he wouldn't draw back tonight. The strange thing, the wonderful thing, was that she wasn't afraid.

A minute later, he forced his head up and looked at her, lying yielding and breathless against him. He touched her breasts possessively before he lifted his eyes to search hers. "You aren't afraid of me like this," he said huskily.

She drew in a shaking breath. "No. I'm not."

His eyes narrowed as he persisted. "You want me."

She nodded. She touched his lips with fingers that trembled. "I want you very much. I like the way you feel when you want me," she whispered daringly, the surprise of it in her expression as she moved restlessly against him. "It excites me to feel it."

He groaned out loud and closed his eyes. "For God's sake, honey, don't say things like that to me!"

Her fingers moved down to his chest and pressed there. "Why not? I want to know if I can be intimate with you. I have to know," she said hesitantly. "I've never been able to want a man before. And I've never felt anything like this!" She looked up into his open, curious eyes. "Matt, can we...go somewhere?" she whispered.

"And make love?" he asked in a tone that suggested he thought she was unbalanced.

Her expression softened. "Yes."

He couldn't. His brain told him he couldn't. But his stupid body was screaming at him that he certainly could! "Leslie, sweetheart, it's too soon..."

"No, it isn't," she said huskily, tracing the hair on his chest with cool fingers. "I know you don't want anything permanent, and that's okay. But I..."

The matter-of-fact statement surprised him. "What do you mean, I don't want anything permanent?"

"I mean, you aren't a marrying man."

He looked puzzled. He smiled slowly. "Leslie, you're a virgin," he said softly.

"I know that's a drawback, but we all have to start some-where. You can teach me how," she said stubbornly. "I can learn."

"No!" he said softly. "It's not that at all." His eyes seemed to flicker and then burn like black coals. "Leslie, I don't play around with virgins."

Her mind wasn't getting this at all. She felt dazed by her own desire. "You don't?"

"No, I don't," he said firmly.

"Well, if you'll cooperate, I won't be one for much longer," she pointed out. "So there goes your last argument, Matt." She pressed deliberately closer to him, as aware as he was that his body was amazingly capable.

He actually flushed. He pushed away from her and moved her back into her own seat firmly, pulling up the straps of her dress with hands that fumbled a little. He looked as if she'd hit him in the head with something hard.

Puzzled, she fiddled with her seat belt as he snapped his own into place.

He looked formidably upset. He started the car with subdued violence and put it in gear, his expression hard and stoic.

As the Jaguar shot forward, she slanted a glance at him. It puzzled her that he'd backed away from her. Surely he wasn't insulted by her offer? Or maybe he was.

"Are you offended?" she asked, suddenly self-conscious and embarrassed.

"Heavens, no!" he exclaimed.

"Okay." She let out a relieved sigh. She glanced at him. He wouldn't look at her. "Are you sure you aren't?"

He nodded.

She wrapped her arms around her chest and stared out the windshield at the darkened landscape, trying to decide why he was acting so strangely. He certainly wasn't the man she thought she knew. She'd been certain that he wanted her, too. Now she wasn't.

The Jaguar purred along and they rode in silence. He didn't speak or look at her. He seemed to be deep in thought and she wondered if she'd ruined their budding relationship for good with her wanton tendencies.

It wasn't until he turned the car down a dirt road a few miles from the ranch that she realized he wasn't going toward the Ballengers' home.

"Where are we?" she asked when he turned down an even narrower dirt road that led to a lake. Signposts pointed to various cabins, one of which had Caldwell on it. He pulled into the yard of a little wood cabin in the woods, facing the lake, and cut off the engine.

"This is where I come to get away from business," he told her bluntly. "I've never brought a woman here."

"You haven't?"

His eyes narrowed on her flushed face. "You said you wanted to find out if you could function intimately. All right. We have a place where we won't be disturbed, and I'm willing. More than willing. So there's no reason to be embarrassed," he said quietly. "I want you every bit as badly as you want me. I have something to use. There won't be any risk. But you have to be sure this is what you really want. Once I take your virginity, I can't give it back. There's only one first time."

She stared at him. Her whole body felt hot at the way he was looking at her. She remembered the feel of his mouth on her breasts and her lips parted hungrily. But it was more than just hunger. He knew it.

She lifted her face to his and brushed a breathless little kiss against his firm chin. "I wouldn't let any other man touch me," she said quietly. "And I think you know it."

"Yes. I know it." He knew something else, as well; he knew that it was going to be a beginning, not an affair or a one-night stand. He was going to be her first man, but she was going to be his last woman. She was all he wanted in the world.

He got out and led her up the steps on to the wide porch where there was a swing and three rocking chairs. He unlocked the door, ushered her inside and locked it again. Taking her hand in his, he led her to the bedroom in back. There was a huge king-size bed in the room. It was covered by a thick comforter in shades of beige and red.

For the first time since she'd been so brazen with him, reality hit her like a cold cloth. She stood just inside the doorway, her eyes riveted on that bed, as erotic pictures of Matt without clothing danced in her thoughts.

He turned to her, backing her up against the closed door. He sensed her nervousness, her sudden uncertainty.

"Are you afraid?" he asked somberly.

"I'm sorry, I guess I am," she said with a forced smile.

His lean hands framed her face and he bent and kissed her eyelids. "This may be your first time. It isn't mine. By the time we end up on that bed, you'll be ready for me, and fear is the very last thing you're going to feel."

He bent to her mouth then and began to kiss her. The caresses were tender and slow, not arousing. If anything, they comforted. She felt her fear of him, of the unknown, melt away like ice in the hot sun. After a few seconds, she relaxed and gave in to his gentle ardor.

At first it was just pleasant. Then she felt him move closer and his body reacted at once to hers.

He caught his breath as he felt the sudden surge of pleasure.

Her hands smoothed up his hard thighs, savoring the muscular warmth of them while his mouth captured hers and took possession of it a little roughly, because she was intensifying the desire that was already consuming him.

His body began to move on her, slow and caressing, arousing and tantalizing. Her breasts felt heavy. Her nipples were taut, and the friction of the silky cloth against them intensified the sensations he was kindling in her body, the desire she was already feeling.

His knee edged between both her legs in the silky dress and the slow movement of his hips made her body clench.

His hands went between them, working deftly on the tiny

straps of her dress while he kissed her. It wasn't until she felt the rough hair of his chest against her bare breasts that she realized both of them were uncovered from the waist up.

He drew away a little and looked down at her firm, pretty little breasts while he traced them with his fingers.

"I'd like to keep you under lock and key," he murmured gruffly. "My own pretty little treasure," he added as his head bent.

She watched his mouth take her, felt the pleasure of warm lips on her body. She liked the sight of his mouth over her nipple, that dark, wavy hair falling unruly onto his broad forehead while his heavy eyebrows met and his eyes closed under the delicious whip of passion. She held his head to her body, smoothing the hair at his nape, feeling it cool and clean under her fingers.

When he finally lifted his head, she was leaning back against the door for support. Her eyes were misty with desire, her body trembled faintly with the force of it. She looked at him hungrily, with all the barriers down at last. Other men might repulse her, but she wanted Matt. She loved the feel of his hands and his eyes and his mouth on her body. She wanted to lie under him and feel the delicious pressure of his body against and over and inside her own. She wanted it so badly that she moaned softly.

"No second thoughts?" he asked gently.

"Oh, no! No second thoughts, Matt," she whispered, adoring him with her eyes.

With a slow, secret smile, he began to divest her of the dress and the remaining piece of clothing, leaving her standing before him with her body unveiled, taut with passion.

She was shy, but his hands soon made a jumble of her embarrassment. She felt her body jerk rhythmically as he suckled her breasts. It was so sweet. It was paradise.

When he eased her down onto the huge bed, she lay back against the pillows, totally yielding, and watched his evening clothes come off little by little. He watched her while he undressed, laughing softly, a sensual predatory note in his deep voice. She moved helplessly on the coverlet, her entire being aflame with sensations she'd never known. She could barely wait. She felt as if she was throbbing all over, burning with some unknown fire that threatened to consume her, an ache that was almost painful.

Her eyes widened when the last piece of fabric came away from his powerful body and her breath caught.

He liked that expression. He turned away just for a minute, long enough to extricate a packet from his wallet. He sat down beside her, opened it, and taught her matter-of-factly what to do with it. She fumbled a little, her eyes incredibly wide and fascinated and a little frightened.

"I won't hurt you," he said gently, searching her eyes. "Women have been doing this for hundreds of thousands of years. You're going to like it, Leslie. I promise you are."

She lay back, watching him with wide gray eyes full of curiosity as he slid alongside her.

His dark head bent to her body and she lay under him like a creamy, blushing sacrifice, learning the different ways she responded to his touch. He laughed when she arched up and moaned. He liked the way she opened to him, the way her breath rasped when his mouth slid tenderly over her belly and the soft, inner skin of her thighs. He made a sensual meal of her there on the pretty, soft comforter, while the sound of rain came closer outside the window, the moonlit night clouding over as a storm moved above the cabin.

She hadn't known that physical pleasure could be so devastating. She watched him touch and taste her, with eyes equally fascinated and aroused by some of the things he did to her.

Her shocked exclamation pulled an amused laugh from him. "Am I shocking you? Don't you read books and watch movies?" he asked as he poised just above her.

"It isn't…the same," she choked, arching as his body began to tease hers, her long legs shifting eagerly out of his way as he moved down against her.

Her hands were clenched beside her head, and he watched her eyes dilate as his hips shifted tenderly and she felt him against her in a shattering new intimacy. She gasped, looking straight into his dark eyes. "I…never dreamed…!"

"No words on earth could describe how this feels," he murmured, his breath rasping as he hesitated and then moved down again, tenderly. "You're beautiful, Leslie. Your body is exquisite, soft and warm and enticing. I love the way your skin feels under my mouth." His breath caught as he moved closer and felt her body protest at the invasion. He paused to search over her flushed, drawn face. "I'm becoming your lover," he whispered huskily, drawing his body against hers sensuously to deepen his possession. "I'm going inside you. Now."

His face became rigid with control, solemn as he met her eyes and pushed again, harder, and watched her flinch. "I know. It's going to hurt a little, in spite of everything," he said softly. "But not for long. Do you still want me?"

"More than anything…in the world!" she choked, lifting her hips toward his in a sensual invitation. "It's all right." She swallowed. Impulsively she looked down and her mouth fell open.

She couldn't have imagined watching, even a day before. "Matt...!" she gasped.

Her eyes came back up to his. His face looked as if every muscle in it was clenched. "It feels like my first time, too," he said a little roughly. His hands slid under her head, cradling it as he shifted slightly and then pushed once more.

Her pretty body lifted off the bed. It seemed to ripple as he moved intimately into closer contact. "I never thought...we could talk...while we did something so intimate," she whispered back, gasping when he moved again and pleasure shot through her. "Yes...oh, yes, please do...that!" she pleaded huskily, clutching at his shoulders.

"Here, like this?" he asked urgently, and moved again.

Her tiny cry was affirmation enough. He eased down on her, his eyes looking straight into hers as he began a rhythm that combined tension with exquisite pleasure and fleeting, burning pain.

His eyes dilated as he felt the barrier. He shivered. His body clenched. He'd never had an innocent woman. Leslie was totally out of his experience. He hadn't thought about how it would feel until now. Primitive thoughts claimed his mind, ancestral memories perhaps that spoke of an ancient age when this would have been a rite of passage.

She was feeling something very similar as her body yielded to the domination of his. The discomfort paled beside the feelings that were consuming her. Glimpses of unbelievable pleasure were mingling with the stinging pain. Past it, she knew, lay ecstasy.

He kissed her hungrily as his lean, fit body moved on her in the silence of the cabin. Suddenly rain pounded hard outside the curtained window, slamming into the roof, the ground, the trees. The wind howled around the corner. There was a storm in him, too, as he lay stretched tight with desire, trying to hold back long enough to let Leslie share what he knew he would feel.

"I've never been so hungry," he bit off against her mouth. His hands contracted under her head, tangling in her hair. His body shuddered. "I'm going to have to hurt you. I can't wait any longer. It's getting away from me. I have to have you…now!"

Her legs moved sensuously against his, loving the faint abrasion of the hair that covered his. "Yes!" she said huskily, her eyes full of wonder. "I want it. I want…it with you."

One lean hand went to her upper thigh. His lips flattened. He looked straight into her eyes as his hand suddenly pinned her hips and he thrust down fiercely.

She cried out, grimacing, writhing as she felt him deep in her body, past a stinging pain that engulfed her.

He stilled, holding her in place while he gave her body time to adjust, his eyes blazing with primitive triumph. His gaze reflected pride and pleasure and possession.

"Yes," he said roughly. "You're part of me and I'm part of you. Now you belong to me, completely."

Her eyes mirrored her shocked fascination. She moved a little and felt him move with her. She swallowed, and then swallowed again, her breath coming in soft jerks as she adjusted to her first intimacy. She loved him. The feel of him was pure delight. She was a woman. She could be a woman. The past was dying already and she was whole and sensuous and fully capable. Her smile was brilliant with joyful self-discovery.

She pulled his head down to hers and kissed him hungrily.

The pain had receded and now she felt a new sensation as his hips moved. There were tiny little spasms of pleasure. Her breath came raggedly as she positioned herself to hold on to them. Her nails bit into the hard muscle of his upper arms.

His dark eyes were full of indulgent amusement as he felt her movements. She hesitated once, shy. "Don't stop," he whispered. "I'll do whatever you want me to do."

Her lips parted. It wasn't the answer she'd expected.

He bent and kissed her eyelids again, his breath growing more ragged by the minute. "Find a position that gives you what you need," he coaxed. "I won't take my pleasure until you've had yours."

"Oh, Matt," she moaned, unbearably touched by a generosity that she hadn't expected.

He laughed through his desire, kissing her face tenderly. "My own treasure," he whispered. "I wish I could make it last for hours. I want you to blush when you're sixty, remembering this first time. I want it to be perfect for you."

The pleasure was building. It was fierce now, and she was no longer in control of her own body. It lifted up to Matt's and demanded pleasure. She was totally at the mercy of her awakened passion, blind with the need for fulfillment. She became aware of a new sort of tension that was lifting her fiercely to meet every quick, downward motion of his lean hips, that stretched her under his powerful body, that made her pulse leap with delicious throbs of wild delight.

He watched her body move and ripple, watched the expression on her face, in her wide, blind eyes, and smiled. "Yes," he murmured to himself. "Now you understand, don't you? You can't fight it, or deny it, or control it..." He stopped abruptly.

"No! Please, don't...stop!" Her choked cry was followed by frantic, clinging hands that pulled at him.

He eased down again, watching as she shivered. "I'm not going to stop," he whispered softly. "Trust me. I only want to make it as good as it can be for you."

"It feels...wonderful," she said hoarsely. "Every time you move, it's like...like electric shocks of pleasure."

"And we've barely started, baby," he whispered. He shifted his hips, intensifying her cries. She was completely yielded to him, open to him, wanton. He'd never dreamed that it would be like this. His head began to spin with the delight his body was taking from hers.

She curled her long legs around his powerful ones and lifted herself, gasping when it brought a sharp stab of pleasure.

His hand swept down her body. His face hardened as he began to increase the pressure and the rhythm. She clung to him, her mouth in his throat, on his chest, his chin, wherever she could reach, while he gave in to his fierce hunger and threw away his control.

She'd never dreamed how it would be. She couldn't get close enough, or hold on tight enough. She felt him in every cell of her body. She was ardent, inciting him, matching his quick, hard movements, her back lifting to promote an even closer contact.

She whispered things to him, secret, erotic things that drove him to sensual urgency. She was moaning. She could hear her frantic voice pleading, hear the sound their movements made on the box springs, feel the power and heat of him as her body opened for him and clenched with tension that begged for release.

She whispered his name and then groaned it, and then

repeated it in a mad, hoarse little sound until the little throbs of pleasure became one long, aching, endless spasm of ecstasy that made her blind and deaf under the fierce, demanding thrust of his body. She cried out and shivered in the grip of it, her voice throbbing like her body. She felt herself go off the edge of the world into space, into a red heat that washed over every cell in her body.

When she was able to think again, she felt his body shake violently, heard the harsh groan at her ear as he, too, found ecstasy.

He shuddered one last time and then his warm strong body relaxed and she felt it push hers deeper into the mattress. His mouth was at her throat, pressing hungrily. His lips moved all over her face, touching and lifting in a fever of tenderness.

Her dazed eyes opened and looked up into his. He was damp with sweat, as she was. His dark eyes smiled with incredible gentleness into hers.

She arched helplessly and moaned as the pleasure washed over her again.

"More?" he whispered, and his hips moved obligingly, so that the sweet stabs of delight came again and again and again.

She sobbed helplessly afterward, clinging to him as she lay against his relaxed body.

His hand smoothed over her damp hair. He seemed to understand her shattered response, as she didn't.

"I don't know why I'm bawling my head off," she choked, "when it was the closest to heaven I've ever been."

"There are half a dozen technical names for it," he murmured drowsily. "It's letdown blues. You go so high that it hurts to come down."

"I went high," she murmured with a smile. "I walked on the moon."

He chuckled. "So did I."

"Was...was it all right?" she asked suddenly.

He rolled her over on her back and looked down into her curious face. "You were the best lover I've ever had," he said, and he wasn't teasing. "And you will be, from now on, the only woman I ever have."

"Oh, that sounds serious," she murmured.

"Doesn't it, though?" His dark eyes went over her like an artist's brush committing beauty to canvas. He touched her soft breasts with a breathlessly tender caress. "I won't be able to stop, you know," he added conversationally.

"Stop?"

"This," he replied. "It's addictive. Now that I've had you, I'll want you all the time. I'll go green every time any other man so much as looks at you."

It sounded as if he was trying to tell her something, and she couldn't decide what it was. She searched his dark eyes intently.

He smiled with indulgent affection. "Do you want the words?"

"Which words?" she whispered.

He brushed his lips over hers with incredible, breathless tenderness. "Marry me, Leslie."

13

Her gasp was audible. It was more than she'd dared hope for when she came in here with him. He chuckled at her expression.

"Did you think I was going to ask you to come out to the ranch and live in sin with me?" he teased with twinkling eyes. His hand swept down over her body possessively. "This isn't enough. Not nearly enough."

She hesitated. "Are you sure that you want something, well, permanent?"

His eyes narrowed. "Leslie, if I'd been a little more reckless, you'd have something permanent. I wanted very badly to make you pregnant."

Her face brightened. "Did you, really? I thought about it, too, just at the end."

He smoothed back her hair and found himself fighting the temptation to start all over again with nothing between them.

"We'll have children," he promised her. "But first we'll build a life together, a secure life that they'll fall into very naturally."

She was fascinated by the expression on his face. It was only just dawning on her that he felt more than a fleeting desire for her body. He was talking about a life together, children together. She knew very little about true relationships, but she was learning all the time.

"Heavy thoughts?" he teased.

"Yes." She smoothed her fingers over his lean cheek.

"Care to share them?" he murmured.

"I was thinking how sweet it is to be loved," she whispered softly.

He lifted an eyebrow. "Physically loved?"

"Well, that, too," she replied.

He smiled quizzically. "Too?"

"You'd never have taken me to bed unless you loved me," she said simply, but with conviction. "You have these strange old-world hang-ups about innocence."

"Strange, my foot!"

She smiled up at him complacently. "Not that I don't like them," she assured him. The smile faded as she searched his dark eyes. "It was perfect. Just perfect. And I'm glad I waited for you. I love you, Matt."

His chest rose and fell heavily. "Even after the way I've treated you?"

"You didn't know the truth," she said. "And even if you were unfair at first, you made all sorts of restitution. I won't have a limp anymore," she added, wide-eyed. "And you gave me a good job and looked out for me..."

He bent and kissed her hungrily. "Don't try to make it sound better than it was. I've been an ogre with you. I'm only sorry that I can't go back and start over again."

"None of us can do that," she said. "But we have a second chance, both of us. That's something to be thankful for."

"From now on," he promised her solemnly, "everything is going to be just the way you want it. The past has been hard for me to overcome. I've distrusted women for so long, but with you I've been able to forget what my mother did. I'll cherish you as long as I live."

"And I'll cherish you," she replied quietly. "I thought I would never know what it was to be loved."

He frowned a little, drawing her palm to his lips. "I never thought I would, either. I was never in love before."

She sighed tenderly. "Neither was I. And I never dreamed it would be so sweet."

"I imagine it's going to get better year after year," he ventured, toying with her fingers.

Her free hand slid up into his dark hair. "Matt?"

"What?"

"Can we do that again?"

He pursed his lips. "Are you sure that you can?" he asked pointedly.

She shifted on the coverlet and grimaced with the movement. "Well, maybe not. Oh, dear."

He actually laughed, bending to wrap her up against him and kiss her with rough affection. "Come here, walking wounded. We'll have a nice nap and then we'll go home and make wedding plans." He smoothed down her wild hair. "We'll have a nice cozy wedding and a honeymoon anywhere you want to go."

"I don't mind if we don't go anywhere, as long as I'm with you," she said honestly.

He sighed. "My thoughts exactly." He glanced down at her. "You could have had a conventional wedding night, you know."

She smoothed her hand over his hair-roughened chest. "I didn't know that you'd want to marry me. But just the same, I had to know if I could function intimately with you. I wasn't sure, you see."

"I am," he said with a wicked grin.

She laughed heartily. "Yes, so am I, now, but it was important that I knew the truth before things went any further between us. I knew it was difficult for you to hold back, and I couldn't bear the thought of letting you go. Not that I expected you to want to marry me," she added ruefully.

"I wanted to marry you the first time I kissed you," he confessed. "Not to mention the first time I danced with you. It was magic."

"For me, too."

"But you had this strange aversion to me and I couldn't understand why. I was a beast to you. Even Ed said it wasn't like me to treat employees that badly. He read me the riot act and I let him."

"Ed's nice."

"He is. But I'm glad you weren't in love with him. At first, I couldn't be sure of the competition."

"Ed was a brotherly sort. He still is." She kissed his chest. "But I love you."

"I love you, too."

She laid her cheek against the place she'd kissed and closed her eyes. "If the lawyers can help my mother, maybe she'll be out for the first christening."

"At least for the second," he agreed, and smiled as his arms closed warm and protective around her, drawing her closer. It was the safest she'd ever been in her life, in those warm, strong arms in the darkness. The nightmares seemed to fade into the shadows of reality that they'd become. She would walk in the light, now, unafraid. The past was over, truly over. She knew that it would never torment her again.

Matt and Leslie were married in the local Presbyterian church, and the pews were full all the way to the back. Leslie thought that every single inhabitant of Jacobsville had shown up for the wedding, and she wasn't far wrong. Matt Caldwell had been the town's foremost bachelor for so long that curiosity brought people for miles around. All the Hart boys showed up, including the state attorney general, as well as the Ballengers, the Tremaynes, the Jacobs, the Coltrains, the Deverells, the Regans and the Burkes. The turnout read like the local social register.

Leslie wore a white designer gown with a long train and oceans of veiling and lace. The women in the office served as maids and matrons of honor, and Luke Craig acted as Matt's best man. There were flower girls and a concert pianist. The local press was invited, but no out of town reporters. Nobody wrote about Leslie's tragic past, either. It was a beautiful ceremony and the reception was uproarious.

Matt had pushed back her veil at the altar with the look of a man who'd inherited heaven. He smiled as he bent to kiss her, and his eyes were soft with love, as were her own.

They held hands all through the noisy reception on the lawn at Matt's ranch, where barbecue was the order of the day.

Leslie had already changed clothes and was walking among the guests when she came upon Carolyn Engles unexpectedly.

The beautiful blonde came right up to her with a genuine smile and a present in her hands.

"I got this for you, in Paris," Carolyn said with visible hesitation and self-consciousness. "It's sort of a peace offering and an apology, all in one."

"You didn't have to do this," Leslie stammered.

"I did." She nodded toward the silver-wrapped present. "Open it."

Leslie pulled off the paper with helpless excitement, puzzled and touched by the other woman's gesture. She opened the velvet box inside and her breath caught. It was a beautiful little crystal swan, tiny and perfect.

"I thought it was a nice analogy," Carolyn murmured. "You've turned out to be a lovely swan, and nobody's going to hurt you when you go swimming around in the Jacobsville pond."

Impulsively Leslie hugged the older woman, who laughed nervously and actually blushed.

"I'm sorry for what I did that day," Carolyn said huskily. "Really sorry. I had no idea…"

"I don't hold grudges," Leslie said gently.

"I know that." She shrugged. "I was infatuated with Matt and he couldn't see me for dust. I went a little crazy, but I'm myself again now. I want you both to be very happy."

"I hope the same for you," Leslie said with a smile.

Matt saw them together and frowned. He came up beside Leslie and placed an arm around her protectively.

"Carolyn brought this to me from Paris," Leslie said excitedly, showing him the tiny thing. "Isn't it beautiful?"

Matt was obviously puzzled as he exchanged looks with Carolyn.

"I'm not as bad as you think I am," Carolyn told him. "I really do hope you'll be happy. Both of you."

Matt's eyes smiled. "Thank you."

Carolyn smiled back ruefully. "I told Leslie how sorry I was for the way I behaved. I really am, Matt."

"We all have periods of lunacy," Matt replied. "Otherwise, nobody in his right mind would ever get into the cattle business."

Carolyn laughed delightedly. "So they say. I have to go. I just wanted to bring Leslie the peace offering. You'll both be on my guest list for the charity ball, by the way."

"We'll come, and thank you," Matt returned.

Carolyn nodded, smiled and moved away toward where the guests' cars were parked.

Matt pulled his new wife closer. "Surprises are breaking out like measles."

"I noticed." She linked her arms around his neck and reached up to kiss him tenderly. "When everybody goes home, we can lock ourselves in the bedroom and play doctor."

He chuckled delightedly. "Can we, now? Who gets to go first?"

"Wait and see!"

He turned her back toward their guests with a grin that went from ear to ear. "Lucky me," he said, and he wasn't joking.

They woke the next morning in a tangle of arms and legs as the sun peered in through the gauzy curtains. Matt's ardor had been inexhaustible, and Leslie had discovered a whole new world of sensation.

She rolled over onto her back and stretched, uninhibited by

her nudity. Matt propped himself on an elbow and looked at her with eyes full of love and possession.

"I never realized that marriage would have so many fringe benefits," she murmured. She stretched again. "I don't know if I have enough strength to walk after last night."

"If you don't, I'll carry you," he said with a loving smile. He reached over to kiss her lazily. "Come on, treasure. We'll have a nice shower and then we'll go and find some breakfast."

She kissed him back. "I love you."

"Same here."

"You aren't sorry you married me, are you?" she asked impulsively. "I mean, the past never really goes away. Someday some other reporter may dig it all back up again."

"It won't matter," he said. "Everybody's got a skeleton or two. And no, I'm not sorry I married you. It was the first sensible thing I've done in years. Not to mention," he added with a sensual touch of his mouth to her body, "the most pleasurable."

She laughed. "For me, too." Her arms pulled him down to her and she kissed him heartily.

Her mother did get a new trial, and her sentence was shortened. She went back to serve the rest of her time with a light heart, looking forward to the day when she could get to know her daughter all over again.

As for Leslie, she and Matt grew closer with every passing day and became known locally as "the lovebirds," because they were so rarely seen apart.

Matt's prediction about her mother's release came true, as well. Three years after the birth of their son, Leslie gave birth to a daughter who had Matt's dark hair and, he mused, a temper to match his own. He had to fight tears when the baby was placed in his arms. He loved his son, but he'd wanted a little girl who looked like his own treasure, Leslie. Now, he told her, his life was complete. She echoed that sentiment with all her heart. The past had truly been laid to rest. She and Matt had years of happiness ahead of them.

Most of Jacobsville showed up for the baby's christening, including a small blond woman who was enjoying her first days of freedom. Leslie's mother had pride of place in the front pew. Leslie looked from Matt to her mother, from their three-year-old son to the baby in her arms. Her gray eyes, when they lifted to Matt's soft, dark ones, were radiant with joy. Dreams came true, she thought. Dreams came true.

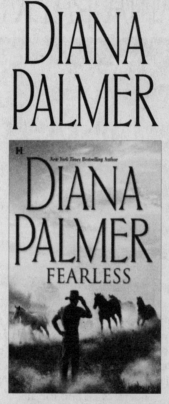

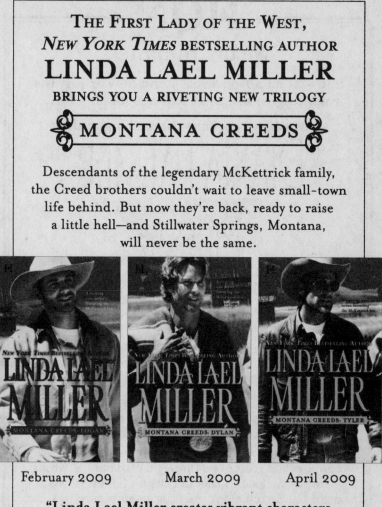